The Indigo Chronicles

Book One
THE PATH KEEPER

Book Two
SON OF SECRETS

Book Three
CHILDREN OF SHADOWS

D1324174

N.J. SIMMONDS

CHILDREN
OF
SHADOWS

The Indigo Chronicles, Book 3

Livonia, Michigan

Poem "Angels Damned" by Robert George Dew. Used with permission.
All rights reserved.

Editor: Jamie Rich
Proofreader: Hannah Ryder

Published by BHC Press

Library of Congress Control Number: 2020937304

ISBN: 978-1-64397-207-7 (Hardcover)
ISBN: 978-1-64397-208-4 (Softcover)
ISBN: 978-1-64397-209-1 (Ebook)

For information, write:
BHC Press
885 Penniman #5505
Plymouth, MI 48170

Visit the publisher:
www.bhcpress.com

For Mum, Jemma, Dad, and Bob
Thank you.

Angels Damned

I grasp at spirals of blue-white light with aching, clumsy hands.
I try to count the countless grains of restless, moving sands.

I ponder depths of deep, dark voids without the thought of choice.
The fingers work, create the words, such powers not the voice.

So gather round, you angels damned, and fear no fear from me.
For deep inside I'm looking on. I am the damned, you see.

You're well aware the price I've paid for what's so hard to gain.
You're well aware my salt glass mines are answers to the rain.

So gather round, you angels damned, come rally—you are chosen.
Be it yours the task to warm the light of hope that's frozen.

—Robert George Dew, 1977—

BEFORE
THE
BEGINNING

19 BC—FIESOLE, ITALY

<u>I.</u>

LIFE WASN'T ALWAYS easy, but it *was* simple. If you wanted it to be.

Luci could have settled anywhere in the world to raise her boy, but she chose Fiesole. The small Italian town perched on the edge of a Tuscan hillside was a vibrant mix of tranquillity and opportunity. Quiet enough that she was left alone, but busy enough that she never felt bored.

With one hand she hoisted her son onto her hip, and with the other picked up her basket full of fruit, wine, and grain. The ears of wheat tickled her back as she balanced it on the crook of her arm.

'You're getting heavy, Zadkiel,' she said to the boy.

She was wearing a white silk dress gathered over one shoulder and tied in the middle with a gold-coloured sash. It was a little extravagant for the market, but the opinion of others was the least of Luci's problems.

Zadkiel hooked his legs around his mother's waist to stop himself from slipping down her body. He giggled as she rubbed her nose into the crease of his sweaty neck and blew a raspberry.

'If I'm heavy then put me down, Mummia,' he said.

'Never. You weren't made to walk, my angel.' Luci smiled, spinning him around. 'You were made to fly.'

The boy laughed, wrapping his skinny arms tightly around her neck.

'Oh, the flowers have gone,' he cried.

Every morning his mother plaited her thick dark hair into elaborate twists, and Zadkiel would carefully thread wild blooms through it. Her hair had come lose in the heat of the day and was now hanging thick around her shoulders.

A jasmine plant grew over a low wall at the entrance to their home. Luci plucked a sprig and handed it to her son.

'Adorn me.'

'They look like tiny feathers,' the boy said, pulling each delicate flower off its stem and pushing them into his mother's hair. Luci smiled at the word 'feathers.' The boy knew nothing of who he was, or the power that surged through his veins. He would know soon enough— but not yet. Not until he was a man.

Their cottage was on the outskirts of the town just over the city wall, nestled in the woods beside a stream. It had taken Luci years to tend the land, to push rocks into the soil to form a path and to collect enough pots and fabric to make the little house a home. *Her* home. The first one she'd ever lived in.

At night she would curl herself around her son, fitting him between her knees and chest as if he'd never left her womb. If anyone were to watch them sleeping, they wouldn't be able to see the boy protected in his mother's embrace—and that's all Luci wanted, that no one but her could get near her son. As long as Zadkiel was with her, he was safe. As long as he thought he was the same as the other dusty boys that ran around the town square playing tag on market day, as long as he remained normal, Luci would be safe too.

'I'm hungry,' Zadkiel said, flopping his damp head against his mother's shoulder. She planted a kiss on his sticky forehead.

'I will make your favourite soup tonight.'

The sun beat down on them, the brown grasses scratching her ankles as she made her way to their front door. She waved at a shepherd she sometimes saw heading up the dirt track, an old man who walked his goats the same route each month, but few knew who she was. *What* she was. The villagers described her as a mother who'd lost her husband to a war, or an illness, or perhaps another woman. As far as they knew she had come from the north looking for work. She made her money as a healer and a midwife—she had magic hands, they said. Half the town feared her for this, the other half sought her out. Luci was good with those who suffered, and she was good with new life. But beyond that, nobody bothered her.

It was cool inside the cottage. Zadkiel immediately perked up and ran off to play with the clay dolls his mother had made him. Luci smiled and hummed as she unpacked her basket, shelling peas into a pot and chopping up onions. All was silent save for the birds making their way to their nests, circling the darkening sky like tiny specks of black against a white canvas.

'The great Lucifer? Cooking?' came a low voice from the doorway.

She'd sensed Gabriel's presence before he'd spoken, but her stomach still twisted at the sound of his voice. The archangel hadn't appeared to her since she'd fallen pregnant. She didn't turn around. Let him come to her.

'Hungry?' she asked.

He laughed, a booming sound so loud it made Zadkiel run in from the other room. The boy's eyes grew wide at the sight of the strange man in his house and he ran off again.

'So that's your boy? The reason why you won't come home?'

Gabriel stepped into the kitchen, creating a shadow over the herbs Luci was chopping.

She turned around, finding herself face to face with one of her closest friends.

'My goodness. Motherhood suits you,' Gabriel said, taking in her flushed cheeks and bright eyes. He picked a flower from her hair, smelled it, and placed it back. Luci shivered at his touch.

'Did Mikhael send you?'

Gabriel didn't know who Zadkiel's father was. No one did. When the realm had discovered that the almighty Lucifer had not only found herself pregnant, but that she refused to return home, there had been much uproar. They presumed Mikhael's special compensation had been because Luci, like him, was one of the original archangels. That he was protecting her out of kindness. He agreed to give her six years to play at being human, to mother a Nephilim child, and then she would leave the child behind and get on with her job.

Nobody knew the real truth—that Zadkiel was no Nephilim. That Zadkiel was strongest of all archangels. Because he was the son of Mikhael himself.

Gabriel, though, was none the wiser.

'Come home,' he said, tucking a stray lock of hair behind her ear. 'Mikhael's angry at your defiance. He's even threatening to pass "judgement" on you, to cut off your wings for disobedience. I think he means it.'

Luci's eyes flickered over to the doorway, but Zadkiel still had his back to them playing with his clay figures.

'It's why I'm here,' Gabriel added, threading his fingers through hers.

'To give me a message?'

He smiled, his eyes glowing a bright jade in the gloom of the evening light. 'Of course. It's what I do best.'

Luci bit her lips together. She wasn't going home. She wasn't leaving her son. Gabriel's fingers stroked hers, his face full of nothing but kindness. How different he was to the man she'd chosen to father her child. Often, she'd wondered what would have happened had she convinced Gabriel to give her a baby instead, to feel *his* arms around her, *his* lips on hers—but the truth was a simple one. Angels laying with angels was the one forbidden rule in the realm, and they'd both be dead right now at the hands of Mikhael's sword. The only way Luci had been able to conceive was via another archangel, and for the baby to survive the child had to belong to the one who made the rules. Mikhael.

He'd clearly kept what they'd done to himself, though. Probably telling the realm the child's father was a shepherd or a passing trader.

'I'm staying,' she said to Gabriel.

A flash of pain passed over his features, so fast she nearly missed it.

'He will come for you. He's telling everyone you've gone crazy.'

'I *have* gone crazy.' Luci laughed. 'Crazy in love with my boy. Crazy to imagine a life without Zadkiel.' She stroked the archangel's cheek and he closed his eyes. 'Crazy to ever leave him,' she whispered. 'I'm staying.'

Gabriel covered her hand with his and brought it to his lips. Then with a slow nod he was gone.

'Zadkiel!' Luci ran to the next room and gathered her son in her arms. 'You need to go.'

II.

How long did she have? How long would it take for Gabriel to tell Mikhael that she wasn't returning? Surely Mikhael wouldn't kill his own son. Would he?

She crouched down. 'I need you to collect firewood,' she said to Zadkiel, doing all she could to keep her voice low and steady.

'But I'm not allowed out on my own.'

'I know, but Mummia needs wood for the fire. To make your favourite soup.'

'It rained yesterday. There's no dry wood,' the boy persisted, looking over at his toys. 'And we already have wood. And it's getting dark.'

Luci had trained her son well, forever warning him of the dangers of being alone. She bit down hard on the inside of her cheek. She couldn't cry. Her tears would scare the boy, would have him clinging to her, and she needed him gone. If he was still here when Mikhael and the realm descended, then… She pushed the thought away and pulled her son closer to her.

'In aeternum te amabo,' she whispered into his hair. 'Forever and ever, Zadkiel. I will love you forever.'

'I know, Mummia,' he said, wriggling out of her embrace. 'You always say that.'

'Because I will always mean it.'

Her skin prickled like a cool breeze passing over wet skin. Mikhael was near. They didn't have long.

'Go!' she cried, pushing her son to the back door leading to the river. 'And don't return until the moon is high in the sky.'

Instead of running out of the door, the child ran straight back into her arms.

'And then we will have supper and you will tell stories and cuddle me to sleep? You won't leave my side?'

She swallowed. How it hurt. 'I will never leave your side.'

Zadkiel didn't see the tears sliding down his mother's face as he headed for the woods. The boy didn't look back.

Luci straightened up and smoothed out her dress. Taking a deep breath, she tied her hair up and walked to the front of the house. This was it. This was the day she'd feared since she'd first thought up her plan of seducing the great Prince of Heaven.

As expected, Mikhael didn't take long. She'd been expecting the sound of rustling leaves and the flurry of sails to slice through the murky light of evening, but no band of angels fell from the sky—instead just one man appeared at the bottom of her garden.

One man. She had to stop thinking of Mikhael as a man—because Luci was no woman. They were the beings who created day and night, light and dark. They had moulded the Earth like it had been nothing but clay and paint. The same Earth she was now refusing to leave.

Mikhael stepped out of the shadow of a tree, his icy blue eyes shining like diamonds in the twilight. The leader of the realm wasn't bedecked in his usual regalia. Instead he'd chosen to blend in with the locals. On his feet were leather sandals, draped over his tall frame was a pale brown robe, and in his hand he held a sword so large no Roman would mistake it for his own. The sword held the power to end all lives—human lives that would never return again, and the angelic lives of those who had gone against him. Yet Mikhael had come alone, which meant he wasn't going to proceed with the "judgement." Regardless of the weapon he was gripping in his pale fists, Luci wasn't going to lose her wings for breaking his rules. Not today.

The King of Angels walked slowly, eyes trained on Luci's, until he was before her.

'You didn't come back to me,' he said.

Back to *him*?

He grabbed her wrist with one strong hand, the other holding on to his sword. 'Gabriel told me you said no.'

Luci gathered herself and considered her options. She could fight...or she could flatter.

'Have you missed me?' She placed her other hand flat against his hard chest. There was no heartbeat beneath her palm. Mikhael had a heart, all human bodies did, but she doubted his had ever done its job.

Mikhael brushed her off, but something still crackled between them like static. Like the seconds before the first strike of thunder.

Luci had lain beneath many a man over the centuries. She'd let them do as they must in order to achieve the one thing she couldn't create alone. A baby. But nothing had worked, and she realised it was because her body was too powerful for mere men. Mikhael had been her only chance to become the ultimate goddess, and she'd done everything in her power to convince him. It had worked. The archangel may have had the mind of an enlightened being—but he also had the body of a young man who liked what he saw. Perhaps he still did.

'Why are you here?' she asked.

'For you.'

'To drag me home? Or because you enjoyed what we did, and you want more?'

Mikhael looked away. 'This union between humans, you treat it like a means to an end. But with physical touch comes much more, Lucifer. You and I. We've known one another since before there was light. I thought...' He stopped, his Adam's apple bobbing in his throat as he swallowed. 'I thought what we did... That it meant something.'

Luci let out a yelp of a laugh. Was the great Mikhael claiming her? Or was this his idea of romance? The archangel had always scoffed at matters of the heart. He saw human beings as nothing more than weak sacks of skin filled with blood and tears. Mikhael didn't feel. He *couldn't* feel.

'Of course what we did meant something,' she replied. 'It meant I got my child.'

His jaw set hard and his lips curled into a sneer. 'You really are an unlovable beast, Lucifer.'

Something sharp twisted inside her chest. That wasn't true. Her boy loved her. He more than loved her, he needed her. She was his oxygen, his water, the very blood running through his spindly body. And from the very moment she'd felt him grow inside of her Luci had fallen in deep and ferocious love with him. A love that terrified her with its intensity. A love she craved and feared and revelled in. She wasn't leaving her boy.

'Go,' she said to the archangel. 'Mothers don't leave their children.'

'We can make more. Come home,' he said, running his left hand over the top of her arm, the other not letting go of his sword. The strap of Luci's dress fell off one shoulder and Mikhael's gaze travelled to her chest.

'No,' she said again.

His grip on her tightened. 'Then let me meet my son.'

He knew Zadkiel was a boy? Who'd told him? Gabriel? She shook her head and he growled. A noise she'd never heard him make before.

'Why do you defy me so, Lucifer? You got to carry a baby, like you wanted. And to play mother, like you wanted. I gave you that much.'

'My life was never yours to give. The same as our son's life is not yours to take. Give me ten more years,' she pleaded. 'Then, when he's old enough, he can join us both and we can tell the realm who he is.'

Mikhael shoved her away, causing her to stumble and fall back on the muddy ground.

'Why do you think I came here alone? The realm doesn't know what we did. They will never know that I, the one who sets the rules, broke the most important one. They don't know I fathered a child with you. They think you've lowered yourself to nothing more than a human whore who fucked a village boy. A whore I need to bring back home.'

'I am Lucifer!' she cried, scrambling to her feet. 'I am the morning star and the bringer of dawn. The ruler of Venus and the angel of light. You will respect me!'

Mikhael laughed, taking in her mud-smeared dress and her wild hair full of wilting flowers.

'Respect you? The great Lucifer, who stops at nothing to get what she wants? Look at the state of you. You chose that womanly body because you thought it would give you control, but you forgot it was a lot weaker than mine.' He pushed her shoulder, and as much as she held her ground her body still stumbled. 'You're pathetic. Feeble. What happens to those who don't obey me, Lucifer? You've seen it, you know. You've stood by my side during many a reckoning. What happens?' he shouted.

Luci had been wrong about her options. She only had *one* option now. To fight.

Rolling back her shoulders she clenched her teeth as the sharp tips of wings she hadn't used in seven years began to rip through the silky fabric of her dress. He back arched, and she relished the sharp painful stabs as the dark plumes unfurled behind her. Giant feathers. Black as death.

'Oh, I know exactly what happens when I say no,' she snarled. 'I win.'

III.

Mikhael had his sword raised before Luci's wings had fully formed.

Night had settled quickly, but thankfully her boy was still far away. She could feel him, she always could, as if the umbilical cord had never been severed. She silently willed the child to keep away. He didn't need to see this. Zadkiel didn't know who his father was, he'd never asked, and neither had he seen feathers as large as the ones rising behind Mikhael's back. White, and as wide and sharp as spearheads, each plume looked like it had been dipped in the blood of his enemies. This was the real Mikhael. The Winged Warrior.

But Luci was not weak. As he raised his sword higher she held out her hands, the power surging from her forcing the archangel back.

'Get off my land,' she screamed.

'You don't belong here, Lucifer,' he shouted. 'You belong with me!'

'I belong with my son. Zadkiel is more powerful than the two of us combined. And when he's fully grown, he'll be the one to take you down.'

Mikhael fought against the force emanating from the palms of her outstretched hands. Like a ferocious gale it whipped at his golden mane, his wings straining like the sails of a galleon ship.

'My son will serve me,' he roared. 'He will worship me. And no one, including him, will ever know who he truly is.' Straining against her powers, Mikhael reached out and grabbed Luci's hair. He wrapped it around his hand and pulled her forward so she fell against him, her chest flat against his. He pressed his face up to hers. Their lips were nearly touching. 'You tricked me once, you disgusting *lupa*. Never again.'

Gathering all her strength, Luci beat her wings and pushed herself into the air, leaving Mikhael on the ground, a handful of her hair in his clenched fist. But in an instant, he was beside her, white feathers against black.

Luci was no match against his sword, and she had no intention of trying to escape and leaving her boy behind. She would have to fight with the little she had. He lunged at her again, his hand grasping around her neck, but Luci was too quick. Dropping and flying beneath him, then behind, she raised her hands and using nothing but magic ripped at his wings. Feathers took a long time to grow back on an angel, and it affected their flight. The ones she pulled from his body floated down to her garden, piercing through the jasmine plant like arrows. Her actions weren't enough to injure him, but it put him off balance long enough to loosen his grip on his sword and make him spin through the air before rising again.

Luci reached for the weapon—if she could just get her hands on the blade—but she didn't make it. With a ferocious cry, Mikhael twisted around so fast his wings smacked Luci in the face, causing her to plummet to the ground.

'You think you can beat me, Lucifer?' he cried, his face ghostly against the night sky. 'You think you can defy me and win?'

Facedown, her back to the archangel and her legs peddling to gather purchase, she tried to right herself. But it was too late.

She heard the blade cut through the air before she felt it. With one strike Mikhael swiped his mighty sword through Luci's wings, leaving a gaping tear between her shoulder blades. Where feathers had once bloomed, there was now a deep dark gash that would never heal.

The almighty Lucifer was untethered. A fallen angel.

The wind was cold against Luci's wet face as her body fell fast, her arms flapping in vain and her mouth wide, frozen in a silent scream.

This wasn't how the "judgement" was passed. There was meant to be a jury, witnesses, a chance to defend herself.

Mikhael couldn't do this. Except he had.

Luci's body hit the damp earth with a deafening crunch of bones, her wings floating down and covering her like a dark shroud. She turned her head, watching one of her loose feathers drift through the air and join Mikhael's crimson-tipped plume on the jasmine plant.

The ground below her shuddered as the archangel landed beside her.

'I will tell the realm how dangerous you are,' he told her. 'You got hysterical and lost control. I had no choice but to kill you. This is what happens when you say no to me, Lucifer. You gave me no choice.'

She tried to speak, but her mouth was full of feathers and her arms wouldn't move. The magic that normally fused her bones together in an instant had vanished, leaving in its wake a long, slow death.

Something cold was pressing against her throat. The tip of Mikhael's sword.

'I should bring back your head,' he said. 'As a lesson to all. But the thought of your wanton body rotting into the very ground you refused to leave satisfies me greater.'

Wrapping her hair around his fist once more, Mikhael pushed off the ground. He flew with Luci trailing beneath him, like an eagle with its prey, her tattered dress leaving a white streak against the black sky.

Running along the edge of the city wall, a thick cluster of trees and overgrown brambles grew. An impenetrable thicket that no one ever visited. Land that belonged to no one. Mikhael threw her limp body into the foliage, thorns and twigs tearing at her skin and dress as she was buried beneath the dry green. Thorns scratched Luci's eyelids, but she couldn't move. Life was seeping out of her where blood would normally flow from a human form. But Luci wasn't human, and now she wasn't an angel either. She was nothing.

'All these years shaping humanity, and you know how you will be remembered?' Mikhael said, floating over her twisted body. 'As a demon. The antithesis of good. As whatever I choose you to be. Because history is written by the victors, Lucifer. And you lost. You're dead.'

Luci had created life on Earth, and she'd also created death, but she didn't think she'd be experiencing them both in such a short space of time. For seven precious years she'd lived, really lived, and she'd loved. But the realm had won, and now the world was losing its light and her feathers would rot alongside her corpse, undiscovered for eternity. Lucifer, the fallen angel, a goddess that would only ever be remembered as the Devil.

'As for our son,' the archangel said, with a final flap of his wings. 'I won't kill him. I'll punish you worse than that. Zadkiel will work for me. No one will know who he is, and I'll make sure he only ever remembers you as the village whore who abandoned her son. The woman who never truly loved him.'

Mikhael's final strike pierced through Luci's heart more violently than any sword. She couldn't move. She couldn't speak. Forced to watch the archangel as he disappeared into the night.

A tear rolled down her torn cheek as her body sank into the earth. Her arms and legs grew heavy, desperation gurgling at her throat. Her son. She had to reach her son.

She opened her mouth, but no sound came out. Air was no longer entering her lungs, her heart already counting down to its final beat. A faint cry carried on a balmy breeze. Not an owl, not the wind, a voice. A child's voice in the distance.

'Mummia? Where are you?'

Luci tried to get up. She managed to move one finger, her lips quivering, then collapsed again. She was sinking, the earth reclaiming her.

'Mummia. I'm scared. You said you would never leave me.'

And those were the last words Luci heard before she died.

IV.

Except Mikhael had been wrong about Luci dying. What he didn't realise was that archangels couldn't die by his sword. They were not like lesser angels—they could rise again. After fourteen years Luci returned, anger and retribution boiling in her new blood, and the first thing she did was look for her boy.

But she was too late.

'I burn, I pine, I perish'
~ Shakespeare, *The Taming of the Shrew*

PART ONE

1

DEATH HAD NEVER been final for Zac—it had simply been a doorway to the next life. When a person died, he got to see them return again. That was how human life worked. Souls moving from body to body.

But that was back then, and everything has to end in the end. Some things go quickly; an inevitable snap of elastic cracking the empty air where a tight stretch had once been. Other things fade slowly; what was once bright, dims. It melts and fills with shadows until nobody remembers it existing. Zac's life, and his preoccupation with the death and rebirth of one special soul, hadn't so much ended but ceased to include him. Pushed him away. Locked him out.

Over one hundred times Zac had watched Ella die. He'd been there in 1613 as she'd swung from the gallows, a broken doll with golden hair blowing on a Dutch breeze. Held her hand in 1941 as the streets of London rained down upon her, his blue eyes the only colour glowing through the grey of her underground tomb. Over the centuries he'd watched her jump off mountains, die beneath horses' hooves, succumb to illness, and get beaten until she was no more. Death was rarely a pleasant business, although sometimes it could be gentle. In a lot of cases he'd simply kept her company during her final moments, when time had been given permission to wear away her body and mind until just paper-thin memories remained. It was her final few breaths he lived for, because it was only then she remembered who he was. And what he'd always been to her.

Zadkiel.

Her everything.

But this time it was different. Zac hadn't been there six years ago, when Josh de Silva's yacht had gone up in flames somewhere off the coast of Santa Monica and killed everyone on board. He hadn't been able to take Ella home this time—because he wasn't able to go home himself. A loop that had lasted two thousand years had finally been severed and there was nothing Zac could do about it.

He leaned over the guitar on his lap and began to tune it, pushing his long hair off his face. Eyes closed, he attempted to take a deep breath, but it made no difference. His lungs no longer filled up to the full. For six years his leaden chest had been hard, heavy, and sharp as mangled iron. Who knew a broken heart could weigh more than a full one?

Running his fingers over the frets and gently plucking each string one at a time, he found himself strumming the same tune he'd played at Ella's dining room table. Had it really been twenty years since he'd made her mother cry, the Spanish melody revealing him for who he was? *What* he was. Twenty years since Ella, his only love, had watched him slice off his own wings and die. It had taken three years to come back to her, yet he'd still missed his chance. She had never known he'd kept his word. And now it no longer mattered.

Shaking his head at the memory, Zac swallowed against the invisible fist closing tightly around his throat. What would the last seventeen years have been like had he ignored his mother's warning and started a life with his one true love? Would he have been able to fight fate and save her from inevitable death? A death he'd known about since the very beginning. A death that signalled the end of her life path; for this life at least.

Unlikely.

He sighed again. What did it matter anyway? Ella was gone, drowned, and he was never going to see her again.

Turning his attention back to the guitar, grounded by the heavy weight of polished wood in his hands, he tightened the last string then glanced up at the clock on the wall. Twelve minutes until the next lesson. But Allegra was always early.

There was a knock at the door and Zac smiled. He never made mistakes…even now.

'Tonio. Allegra. Good afternoon.'

A woman stood in the doorway to his apartment, her grinning mouth slick with newly applied lipstick. Both arms were draped casually around the shoulders of her son, who was holding a guitar in one hand, eyes glued to the phone in the other.

'*Come va, Señor Zac?*' she asked.

'Very well, thank you. Come in. Ready for your lesson, Tonio? I see you have your new guitar with you.'

The boy made a noncommittal sound as he walked past his teacher and into the living room. Placing the instrument gently on the ground, he flopped onto the sofa, the light from his phone highlighting cheekbones the colour of freshly varnished wood. The room filled with the faint ring of electronic music as the boy's fingers moved deftly over the screen.

'You like it?' Zac asked, pointing at the guitar at his feet.

Tonio looked up, blinked, and muttered something resembling a 'yes, thank you' before turning back to his phone. To anyone else the boy's disinterest may have appeared ill-mannered, but Zac was proud of his student. When they'd first started lessons, the boy was hardly talking.

Allegra hovered beside Zac, so close her arm pressed against his. He shivered. It had been a long time since he'd had any physical contact with anyone. The only people he ever spoke at length to were the parents of the children he taught, and even then conversation was stilted and formal. Most parents dropped off their children and collected them at the end of their lesson; but this mother was never in a rush to leave.

'Is there anything I can help you with?' he asked.

Dark, liquid eyes looked up at him. 'Yes, I need to talk to you, Señor Zac.' She patted him lightly on the shoulder, causing another shiver to run down his spine. 'In private, please? Before the lesson starts?'

There it was again, the inability to fill up his lungs with one deep breath. He led her into the kitchen and gestured at the silver-and-black coffee machine on the counter.

'*Grazie,*' she said, pulling her hair out of its ponytail and running her fingers through it with both hands. Her thick hair framed her face and brought out the amber in her brown eyes. Eyes just like her son's. Zac had never noticed how much Tonio looked like his mother, or how much younger the woman was compared to the other mums.

'Espresso?' he asked.

She nodded.

January in Tuscany meant blue skies and a bitter bite in the air, yet Allegra was wearing a thin skirt and a brightly coloured shirt that clung to her chest so tightly the top button was only half fastened.

Her dark eyes followed him around the kitchen as he directed his gaze to the ground, picked up two tiny coffee cups from the cupboard, and filled the machine with water. It was the first time he'd made coffee for a parent, refusing to let anyone inside his home beside the living room and hallway. Zac cherished his privacy as much as he did the apartment he'd bought three years ago. It was the first place he'd been able to call his own.

How long would he be staying in Italy this time before being forced to move on?

The kitchen, like the rest of the apartment, was new and modern in design. Zac no longer had any interest in old buildings; history had been far from kind to him.

'You have a lot of recipes,' she said, squinting up at the cookbooks displayed neatly on the shelf.

'Yes, one of my few vices,' he replied. 'I like to travel. Every time I visit a new country, I bring home a reminder of their culture. Love of food and family is the one thing all nationalities appear to have in common.'

She nodded, although Zac knew there was no way she'd understand how much he valued family. Nor would she be aware of the vast hole that had been left in his life after losing any hope of a normal life with the woman he loved.

'You like to cook?' Her voice was filled with the same smooth, caramel tones as her hair.

'Yes, although I rarely have anyone to cook for.'

The look she gave him was difficult to decipher. For seventeen years he'd been as close to human as he could possibly be, yet he still missed having the power to feel what others felt. It was a continuous struggle to read people just by their facial expressions, even after all this time.

'That one is in Japanese, and those two in French,' she said, pointing at the bookshelf. 'You read them all?'

'I speak many languages.'

'I thought you were Italian. You sound like a local.'

'It's complicated. I'm not from anywhere really, although I was born close to here. In Fiesole.' He handed her a tiny cup. 'Careful, it's hot.'

She took a sip, her red lipstick leaving a heart-shaped mark on its rim.

'If you speak so many languages why did you return to Tuscany? You could have settled anywhere.'

The espresso scalded his throat as he downed it in one gulp, placing the cup back in the machine to make another. Why *had* he returned? Perhaps it was morbid curiosity. Wanting to be close to the place where it had all started, where he'd first met Ella—or Arabella as she'd been back then. He'd wanted to see how much the town had changed in two thousand years, search for the clearing in the woods where his cottage had once stood. Now there was no future for him, his soul yearned to get as close to his past as possible. Needless to say, Fiesole was virtually unrecognisable. He hadn't returned since.

'I came back because of family,' he replied.

'But you have no wife or children?'

The invisible fist was back again, this time twisting his guts.

'No. I don't want children of my own.'

What he really meant to say was that he *couldn't*. That if he ever dared father a child and his mother found out she would possess the last piece of her puzzle. She would change the world in ways no one could imagine. He wasn't prepared to give her that.

'I do love children, though,' he added quickly. 'It's why I set up the charity, for kids like Tonio.'

The sound of guitar music floated through the gap in the kitchen door, making him smile.

Allegra was smiling too. 'He's eager to get started, but I want to say one last thing.' Without taking her eyes off Zac, she reached behind for the kitchen door handle and closed it quietly. 'I want to thank you for buying him the guitar for his birthday last week. It was too kind. He hasn't put it down since.'

'Tonio's a good kid.'

Her voice dropped to a hush tone. 'I've never known a man like you, Señor Zac.'

It was difficult to keep from sighing at the irony of what she was saying. Of course she'd never met a man like him before, because he was the only one of his kind. He'd never *been* a man—and now? He had no idea what he was now.

There was worry in her dark eyes as she gazed nervously up at him. But he wasn't going to reply. Not because he didn't want to, but because he feared the words that formed behind his tightly pressed lips.

She tensed as he took the coffee cup back off her, his fingers brushing hers. It would have been easy to look up, meet her gaze, but he wasn't ready yet. He needed more time. Luckily time was something he had an abundance of.

'Would you like another coffee?'

'No, thank you.'

The right thing to do would be to get rid of this woman, this distraction, and save them both the inevitable heartache of starting something new. Yet pushing her away wouldn't be fair to her son. The boy needed him. He couldn't let his own emotions hamper Tonio's potential.

As well as having founded the children's music charity, Zac was also a volunteer at the local community centre for underprivileged children. It was where he had first met Allegra and Tonio. Thanks to Zac's abilities it was easy for him to convince companies and rich people to part with their money for a good cause, and to get the word out to families that needed help. It felt good to have a worthy purpose again. He'd hoped to form a strong bond with the children who needed him, but he hadn't anticipated this…emotional turmoil.

The day Ella died had been the beginning of his unravelling. There were gaping holes in his memory of the dark weeks that followed the accident, and the argument he'd had with his mother. He couldn't remember where he'd gone afterwards or what he'd done to numb those incessant, sharp stabs of grief. Eventually the fog of pain had lifted, and he'd vowed to focus on something more important than one person. Even though Ella had ruled his very existence for two thousand years, and every minute without her was a reminder of the life he was unable to have, she was still just one woman out of millions of souls.

At least that's what he told himself. Not that it made any difference to his twisted guts and strangled heart.

Yet here was another woman, one that was very much alive and looking at him like the pilgrims had when he would appear to them in all his glory. Looking at him with the wonder and reverence he missed.

'What are you thinking, Allegra?'

She stepped closer, the scent of her perfume permeating the space between them. Spring meadows and wildflowers. The hairs on his arm rose as she placed her hand on him, her touch too warm, too soft, too gentle. Again, only a fraction of his lungs filled as he tried to take a breath.

'For two years I've brought Tonio to your apartment for guitar lessons. Every Monday afternoon.'

'You want to stop coming?'

'No! It's his favourite part of the week. I just think I should pay.'

Zac shook his head. 'I've told you before, the charity pays.'

Over the last couple of months Allegra had been trying to pay him for his time and had started to make excuses to stay and watch her son play. Zac could have done something about her interruptions, it wasn't fair on Tonio, but in all honesty he'd begun to look forward to his Monday afternoons. Sometimes he'd even stall her at pickup time, tell her how much her son had progressed and how proud she should be. He liked to see her smile and watch her amber-flecked eyes, so often filled with worry or nerves, crease in the corners. Her lips were full and pale against her sun-kissed skin, and he often wondered what they would feel like brushing his skin.

'If I cannot pay, then let me do something for you in return,' she said, then covered her face as she realised how that sounded. 'I mean, let me help you too.'

Zac didn't know much about her past except that she was a single mother, Tonio her only child, and she still lived with her parents. After some digging, he'd also discovered she was in her second year of medical school and worked in a local restaurant by night. The woman before him didn't look like someone who had little rest and so much responsibility to shoulder—she looked like a teenager waiting for her crush to text her back.

'There's no need to thank me, Allegra. Your son is a talented boy, and he deserves to shine. With a mother like you there's no doubt he will do well.'

With a shaky smile she placed her hand on his arm again. Her touch felt hotter this time, matching the growing heat forming in his centre. For seventeen years he'd been denying himself physical contact with anyone—telling himself he wasn't human, that he didn't have the same needs as others. Except he did.

It had been easy in the past to resist that pull, any desires that didn't involve Ella, but he'd been a different being back then. Now he was as close to human as possible, that is, if humans never aged. He knew it made no sense to act on his wants. After all, he couldn't possibly maintain a relationship without the other person growing suspicious of him and his past. Yet it was getting increasingly difficult to turn away potential happiness each time it presented itself.

Like right now.

He cleared his throat. 'I better start Tonio's lesson,' he said, his voice thick and slow. Had Allegra sensed the shift in the air between them?

He reached for the door handle behind her. 'You can stay if you want.'

· · · · ·

For the next hour Zac taught Tonio a new melody and Allegra watched. Seated at the dining table, her head resting on her hands watching them play, Allegra's eyes filled with such intense love for her boy that Zac struggled to concentrate on the sheet of music in front of them.

Knowing he would never be a father was a relentless, gnawing ache in his guts. The discomfort refused to cease, no matter how much time he spent helping his students. Zac would never know what it was to look at his own flesh and blood, see himself in the face of a child, experience a magnified version of their joy and pain. How did parents do it? How did they survive each day watching a piece of their heart walk around outside of their body, forever attached by the thinnest of threads? How did they function while constantly toying between wanting to set their children free, yet keeping them as close as possible?

Then it hit him, the reason why he was trapped no matter what he did nor where he went. Looking at Allegra's face, so in awe of her son, Zac realised he'd never be able to rid himself of his mother's fierce love for him. The bond between mother and child was forever—time and distance made no diffcrence—he would never be free of Luci's hold over him.

But he yearned for a different kind of love. A love based on want, not need.

Allegra's eyes flickered from her boy to Zac and he quickly turned his attention back to his student.

'I think that's enough for today, Tonio. I'm very impressed with your progress.'

'It's this guitar, Señor Zac!' the boy cried, his face filled with the open wonder only children possess. Zac wondered how long it would take for life to reveal her cruel nature to the boy. 'I practice every day like you told me to. Even on the toilet. The guitar sleeps beside me at night, so if there's an emergency I can take it with me.'

Zac ruffled the boy's hair. 'There won't be any emergency. You just work hard at school and keep practicing and you'll see how quickly you pass to the next grade.'

Tonio gave Zac an impulsive hug, then remembered it wasn't cool for ten-year-old boys to hug their teachers and turned to his mother instead.

'I have to pee, Mummia. Then we go, OK? I want to show Nonna and Nonno what I learned today.'

The living room door slammed behind him as he ran into the hall-way to the bathroom.

'I meant what I said earlier,' Allegra whispered, taking the guitar from Zac. Feeling brave, he let his hand hover beside hers for a moment too long before she placed the instrument back in the case. 'If you won't take my money then let me cook for you. I will make you my famous ravioli.'

This time, when he took a deep breath, his chest let in a little air. 'I'd like that.'

It was out before he'd had time to think. *Careless!* How could he date a woman, run the risk of falling for her, without revealing what he was? He and Ella had been disastrous enough, but at least she'd been aware of his past. This thing Allegra was attempting to start would only end in tears—not just hers, but her son's too.

'Actually, Allegra…'

'Zac.' She glanced at the door, then placed a hand on his chest. He closed his eyes at her touch. Damn, it felt good. 'You are a wonderful man, and to my son you are a hero. I look forward to spending more time with you.'

Say something! He parted his lips, ready to speak, but his mouth was too dry, and the words wouldn't form. The look she was giving him, it was too much—his body was responding as if it were her soft finger-tips, and not her eyes, that were caressing his face. The space between them was getting smaller, one of them had stepped closer. Maybe both of them.

What would happen if he kissed her? People did that all the time. He'd seen it in bars and clubs, strangers locking lips then walking away as if it meant nothing. What would happen if he clasped her beautiful face in his hands and kissed her until he was drunk from her? Would the kiss cancel out seventeen years of pain, bridge the gap from when he'd last felt lips on his? Perhaps, if he closed his eyes, he could pretend Allegra was Ella. Their kiss would be like water quenching his cracked clay heart, and perhaps over time he'd be able to think of this woman instead of his one true love every time they embraced.

The sound of the toilet flushing made Zac jump. Tonio was returning. They didn't have much time.

'One more thing, before you go,' Zac whispered, cupping Allegra's face in his hands.

Swirls of brown and amber flecks swam before him as he stared deep into her eyes, liquid eyes that misted over as she awaited his kiss. His voice was low and fast, he had to tell her before the boy interrupted them. She had to know how he felt.

'Allegra, from now on you will no longer feel anything romantic toward me. You will not be attracted to me. Neither will you ask questions about my personal life. I will be nothing more to you than your child's music teacher. Do you understand?'

'Yes, Zac,' she said, a stupefied smile on her tanned face.

He was going to miss that smile.

Tonio entered the room just as Zac let her go. The boy pulled his mother by the hand and gave his teacher a high five on his way out.

Zac held open the door for her. 'Good night, Allegra,' he said, increasing his grasp on the door handle to stop his hand from trembling.

'Good night.' Her smile was still slick red with lipstick but no longer filled with longing. Zac thought back to the crimson heart she'd left on the rim of his coffee cup and watched them step into the lift.

Shutting the door with a quiet click, he leaned his back against it and let out a long breath as he slid to the floor. How long would he have to wait until he no longer feared living?

2

THE INSIDE OF the calzone was hotter than molten lava. Zac flinched as the scalding mozzarella burned the roof of his mouth. In an instant he was healed. Although there were plenty of downsides to being immortal, at least he never had to worry about blowing on his dinner to cool it down.

It was early evening and the sun had been replaced by shadows, the cobbles beneath his feet lit up by the amber glow of cosy trattorias and wine bars. In the summertime Florence was a crazy din of tourists, but in January the dark, chilly streets were empty save for the odd couple kissing against the river wall and shoppers bustling against the wind.

Walking along the Ponte Vecchio, he thought back to the first time he'd crossed the river Arno at this point, over two thousand years ago. The Roman bridge had originally been built from stone and wood, the landscape nothing but fields back then. Every week he would venture down to the city from Fiesole to trade his goat's meat and milk, pushing his heavily laden cart down the hill and along the dusty tracks. The hour's walk took much longer back then.

Fiesole had lost its charm after losing his girl and his life there two thousand years ago. Zac had returned only once since then, but he hadn't stayed long—it had hurt too much to retread the steps of the world he'd briefly shared with Arabella. But he never used to know where his work as a Path Keeper would take him, and in the past he'd occasionally been sent back to nearby Florence. When he found himself in this city, the first thing he did was visit the famous bridge and note its changes, such as its rebuild after the floods of 1117 and the way shops had sprung up along its side, perched over the edge as if clinging on for dear life. Back then it was butchers who dominated that bridge; for hundreds of years it was the place to go for the best meat in Florence, a crazy scramble of eager locals weighing down its fine arches with their greedy needs. Now it was a tourist attraction, fancy stores selling jewellery, fine art, and souvenir trinkets. Zac shook his head, smiling to himself. Everything in life insisted on changing, yet always remained the same.

As he reached the other side of the river he turned right, ignoring the cries of the gelato vendor mistaking him for a tourist. In Florence, ice cream was always in demand—even in winter.

If he squinted and ignored the tiny cars and Vespas parked on the side of the road it could be any year over the last four hundred. Florence had always been a veritable canvas, ornate buildings, carvings, and fountains scattered haphazardly at every turn, but it was during the Renaissance that the Tuscan city had shone its brightest. Which was why Zac was on his way to the Uffizi Gallery—to relive the heady days when he'd been in the thick of it, basking in the glory that angels had once been permitted.

Taking a final bite of his calzone, Zac brushed the crumbs off his hands and stared up at the darkening sky. He still had a couple of hours until the gallery closed.

To reach the Uffizi, visitors had to walk beneath the arches and past the queues. But Zac wasn't just anyone—he was special. He had the luxury of skipping the throngs and walking straight in. Just as he did every week, he nodded at the security guards then greeted the receptionist who waved him through with his all-access pass. Anyone who mattered in the old city knew Zac. He'd convinced them, in his own special way, to allow him full reign to do as he pleased. He gave a lot to the community, he reasoned, so not paying to see the paintings he helped create wasn't the worst misuse of his power.

It was late on a Wednesday and the middle of winter, which meant the gallery was at its emptiest. First stop, the Botticelli rooms.

Florence during the 1470s had been a spectacular sight, at least for those who had money. Zac had spent a lot of time in the centre and had found himself swept up in the new wave of creativity. He'd even posed for a selection of artists. No photos of him existed before that rain-soaked night in the Spanish hills twenty years ago, when he'd forfeited his wings for the chance to return as human. And even now, whether out of habit or to remain hidden from his mother, Zac still avoided having his picture taken. But having appeared in classical works of art through the ages meant that the Uffizi gallery had become Zac's very own photo album, a glimpse back at a simpler time when angels were revered, and love was less complicated.

Botticelli's Primavera was one of his favourite paintings, and he was in it. Back then, the only reason he'd visited the artist's studio was because of Aria, the girl in the centre of the painting. But he'd ended up staying for days. It was somewhat poetic that the famous oil canvas had never left Florence, as if the soul of that special girl had kept it rooted so close to where her and Zac's story had begun. Hair like molten copper, Aria had been a Florentine whore who'd sat for artists in exchange for money. The eighty-third reincarnation of Arabella, she'd been a melancholy girl who spoke very little. For days, as they'd been forced to hold their pose, the other models had talked among themselves, but she'd stayed silent, her gaze fixed on Zac. Botticelli had captured her longing and pain perfectly. Over the short time Zac had watched over her Aria had remained quiet and guarded, always twitchy and nervous around him. Their relationship had been filled with nothing but gentle guidance and support, not like the passion he'd shared with Ella or the deep sense of protectiveness he'd felt for Arabella. It never ceased to amaze him how every version of his girl had been so different, yet at their core they still possessed the same mix of strength and vulnerability.

He rubbed his face. Memories were exhausting. And what did it matter now, anyway? Ella was gone now, like every other version of her.

He joined a group of tourists at the base of the large Botticelli canvas and looked up at the depiction of the three graces—a whimsical trio of scantily clad girls dancing in a ring. And there he was beside them, Zac pretending to be Mercury chasing away the clouds.

The invisible fist was back, pulling at something deep inside of him.

His and Aria's time together *had* mattered, he *had* been important to her. He could see it in the way the girl in the painting was looking at him. Nothing had been wasted. Zac and his soulmate, together on canvas, subjects of a creative masterpiece that would last the test of time. At least something more tangible than just painful memories of their love had survived.

He'd been staring at the painting for at least ten minutes when his phone vibrated in the back pocket of his jeans. Zac had learned many things over the last two thousand years but, due to his previous inability to use anything electrical, technology wasn't one of his strong points. But he'd managed—which was more than could be said for the person messaging him right now. His screen was flashing with line after line of text, each word sent individually.

I Miss yiu
Zadkiel.
Get IN toch.
You cant ig.nore me
forever.

His phone vibrated again.

P.S. This is Luci. You r mOTher.

She never gave up! For the third time in six years he blocked the number without replying. Luci could go to hell where she belonged. It was bad enough she'd wiped Ella's memory seventeen years ago, but after what she'd done to him the week Ella was destined to die, he never wanted to see her again. It was unforgiveable. For six years he'd managed to successfully evade his mother, and he had no intention of answering her pleas any time soon.

His jaw cracked as he moved it from side to side. He covered his face and let out a low groan into the palms of his hands. Why did she have this effect on him? No matter what he was doing, his mother always managed to ruin a special moment.

His shoes echoed far too loudly as he marched out of the Botticelli rooms, rushing aimlessly from gallery to gallery, his head swimming with all the things he wanted to say to Luci—even though he never wanted to speak to her again. He didn't slow down until he spotted an art guide standing before a large painting.

Zac listened for a moment and then, lips twitching, he rolled his shoulders and stood beside the group of tourists fixated on the guide's every word.

'This work of art by Da Vinci is called the Annunciation,' the Italian woman explained to the crowd forming around her. Her smile looked encouraging, but her eyes spoke of the hundreds of times she'd stood in that exact spot, saying the same words over and over again. 'It was believed to be a collaboration between a young Da Vinci and his master Verrocchio. The angel is Gabriel, and this here is the Virgin Mary receiving news that she is pregnant.'

Zac let out a sarcastic laugh. The woman turned to him.

'*Signor*, perhaps you would like to enlighten us as to why this painting amuses you?'

He raised his eyebrows as dozens of pairs of eyes stared at him. Did he dare?

'I laughed because Archangel Gabriel doesn't look like that. Mary didn't look like that either. Plus the tiny wingspan in the painting is very offensive. When it comes to wings, angels believe the bigger the better.'

A girl beside him giggled and he flashed her a lopsided grin. The guide wasn't laughing though.

'It's true that Archangel Gabriel has been portrayed in many ways throughout art history,' she said, mouth puckered, and brow creased. 'But this was painted during the Renaissance, when angels were depicted with flowing locks and the Virgin Mary was—'

'White with blonde hair? Mary was a Jewish woman from Galilee, not a twelve-year-old girl with porcelain skin. Women from there never used to look like that,' Zac answered, his lip curling into a sardonic smile.

Luci had already pissed him off and he wasn't in the mood for anyone else's nonsense.

'And it was Verrocchio who was to blame for most of that painting, not Da Vinci. Leonardo was young back then and was only permitted to paint some of Gabriel and the background.' Zac was warming up now. 'Originally, Da Vinci gave the angel dark skin and *huge* wings, massive golden-tipped feathers that obscured the trees behind him. His master went crazy when he saw it and insisted that his other student, Domenico Ghirlandaio, paint over it all. The lesser-known artist changed the skin tone and copied the structure of a bird's wing, giving the angel an overall lacklustre demeanor. Leonardo wasn't happy, which is why he disassociated himself from the work. Most people attributed this painting to just Verrocchio and Ghirlandaio until 1869.'

The crowd had grown and were now gathering closer to Zac, but the guide had her arms crossed.

'No one can say any of that for certain,' she replied. 'Did you read that nonsense on the internet? Like many of Da Vinci's works, speculation is rife, but unless you were actually there between 1472 and 1475 when it was…'

'1473. It was painted not long after Da Vinci became an apprentice.'

The woman sniffed and shook her head. '*Signor*, these statements are unfounded. I have been studying Renaissance art for thirty years and have worked at this gallery for twenty-four of those years. Unless you were beside Da Vinci while he painted this masterpiece there is no way you can know any of that as a fact. Were you there? Hmm?'

With a shrug and a ghost of a smile on his lips, Zac turned back to the painting as the guide led the tourists to the next masterpiece.

Of course he'd been there. He and Gabriel had stood beside Leonardo in the studio the day he'd been left alone to paint the angel. Zac remembered it as if it were last week. The smell of turpentine and oils, the room filled with feathers and colourful fabric which the artists had been sketching for days, perfecting the intricate folds of the Virgin Mary's skirt and the angel's robe.

'Where are my sexy wings, my man?' Archangel Gabriel had boomed, making Leonardo jump and smudge one of the trees in the background. 'If you're going to paint me as an effeminate white man, at least show my pretty feathers. These bad boys are my pride and joy! Whereas these *things*, that your master has sketched for you to colour in, wouldn't raise a sparrow off the ground.'

Zac had grinned, much as he did now, but Gabriel hadn't finished.

'I'm sick of the weak-looking angels you're all painting nowadays. Leonardo, you know your father doesn't look like this prepubescent man-child you're depicting. Azantiel is a warrior in our realm, brave enough to father you and risk the wrath of Mikhael. At least honour our kind and give me some decent wings.'

Leonardo had only been young back then, no more than twenty-one years old. His mother Caterina, a peasant girl, had been unmarried when she fell pregnant with the child of an angel. Azantiel had begged Gabriel to keep an eye on his boy and ensure his safe arrival into the world, knowing the archangel had watched his own Nephilim son suffer at the hands of Mikhael. It was Gabriel who had found Caterina a husband, a notary called Piero da Vinci, whose true love was a rich and powerful gentleman in Rome. Piero was more than happy to claim the boy as his own and dispel any damaging rumours. But it was Azantiel who raised Leonardo in his shadow, making him the great man everyone knew today. It still shocked Zac how accepting the world had been of the artist being so ahead of his time, without ever questioning why.

'Your task in this lifetime, son, is to ensure that our truth will be discovered one day,' Zac remembered Azantiel telling Leonardo when he was just twelve years old. 'You have many of my gifts and you will use them to communicate our plight. In the future, people will look at your work and understand that we live in a godless world governed by angels—and that one day the two realms will unite. I will father as many Nephilim as it takes to pass on my knowledge to humans. I won't stop until the day Archangel Mikhael loses his power.'

Back then Zac hadn't known he was the son of their master, but he'd always known their archangel leader would do anything to remain in power. Leonardo wasn't Azantiel's only child. Zac's mother Luci had recently told him about Marisse, the German witch in the Dutch city of Roermond who'd also been fathered by the rebel angel two hundred years later. It was she who'd made the jewellery Luci said would bring down the realm. Azantiel had brought many secret Nephilim into this world until, along with a handful of other rogue angels, he'd eventually been murdered by Mikhael. But the warrior angel had done his job by then—the seeds of doubt among those that mattered had been sown.

And Leonardo's works, and the secret messages hidden among them, had lived on forever.

'Look at those damn pigeon wings. I should have destroyed that painting centuries ago,' a deep voice boomed behind Zac.

The air was instantly sucked out of the room, leaving his skin covered in tiny goose bumps. Only one being had the power to do that. Turning around slowly, his face splitting into a giant grin, Zac found himself eye-to-eye with his best friend. The most famous archangel in history.

3

'GABRIEL!'

The angel threw his arm around Zac's shoulders. Heavy and reassuring, his embrace reminded him of a time that now felt more fantasy than memory.

'And how are you, brother? I saw you giving that tour guide a hard time.'

Zac shrugged, making Gabriel laugh and pull him into a bear hug.

'I've missed you, boy. It's been too long.'

'Ten years. You're not easy to track down,' Zac replied, leaning back to look at his friend.

'Yeah, well, we angels don't have those fancy computer phones you lot have now. I always find you in the end though, right? So, you're looking at our family photos.'

They were surrounded by paintings of winged beings and saints.

Zac laughed softly. 'I come here to think about the past sometimes. You know?'

Gabrielle nodded slowly, his pale green eyes narrowing with concern.

'Come! You need some fresh air, my friend. You're getting maudlin. Let's go for a walk.'

Zac followed him out of the building, in the opposite direction to the river. The evening had turned to night and the sky was bruised in shades of indigo and purple, the stars yet to appear. Piazza della Signoria was Zac's favourite square. It was dusk and the Palazzo Vecchio was lit up, shining gold against the velvet sky. It loomed over the hustle and bustle of tourists and postcard sellers, its castle-style roof and tower straight out of a fairy tale. The sides of the piazza were lined with arches and statues from the gallery, the pretty wooden shutters of the apartments above the restaurants locked tight against the crisp night air. Even though an icy wind blew, a few couples were still enjoying their evening, sipping their coffees, scarves wrapped loosely around their necks.

The two friends, one a famous archangel and the other fallen and broken, sat on a stone bench beneath the arches. There was something about Gabriel that made Zac want to talk for eternity. To spill his soul at his feet. But tonight, instead, Zac rubbed his eyes with the heel of his hand and swallowed down the loneliness he'd been battling since the last time they'd met.

'That's you, isn't it?' Gabriel said with a smirk, pointing at the replica statue of Michelangelo's David guarding the door to the Palazzo.

Zac rolled his eyes but didn't answer.

'Come on, I know it is. You were a right artist's plaything back then. In and out of those studios more times than you could say "strike a pose."'

A small laugh escaped Zac's lips as he glanced up at the statue. The original was bigger, marble, and the sculptor's most famous work. This was one of many imitations of David scattered all over the city.

'It's not in proportion,' Zac mumbled. 'The hands are too big and the...' He nodded at the magnificent carving. 'You know? The...'

'You saying Michelangelo made your dick too small?'

Zac rubbed the back of his neck. 'Well, yeah. I offered to pose for him, and he was a bit...enthusiastic, about how much I should show. I said I wanted to keep my dignity and we argued. So he did that.'

Gabriel's laugh was so loud it reverberated through the arches, causing a couple on the other side of the square to stop taking photos and look over at them.

'Oh, come on, Zadkiel! You *loved* the attention. I bet half the Renaissance paintings of naked guys are you.'

'I did it for Aria.' Zac registered his friend's confusion and waved his hands impatiently. 'Arabella? Ella? Aria was one of her incarnations. She modelled for artists. That's why I offered my services, so I could stay close to her.'

'Of course, the prostitute. Florence was full of them back then.'

Zac had never thought of Aria that way, but his friend was right. The same streets he'd walked down that afternoon used to be crowded with groups of women wearing high heels under their long skirts, the air sweet and sickly from their scent.

Gabriel continued. 'Remember the tinkling of the bells around their wrists and necks? It was a colourful time back then. Such a sense of freedom and hope after the Black Death. So much love. Men with men, girls with girls. Remember how everyone was having sex but no one was having babies anymore?'

'I can't remember,' Zac muttered, his mind filled only with images of a half-dressed Aria, posing for Botticelli while staring intently at him. She was the only thing that had filled his mind and time for years.

'You *must* remember! The pope was getting desperate, worried the city would never repopulate again, which is why he made prostitution legal. You know, to get the gay guys randy enough to marry women and fill up Florence again. "Redirection of male lust," he called it. All these beautiful painted women, tottering around the streets fighting over any man who walked by. It was a joke, as if you can redirect lust! All that happened was married men and priests got more action than usual.'

Zac remembered it differently. It wasn't as vibrant and amusing as Gabriel made out. It was a time of hardship, loss, and illness. The stench of death permeated every inch of the city, hanging like smoke above the buildings, winding its way through narrow, cobbled streets and up to the lofty heights of the rich and powerful. Death had no preference for class nor wealth.

'Aria was different from those women,' Zac said. 'She loved art and had dreams of being a painter. Botticelli took advantage of that, convincing her to pose in exchange for lessons that never happened. I was only there to keep an eye on her.'

'Yeah, OK. Ever the heroic Zadkiel, the self-deprecating martyr. Admit it, you were desperate to be near her and desperate to be in a painting. Don't look at me like that, bro. You know it was always me and Mikhael on stained glass windows and church frescos. You wanted in on the action.'

Perhaps his friend was right, perhaps there *was* a part of him that wanted to last forever. Zac didn't have the big legacy, like the archangels who appeared in the Bible. Gabriel, Mikhael, even Rafael—they were the ones people talked and wrote about. Perhaps, considering that every version of Arabella forgot who he was life after life, perhaps Zac *did* want to be remembered in some way.

'I loved that beautiful girl, just as much as I have loved every version of Ella before and since. Did you know Aria died of the Great Pox in 1501?'

Gabriel screwed up his nose in disgust and Zac frowned.

'Hey, sorry, man,' Gabriel said, his hands up in mock surrender. 'You just reminded me of the smell…and the boils.'

Zac ignored him. 'I was heartbroken. I made her a promise on her deathbed, that I would help create the most beautiful thing that has ever been sculpted by human hands. That's why I posed for Michelangelo di Lodovico Buonarroti Simoni the following year. Good job he's only known by his first name now.' He gave a half-hearted laugh, then sighed. 'I never appreciated how much easier things were back then, Gabriel. When I lost Aria, I knew I would see her again in a different guise. Yet this emptiness I now possess is eating me up from the inside. I wake up some mornings expecting to have been swallowed whole by it and there to be nothing left of me but dust and memories that no one can recall.'

'My dear friend, your melancholy is positively Shakespearean.' Gabriel squeezed his friend's shoulder and looked up at the sky, now studded with the first few pinpricks of stars. 'There's a simple way to overcome this loneliness and despair, you know. There's one other person who knows exactly how you feel.'

Zac stared straight ahead, his jaw twitching. 'I'm not interested.'

'Call your mother, Zadkiel. Now that *is* a woman who knows all about love. Lucifer spent two thousand years searching for you and suffering who-knows-what in order to find you. And *this* is how you repay her?'

Zac wasn't going to sit and be lectured to by his oldest friend, and neither was he going to argue about it. His mother didn't know the first thing about love and sacrifice. He stood up.

'Zadkiel, don't go. I came to…'

Gabriel had no clue what Luci had put him through; he'd never understand. Zac took two steps forward, but his friend wasn't finished yet.

'Zadkiel, *sit down!*'

The archangel's deep voice reverberated around the piazza. A flock of pigeons took flight and for a short second it was as if the entire city stood still, frozen, waiting to see what would happen next. Zac closed his eyes and raised his face to the heavens. There were times he wished that a god *did* exist, just so he had something to pray to. With another exaggerated sigh, he sat back down on the cold bench.

Fine, if Gabriel wanted to talk, then they'd talk. But the archangel wasn't permitted to lie, so it was time for some tough questions.

'Did she send you? Did Luci tell you to come here?' Zac asked, his voice so quiet Gabriel had to shuffle closer to hear him.

'Why would you think that?'

'Because it's your job. You're the Holy Messenger, for crying out loud! It's in your *nature*. You only visit when you have important news to impart.'

Gabriel said nothing. His silence spoke volumes.

'She *did*, didn't she! Luci sent you!'

'Yes. I saw her yesterday. She told me you were here.'

There it was again, the iron fist clutching at Zac's chest and squeezing the air out of his lungs. His fucking mother was never going to give up.

'She sent me a text message a few hours ago,' Zac said. 'How did she track me down this time? Those creepy whisperers of hers?'

'Of course. I don't know how she does it, how she has a constant stream of people working for her around the globe feeding back information about Nephilim and sightings—but it works. That woman is something else.'

She was indeed, except Gabriel hadn't said it with the same disgust and fear Zac felt. When Gabriel spoke of Luci he did so with awe. Another fly trapped in her dewy, irresistible web.

'She's not the great goddess you think she is. She's a bad person, Gabriel. She makes people do things against their will. How's that a good thing?'

'If you're talking about sex, she simply brings out their latent desires. You think your mother, of all people, would force anyone to sleep with her? She merely strips them of their inhibitions, because deep down everyone wants someone to give them permission to let go. You make her sound like a rabid animal.'

Zac wasn't thinking about sex. He was thinking of the way Luci always got what she wanted, no matter who she hurt.

'You tell yourself that, Gabriel. But Luci is reckless and dangerous, and you know it.'

'Give her a chance, Zadkiel. She's your mother and she loves you very much.'

'Love? She has no idea what that means.'

Gabriel rubbed his face. 'You forget I was there, at the very beginning. I saw you as a boy, and I saw the true power of a mother's love. Lucifer died for you, Zadkiel. She put you before the entire Angelic Realm!'

'And what did she do when she returned? She ruined my life.'

'Hey, that's *enough!*' Gabriel cried, pointing a finger at Zac as if he were an errant schoolboy. 'You need to let it go. Man, I've never known a being hold a grudge for as long as you. When you get fixated on something, you really get fixated.'

Zac rounded up on the archangel, their faces inches apart.

'Luci took away my only chance to be with Ella!' he spat. 'It wasn't up to her to decide when I said goodbye or how. She took that away from me, and I'll never get that moment back.'

Gabriel closed his eyes, and when he opened them there was a softness there. 'I was in Spain too, remember? The day of Ella's wedding was a mess. Your mother murdered a man and impaled him on a goddamn crucifix. In a chapel! And Mikhael had one of his minions, that Paloma girl, spying on Ella to make sure the ceremony went ahead and she'd stick to her path. Yet you *still* think, after all these years, it was worth risking Ella's life for the sake of a happy ending? Revealing our rebellion? Letting the realm know that you and Lucifer had survived and that I'm working against our leader? Ella had eleven years of her life left, Zadkiel. That's nothing. It wasn't worth destroying all our hard work, and all our lives including hers, for that. Your mother did what she had to do. Wiping Ella's memory was an act of kindness. The girl went on to have a happy life, just like you wanted for her. You spent ten years travelling around the world with your mother after that, looking for Nephilim, having fun. I thought you'd got over it all.'

Gabriel had no clue. This was typical of Luci, managing to control people's perception of her at every opportunity.

'She hasn't told you, has she?'

The wind had picked up since they'd been sitting on the stone bench, and now the sky was pitch black, the stars struggling to be seen against the haze of the city's lights. Angels didn't feel the cold, but Zac did, and his behind was getting damp and numb. He shifted his weight. Of course his mother hadn't told Gabriel what she'd done. Why would she? She needed the archangel on her side.

'Told me what?' his friend replied.

'I've known the day Ella was meant to die since before she was born. The tenth of July. Aged thirty-four. Drowning. That was all I knew—what all the Path Keepers and archangels knew. Had I remained an angel I would have been there, felt her, and been by her side to take her Home. Like I have done at every single one of her past lives. But this time, all I knew was when and how she would die, but not where.'

'Zadkiel, I know it must have been difficult but…'

'Listen, Gabriel. *Please!* This is important. You're right, my mother and I had fun for ten years. I reasoned Ella was happily married and living the highlife in California, so I tried to move on. Luci and I saw a lot of the world, and although I had no romantic interest in anyone else, I did manage to relax and live a little. My mother convinced me that if we found the Nephilim in those ten years, we might have time to save Ella. There was no way of making her live forever, but at least if Mikhael was out of the way I could spend Ella's final years with her. I can use electricity now, but I tried not to follow her progress on the internet. It was too painful to watch her on the red carpet, beaming beside Joshua de Silva, the man she was always destined to be with.'

Zac took a breath, but Gabriel remained respectfully silent. Waiting.

'Josh was a good man, and they were right for each other. I didn't hate him. I should have, he had the life I'd spent two thousand years longing for, but I didn't hate him. I found out they had a house in Santa Monica and so, in Ella's last week, I decided to look for her. She was going to die anyway, so I wasn't going to be able to change her life path, but I needed to see her. Surely you understand that, Gabriel? I needed her to know that I loved her, that I came back for her. Just as I'd promised.'

Gabriel nodded. It was clear he was bracing himself for something big—and so he should.

'I went to Santa Monica and asked after her. You know I can convince people to tell me anything, so I found out where she lived very quickly, and I watched her… Yes, I know you think I'm a love-sick creep, and a wimp, but I needed to convince myself she was happy. And she was. I wanted to talk to her, but the more I saw her laughing with friends, having lunch meetings and romantic walks along the beach with Josh, the more I realised what I was doing was wrong. So I decided to leave her alone and only see her the morning of her death. A quick and final goodbye.'

'What happened?' Gabriel asked.

'Luci happened. What could have simply been a ten-minute visit, a chance to hold Ella again and tell her I loved her on the last day of her life, became the worst few days of my existence.'

Was there any point in carrying on? Would Gabriel see it for the horror that it was, or was Zac—as his friend had called it—holding a grudge for no reason?

'My mother turned up in Santa Monica. I have no idea how she found me, her whisperers I guess, but there she was. It was the ninth of July, the day before Ella was due to die, and I was sitting on the beach watching the sun set and eating a burger. What? Nothing beats a burger on the beach.' Gabriel smiled, giving Zac the courage to continue.

'Then suddenly there she was. Luci, towering over me, wearing a silky, flowing caftan and stupid flowers in her hair. She looked totally over-the-top as usual, like some festivalgoer from the 1960s. Honestly, that woman has a warped sense of occasion.'

Gabriel laughed, but Zac hadn't meant it to be funny.

'She sat down beside me, offered me a lick of her ice cream, then carried on looking out to sea as if we'd been on the beach together all day. I was happy to see her. We'd been getting on so well and over the years she'd told me all the stories about her having helped Ella in the past—how she allowed the Roman soldier to attack her, so Arabella could escape, and how she tried to stop Elien from being hanged. She seemed to be on Ella's side. That's why it didn't surprise me she was there. I thought perhaps she too wanted to say goodbye. Luci knew how hard this was going to be for me. I can't believe I was stupid enough to think she was thinking of my feelings...'

Zac's voice began to crack. Maybe it was that which hurt the most, not what his mother did but the fact that he'd trusted her. That her being there had felt like kindness, proof of her love for him. He should have known better—he should have known that the bitch only ever thought of herself.

'What did your mother do?' Gabriel asked, placing his hand on his friend's shoulder. Zac left it there; the weight of it was grounding.

'She tricked me.' He played with the cuff of his coat, his fingers now pink from the cold. 'She said she'd found her, that Ella wanted to speak to me. Gabriel, I've never got to my feet so fast in my life. "Where is she?" I cried. Luci smiled and walked away without saying another word, so I threw my half-eaten burger in the bin and followed her. We walked for about fifteen minutes, the whole time my eyes darting from face to face in the crowd looking for my love. I felt sick with anticipation and excitement, desperate to hold my love again and hear the sound of her voice. All the time I'd been watching Ella I'd been surprised by how little she'd changed in ten years; she still looked so young.

I would have noticed her beautiful smile among those of a million people. We stopped outside an old abandoned warehouse and my mother told me Ella was inside.'

Gabriel raised one eyebrow. It sounded so stupid saying it aloud. A bloody *warehouse*! The archangel was right to be suspicious. Anyone else would have asked Luci why the hell Ella was waiting for them in a dilapidated building fifteen minutes away from the seafront, but Zac hadn't. He'd trusted his mother and he'd been desperate to speak to Ella. To hold her hand. To breathe her in.

'So? Was your girl in there?' Gabriel asked, although it was clear by his flat voice that he'd already guessed the answer.

'Of course she wasn't. Luci locked me in, walked away, and I never saw Ella or my mother again.'

Zac blew into his frozen hands and shifted on the hard bench again. They were the only people left on that side of the piazza. Everyone else had either gone home or out to dinner. Even the eager photographers and art-lovers had been driven away by the bitter wind.

'Back up, Zadkiel. You are the one true archangel—son of Mikhael and Lucifer. Are you telling me you couldn't get out of a warehouse?'

Zac shrugged. 'I couldn't. I have no idea what she did, some magic spell she learned in Roermond from that old witch, no doubt. I couldn't get out. There were no windows and just one huge metal door. I screamed, shouted, kicked at the walls, banged at the door. Nothing. I punched my way out of a *tomb* the day I woke up after dying, remember? Yet I couldn't get out of that building. I was there for four days. Do you have any idea what that feels like, Gabriel? To be trapped, when all you want to do is say goodbye to the one you love? Knowing your girl is fifteen minutes away, and about to die, and not be able to get to her? To know that by the time you do she'll be dead...forever?'

Zac sniffed and rubbed his eyes. He'd never told anyone what he'd been through in that filthy old building. Eating and sleeping weren't something his immortal body needed in order to survive, but they'd become a habit over the years. He knew his hunger wouldn't kill him, but being hungry and thirsty had still been unbearable. He lay on that dusty concrete floor for days, rats scuttling at his feet, his voice hoarse from shouting and his nails bloody and torn from their beds. He hammered on the warehouse door and kicked at the walls for hours, breaking bones in his feet that healed immediately, the flesh on his hands tearing apart then knitting back together again. Nothing gave way, not even the grimy glass panels in the roof. Some magical force was keeping everything intact and him firmly trapped. His body broke into a million pieces then righted itself over and over again during those four torturous days, but his soul never healed. Each hour that went by his heart developed a new crack, until finally it crumbled into the pit of his stomach.

He had no idea where Ella was. All he knew was that it was the day before Ella was going to die. Then that it was the day Ella was due to die. Then that Ella was dying. And finally, that Ella was dead. Yet there he was, minutes from her house and unable to get to her.

'What did you do to escape?' Gabriel asked.

'Nothing. On the fourth day the door opened by itself as if someone had been on the other side all along, waiting for the right moment to let me out. The sun was shining, and the world had carried on as normal. I ran out, my hair matted with sweat, and my clothes covered in my own dried blood. I must have looked like a madman. I ran up and down the beach screaming out Ella's name *and* my mother's. I wanted to save one from dying and murder the other. Then I saw it, a man in a café reading the local paper. DE SILVA YAGHT TRAGEDY. NO SURVIVORS. That was all I needed to know. It was over. I went back to my hotel, got showered and changed, and came here to Italy. I haven't spoken to Luci since.'

They sat in silence for a long time, both lost in their own thoughts. Zac knew this would be difficult for Gabriel to hear. The archangel idolised Luci—the two of them had literally built the world together millennia before Zac was born. Gabriel thought he knew the real Luci, the kind and loving mother that Zac remembered. But there was another Luci. Evil, calculating Lucifer, the devil image that Mikhael had painted over the years. Perhaps his father had been right about the fallen angel all along. Perhaps she wasn't an innocent victim of their master's grand plan.

'It makes no sense,' Gabriel said finally, still staring out over the empty square.

'What doesn't? That your precious Luci could do that to me? That she would rob her only son of a couple of minutes with the woman he loved, out of spite and jealousy?'

A deep groove formed on the angel's brow as he shook his head slowly.

'Zadkiel.' He turned to face him, jade eyes pinning him down. 'There's something important you need to know. Something that not even Luci is aware of.'

Gabriel was a being who glided through life with a smile, his feathers rarely ruffled, yet right now the look on his face was making Zac nervous. Why was he hesitating?

Zac clasped his cold hands together, which were already clammy with anticipation. 'What? Gabriel, tell me. What do I need to know?'

The archangel bit his lip and looked deep into his friend's dark blue eyes.

'Ella's not dead. She's very much alive.'

4

JAGGED WHITE LINES ran up Ella's abdomen and a dark red scar skimmed her pubic bone. How was it so red and angry after sixteen years? She traced her fingers over them, rough rips papered over with silver, a constant reminder of motherhood and how close she'd got to never having experienced it. Doctors had been amazed her daughter's birth hadn't killed her. Then ten years later they said the same words again—*you should be dead.*

Ella the survivor, the woman who refused to die. How had she managed to evade death twice in sixteen years? Doctors called it luck, but Ella knew there was no such thing. Coincidences didn't exist, only miracles. She'd seen them happen with her own eyes.

'Yes, I'm still here,' she said, clasping her mobile phone between her ear and shoulder. Talking to Mai Li was not easy nowadays, but she needed to hear her friend's calming voice before she totally bottled it. They rarely spoke, not since Mai Li's fourth child had been born, but Ella was going to a big work event tonight and was having a major crisis of confidence.

'Sorry, it's a bit crazy here,' Mai Li shouted over the squeals in the background. 'What were you saying about an awards ceremony? Whatever you're up to, I'm jealous. I never go anywhere that doesn't involve nappy bags and nipple pads. A solo trip to the supermarket feels like a spa day.'

Ella chuckled and pulled on her underwear, struggling to get her knickers over her thighs. She adjusted the lace sides, so they lay flat against her hips, but it made no difference, her stomach still hung over the top like a cupcake that had risen too high over its casing. No matter what exercise she tried, she still had a paunch that resembled a week-old balloon which had gradually lost air and was now wrinkly and deflated. That's what she was now—an old, wrinkly, useless, lifeless balloon.

'It's just some photography awards thing,' she said, grimacing at her reflection. 'I've been nominated, so I have to go. But I'm shitting myself.' She rolled her pants back down and kicked them into the corner of the room, replacing them with large knickers that went all the way up to her rib cage. 'I want to stay home. I'm old and fat and having serious imposter syndrome.'

'You're not old or...'

'I am! Want to know what I did last night? I went outside at nine o'clock and shouted at those kids who keep sitting on my garden wall. They all wear hoodies, smoking and shouting all night. It's been driving me crazy for ages. So that's me, the old bag in her dressing gown having a go at teenagers. Mai Li, stop laughing. I'm *forty* in April.'

Fucking forty. She flinched at the words as she said them out loud. She'd spent most of her thirties mourning her husband, going from wife of Hollywood heartthrob to a self-employed photographer, single mother, *and* widow by thirty-four. And here she was now, six years after his death, practically middle-aged.

It was never meant to be that way.

When she'd got together with Josh she'd been following her life path, just as Zac had instructed her to before he died. Her and Josh were destined to be together. At no point did anyone tell her that her marriage would only last eleven years and that one day she'd be explaining to her ten-year-old daughter that her father was dead. Ella had experienced two true loves in one lifetime, and they'd both died beside her.

Her life wasn't fated. It was cursed.

'I'm sure you look lovely,' Mai Li said, bringing Ella back to her current crisis.

She sniffed and rubbed at her nose. Her makeup was already done, now was not the time to start crying.

'Hey! Have you heard the latest about Kerry?' Mai Li whispered, like she always did when sharing gossip.

'No, what's that cougar up to now? Is she still in Melbourne looking after her mum?'

'Yes. The operation went fine, and her boss extended her sabbatical. She's lecturing at a big uni out there now *and*—she paused for dramatic effect—'she's shacked up with a surfer.'

They both squealed at the same time. Ella could feel the years slipping away, once again the two of them living vicariously through their single friend's love life.

'Is he really young?' Ella asked as she applied her lipstick. Was that shade of red too bright? Too late. No one would be looking at her anyway.

'Of course he's young. He's...'

'Twenty-six,' they chorused together, erupting into laughter.

'No matter how old she gets, her boyfriends never age.' Ella laughed. 'God, that old tart has it good. Travelling the world giving talks on anthropology and shagging fit guys.'

Mai Li, Kerry, and Ella had been friends since university, and although Ella's life had lurched from drama to drama, her friends had never left her side. She'd moved to Spain after Zac's death, then to California to be with Josh, and finally back to London after the accident—and throughout it all Mai Li and Kerry had been there to pick up the pieces. They'd been her bridesmaids. Ella was godmother to Mai Li's first child and Kerry had even moved in with Ella for three months while she'd packed up her old life in America and tried to settle back in London. She was lucky. Not everyone could say they had friendships that had lasted twenty years.

'Is it bad that I'm a little bit jealous of her?' Ella sighed, sitting on the edge of her bed with a thump.

'No. But why are *you* jealous? Your life's perfect.' There was a short beat before her friend rushed in. 'Oh god. I mean, not the parts with Josh passing away and you nearly dying—twice—and all that horrible stuff that happened to you when you were younger and…'

Ella gave a small laugh. 'Hey, I know what you mean. I'm lucky, I know I am. I have a lot to be thankful for. I was envious of you too for a long time.'

'Me? I live in a shitty flat in Wood Green and my husband works in IT. Yeah, glamorama.'

'Mai-Li, Adam adores you. And you have four amazing kids, plus all your family live nearby and you make life look easy. You have no idea how long Josh and I tried to have a second child, but nothing worked. It was really tough with our parents living so far away and my little girl begging me day after day for a baby brother or sister.'

'But you *do* have the most perfect daughter. Even though you named her after a nightclub.'

Ella laughed. 'True. Indigo is the only thing keeping me going sometimes.'

They both fell silent for a moment. Ella could hear the distant squeak of a child's voice on the other end of the phone, and the rustle of something being opened. She pulled on her trusty black dress, the one she'd worn to every special occasion in the last five years, then attempted to do up the zip herself while still balancing the phone between her ear and shoulder.

'It's been so nice catching up. We really should meet up soon. Maybe do a gym class together or cocktails or…' Mai Li was interrupted by the high-pitched cry of her youngest. Ella could hear Adam trying to calm the baby down, but whatever he was doing wasn't working.

'I better go before Adam starts crying harder than the kids,' Mai Li said. 'Have fun tonight. Be that glam, successful, creative woman I've always dreamed of being.'

Ella grinned, trying not to drop the phone as she adjusted her bra straps. 'And you keep being awesome. We'll talk soon and arrange a night out. Let me know when things are less crazy.'

'Great. I'll call you back in about eighteen years.'

Ella blew her friend a kiss and was still grinning as she threw her phone on the bed. Her life wasn't always easy, but at least she didn't have four kids under the age of seven.

'Mum? Oh, you're in here.'

Indie's reflection appeared beside her mother's, making Ella's heart instantly swell ten times larger. It was like seeing herself at sixteen, but without the undercurrent of uncertainty and resentment that had plagued her teen years. Her daughter's delicate features were framed by bouncy dark curls which she always insisted on wearing loose, even though her hair fell in her food and blew into her mouth on windy days. Indie's eyes were also the same deep dark chocolate shade as her mother's. There was nothing of Josh in their daughter's face. Years ago, it had given Ella a secret thrill, but now it made her sad to think that no one would look at her beautiful daughter and be reminded of the unforgettable Joshua de Silva.

Indie threw herself on Ella's bed and stared up at the ceiling. 'You wearing that? Again?'

Taking a deep silent breath, Ella counted to ten in her head. It was uncanny how much of her own mother's personality had filtered through to her daughter. Indie was a good kid, but she didn't mince her words. Just like her grandmother Felicity, or Lily as everyone called her now.

'Can you help me with the zip, sweetheart?'

Letting out an exaggerated sigh, Indie rose from the bed and joined Ella at the mirror.

'You always wear this,' she said, pulling up the zip in one swift motion. 'You going somewhere important tonight?'

Was the event important? Ella wasn't sure. She wasn't going to go at first, even though she'd been nominated for an award, but when she heard who would be at her table she'd changed her mind. The knots in her stomach were doing their best to remind her that it had been a long time since she'd felt excited about meeting someone new.

'It's the New Year's ball for the Association of British Photographers,' Ella said, turning around to face her daughter. 'They're giving out a bunch of awards.'

'But it's not New Year's,' Indie replied. 'That was ten days ago.'

'I know.'

'And if it's a ball why are you wearing a dress that looks like you're going to ask a bank manager for a loan?'

Is that what she looked like? Boring and frumpy? She never used to be boring and frumpy. Not that long ago, Ella had lived in a beach house in LA with Josh and Indie and hosted swanky cocktail parties for film stars. In her youth she'd downed tequila shots in Spanish bars while wearing cowboy boots and singing karaoke. And as a teenager she'd flown from the highest rooftop in London wearing a sequined gown the colour of midnight and frolicked in the snow with an angel. But all of that was another lifetime ago. A time that hardly felt real anymore. *This* was real life—a widowed single mother, living in North London, failing to get rid of her muffin-top stomach.

'Here,' Indie said, opening the wardrobe and passing Ella a long emerald dress. 'You've never worn this and it's nice. You're excited. How come?'

This was another Indie thing. Josh used to call her intuitive, her teachers used to say she had high emotional intelligence, but Ella knew it was more than that. Quiet and pensive in public, Indie was overly empathetic to the point of debilitation. As a child she would cry before hearing bad news or jump up and down with glee before Ella had the chance to tell her good news. It was impossible to surprise her daughter.

'I'm not excited,' Ella said, wiping her damp hands on the back of her Spanx before wrestling her way into the green dress. Her daughter was right, it was a beautiful outfit. It hung low at the back and there was a long slash up one side showing off her shapely legs. The one part of her that wasn't wobbly. Yet…

'It's not too sexy,' Indie said, reading her mind as usual. 'You look amazing, Mum. And you don't look as old as you are.'

Ella supressed a smile at her daughter's attempt at flattery.

'You're right. I'm a bit nervous.'

'Just remember not to bite your nails,' Indie said, lifting her mother's hand and nodding when she saw the fake nails in place. 'Ha, good. Your hands look prettier like this.'

'I'm up for an award, for that Life Uncovered project.'

'Really? That's so cool. You totally deserve to win. The portraits you did of those women in Tibet were amazing. Who you meeting there?'

'No one special.'

It was the truth. Even though she knew a lot of guests invited to the event—fellow photographers, press and magazine people—none of her actual friends were going. Although there *was* one photographer she was excited to meet, and rumour had it he was also nominated for an award. Ella was secretly hoping to talk to him, or at least say hello.

'You're such a crap fibber,' Indie replied, giving her mother a half-smile. 'It's fine if you're meeting a man. It's not a big deal.'

It *was* a big deal. Ella's heart quickened at the thought of another man in her life. It had been six years since Josh died. Their daughter was ten years old when she'd watched the family yacht go up in flames from her bedroom window and seen dozens of her parents' friends wash up dead on the shore. Indie had been there when the ambulance arrived and rushed her dying mother to the hospital. She'd received counselling every week of her life since the accident, even though she insisted she didn't need it anymore. Yet Ella and her daughter rarely spoke about it. That's why Ella had decided to move to London after the accident. The city brought with it a mix of emotions and memories, not all good, but at least it was where work, friends, and public anonymity was. A fresh start and a chance for Ella to stand on her own two feet again.

'I'm not meeting anyone special,' Ella said again.

Technically she wasn't lying. There was no one who could ever compare to her Josh. Her destiny. The man who fate had pushed into her arms, then just as quickly ripped away again.

'You OK, Mum?'

Indie's face was frozen in concentration as she assessed her mother. That was something else her daughter did—she stared. Every time Ella was thinking of something, even back when Indie was a baby, her little girl would go still as a statue and stare at her. Eyes narrowed, head cocked to one side, as though she was listening to a silent conversation that only she could hear. It had creeped Ella out at first, but she was used to it now. Serious and studious, Indie rarely smiled. As soon as their daughter had been old enough, Ella and Josh had taken her to see the best doctors in the country to discuss her development. Every psychologist and specialist they consulted confirmed that physically, mentally, and socially their child was absolutely fine.

'She knows how to interact with others and is fully aware of her surroundings,' they were told. 'She just has her quirks; some children are simply not big smilers and like to be left alone.' Indie's dislike of physical contact, and her constant staring, was apparently neither a concern nor did it fit into any of the usual spectrums. It was a relief to hear it wasn't anything serious, as much as it pained Ella to miss out on sofa snuggles or be able to rock her baby to sleep.

'She'll grow up to be like every other child,' the doctors told her. 'No need to worry.'

Except Indie never did grow out of it. And Ella never stopped worrying.

'I'm fine, sweetheart,' Ella said, placing her hand on her daughter's cheek. Indie instinctively pulled away and Ella tried not to show how sad it made her. 'There's no man. Your father was the only man I ever loved.'

It wasn't technically a lie, although Ella had definitely loved before. A frown appeared on Indie's face and just as quickly disappeared. She placed a hand on her mother's arm and squeezed it. It wasn't much, but coming from her daughter it was a huge gesture.

'I know how much you loved Dad, Mum. I'm just saying it's cool if you want to go out more with friends, or go away for work, or date guys. You're not *that* old. You're still technically in your thirties.'

Ella snorted. 'For three more months.'

'Yeah, well, Dad wouldn't have wanted you sitting at home every night watching TV.'

Ella stroked her daughter's hair and planted a kiss on her cheek.

'When did you get so wise, eh? When I was sixteen, I was an insecure mess. I was your age when Nana Lily got married. Did you know that?'

'When Nana Lily married Abuelo?' Indie asked. Ella shook her head.

'Oh no, my mother and father married many years later. This was years before that. Remember I told you how your Nana was married to that lovely older man, Richard Fantz?'

A chill ran up Ella's spine at the memory of her mother's wedding, and she suppressed a shiver. How innocent she'd been that day, the bridesmaid in pink, and how awful her life had become soon after. She couldn't bear the idea of her daughter being that vulnerable.

'Did I ever meet this Richard?' Indie asked.

'No, sweetheart. He died a couple of years ago. Such a kind man.'

With a brief smile, clearly not interested in her family history, Indie handed her mother a long pair of earrings. Emerald drops set in silver. Ella held them up to her ears.

'Not too much?' she asked, moving her head from side to side in the mirror and seeing what she looked like with her hair up, then down, then up again. She could see Indie was getting impatient with her, which in turn made her jumpy.

'What are you worried about, Mum?'

'Nothing. Well. It's stupid. I just…I feel like a fake, sweetheart. I'm going to be surrounded by much younger, more interesting, and much more talented photographers tonight and they're all going to be super sweet and nice to me because I'm Josh de Silva's poor widow. It never gets any easier.'

Indie's face fell, and Ella instantly felt guilty. Her daughter rarely cried, but right now her dark eyes were shimmering in the half-light of the dimly lit bedroom.

'Just go and have fun, Mum. You worry too much. And if there are nice people there, especially a nice guy, then even better. Honestly, it's OK. I'm cool with it.'

Scooping her up into a giant bear hug, Ella squeezed her daughter harder than she'd done in a long time.

'How did I get so lucky? You're the best daughter in the world, you know that? So wise and clever and grown up,' she whispered into her hair, blinking quickly, conscious of all the black eyeliner framing her tired eyes.

Indie squirmed beneath her embrace, but Ella didn't let go. She never wanted to let go of her little girl—she was the only magical thing left in her life.

5

INDIE WAVED OUT of the window as her mother's taxi turned the corner of the street. Once it had disappeared, she pulled down her bedroom blinds and threw herself on the bed.

'Fucking hell,' she whispered under her breath.

It never got any easier. Slowly at first, then with a sudden urgency, all of her mother's emotions left Indie's body like water disappearing down a plughole. The trickle turned into a deluge, starting at the top of her head and finishing in a whirlpool in the pit of her stomach. Finally, she was empty, if not a little soiled around the edges.

Every person was different. Some energies were strong and all-consuming, others lighter, but her mother was beyond intense. She never had just the one emotion—and half of them didn't even make sense.

Dozens of glow-in-the-dark unicorn stickers shone down on Indie from her bedroom ceiling. She'd been meaning to peel them off for years. Silence washed over her, like waves lapping over badly made sandcastles until only smooth sand remained. It always took a while to adjust to the freedom of being alone again. Her mother leaving the house was like shrugging off a heavy backpack filled with rocks. Indie could only carry the weight around for so long.

Tonight, her mum had radiated a kind of hope speckled with tiny bubbles of excitement. Nerves had popped away in Indie's stomach as if it were her who had a party to look forward to. It wasn't entirely unpleasant, although coming from her own mother it was unusual. Ever since Indie's father had died, Ella's energy had been covered in a thick cloying tar. Dark and sluggish, it carried nothing but pain and guilt which permeated every spark of happiness she dared to feel. A heavy blanket of suffocating sadness that wouldn't allow any space to breathe.

Today was different though. Today was the first time in six years that Indie could see that black cloud lift a little, parting just enough to let a glimmer of light shine through. Her mother was made of three tiers of emotion. The first was unique just to her—a serene first layer, like a base coat of calm. The second layer was whatever that day's emotion was. And covering it all was a thick blanket of grief. That unusual base coat of her mother's had always been there though, way before her father had died, and it never changed. Indie couldn't see inside people's heads or read their thoughts, but sometimes their emotions had colours and textures. Ella's first layer of emotion was something akin to an aura—a magical lilac glow, a silent stream running deep beneath Ella's foundations. Ancient. Her mother didn't seem aware of it being there, but sometimes when she spoke of fate or her old life in Spain, her gaze would soften into the distance and that magic would rise to the surface. Were those old feelings connected to a person, a place, a memory—or perhaps a mix of all three?

Once Indie's mind felt clear again, she reached over to her bedside table and picked up her phone. She'd be lost without social media. For her friends it was simply a way to show off what they were up to, or to pass the time of day, but for her it was the only way she could chat to other people without being engulfed by feelings that didn't belong to her.

Jesse had sent her a message. A movie. The triangular white Play symbol winked seductively, and she clicked on it. It was a montage of old movies condensed into a twenty-second clip. Film was how her best friend communicated with her and it made her laugh out loud every single time. The film showed The Pink Ladies from Grease arriving at Rydell High and saying they were going to rule the school, then a clip from Mean Girls with the 'too gay to function' line, another from Twilight with Bella looking like her usual moody self, and finally the 'Who's that Guy' song from Grease 2.

Jesse picked up on the first dial tone.

'So? Did you like it?'

He was such a dork. She could imagine him sitting by his phone waiting for her call as soon as he'd sent it.

'What's your obsession with these ancient movies?' She was laughing so hard she could hardly get the words out. 'Have I ever told you that you're the dweebiest, campest, most hopeless gay guy I know?'

'Er, I'm the *only* gay guy you know. Actually, I'm the only *guy* you know. Correction—the only *person* your own age you speak to.'

Indie rolled her eyes. He was right, but that wasn't the point.

'So? Did you get my mini-movie montage?'

'Yeah, I just told you I liked it.'

'No, I mean did you *get* it? Did you understand what I was saying through my creative use of classical film clips?'

Indie grinned, plumped up her pillow, and lay down on her bed. Jesse clearly had something important to say and she knew this wasn't going to be quick. The boy lived for gossip like people needed oxygen.

'Spill. What's going on?'

'Well…' She could hear the rustle of cushions as he got comfortable too. 'The first bit of my film is us going back tomorrow and ruling the school because we're awesome.'

'Except we're far from cool, and we're only halfway through our first year of A-Levels. It would have been better if you'd used that clip to illustrate our *last* year of school.'

'Yeah, OK. You're a tough crowd to please, de Silva. Anyway… Then the rest is you and me…'

'Why do I have to be Bella?'

'Because you have a permanent resting bitch face.'

'I'm pensive.'

'You're sullen. Anyway, then it's about the new people starting in our year.'

'Who?'

Indie didn't like it when new students joined her class. Not just because they didn't know to avoid her, so they tended to be extra friendly and it got mega awkward, but also because she never knew what to expect. Sixth form wasn't that big, so it was rare to have new people start mid-school year. Would they be joy-suckers or so highly charged that even walking past them would make her dizzy? It was the unknown that freaked her out. That's why she preferred doing the same thing all the time with the same people. She knew what to expect.

'I heard they're brother and sister, twins, from somewhere up north,' Jesse said.

'So that was the "Who's That Guy?" reference? Are you saying you fancy the new boy already?'

The line went quiet.

'Jesse! Are you nodding or shaking your head? Because you know I can't see you, right?'

He sighed. His sighs were so melodramatic that sometimes he even put a hand up to his forehead. 'I was shrugging, sweet-cheeks. Jesus, I've no idea if he's hot or what his sister looks like either. I don't even know what their names are. It's quite exciting really.'

Jesse thought everything was exciting. That's why he'd remained Indie's only friend. He was never sad or stressed or anything negative at all. Hand on heart, in four years she'd never seen him less than happy. Some people said his happiness was all an act, because no one could ever be that chipper the whole time. Well, that was bullshit. And Indie was probably the only person qualified to know exactly what was going through her best friend's mind, because she felt everything he felt and it was all good.

Most of the time Jesse was bouncing-about-like-a-demented-lunatic happy, and on bad days he was simply upbeat. Being around him was fun, easy, and light. Indie wasn't sure if Jesse's constant jolliness meant he was shallow or stupid, or if she was being selfish being his friend mainly because nothing ever dimmed his glow, but she wasn't complaining. Hanging out with him was simple. How often could that be said for a person?

'Quarter to eight, tomorrow? Same as usual?' she asked.

They'd walked to school together for years, always meeting at the corner where their two roads met. Indie walked because public transport and dozens of people crammed together was too intense, and Jesse walked because he had too much energy to sit still on a bus. It suited them both.

He still hadn't answered.

'Jesse! Are you nodding or shaking your head? I swear to god if you don't learn how to use a telephone we'll have to video-call only.'

'I'm nodding. I'm nodding. Actually, let's make it seven thirty. Might be worth getting to school a bit earlier to see if the new boy is hot. You better not be screwing your nose up, Indie. I know you. One day you *will* like a boy, or a girl, or even a platonic dog in the street, and you *will* smile and talk to them.'

'See you tomorrow, Jesse. You've exhausted me already.'

'I haven't even told you about New Year's yet,' he said. 'OK, fine, I'll save that for the walk to school. You will never guess what Naomi said to Rochelle…'

'See you tomorrow.'

'Way worse than the fight they had at the Harvest Festival assembly in year eight…'

'Bye, Jesse.'

Indie hung up, her cheeks aching from grinning. Her best friend was literally the only reason she got out of bed in the morning.

6

ELLA LOVED THE Embankment. Years ago, when she first lived in London, she'd enjoyed walking along its narrow gardens running parallel to the Thames, forever in bloom and full of office workers eating lunch and chatting. The view from Waterloo Bridge had always been her favourite—St Paul's Cathedral, Houses of Parliament, and the London Eye all vying for the attention of selfie-taking tourists.

That evening's event was at The Savoy, one of London's most famous hotels that looked proudly out over the gardens and river. She'd stayed there a lot during her married life, back when Josh had junkets and press trips for his latest movie. He would insist his family accompany him back to the capital, so they could visit his mother and take in the sights. It was strange to be back at the hotel after so many years, especially now Ella was single, older, and no longer the young wife of a movie star. After the yacht accident there had been a very public legal battle with the family of the deceased suing Josh's estate for damages and negligence—as if Ella hadn't watched her own friends burn and drown. Not only had she nearly lost her life, but after the court case she'd also lost most of their money. She still had their modest house in north London, and some savings, but nothing compared to what she'd grown accustomed to. Ella had spent most of her adult life as either the stepdaughter of a rich hotelier or the wife of a film star, and now she was simply Ella Santiago de los Rios. Photographer, widow, and single mother. A woman simply doing her best.

Standing at the hotel's river entrance, looking up at its art de-co-style doors, she willed herself to climb the steps to the foyer. How bad could this dinner be? All she had to do was sit at a table, smile at a few people, and try not to look too upset when she didn't win the award. After all, everyone knew the nomination was nothing more than a sympathy vote and PR opportunity for the photography association. She wasn't short of work, but she wasn't that renowned for her art, either. Nothing compared to the talented creatives who, at that very moment, were inside sipping champagne, making small talk, and not thinking of her in the slightest.

'Ella! I knew it was you.'

A middle-aged woman with a sharp chestnut bob stepped out of a black cab. Even though it was already dark outside, she was wearing large sunglasses which kept slipping down her perfect, slender nose.

'Renée! How lovely to see you,' Ella replied, her fake smile shaking.

She air-kissed the fashion editor and remarked on her design-er trouser suit, all the while wondering whether her own floor-length green dress, with its high slit up one side, was too showy and old-fash-ioned for such a cutting-edge event.

'Come with me,' Renée said, taking her arm. 'We're on the same table, near the front. So many people I've been desperate to introduce you to.'

Ella begrudgingly climbed the stairs, discarding all thoughts of settling for a bowl of noodles and a pint of cider on the Southbank instead.

It wasn't the first time she'd attended a fancy evening at the hotel's grand hall, but each time she was there it looked completely different. Tonight, the event coordinators had themed the decor 'Flamingos and Flamenco' in honour of…Ella had no idea. Some charity or other. There were huge pink feather table-centres, polka-dot plates, and bread rolls shaped like castanets. The guests were already filling their Instagram accounts with tasteful shots of the not-so-tasteful adornments.

'Ella!' Renée cried out again, as they took their seats. 'You must meet Elf. I believe he's seated beside you. Elf started out at the magazine as an intern and within two years became our creative director. He's worked with so many of the photographers here tonight. He's also a very successful blogger.'

Ella shook the hand of a boy who looked the same age as her daughter. His trousers were orange corduroy, and he was sporting a bowtie that appeared to be made from tinfoil. His tightly curled hair, the same colour as his trousers, had been back-combed into a giant powder puff.

Ella gave the boy her most encouraging smile. 'Elf. Interesting name. Is it short for something?'

He shook his head.

'What's your blog about?' she continued, wondering at what point someone was going to give her a glass of something alcoholic.

'Paving slabs,' he replied.

'Paving slabs?'

'Yes. I take creative shots of paving formations, their various colours and geometric designs. Pavements can be fascinating.'

'Oh.'

She glanced at the empty chair to her left, wishing she had at least one other conversation option, then went back to staring at her castanet bread roll. Why the fuckety fuck had she let Mai Li and Indie talk her into going to this ludicrous event? She could have been tucked up in bed right now, in her warm pyjamas, watching…

A shadow loomed over her. 'Hey, everyone.' Someone was standing behind her, his voice made of gravel and velvet. 'Took me a while to find the right table. I was dazzled by all these giant feathers.'

Ella looked up, then let out a strangled gulp. Towering above her, beaming a megawatt smile, was the only reason she'd come to the event that evening.

'I'm Enzo,' he said, taking it in turn to shake the hand of everyone around the table.

'Oh, we all know who *you* are,' Renée simpered. 'And you've *both* been nominated for an award. How lovely.'

'Both?'

'Yes, Ella here is up for Best Female Portrait Photographer. That thing she did in Timbuktu.'

'Tibet,' Ella mumbled, rubbing her cheek to see if it was as hot as it felt.

Enzo sat down beside her and gave her his full attention. It was like a spotlight being shone in her face. She blinked and leaned back as he gave her another large smile.

'Ella Santiago de los Rios, right? Did I pronounce it correctly?'

'Yes. Um, it's Spanish,' she mumbled as he shook her hand.

Holy shit, the man was even more spectacular up close. Huge and tanned, the kind of build you get from being outdoors all day doing active, heroic things. He had the features of a warrior from a fantasy movie, small unruly beard, long, tousled hair pulled up in a man-bun, and ears and fingers glinting with silver. Most of the skin on his arms and hands was covered in tattoos and, although dressed in dark trousers and a white shirt, he wore the top button undone, displaying an array of pendants hanging from tatty pieces of string and leather around his neck.

Her hand was still in his, and it looked like that of a child's. Clearing her throat, she willed her face to unfreeze, no longer remembering what her mouth and eyes and cheeks were meant to be doing.

'What category are you up for, Enzo?'

God, she sounded like a mum asking her daughter's friends what they want to be when they grow up! Why was she even trying to strike up a conversation with this guy?

'News Documentary. I'm a war photographer.'

There was that voice again, stone on stone, low like the rumble of clashing skies before a storm. His entire body leaned into hers, like there was no one else sitting at their table. It had been a long time since anyone had looked at her like that. His dark eyes, framed by thick lashes, weren't brown but inky black, and shining as brightly as wet pebbles in a stream.

A war photographer. Of course. A man like that wouldn't be seen poncing about on the side of catwalks or calming down hysterical brides; he was on the front line where the action took place. Enzo made a living dodging bombs and capturing the drama and destruction of worldwide disasters. A modern-day hero. The kind of man who…

'Wine?' he asked.

Ella nodded and the waiter poured her a glass of red. She raised it at Enzo who was holding his own glass aloft.

'What shall we drink to?' she asked.

'May fate find us, and destiny guide us,' he said, his eyes widening as he stressed the word 'destiny.'

The wine in her glass sloshed from side to side as she tried to control her trembling hands. Fate? Why was he talking about fate? Her mouth was dry, and it was a struggle to swallow down her nerves. She always got like this whenever anyone mentioned destiny. How could she not? But she was being silly. His toast was just a coincidence. Surely *some* coincidences still existed? Her hand was still trembling as they clinked glasses, and he smiled at her over the rim of his goblet as he took a sip.

Come on, Ella! Now was the time to say something interesting, something witty and funny and fascinating.

Too late, a woman on his left wearing a beautiful golden sari was already asking him a question. Ella finished her glass of wine in three hungry gulps and turned to her right. Perhaps Elf wanted to have a scintillating conversation with her.

He didn't. He was taking photos of the floor tiles.

She played with the stem of her glass while eavesdropping on Enzo's conversation. Ella realised who the woman was, she'd been featured in an article in *The Times* recently about up-and-coming photographers. Enzo's wild and tough exterior contrasted incongruously with both the petit woman beside him and the table's backdrop of fluffy pink feathers. He didn't belong indoors, and Ella didn't belong at that table—or anywhere near such an award ceremony.

The food was served, and she sipped her soup while she listened to the photographer's war stories.

'…Bosnia was difficult…'

'…Afghanistan was so beautiful until…'

'…what happened in Cambodia remains one of…'

There was no way he'd documented all those wars. He was far too young.

Eventually they stopped talking and the Indian photographer turned to the man on her left, leaving Enzo and Ella to focus on their watery tomato soup.

'I'm a big fan of your work,' he said after a long silence, so quietly she didn't realise he was addressing her. 'I looked you up when I saw the award nominees. Your photography has a depth that I've rarely seen anywhere else.'

What was this godlike man talking about? Ella took a deep breath, ready to bat away his compliment, then began to choke. Shoulders hunched and hair dipping in her wine she coughed and coughed so violently she thought she was going to be sick. Acid bile from the soup burned her throat as she struggled to breathe. Attempting to grasp her glass of water, she knocked it over instead, leaving a large wet patch on her lap.

Enzo stood up calmly, passed her his own glass of water, then gently lay his hand on the small of her back until she regained her composure. The fabric of her dress dipped low at the back, and the heat of his hand on her bare flesh sent sparks up her spine. No man had touched her bare skin since Josh had died.

'Breathe,' he said quietly, so close that his own breath tickled her ear. 'You scared me.'

The rest of the guests in the grand hall pretended not to look at her, even though her face was probably blotchy and red, and the water she'd spilled was dripping from the table and pooling at her feet.

'Thanks. Sorry. Went down the wrong way,' she said to Enzo, her voice still wobbly.

Renée, Elf, and the others around the table visibly relaxed as she composed herself. They turned their attention back to their soup, but Enzo remained beside her. He handed her a clean napkin and signalled at her wet lap. She dabbed at the damp patch.

'As I was saying,' he continued, his eyes sparkling like onyx. 'I'm a big fan of your work.'

Ella bit her lip and looked down at the wet stain on her dress. 'Thank you, but I have no idea what I'm doing here—let alone why I'm up for an award.'

He handed her another clean napkin and sat back down.

'Nonsense, you're more than worthy. I've never seen anyone capture a person like you do. You don't photograph faces, you draw out their souls.'

Ella meant to giggle in a humble and endearing way, but it came out more of a snort.

'Cheers, but I've only been doing it professionally for ten years. Some people here have been…'

'Don't worry about "some people." The only person you need to compare yourself to is yourself.'

What was she meant to say to that? She focused her attention on dabbing her wet lap with the napkin. As she crossed her legs, the slit in her dress widened up to her thigh. Enzo's gaze flickered to her legs, then away just as quickly. Her gown was too revealing. Why hadn't she worn her trusty black dress? She pulled at the silky fabric, but it kept slipping back down.

Enzo pointed to her leg, just above her knee. 'Interesting scar. Looks like a crescent moon.'

'Birthmark,' she said, trying to keep her voice steady. She traced its shape with the tip of her finger, aware that Enzo was watching. Luckily everyone else at their table was too busy making inane small talk to notice their interaction.

'Apparently there have been studies proving that birthmarks are linked to past lives,' she said quietly. 'Someone once told me I was injured badly in a former existence right here, in the same place, just above my knee. He said my soul still remembers.'

That someone was Zac. She tried to keep her features neutral but failed as her mind dragged her back twenty years to the first night she'd made love to the mysterious blue-eyed boy at her parent's house in London. The way Zac had kissed her birthmark, then worked his way higher and higher, whispering that he had fallen for her. Literally fallen from grace and the heavens. For her. She shivered.

'Are you cold? Would you like my jacket?' Enzo asked.

She shook her head and gave him a small smile, making sure to look at his face properly this time. She wasn't imagining it, there was something about the way his eyes shone that was unnerving. The sight of him tugged at a memory, pulling her back to a rain-soaked mountain and a ring of people with eyes not quite…human.

She had to stop thinking that way. For ten days of her teenage life she'd lived in a world of magic and angels. Just ten crazy days. Zac,

Mikhael, Gabriel—she'd seen their wings and their power. Her father, Leo, had told her of his work with their realm, and the love of her life had died at her feet. Those few days had changed her life, but since then she'd not witnessed any angelic apparitions, no magic, no feathers. Her father had even stopped working with them after Zac had died, yet Ella still looked out for angels everywhere. She would scrutinise the colour of people's eyes and was always on the lookout for anyone who healed too quickly, appeared blurry in photos, or couldn't use electricity. Of course, she never discovered anyone that was anything but human. In twenty years she'd seen nothing out of the ordinary, yet she couldn't shake the feeling that angels were still watching her. That Mikhael wasn't finished with her yet.

The waiter took away their plates and poured more wine, while Enzo nodded at something Renée was saying to him.

'Excuse me.' Ella tapped him on the arm. It was a silly idea, but she was curious. 'Would you mind plugging in my phone, please? It needs charging. The socket is right by your foot.'

Enzo gave her another beaming smile and took the charger and iPhone off her. The battery was at eighty-three percent, but he didn't seem to notice.

He plugged it in and switched it on at the wall. Her phone lit up and he continued his conversation. Oh well, that was *that* theory crossed off the list. If he could interact with electricity, he wasn't an angel.

Ella sighed. Of course he wasn't a bloody angel! Not every handsome man with shiny eyes was celestial. Luckily, Zac had also told her gods didn't exist—because that would have been her second guess. Enzo was the least human-looking human she'd ever met.

The main course and dessert came and went, and nothing exciting happened for the rest of the meal. Ella managed not to choke or douse herself in water again, and Elf eventually stopped taking photos of the floor long enough to declare he couldn't eat his white chocolate mousse as there was a small lilac flower on it and it wasn't fair to bees. Luckily the wine was flowing, and it was decent stuff.

A *tap, tap* sound came from the stage where a man in a maroon dinner jacket stood behind a plinth, his mouth far too close to the tiny mic.

'Your attention, please. Now for the part of the evening you've all been waiting for! Time to hand out the awards to some of the country's most creative geniuses.'

Well, Ella definitely wasn't a genius! She snorted again. Oh no. Was she drunk? How had that happened? It was fine, at least she wasn't driving and didn't have to get up to collect an award. She was perfectly safe sitting down.

'Let's start with the women…' The man's voice droned on and Ella fought to keep her eyelids from drooping. She'd been up late the night before editing a collection of images of boring politicians she'd shot for a magazine and was ready for bed already.

'And the award for Best Female Portrait Photographer goes to…Arabella Santiago de los Rios, for her Life Uncovered campaign in Tibet.'

Ella's head jerked up as her work was projected on a big screen behind the man with the mic. *Shit!* Shit, shit, double shit. Would it look strange if she pointed out they'd made a mistake? Surely the man didn't mean *her*? She stumbled to her feet, Enzo's hand reaching out to steady her. He grinned and her stomach dropped to the floor. Oh god, his smile. And the stage. It was a million miles away.

'You deserve this, Ella. Go!' he whispered.

She managed to collect her award and return to the table without any mishaps, although she hadn't planned a thank you speech so had no idea what she'd blabbered into the mic.

Back in her seat, clutching the big glass orb, she blinked back tears and wondered what Josh would have said had he been beside her instead of Enzo. Her chin trembled and she bit her lips together to hold back the tears. Proud. He'd have been immensely proud, like he'd been about everything she'd achieved since marrying him. It was Josh who'd first convinced her to be a photographer, ever since she'd taken his photo in Tarifa all those years ago. He was the one who'd always believed in her, even when she stopped believing in herself. *Especially* when she stopped believing in herself. Where was he when she needed him? Why did she always have to lose the ones who loved her the most?

The touch of a hand on her arm made her look up. Enzo's solemn face was etched with concern, his eyes deep as a starless night.

'I'm sorry for your loss,' he said. Ella wasn't surprised, everyone here who knew her also knew who she'd once been. 'You must really miss him.'

'I do,' she replied, realising it wasn't just Josh she missed.

God, her life was a bloody mess! A life filled with dead, dead, dead men and now a man who was giving her butterflies but was way out of her league. Fuck men and fuck everything. She reached for a bottle of wine, red drops splashing onto the tablecloth as she filled her glass to the brim.

Enzo was looking at her legs again. Was he really checking her out? *Really?* There she was, drunk and teary about losing every man she'd ever loved, and he was eyeing her up?

'How come, when he announced your name for the award, he called you Arabella?' Enzo asked, ignoring Ella's cutting look and the bloodlike blotches of wine on the table.

'Arabella is my full name,' she replied curtly. 'But I never use it. There has only been one person who has ever called me that, but it was a long time ago.'

Enzo didn't ask who, and Ella wasn't going to tell him.

More awards were handed out, including one for Enzo and the woman beside him, until eventually guests began to say goodbye to one another and meander to the exit. There was no more red wine left, so Ella moved on to the white. She peered through her glass award, people looking distorted and wobbly through the crystal.

'Want me to call you a taxi?' Enzo asked.

He was the only one left at the table. Not even the fashion editor Renée or Elf the pavement-lover had bothered to say goodbye.

Ella swayed as she got to her feet. Crap! She hadn't meant to drink so much, but then she'd started thinking about Josh…and then Zac… and then….

She managed perfectly well day to day, especially as she only drank alcohol on special occasions. As long as she kept busy her mind stayed clear, and she was able to block Josh and Zac out and get on with things. And when she was angry or sad, she was also fine—she could re-direct her emotions. But as soon as something nice happened, like winning tonight's award, then the enormity of her life without either man hit her hardest. And that's when she drank too much.

'He should have been here,' she said to Enzo, her voice slow and blurring at the edges. 'My husband should have been here to see me win this, but he had to go and die. I was meant to die too, you know. Actually, I *did* die, but I came back.' Her voice rose with every word. 'How the hell is that fair? Even fucking angels can't return from the fucking dead, *but I can.*'

'Angels?'

She wasn't listening to him. 'I'm a living miracle—did you know that? Ha, well, I stopped believing in miracles a long time ago. Fucking liars, the lot of them.' She jabbed his chest. 'Men. You all lie. You say you'll love us forever, and then you die. You say you'll return, and then you don't.'

A large hiccup turned into a sob, which turned into a silent wail. Enzo manoeuvred her to a quiet corner of the hall and let her fall into his wide chest. Oh god, she had to stop doing this, she had to stop breaking down in tears at random moments. She'd even sobbed in front of the security guy in Marks and Spencer last Christmas when she'd spotted a tie Josh would have liked. Maybe she should speak to Indie's therapist. Ella probably needed more help than her daughter did.

Enzo held her to him, her head hardly reaching his shoulder, and didn't say a word as she cried big ugly tears all over his crisp white shirt.

'I'm getting makeup on you,' she said, which only made her cry even harder.

'Don't worry about it. Grief is a difficult thing. It's impossible to know when it will strike next. When you lose someone important to you, you can't control when or how their memory will resurface. Pain isn't measured in years, Ella, it doesn't care that you're ready to move on. It will always find you and remind you of how much you were once loved. How life will never be the same again.'

Ella sniffed loudly and gave him a watery smile.

'I'm sorry. I've been a bit of a mess lately. I'm normally a lot stronger than this.'

'I know,' he said, handing her the award she'd won. 'I've heard some very impressive things about you.'

Outside, the sharp night air was like a slap in the face, sobering her up enough to realise she really had to get to bed. Her first night out in ages and she'd made a complete tit of herself. Clearly approaching forty made no difference to her lack of control when it came to free alcohol and the kindness of strangers. Enzo hailed her a cab and helped her get in, making sure she'd given her address to the driver.

'Thanks for being so nice,' she said. 'It was lovely to meet you.'

'We'll meet again,' he said, his smile easy like they were lifelong friends. 'I'm sure you'll be around for some time yet.'

She swivelled in her seat as the taxi pulled away, but Enzo didn't head back into the hotel. Instead, he stood and watched her drive away until he was nothing but a speck in the distance.

7

THE SWEET STENCH of ripped bin bags and discarded chicken bones hung like a fine mist over the deserted street. A neon sign flashed above Luci's head—green to pink to blue—projecting a ghoulish tint over her flawless face. It was dark, but it was far from quiet. All night, the bass thud of the nightclub behind her had become a second heartbeat, monotonous shock waves travelling up her freezing bare legs and into her very core. It hardly counted as music. Somewhere in the distance two women were fighting to the soundtrack of a car alarm wailing in protest.

Just another night in Redwood, north London.

'Jesus loves you.'

A bearded man, skin like cracked leather and fingers thick and dry, peered into Luci's face. He smelled of piss-soaked alleyways.

'Jesus loves you,' he said again.

Luci gave him a pitying smile. 'I assure you, Jesus has never loved me.'

'He loves all his children.'

The man was right, Jesus *had* loved his children. Luci had been there the day Jesus's family had gathered around the cross from which he hung, his wife bathing his feet and his four daughters soaking his legs with their tears. He'd been close to death by then. Finally quiet. Depicted throughout history as the docile bearded son of God, the truth was very different. Jesus had fought his capture every step of the way, earning him hundreds of lashes and broken bones before being nailed to the cross. He'd screamed out the truth for days, the searing sun beating down upon him until his bloody face dried into a crimson mask of agony. Birds of prey had hovered like puncture wounds against the light blue sky, their piercing screams mirroring Jesus's own torment as they waited for him to finally fall silent. He'd cried out about injustice, how the leaders of the land had invented an almighty god to control the masses and that he'd done nothing wrong. But nobody cared. To witness the demise of another was sport back then, and so much more enjoyable when the accused was greater than the average man. Even if that greatness had been thrust upon him.

Luci hadn't known Jesus and his family for long, but she did know that he'd forever been a pawn in Mikhael's game. The messiah's death had been nothing more than a warning to his father, Gabriel, and to all of humanity. No more Nephilim. No more mixing of humans and angels. Proof that no one could fight against the angelic leader, not while he governed with a sword that had the ability to end the lives of both angels and humans. So now the people had their fictitious god, and Mikhael continued to rule the Angelic Realm, knowing his downfall lay solely in the unity of two worlds. Something he would never let happen again.

Mikhael was the worst kind of bastard. The *secret* kind.

Luci turned her face away from the acrid fumes on the old man's breath and focused on the end of the street. Where was the boy? She'd been waiting for him for hours.

'Have you spoken to Jesus?' the man continued.

'Not for a while,' she muttered. 'He was never much of a conversationalist. Good at parties though. We never ran out of wine.'

The old man physically recoiled at her blasphemy and pointed a gnarled finger in her face.

'Heathen bitch,' he hissed, spit speckling her cheek. 'Hell has a place for women like you.'

Luci wiped her face with the back of her wrist and watched the old man shuffle into the shadows.

'I *am* Hell,' she screamed.

An icy wind blew, and a discarded burger wrapper impaled itself on the heel of her stiletto. She flicked it off. How much longer would she have to wait for this little prick? The boy was the next kid on her list, but he'd been difficult to track down. Her whisperers had told her all about him. The situation wasn't ideal, but she wasn't exactly spoiled for choice.

She took a swig of vodka from the small bottle she kept in her handbag. The thick liquid settled into the pit of her stomach, warming her up from the inside out and doing the job her flimsy, tight clothes were not.

'How much?' a voice called out.

A man in a crumpled suit was weaving his way toward her. His tie had been loosened and his cashmere coat was stained with dribbles of brown sauce. Swaying on his feet, it took a while for his eyes to focus on hers.

'For a blow job. How much?'

His droopy cheeks wobbled as he struggled to form the words, lips slick with saliva. He put down his briefcase and showed her his wallet stuffed with fifty-pound notes. 'I have cash. Lots of it. Perhaps there are other, *more interesting*, things you'll do for the right price?'

Luci leaned against the grimy wall behind her and ran her hand through her long, dark hair. She'd learned many things over the last two thousand years, one of which was that if a woman stood long enough on a moonlit street corner, a man would eventually come along to either save her or try and stick his cock in her mouth. Sometimes both.

He placed a hand on her shoulder and gave her a lascivious smile. His yellow teeth shone in the haze of the lamplight, and the edges of his mouth were crusty with dried spit.

'Oi! Get the fuck off her.'

A young man was marching toward them. The drunk instantly backed away, his head jerking up in realisation as the guy came into view. Luci had been expecting a teenager, but this kid looked older than his years. Rough streets did that to boys.

The drunk was spluttering now. 'Oh, my goodness. Bugger. I'm ever so sorry. I didn't know she belonged to you.' He pointed at the neon sign above Luci's head. 'I thought she was a stripper from the club.'

'I'm not a pimp, knobhead. I just deal,' the young man spat. He nodded his head as he spoke, swaying to his own private beat. 'Where's the money you owe me, Graham? Three grams. I'm not a fucking charity.'

Although the drunk man was double the size of the boy, his fingers trembled as he counted out note after note, laying it into the drug dealer's outstretched palm.

Luci watched. Eyes unblinking. She'd been waiting all night for this, but she still had to be sure.

'There, that's everything I owe you,' the man spluttered, his eyes fixed on the littered pavement.

'Good. Now fuck off back to your poncey house in Kensington, *your honour*,' the boy said with a flourish, bowing deeply in mock respect. 'And leave the whores alone. I feel sorry for your wife.'

The man nodded vigorously then scurried down the unlit street, his leather-soled shoes making tiny slapping sounds along the wet pavement.

The boy turned to Luci who was still leaning against the wall, her face bathed in neon indifference.

Taking in her high-heeled shoes, short skirt, and ample chest, his eyes eventually met hers. They shone a scarlet red, the club's lighting reflecting off his pupils, giving him a devilish appearance. Luci's lips turned up at the edges—there was only one devil around here.

'You're new,' he said.

'No. I'm very, very old.'

It was her turn to look him up and down, and he didn't like it. He was short with tanned skin and a slight frame. No older than eighteen—twenty at a push. Too young for the life he was living. His dark hair was slicked back, reaching the nape of his neck, a diamond glinting in his left ear and another in his front tooth.

'You're not that old,' he said, stepping closer.

Luci let him, for now. It had taken years to find him—there was no need for him to fear her just yet.

'What are you? Late twenties? Early thirties? Older than most of the birds on this street, but you still got some bounce in there. You get me?'

Luci stayed quiet. She knew the less she said, the more he would talk.

'What's up? Nothing to say?' He kissed his teeth. 'Get the fuck outta here. These are *my* streets.'

He had a rough London accent, tinged with a South American twang. Luci didn't move. Her stillness clearly unnerved him, but he was putting on a good show.

She stared deep into his crimson eyes. 'Go home,' she whispered.

He laughed, gold fillings glinting at the back of his mouth, but he didn't step back. He'd passed the first test and didn't even know it.

A flurry of excitement unfurled in the pit of Luci's stomach, but she fought back the urge to tell him why she was there. Patience. Not long now.

'You want me to go home?' he scoffed. 'Jokes. Who's your boss?'

Luci shrugged. 'I don't have one.'

The boy nodded, his teeth working over his bottom lip as if he were chewing on something.

'Want to make good money? I don't mean selling your sweet arse on the streets, I mean *good* money. Safe, fun, you manage your own hours.'

So this is what happened when young and hopeless Nephilim had his power. Luci had seen it before. Pirates, thieves, witches, and rogues—but not teen drug dealers. He could be so much more than this. And he would be, she'd make sure of it. The kid would be turned into something worthy. But there was still a long way to go.

Luci pushed back against the wall and stood up straight, forcing him to step back a little. Toe to toe, in her towering heels, she was a couple of inches taller than him.

'Work for you?' she purred. 'No. *You* are going to work for *me*.'

The boy kissed his teeth again.

'I'm busy, lady. I ain't here for no bullshit.'

He turned to walk away but Luci stepped in front of him, blocking his path. He clearly wasn't used to being confronted.

'Get out my face, yeah. You don't know who you're messing with. This ain't no game.'

'Oh, but it is,' she said, running her finger along his face. His chin was strong, and his eyes burned a deep red. She smiled to herself. It was nice to see Chamuel's chiselled features and bloodthirsty glare again. She wondered what else the boy shared with his Viking-warrior father, an archangel this kid was never likely to meet.

The boy swatted her hand away from his face, grabbing her by the wrists.

'You winding me up, lady?' he snarled. 'Do you have any idea who I am? I'm Scar. I own this street and everyone working on it. People don't mess with me, because I'm not like most people.'

This was it. The part Luci had been waiting for. Her wrists smarted under the boy's tight grip. He was stronger than he looked, but that was a good thing. She was searching for someone strong, reckless, and brave; he just needed his edges sanded down.

'You think I'm going to work for a whore?' he continued. 'Some slut trying to tell *me* what to do? I was raised on these streets, bitch. No one's told me what to do since I was twelve. I never needed no one—I'm my own boss.'

So that was his story, living alone from a young age. It explained a lot. Luci waited for Scar to let her go. Then just when he thought he'd made his point and went to walk away again, she lifted him up off the ground with nothing but a flick of her finger and deposited him on the roof of the nearby bus stop. His eyes flashed like garnets, his face burning the same shade of red.

'Are you prepared to listen to me now?' she asked quietly.

He looked around wildly, either for help or to ensure no one had witnessed his humiliation. The street was eerily quiet—even the car alarms had stopped bleating.

'Who the fuck are you?' he shouted.

'Scarlet, that's your name, isn't it? Such a pretty name for such a tough little boy.'

'How do you know my name? You the police? You ain't got no right to manhandle…'

Luci raised her hand again, causing the bus shelter to rock. The boy threw himself onto his stomach, gripping the side of the roof like a novice surfer.

'Sit down and listen to me, you little brat.'

He did as he was told, inching to the edge and sitting up until his legs were swinging over the bus stop roof. His ragged breaths were the only sign of his diminishing bravado.

'My name is Luci, and I've been looking for you.'

'You've got no proof that I…'

'You're not in trouble, Scar. I need you. I need people like you.'

His eyes narrowed into fiery slits. Good, he was listening properly now.

'Get down. We need to talk.'

He jumped effortlessly, landing like a cat at her feet, and brushed himself down. Then in one swift movement he swiped his hand in an arc, emanating enough power from his fingers to send Luci flying headfirst into a pile of putrid bin bags. Not nice, but she'd been expecting worse. The sound of his thundering footsteps echoed through the nearby alleyway, his skinny legs rounding the corner and out of sight.

Luci laughed out loud. Stupid, stupid boy.

She pointed in his direction, then watched his writhing body being dragged backwards toward her, the boy's cheek scraping along the wet pavement. People never learned. Even after witnessing her abilities, her victims always tried to run…but they only did it once.

The kid, now a crumpled heap at her feet, winced as she helped him up and straightened the collar of his tracksuit jacket.

'There. Good as new. Are you prepared to listen now, Scarlet?'

His face had turned a sickly shade of grey.

'It's Scar.'

'I don't care. What I'm offering will give you power beyond your wildest dreams. Much more than making a profit from vulnerable addicts and sordid men in these stinking backstreets. This life is not acceptable for anyone. Understand me?'

He nodded, knowing when he'd met his match. She had him now. He wouldn't run again.

'Working with me means becoming invincible. Are you interested?'

Of course he was, boys like him always were. His face remained passive, but he nodded, his left eye twitching nervously. Scar had good reason to fear her, because Luci had the ability to change his life forever.

'Get in,' she said, walking toward a sleek silver convertible parked in the shadows. His eyebrows shot up. No one in Redwood owned a car like that.

'Where we going?' he asked, ducking his head as he slid into the passenger side.

'Away from here. I'm going to show you the kind of life you could have.'

'You don't know me though,' he mumbled, his eyes now a pale orange but still wide with fear. 'Why would you do that? What do you want from me?'

'I know your father,' she said. 'And I know others like you. Are you ready to be the toughest badass there is?'

He smiled hesitantly and she ruffled his hair, surprised he let her. Perhaps he wasn't going to be as hard to train as she'd imagined.

Scarlet was nothing more than a scared and scarred little street rat—a damaged boy hiding behind a celestial gift he hadn't yet learned how to master. But Luci knew all about scared little boys, and she knew exactly how to turn them into powerful men.

The difficult part was keeping them close.

8

ZAC RAN HIS finger over the photo of Ella. Gabriel had ripped out the page from a magazine and was now holding it out to him. The thin paper, one edge ripped, fluttered in the cold night air. It was her. The photo was definitely of Ella.

But how was she still alive? It didn't make sense. She died six years ago. She couldn't have avoided it—it was her death date. Zac had even seen the news of her passing on the front cover of a newspaper the next day: NO SURVIVORS, the headline had screamed.

The square was empty now. The only noise was that of restaurants locking their doors and bar staff rushing home, heads bowed against the chilling wind. Zac no longer felt cold: he didn't feel anything at all.

The italic writing at the top of the page was tiny and he had to squint in the dark to read it. *Photographers Unite Magazine*, it read, dated just five months ago. Zac's hand was clammy as he took the piece of paper from his friend, his chest filling with warmth at the sight of Ella's face smiling back at him. According to the write-up, the photo was recent, yet it could have been taken the last day he'd seen her. She hadn't changed a bit.

'How…? Where…?' he stammered.

Gabriel put his hand on his friend's shoulder and gave it a light squeeze. His eyes shone with compassion and something else. Pity? Regret?

'I saw her photo completely by chance. As you know there are no mistakes in our world, Zadkiel—it is *us* who make the coincidences happen—so I have no idea how I was lucky enough to discover it. I'd been sent to speak to a dentist in Birmingham, to pass on some news that would change her life. You know, the usual stuff. I was sitting in the waiting room and there was Ella's face. It was only a small photo on the bottom left of the cover, something about the rise of female portrait photographers. At first, I presumed it was an out-of-date gossip magazine—she used to appear in them sometimes if Josh had a film coming out. Yet this one was dated September of this year and the headline said she'd moved from America to Europe. I turned to the article and there she was. As soon as I discovered your whereabouts, I came immediately.'

A solitary tear rolled down Zac's cheek, but he didn't wipe it away. Ella was alive. In the two thousand years he'd been an angel, watching people being born, dying, then being born over and over again, he'd never once seen any human escape death. People always died on the day allocated; you couldn't run away from your end of days. On the rare occasions Zac had tried to save the various versions of Ella in the past—and at first, he'd tried *so* hard to save her—death had always arrived as planned. You couldn't compete against your inevitable end. Yet Ella had…and she'd won.

'Is Josh alive too?'

Gabriel shook his head.

'So how did Ella live? I don't understand, they were meant to die together. It doesn't make sense. Gabriel, I've wasted all these years pining for her and all along she…'

'Hey. Take a deep breath,' the archangel said, handing his friend a tissue. 'It's all good. The game's back on, brother.'

Zac gave a shaky smile up to the heavens. The sky was the colour of raven wings studded with diamonds. So many stars shining down on them, and somehow, they'd aligned to create the impossible just for him. For him and Ella.

'I never thought I could be this lucky,' he muttered to himself. All those fictitious gods worshipped by fools never smiled down on their people, except for tonight.

'This isn't luck, Zadkiel. This is some kind of magic. Perhaps I should have asked your mother whether she's seen this happen before.'

'Wait! She doesn't know about Ella, does she? Please tell me you didn't…'

Gabriel shook his head. 'Relax, Zadkiel. I like your mother, a lot, but I'm not stupid. We've met up a few times over the last few years, but I'd never meddle in the things that come between you both. Especially not this.'

'What do you talk about then?'

'She likes to update me on her Nephilim quest, and we reminisce. It's nice to remember the old days together.'

Zac wanted to roll his eyes at the absurdity of his best friend and mother being so cosy, but he had much more important things to focus on now. Ella being alive changed everything. She'd fallen off her path before, but now she no longer had one! Neither did she have her soulmate Josh by her side.

Zac swallowed down the ache building in his chest—it was wrong to take pleasure from such news. Yet it felt so good.

Then he thought about Ella, what she'd gone through in this lifetime, and that short-lived joy quickly faded. The woman he loved had watched him slice off his own wings and die at her feet, then merely fourteen years later she'd lost her husband. She had nothing left, nothing but the guilt of having been the sole survivor of a tragic accident where she should have died. How had she carried on, managing all that fear and loneliness on her own? Zac should have been there for her instead of moping around Italy considering kissing the mother of one of his students!

He turned to the angel beside him. Gabriel was staring across the square at an elderly couple sitting on a bench, hand in hand. Regardless of the cold weather, the old man was holding a gelato cone and they were sharing it, passing it from one to the other as they took turns to lick the ice cream.

Zac smiled. He and Ella still had time. Love didn't have a use-by date.

'Gabriel, I'm forever indebted to you,' he said, putting his arm around his friend's shoulders and squeezing. 'I need to go to her right away. Where is she?'

The angel shrugged.

'How do you not know?'

Not again. Zac screwed up his eyes, his ears drumming with the beat of his heart. How many times were he and Ella going to evade death, only to find themselves separated further? It had taken a week to track her down last time, but at least he'd had Gabriel's help back then.

'I can't feel her,' Gabriel said quietly. 'I'm sorry. It's like she's dead. Mikhael believes her dead too—which is no bad thing. He even told me how relieved he was he no longer had to keep an eye on her, that with you and her both gone he could finally relax. What a piece of shit that creature is. Anyway, I can't help, I'm sorry. Read the article.' He pointed at the page still in his hand. 'She goes by the name of Ella Santiago de los Rios now. Interesting.'

Rivers. A warmth spread across Zac's chest as he scanned the page, picking out certain words and phrases.

'Why would she drop her husband's name?' he mused.

'I don't know. Did you see the part about her kid?'

Zac read on, frowning at the only sentence where a child was mentioned. *Josh will always live on in our only child. Our little miracle. I wanted a new start for us both, which was why we left America and settled in Europe,* it read. It didn't even mention which country she'd moved to.

'That doesn't make sense either,' Zac said. 'In this life Josh was infertile and they were meant to adopt—three children, to be exact. And the entire family was meant to die that day including the kids. But their child is clearly not adopted, and neither is it dead.'

'This is all I have,' Gabriel added with a small shrug. 'Why don't you look on that internet thing you can do now, use your magic phone and computers and such. You managed to find her last time.'

Zac took out his phone and typed in *Ella de Silva, Ella Santiago de los Rios, Ella Fantz, Ella Rios photographer.* Photo after photo of his beautiful love filled his screen. His fingers shook with cold and nerves as he scrolled through every link and photo.

Why had he never done this before? Because it hurt, that's why.

Gabriel peered over his shoulder, making the odd humming sound of interest or surprise as Zac dipped into news and photography sites. Although the blogs and clippings praised Ella's work, they revealed very little about her personal life.

'She's probably involved with someone else by now, bro. Maybe even remarried,' Gabriel said. 'It's been six years since Josh died. That's a long time for young humans.'

Zac breathed angrily out of his nose. 'I don't care, Gabriel. Ella's destiny ran out a long time ago. There are no rules now. Nothing and no one can stop me.'

Gabriel nodded slowly then continued to read over his friend's shoulder, occasionally coming up with suggestions as to where she may be living.

'This article says she doesn't travel much for work because of her child. What are you going to do with a kid on the scene?'

Zac wasn't going to be deterred. Not this time. 'I'll be there for them *both*, Gabriel. I love Ella and I will do whatever it takes to make her life better. She thinks I died and never came back, but I did. I let her marry a man I knew would make her happy, even though it shattered my heart. I left her alone, when all I've ever wanted was to have her beside me. I missed out on saying goodbye, because of my bitch of a mother, but I have the perfect chance to right my wrongs now. I thought I would never see her again. I'm going to find her, Gabriel, and I will be there for her and her child—in whichever way she needs me. The magazine says she's in Europe. I'll go to Spain, to London, every single place we ever visited together. I *will* find her, and I will tell her I'm sorry that I let so much time pass between us.'

'Take a breath, my friend,' Gabriel said with a smile.

'Thank you. Thank you so much, I'll never be able to repay you for this.'

Zac pulled Gabriel into a tight bear hug and the archangel laughed softly into his shoulder.

'Hey, I'll always have your back, bro. So, what's the plan? You going to do some more research, make some phone calls?'

Zac stepped back and grinned at the angel, the cold air blowing his hair into his eyes and pinching his cheeks. He'd never felt more alive.

'No, I'm off. I'm going back to Spain to see what her parents have to say.'

'But you can use the internet and telephone now. Don't be foolish.'

'I need to see them face-to-face. I don't want them to warn Ella that they've spoken to me.'

Gabriel pursed his lips. Zac knew that look—it meant the archangel didn't approve. He didn't care.

'When are you going?'

'Right away. I'll get the next flight to Gibraltar. I'm going to visit my old friends Leonardo and Felicity, find out where their daughter lives, then I'm going to get my girl.'

'Don't do anything rash, Zadkiel. Think it through. Don't forget both Ella and her parents still think you're dead. No one remembers what happened the day she got married.'

'Don't worry,' Zac shouted, as he walked backwards across the piazza. 'I know what I'm doing. Ella is alive, Gabriel! I'm going to tell her I love her, and hopefully she still loves me too. Everything is going to be perfect.'

'What about your mother?' Gabriel shouted out. 'You know she's still out there hunting for Nephilim. She needs you, Zadkiel. You will have to speak to her eventually.'

'Everything my mother has ever done has been for her own gain,' Zac shouted out, arms outstretched. 'She means nothing to me. Ella is my family now.'

The archangel opened his mouth to reply, but he was too late. Zac was already sprinting across the square so fast he looked like he was about to take flight.

9

INDIE HAD HARDLY slept. It was the first day back at school after the Christmas break and her eyes ached, scratching like they were full of grit every time she blinked. But bad nights were nothing new.

After her father died, Indie had spent every moment she should have been sleeping fighting against the avalanche of her mother's emotions. Invisible tendrils of grief would reach out to her through the walls of their house like ghostly hands. Just ten years old, she'd been deprived the opportunity to come to terms with her own loss. The emotions of her mother, family, and friends after her father's death had been so strong and all-encompassing that some days Indie had been unable to get out of bed. Everyone thought she was depressed, which would have been understandable, but it had been more than that. The truth was she'd been paralysed beneath the weight of the grief of others. As she'd been so young at the time she'd never been left alone, not for a minute, which meant the grief only multiplied.

Even now there were times her mother's blanket of despair would wake her, like a suffocating fog seeping through every pore of Indie's body. It rendered her motionless, unable to breathe through racking sobs. Other nights it was the tinkling jangle of nerves tapping their way under her skin, her heart thudding against her rib cage. But last night had been different. Last night her mother had come home drunk.

Indie was running late for school. She checked she had her keys then shut the front door quietly behind her, conscious of her slumbering mum passed out on the sofa. It was the first time Indie had seen her like that.

It was gone midnight when she was woken by the front door slamming shut and her mother muttering something about 'fucking angels' and 'fate bollocks.' Indie had attempted to get up and see if she was OK, but her own head was too light and swimmy and she had to lay back down. *Typical!* The first time Indie had experienced being steaming drunk and it was courtesy of someone else. She'd never even *tried* alcohol and definitely didn't want to now because what she'd felt last night had been horrific. She was just pleased she didn't have to be near her mother for today's inevitable hangover.

Emotions were always described as a conscious thing, something you could only feel while awake—but Indie knew differently. She felt dreams too, and they were just as violent as any conscious thought. Last night her mother's dreams had been filled with cloying lilac, anger, and a tiny inkling of hope.

Indie rubbed her eyes as she shut the garden gate behind her, wincing at the stark brightness of the white January sky.

'Windy Indie, you look like shit,' Jesse sang, sidling up to her as she rounded the street corner. He blew her two exaggerated air kisses then turned his back to her. 'Check out my new schoolbag.'

It took all her will not to laugh out loud.

'Fluorescent rainbows and heart-eyed kittens? You know that bag is made for six-year-old girls, right? It looks like a unicorn has shat all over your back.'

Jesse grinned, as if she'd given him a huge compliment, then grabbed her hand and swung it back and forth.

'We're gonna ruuule the schoool,' he said in a terrible Rizzo accent.

'No, we're not. We're going to remain exactly the same awkward nobodies that people neither love nor hate. You'll carry on being inappropriately extra, although the novelty has totally worn off and no one laughs anymore, and I'll...'

'Continue being a miserable cow?'

'Probably.'

She felt his good mood drop a notch, but she didn't care. She knew she was being mean, but she was tired, grumpy, and cold, and didn't have the energy to deal with Mr Hyper With Added Glitter.

They walked on in silence. It took half an hour to get to school by foot, but in winter they could do it in twenty. Neither of them liked the cold, so they talked less on frosty days like today and half jogged to keep warm.

'We finally get to check out the new people,' Jesse said, still swinging her hand. 'I wonder what their names will be.'

'I couldn't care less,' she said, meaning it.

Jesse was her only friend. She had no girl mates and had never dated. In fact, she'd never even kissed a guy. Indie didn't need new people in her life, which was why she had no intention of going out of her way to talk to the newbies, especially on their first day. She hadn't slept enough to deal with the secondhand nerviness of a new kid at school or their inevitable overeagerness to fit in.

As they reached their school road, they were met with the usual throng of students dressed in dark blazers and white shirts. As sixth formers, Indie and Jesse were given the luxury of the use of a common room and private sixth form toilets, plus they no longer had to wear a school tie or blazer. This meant that every weekday Indie, in her black trousers and white blouse, looked like a waitress.

Someone shoved her right shoulder, causing her backpack to fall to the ground. She bent to pick it up, only to be knocked to the ground by a herd of stampeding kids.

'Exactly where you belong, in the gutter.'

Indie knew that voice only too well. She normally felt the uneasy prickle of Alyssa before she saw her, but in a crowd, it was easy to miss someone creeping up on you. A globule of spit landed next to Indie's hand on the pavement, accompanied by a wicked laugh. She looked up, but her classmate was already lost in the crowd before Indie had a chance to say anything.

'Oh. My. God. Indie, you OK?' Jesse helped her up and handed over her schoolbag. 'Alyssa's such a bitch. Why has she always been so horrible to you? Do you think she's jealous, you know, because your dad used to be…'

Indie let Jesse's words wash over her. The more he babbled the more she had a chance to think about what had happened. It annoyed her that she was so tired she hadn't felt Alyssa creep up on her. Not that it mattered anyway. The girl had issues—they hung over her like a veil. It was hard for Indie to hate her when the person who hated Alyssa the most was Alyssa.

'We should report her,' Jesse announced, as they reached the sixth form common room. 'Alyssa Fleur is a nasty bitch, and she needs to be punished.'

'What you saying about my mate?' came a voice behind them. Cassidy and Rochelle. Great. Ella blinked slowly. They'd been back at school less than ten minutes and already the bitchy girls were in full force. It was so cliché. Didn't they have anything better to focus their energy on?

Jesse stared at his feet. For all his showmanship and bravado, he hated confrontation.

'I heard what you said, *gay boy*!' Rochelle added. 'You and Indie think you're so cool being all alternative and diverse. Just because you're mega camp and she's a swot doesn't make you interesting. It just means no one else likes you and you have nothing worthwhile going on in your lives.'

Indie smiled and rubbed Cassidy's arm.

'Have some breakfast. You'll feel less angsty if you have a slice of toast or something.'

'What you trying to say? You calling me fat?'

She wasn't. She could feel the gnawing ache of Cassidy's hunger eating away at her own stomach. As Alyssa's best friend, Cassidy struggled to keep up with her—in both grades and looks—forever starving herself in fear that her best friend would one day notice she wasn't naturally slim and drop her. Indie felt sorry for her, while at the same time thankful not to have to worry about fitting in. Cassidy had been Indie's friend for a while, back in year eight, but now she joined Rochelle and Alyssa in entertaining herself by making Indie's life hell. Or at least thinking they did. They had no idea their nasty comments were the least of her troubles.

'You want me to eat something? Well, I have this in my bag,' Cassidy announced, bringing out a yogurt pouch and unscrewing it. She aimed it at Indie and squeezed, sending a splattering of white over her black trousers. 'Ha, now it looks like you got lucky with some guy. About the closest you'll ever get, *Indigo!*'

A group of sixth formers had gathered around them and were now pointing and laughing. Indie could feel the mix of hilarity and shame rising through her body, starting at her feet and filling her up bit by bit. Everyone wanted her to react, but the truth was she genuinely didn't care. How could she feel sad or angry when the overbearing emotion that was currently taking her over was everyone else's amusement? She rolled her eyes and headed for the sixth form girl's toilet, Jesse trotting behind making placating noises. Fat lot of good he was in an emergency.

'Let me go in with you,' he whined.

She shook her head. She needed to be on her own, even if it was just for a few minutes in the loo. The door swung open with a bang, but there was someone already in there.

'Hey,' Indie said quietly to the girl blinking into the mirror.

'Fuck!' she cried, although it sounded more like 'foogh' with a hard *h*. 'I didn't hear you come in. Creeping about like that!'

Indie gave an apologetic smile and grabbed a handful of paper towels. She attempted to wipe the yogurt off her trousers, but all she managed to do was create a bigger smeary stain full of paper fluff. The bell rang for registration and she groaned.

'You wanna hand?' the girl asked. 'You're making a right mess of that.' She didn't pronounce the *t* at the end of her words. Indie had no idea where the accent was from, but she liked it.

'Are you new?' Indie asked her.

'Yeah, I'm Jade,' she replied over her shoulder as she ran something under the tap. She held up a ball of black fabric. 'Spare tights. They're clean. I had them in me bag.'

Scrunching them into a ball she rubbed the tights on Indie's trousers, occasionally glancing up and frowning, then looking back down.

'There you go. Now you look like you pissed yourself, but it's better than cum marks.'

Indie bit back a smile. Jesse was going to be mad that she got to speak to the new girl before he did. 'Thanks. I'm Indie. We're in the same year. What's your first lesson?'

'Art.'

'Mr Parson?'

The girl nodded.

'Cool, me too. I'll see you there.'

Jade didn't smile or say anything back, she just silently watched her walk out of the toilet. It wasn't until Indie reached her form room that she realised she hadn't felt anything emanate from the new girl. No emotion, no feelings. Nothing.

10

THE SKY WAS chalky white with dark smudges of grey. It was too cold to rain, too warm to snow, and too miserable to be out in. After a day at school, her head buzzing with the overwrought emotions of her classmates, Indie craved silence and solitude. Instead, she found herself in the school field, sitting on her damp rucksack, with a jittery Jesse beside her.

'What are we doing here?' Indie asked, pushing her scarf deeper into her coat.

'Watching the boys play football.'

She pulled a face. 'OK, let me reword my question—*why* are we sitting in a wet field watching the boys play football? I'm freezing.'

'Because Xavier is the new team captain and I want to gaze at him adoringly, but not so adoringly that it's obvious. There's nothing to see here! I'm no different to any other boy who enjoys watching sweaty footballers running about on a freezing cold January afternoon. I'm just a guy, watching another guy, and admiring his very muscly legs in those very tight football shorts.'

Her friend's nerves fluttered like spikey leaves rustling beneath her skin. This was ridiculous. Jesse had fancied Xavier since he'd joined sixth form back in September, and Indie could sense that the footballer felt exactly the same way about her friend. Yet the two of them continued to skirt around each other like a couple of brightly coloured birds ruffling their feathers—desperate to be noticed yet flapping away at the merest chance of anything happening. Indie wished Jesse would calm the hell down, because the fizzing and popping sensation of his imagined unrequited love was making her feel ill.

'Jesse, you don't look anything like the other boys from our class. They're on the other side of the pitch, cheering and eating hot chips from the burger van, and you're sitting under a tree with me, miles away from the match, painting your nails neon pink and sucking on a lollipop.'

Jesse licked the lolly suggestively and made a groaning noise. She stifled a laugh then whacked his arm, making him jolt.

'Hey! You smudged my nails. You're such a stiff. You know what you need? A hot man. Or a hot woman. *Anyone!* Indie de Silva—you need to get kissed so hard your legs shake and your fanny flutters so much you can't remember your name.'

'You're disgusting.'

This was their daily conversation. Since year ten, when Jesse received his first snog at a campsite in France on a family holiday, he'd been telling her that the answer to every single one of her problems was a tongue in her mouth. Indie wasn't interested. Not in boys, girls, or anything that involved a complete stranger getting that close to her. It was bad enough knowing when people fancied her, and the discomfort that caused, but the idea of being able to read their emotions and know when they were going off her before she'd even warmed to them was beyond agonising. No way, she wasn't going to do that to herself.

She wasn't like other people, which meant she couldn't enjoy the things they did. Except no one knew she was a freak, so Jesse was never going to give up being Mr Matchmaker.

'I spoke to the new guy in maths this afternoon. Wait until you see him tomorrow. I think he's in the same history class as us. He's the cutest. Totally your type.'

'I don't have a type.'

'He's *everyone's* type.'

'No such thing. You're seriously tiresome, Jesse. I'm fine on my own.'

'No, you're not. You're an uptight pain in the arse who deserves a cuddle from a sexy someone. So, what do you want—girl or boy? He has a twin sister, you know.'

Indie sighed. 'Yeah, I know about his sister. And I'm fine, thank you very much.'

'Maybe you're ace? Like asexual? That's cool. You need to make sure you update your Twitter so everyone knows.'

Indie shook her head slowly, there was no point arguing with Jesse when he got like this. She *did* fancy people. No matter how hard she fought it, there were plenty of people she liked. Boys. She fancied boys. But she wasn't going to tell her friend, or he'd relish the find-Indie-a-boyfriend mission and she'd never hear the end of it.

Jesse blew on his nails and flicked his hands through the air like a flamenco dancer, all the while squinting at the footballers. 'Who's winning? I can't see because my hair is in my eyes, but my nails are wet so I can't brush it back seductively.'

Indie looked over her shoulder at the group of lads in the distance. Their stripy red shirts were streaked with mud, and they were hugging each other. She turned back around.

'We've just scored, I think. That's the whistle for halftime. I might head home before it gets any darker. It's going to rain.'

Jesse did one of his dramatic sighs and screwed the lid back on the nail polish bottle.

'Indie, don't go. Don't leave me. I need my wingwoman for when I find the courage to sit closer to the pitch.'

'Just go and say hello to Xavier. Look, he's over there sucking on an orange. Go on, talk to him! He likes you.'

Even from this distance she could feel the warmth of Xavier's desire for Jesse. His feelings toward her friend were strong, so strong she was surprised Jesse hadn't been knocked over by the intensity of the captain's dirty thoughts. Xavier had it bad. If those two ever got together she hoped they'd find somewhere with a lock on the door.

'Yeah right!' Jesse screeched. 'As if Xavier likes *me*! A strapping, sexy Latino like that is not going to want to be seen with this princess. He probably has a bunch of big-tittied girls on the go at once. No, I'm not embarrassing myself. I'll just continue gazing adoringly at my doomed crush, drool over my parka, then hate myself later.'

This could go on for hours and she didn't have the energy for her friend's dramatics. Although Jesse's excitement and nerves ran through every fibre of her being, running beneath it all was a steady, sludgy stream of her own exhaustion.

'I'm off.'

'Wait! Indie!' Jesse shouted, jumping up and spreading his arms apart. 'Don't leave me this way…' he sang. How was it that he knew all the words to so many old pop songs? With the lollipop still in his mouth, he bellowed out the lyrics while pirouetting on the spot. Indie was used to his theatrics, and although she never joined in, she'd usually laugh. Not this afternoon though. She was numb with cold, she was tired, and she had art homework due for the next day.

'Oh, my bloody god,' Jess sang to the tune of the song. 'Xavier just looked, over at me. I think I need a peeeee. He's so effing hot!'

'Of course he looked at you. The whole school is looking over. You're doing jazz hands at a football match.'

Jesse's gaze fell over her shoulder and his face lit up. She felt his emotions shift from nerves to excitement. Oh no. Things were about to get a whole lot worse.

'That's him! That's the new boy I was telling you about.'

Indie didn't have a chance to say anything before Jesse sprinted across the field to a group of boys by the chip van. She knew them all from her year, all except for one. She picked up her schoolbag and slung it over her shoulder. The last thing she was in the mood for was making small talk with a stranger. But it was too late, because Jesse was already gesticulating wildly and pointing at her. He was dead. *So* dead. She walked slowly toward them, telling herself she had to go that way anyway to go home.

'This gorgeous but scary girl is Indie,' Jesse said with a flourish to the boy next to him, 'and this, oh surly one, is the newest of new boys, Blu. That's blue like the colour, but without the *e*. Is that right?'

The boy standing next to him nodded, a faint smile on his lips. When his eyes settled on Indie his expression changed. Brows knitted together, he stared, as if she'd asked him a question that he was struggling to answer.

Jesse hadn't noticed, of course he hadn't. He was bouncing on the spot, hands twirling in the air encouragingly.

'Nice to meet you, Blu. Nice to meet you, Indie. Shake hands. Hug. Make out. Say something. *Smile!*'

'Don't worry about him,' Indie mumbled. 'He's not on drugs; he's always like this. Thank you, Jesse. You can go back and stare at the footballers now. I can say hello on my own, and then I'm going home.'

Jesse held her face between his hands and gave her an exaggerated kiss on both cheeks.

'Mwa! Mwa! *Ciao, bella.* Get home safe. I'll message you tonight and you can thank me for introducing you to Mr Hot Stuff. Bye, Blu,' he added, before winking at the new boy and running back to his spot beneath the tree.

'Nice to meet you,' Indie said, giving Blu a tight-lipped smile. 'I'm sorry about Jesse. He gets easily excited.'

He nodded slowly, his face still. 'He's funny. He was talking about you all through maths this afternoon.'

Indie's cheeks prickled at the thought of what exactly Jesse had said about her. She wouldn't be surprised if he'd made business cards with her face on them to hand out to anyone vaguely attractive, selling her virtues as if she were an old car he was trying to get rid of. Blu must have noticed her face reddening because he was quick to fill the silence.

'It was all good. He thinks you're amazing. Said I should meet you.'

He had the same accent as his twin. They sounded like they were singing when they spoke.

'I met your sister today, in the loo,' she said, because she couldn't think of anything else to say. 'Then we had art together. She seems nice.'

'Then it can't have been Jade,' Blu said with a smile. 'Me sister's a rude bitch. She makes Darth Vader look like a Butlins Redcoat.'

Indie laughed out loud. Then stopped just as quickly. That was strange. If she was feeling amused then that meant she was feeling her own feelings and not Blu's, which meant that… She took a deep breath and looked at him. Waited. Nothing. Just like with his sister, she couldn't pick up a thing. No emotions or sensations emanated from him. Nothing. She couldn't remember the last time she'd been able to talk to someone without feeling what they did. Two people in one day wasn't normal, plus she hadn't felt Alyssa creep up on her in the crowd earlier either. Was she finally growing out of her weird affliction?

Jesse was a walking, talking can of energy drink. Hanging out with him that afternoon had been like a jittery drug keeping her awake. But Jesse was at the other end of the field now and the other boys from her year had also wandered off. It was just her and Blu left, and all she felt was…herself. As if she were on her own, but in a good way.

'You OK?' he asked.

'Yes, sorry. I'm tired. I was just heading home.' She waved in the general direction of the school gates. 'I normally walk.'

'Want me to walk with you?' he asked. She must have made a face because he quickly held up his hands in surrender. 'Sorry, I don't have to. It's just that the first day at a new school can be a bit full-on and I could do with a walk. You know? Clear me head. If that's OK. I don't have to.'

Walk her home? She didn't even know him, why would he want to walk her home? It would be proper dark soon, but still—she didn't need an escort.

'Sorry,' he said, backing away. 'I'm being overly friendly, aren't I? Jade says I'm dead creepy when I do that. It was just an idea....'

'I don't mind the company,' she heard herself say, even though company was the last thing she normally enjoyed. She headed for the school gate and turned left toward the bus stop, Blu's quick footsteps following behind her.

They walked in silence for a couple of minutes. Normally she would tune into the other person's emotions. She'd assess whether they were eager to talk or wanted to be left alone, whether they were happy, sad, or anxious about something. It made choosing conversation topics easier. But with Blu all she got was an empty silence. Was that what it felt like to be normal? Like every other person who was free to focus on their own emotions instead of someone else's all the time? How *was* she feeling?

Light. Relaxed. Curious.

She looked over at him just as he glanced up at her. Jesse had been right, he was cute. Although it was easy to find someone attractive when their feelings about you weren't permeating every thought you had.

'Where you from?' she asked. Her voice sounded tiny now that it wasn't vying for attention against another person's needs. It was like whispering into a huge, empty cavern.

'Liverpool,' he said. 'Me accent not obvious enough?'

Everything he said sounded like a question and was accompanied by a smirk. Not the leery kind, but the kind that made the tip of Indie's ears itch with heat.

'I didn't notice, sorry. I moved to the UK when I was twelve,' she replied. 'It means I'm crap at local geography and accents and stuff.'

'Ah, that explains why your own accent's so strange. Like an American pretending to speak Cockney.'

She screwed up her nose in jest. No one had ever said that to her before, not that she spoke to many people. They passed East Finchley Tube station and headed up the steep incline to Muswell Hill. Blu didn't seem at all concerned about where he was going or about getting home at a certain time.

'Wait a minute. You weren't asking about me accent, were you?' Blu said, giving her a light nudge with his elbow. He was one of them, the kind of person who felt instantly comfortable enough to touch someone they'd just met. It took Indie at least a week to build up the courage to make eye contact with most guys, let alone elbow them in the ribs. 'When you asked where I was from you were referring to this, yeah?' He circled his face with his hand. 'Me pretty eyes, these cheekbones, me dark skin.'

Oh god, he thought she was being racist. That wasn't what she meant at all! He *did* have amazing cheekbones and really nice skin but that wasn't the point. Her question had been genuine, and now he thought she was one of those people who demanded to know someone's heritage just because it wasn't immediately obvious.

She concentrated as hard as she could but couldn't pick up any of his emotion. Was he angry with her?

'It's a sexy combo, eh?' Blu grinned as he spoke, like it was part of a stand-up act, and Indie breathed a sigh of relief. 'You curious about me parents now, eh?'

With his mile-a-minute chat and self-assured cockiness, Blu was exactly the kind of guy Indie stayed away from, far too intense and expectant. But because she couldn't feel any of his emotions it was strangely OK. She could actually think around him, free to enjoy his one-man show.

'I wasn't thinking any of those things. I promise. Your family history is *your* business.'

'Yeah, well, I'll tell you me story anyway, because all the girls ask. I've never met me mam or dad,' he said, eyes wide, expecting a reaction. She kept her face straight. It wasn't for her to ask details. She didn't exactly have a normal background herself. 'I live with me aunt and her wife. Me mam was Japanese but died the day me and Jade were born. Car accident. Doctors saved us but not her. And I don't know who me dad was, but I'm guessing he was black because…' He pointed at his face. 'Handsome, eh?'

'That's sad about your mum. I'm sorry.' She wasn't going to give him the satisfaction of telling him how attractive he was. He knew that already, and clearly was used to girls telling him. 'What about your name? Is Blu a Japanese word?'

He laughed and nudged her again.

'No!' he shouted out with a laugh, making the word sound like 'neuw.' Indie decided there and then that she was going to make him say 'no' as often as possible because it was the cutest sound. 'You're funny, Indie. Blu is an acronym. You know, acronym as in…'

'I know what an acronym is.'

'Sorry. Me mates from me old school didn't know any words longer than two syllables. Where was I? Oh yeah. Me real name is… OK, promise not to laugh.'

Indie placed her right hand over her heart and nodded solemnly.

'Me real name is, and don't tell anyone because people will take the piss…' Indie raised her eyebrows in mock exasperation. 'It's Bristol Levington Usaki. Fucking Bristol. Like the city.'

Indie waited to feel his shame wash over her, or anger or something. Anything. But there was no emotion at all. Strange. She must have been staring at him because he was waiting for her to say something.

'It's not that bad.'

'Oh, behave! It's totally crap. You're not a real Londoner, so I take it you don't know what Bristols are in Cockney rhyming slang?'

She shook her head and he grinned.

'Good. At least me sister's name is normal. Jade is a normal girl's name. When I realised me initials spelled a colour too I told me aunt and Tara, that's me other mam, that I wanted to be called Blu.'

Indie didn't blame him for changing it. Her own mother had told her all about the Ella Fantz taunts she used to get at their age. Blu was a cool name, though. It suited him.

They continued to walk in silence. He didn't ask anything about her in return, and she was thankful for that. It was only quarter to five, but the sky had already turned gunmetal grey filled with black specks of birds heading for their nests. Light was one of the things Indie missed most about LA—London was always so dark. Even in the day, the sky went from grey to white to black without any blue sky for days.

The people here were just as bad as the weather, especially in winter. Emotions that pulsated from the crowded streets of London in January were a mix of impatience, disdain, dissatisfaction, and frustration. No one was outwardly evil or cruel, just constantly irritated—as though they were imagining that anything was better than what they were experiencing in that moment.

But that wasn't the case right now. Right now, just her and Blu walking along the quiet backstreets of Muswell Hill, felt good. Light. Normal. Even though it was so cold her lungs were crystallising each time she inhaled, and her breath puffed out like smoke as she spoke, life felt easier than it had for a very long time.

'When did you move to London?' she asked.

Jesse had already dug for juicy info about the new twins and had shared with her all he'd discovered, but gossip wasn't always reliable at their school.

'Just before Christmas,' Blu said. 'Me mam, Tara, the one that's not me biological aunt, she's Australian, but she's been here about eighteen years. She's a tattoo artist, which is kinda cool. She used to live not far from here, Archway, I think. She moved up to Liverpool to be with me aunt when we were born, but always wanted to get back to the big smoke. Said there was better work down here and more opportunities, you know?'

Indie nodded. It was the kind of thing her own mum would say.

'She's got this friend,' Blu continued. 'Zac, his name is. She did him a tattoo way back and they kept in touch. She says he's a bit loo-la, one of those rich eccentric guys who never ages, you know? He sounds dead nice though. Anyway, he gave her a big load of money for her fortieth birthday last year and she bought a tattoo studio in Covent Garden with it. Comes with a flat above it. Me aunt is an illustrator, freelancer, so she can do her job anywhere. Plus, Jade was getting into trouble at school. It made sense to move south.'

Blu's family sounded more interesting than hers. People thought Indie's mum was cool and creative too, just because she was a photographer and used to be married to an actor, but the truth was Indie's life was dull. They'd moved to London under the cloud of her mother's grief and anonymity, then Indie became the quiet kid at school everyone avoided. She hardly remembered her old life in the sunshine, back when her family was a solid unit, and everyone was happy.

'Your mums and sister sound nice,' she said.

'Yeah, it's OK. It can get a bit much sometimes though. A bit intense. I live in a house with three women—someone is always bitching at someone. And once a month I have to stay away for a whole week because they all hate men. More than normal, I mean.'

Indie laughed. 'Really?'

'No.' He grinned. 'They're like that *all* month. What about you? You got brothers and sisters?'

'No. It's just me and my mum.'

'What's that like?'

Why did people ask those kinds of questions? What was she meant to say? *Oh, it's terrible. My mum cries herself to sleep most nights because my famous dad was blown up on his yacht, and I have no one to talk to about it because no one knows what it's like to be me. To be a complete freak.*

'It's fine. Chilled. Birthdays and Christmas can be a bit quiet and boring, but it's OK.'

'Sounds nice. I'd love a chilled birthday. Me family is so full-on our house turns into a real-life Pinterest board every time there's a big occasion. Me mams are into decoration big-time, you know, bunting and cake and wrapping paper all matching. Last year, for me and Jade's sixteenth, the party was superhero theme, and our mams invited all our mates around as a surprise. They made this crazy cake and me aunt even had gift bags for everyone. She'd drawn pictures on each bag of my friends as a different superhero and filled them with stuff, like we were six years old, except instead of a yo-yo and a bag of sweeties she filled the party bags with beer and cinema vouchers. They're crazy.'

Indie rolled her eyes because it was expected, but she actually thought it sounded amazing. Although if her mum had gone to that much trouble it would have been just the two of them and Jesse, standing in the living room, with a plastic cup of orange juice.

'My birthday is the second of January. No one ever wants to celebrate the day after New Year's,' Indie said.

'You're seventeen already? You're six months older than me and Jade.'

Indie had just turned sixteen, but no one knew she was a year ahead. The school had accidentally put her in the wrong class at twelve years old, and her therapist had said forcing her to resit a year would be too damaging to her mental health so the school left it. Plus she was smart, so no one noticed. It would be so easy to say nothing—she'd only just met Blu after all. But something about the way he was looking at her, friendly and open like a trusting dog, made it too hard to lie.

'I'm sixteen. Literally turned sixteen last week. I'm a year ahead.' The words were out of her mouth before she could stop them. 'Please don't tell anyone. People at our school don't need much to make someone's life hell.'

Blu frowned and nodded his head in small movements, like he was incredibly impressed.

'Cool,' he said. And that was that.

Indie tucked her hair behind her ear and kept her eyes trained on the pavement. God, he probably thought she was a stupid child now. She made a mental bet with herself that today would be the last time he talked to her. In fact, she wouldn't be surprised if he made his excuses right away and jumped on the next bus. Of all the people at school, why would he want to make friends with someone in the year below?

They walked in silence for a minute more, then Indie stopped in the middle of the pavement.

'Wait up. Didn't you just say you live in Covent Garden?' If he wanted an excuse to stop walking with her, she was giving him his chance. 'Only, we passed the Tube station ages ago. How you getting back to the centre of town from here?'

Blu shrugged. 'Dunno. I might walk you home then walk back.'

'What? Walk to the Covent Garden? But that will take *hours!*'

'Yeah, about two hours. It's OK, I hate the Tube and buses. I might start cycling into school soon, but I don't mind walking today.'

'You're mad, but I know what you mean. I hate public transport too. Too many...'

'People?'

'Yes, totally. I hate people.'

'Me too.' He smiled, his brows coming together in a half-frown, half-smirk. Did he find her amusing or strange or…? Unlike anyone else she'd ever met, right now Indie wished she had an inkling of what Blu was thinking.

They walked on in silence, the streets around them varying shades of grey and navy in the bitty evening light. It was so quiet in her neighbourhood, even the birds had settled for the night. Blu was in no apparent rush, taking everything in like a tourist who had no place to go.

'Do you like London?' she asked.

He answered immediately. 'I like it more now.' Then he stopped, throwing his hands in the air in mock surrender, making Indie jump back. 'Sorry, sorry, that sounded wrong. I wasn't hitting on you. I just meant…you're cool. You know? I'm enjoying our walk. London is big and busy, and I don't know anyone and, well, now I do.'

He thought she was cool! And he made the word rhyme with 'yule,' which was beyond cute. Blu was cool too, maybe this was what Jesse meant when he said she needed more friends.

She grinned and he grinned back, and they carried on walking without talking, their steps synchronising after a while. They turned into her street and she watched him take in the big houses and tidy front gardens, eyes narrowed like he was figuring out what kind of people lived there. What kind of person Indie was. Walking with Blu was a refreshing change from hanging out with Jesse, who bounced and twirled and skipped with every step. It took at least an hour every afternoon to shake off her best friend's excitement after walking home together. His energy would course through her veins well into the evening, fizzing and popping like a glass of Coke slowly going flat. Whereas now Indie felt…empty. In a good way.

'We're here,' she said, nodding at her front door. 'Thanks for walking me home.'

Blu didn't say anything, he just stood there with his head cocked to one side, like he was listening to something.

'You're really unique, Indie.'

'What?'

'I just mean, I dunno. I get a…feeling about people, sometimes.'

Was he flirting or taking the piss? She had no idea, and it was freaking her out. He seemed friendly enough, but not being aware of his emotions was unsettling.

'Right, well, see you tomorrow then,' she said, tugging on the straps of her backpack and pushing open her front gate.

'Hey,' he shouted out, as she reached her front door. 'I forgot to ask. What's with Jesse and that footballer? The Colombian guy?'

'Xavier?'

'Yeah. Those two going to get it on, or what?'

Nobody but Indie knew Xavier was gay, and Jesse hadn't told anyone about his crush except for her. He definitely wouldn't have confided in Blu! Indie focused as hard as she could, desperately attempting to burrow into his mind. Still nothing.

'I don't know what you're talking about,' she said. 'Jesse doesn't fancy straight guys. Don't go starting any rumours, eh new kid!'

Blu placed his hands in mock surrender again and backed down the street, his eyes fixed on hers.

'I won't say a word. Stay happy, kiddo.'

She shut her front door, kept the lights off, and ran to the living room window. It was nearly dark, and she could just make out Blu's silhouette as he walked down her road like he had all the time in the world. Then he turned back, looked at her house, and shook his head, before rounding the corner.

Indie stood in the dark of the living room for a long time, staring out of the window and wondering what the bloody hell had just happened.

11

'SO? *SO?*'

Jesse hadn't left Indie alone since she'd met him at the corner of her street that morning, and now they were approaching the school gates and he was still jabbering on in his usual hyper way. How did he never run out of energy? The boy was a scientific phenomenon.

'*So* nothing!' she said, for the tenth time.

'Bullshit. Blu likes you, I could see it. He walked you home. First day in a new school and he walks you home. I mean, who *does* that? And you *let* him! You can't hide it, Indie, you like him. You *like* him! Blu and Indigo, sitting in a tree. K–I–S…'

Jesse stopped singing and began to laugh. A small giggle at first, which quickly grew to ridiculous hysterics, his body shaking so hard he had to stop in the middle of the pavement, hands on his knees, doubled over. Why the hell did he have to be so extra in everything he did? Even laughing was a huge theatrical performance.

'What?'

'Your names! Oh my god, Indie. You have matching names. This is too much. You have to date him now and marry him and be with him forever, just so that I can see your names together on the wedding invite. Blue and Indigo, perfectly colour-coordinated. Oh god, wait until I tell everyone... Ow! Why did you hit me?'

Even though the wind had been relentless all morning, and Indie's woolly hat was soaked through from the fine drizzle misting over them, she could feel her cheeks glowing red with embarrassment. Jesse's hilarity burned through her, a million pinpricks of her own shame combined with his mounting bubbles of mirth. It was a weird combination and not one she had any intention of getting used to. Blu was the first straight guy she'd talked to in years and now her best friend was making it the butt of the world's biggest joke.

'It's not funny, Jesse. Grow up. Blu and I were walking in the same direction and had a chat. Big deal.'

'It's funny. Admit it.'

'No!'

'Oh, come on! Lighten up, miserable moo. I'm just saying that it was good to see you talk to someone. He seems like a nice guy. You need more friends.'

'No, I don't. I have you, and that's more than enough for one person.' Her cheeks had cooled down and her blood had quickly gone from boiling to a light simmer. Her emotions, on the rare occasion they fought their way through the feelings of others, rarely hung around for long. Jesse, relieved she was no longer upset, was now pirouetting through the school gates singing 'True Blue' in a high '80s Madonna voice.

Indie rolled her eyes and stomped behind him. How could she stay angry with such an adorable fool?

• • • • •

As usual the school corridor was a sea of sweaty winter coats and a jumble of overwrought emotions. Indie pushed through the throng, doing her best to block out the onslaught of angst-ridden dramas that hovered around her head, so many emotions swarming around her like angry wasps refusing to leave her alone.

'We have history first thing,' Jesse shouted over the bell, as Indie threw her bag into her locker and took out her folder and pens. 'Blu will be there, remember.'

'Give it a rest, Jesse. You never know when a joke's over.'

'You're the biggest joke here,' purred a voice over her shoulder.

Indie didn't need to turn around to know that Alyssa, and most likely her two goons Cassidy and Rochelle, were standing behind her. She could sense them—uncertain, spiky insecurity enveloped in the pink bubble gum goo of bravado.

'Piss off, Alyssa,' Jesse spat, although he was a good two inches shorter than the trio of girls. 'You were out of order yesterday, and so were you, Cassidy.'

'Ignore them,' Indie muttered, physically shrugging as if she could literally release their desperate weight from around her shoulders.

Alyssa wasn't going to let them walk away without a fight. 'Running away again, are you? Pathetic. No wonder you've never had a boyfriend, Indie, when you're so miserable and your best friend is more of a girl than you are!'

Indie placed her hand on Jesse's chest as he made to lunge forward, although they both knew he had no intention of starting anything. Jesse wasn't a fighter. He didn't even like playing rugby or getting muddy during PE.

'I don't get it,' he hissed as the girls sauntered off down the corridor in the opposite direction. 'What's her issue? I can't even remember why she hates you so much.'

'Year nine. She fancied that boy Lee, remember? But he asked me to the summer dance instead. Even though I said no to him, and he left for another school that year, she's always claimed I stole her boyfriend.'

'What? That's it?'

Indie shrugged. 'I suppose so. I can't think of anything else.'

Jesse's adrenaline was still pumping through her. The sick feeling sloshing around in the pit of her best friend's stomach was now also making her feel queasy. Jesse didn't even look up as Xavier walked past. He had to be mega worked up to not notice the look the footballer had just given him.

'Hey, don't worry about it,' she said, giving Jesse a quick hug. 'Just ignore her.'

Jesse's eyes were glassy, and he was biting his lower lip. 'I don't understand. Why don't you ever say anything to that bitch? She's been horrible to you for years and you just take it!'

What was Indie going to say? That she could feel Alyssa's pain and the girl was more messed up than she was? That Alyssa's parents argued nonstop, so their daughter cut the tops of her thighs every night so the physical pain replaced the one in her soul? That Alyssa was bitter because she was convinced everyone had a better life than she did? How could Indie hate someone who hated herself so much? No one knew Alyssa's secrets because she did a great job of keeping her distress to herself—but Indie knew. Indie knew everything that her classmates fought to keep hidden. Even the things she wished she'd never have to feel. As for Alyssa's friends, they were just as insecure and weak too. They had no idea their friend was in such turmoil. They hung out with her because they needed to feel special. At the root of everything anyone did, Indie saw their humanity. Their pain. Their justification. It was hard to hate someone who did what they did because it helped them hurt less.

'You're a bloody saint, that's what you are,' Jesse said as they entered the classroom. 'A saint or a stupid idiot. I haven't decided yet.'

He blew her a kiss and settled at his desk, then raised one eyebrow as Blu and Jade entered the classroom. Jade sat behind Indie, completely ignoring her as if they'd never spoken before. Blu, on the other hand, grinned at both Indie and Jesse, then made a beeline for the desk next to hers. Her best friend's eyebrows rose even higher, making his forehead crease into three deep lines, and Indie widened her eyes in return as if to say 'calm down, it means nothing.' Too late. Jesse was already scribbling something down. As Mr Dowding entered the classroom Jesse held up the piece of paper so Indie could see. It was two squares, coloured in different shades of blue, with a heart between them. Idiot! She still laughed though.

'OK, class,' Mr Dowding began. 'I see we have a couple of new faces here, but as you're practically adults, I'm not going to waste my time making Bristol and Jade introduce themselves. Say hello to them after class and don't be your usual rude, antisocial selves.'

A buzz travelled through the classroom, bodies swivelling around to look at Blu and his sister. The word 'Bristol' could be heard among the excitable titters and snorts. Indie hadn't missed Dickhead Dowding over the Christmas break. The man got his kicks from humiliating children, as if it was his only pleasure in life.

Blu's hand flew up, but Mr Dowding ignored him.

'Last term we were looking at the importance of the Dutch East India trading company, and this term we will be investigating what that meant in terms of commerce and how the trade routes shaped our nation.'

'Sir,' Blu called out. 'Excuse me.'

'First of all, we are going to discuss how...'

'Sir!'

Mr Dowding had his back to the class, jabbing at the electronic whiteboard, trying to make a video play. '...how the spice route influenced...'

A huge crash erupted at the back of the classroom as a framed map of Europe fell and smashed to the floor, sending shards of glass skittering across the tiled floor. Mr Dowding swung around, giving Blu the opportunity to finally get his attention. He jumped up and gave the teacher a large smile.

'Please, sir, my name is Blu. It's not Bristol, it's Blu.'

The classroom erupted into chatter again as Mr Dowding nodded his pasty bald head impatiently at the new boy then marched out of the classroom, muttering something about a dustpan and brush. Blu grinned at Indie and something inside her chest swelled like an overinflated balloon. She looked away, but not before catching the tail end of his sister's whispers to him.

'…dramatic, no? Can't you behave for once?'

Blu gave Jade the side-eye as he leaned closer to her.

'The teacher wasn't listening. I didn't hurt anyone.'

The rest of the lesson went by in a blur of dates and charts and maps, with red dashes signalling trade routes and a short documentary about cinnamon. With ten minutes left until the end of class, Indie's hand was beginning to cramp as she frantically scribbled in her notebook.

It had taken all her willpower not to look at Blu again throughout the lesson. A few times, out of the corner of her eye, she'd seen his head turn in her direction, but she hadn't dared meet his eyes. That morning she'd wondered whether yesterday had been a weird anomaly. If perhaps today she'd be able to feel the twins' emotions. But no. As before, nothing emanated from them. With ten minutes until the end of class, Indie put down her pen and stretched, accidentally swiping it off her desk and sending it skidding across the floor of the classroom to the other side. Indie didn't have another pen. Crap!

Mr Dowding was back at the whiteboard, pointing at a long quote.

'Homework,' he said. 'This is a famous quote about the East India Company. I want you to write it down and by next week produce a two-thousand-word paper on how these new trade routes impacted seventeenth-century colonialism.'

How was she going to copy the board when her pen was under Jesse's desk? She hissed her friend's name, but he was too absorbed in his own work to hear her. She called him again, this time too loudly.

Mr Dowding turned to face her. 'Miss de Silva, do you have a problem?'

A wave of amusement washed over her as everyone's feelings poured out of them like a tsunami, even though every student was looking down, and no one was making a sound. Everyone except Jesse, who was grimacing at her. He knew how much she hated the spotlight.

'I dropped my pen, sir.'

'Well, then you'll have to copy someone else's work after class,' Dowding shouted, giving her one of his signature head-wobbles. 'Don't interrupt my lesson again.'

Indie swallowed down her humiliation and stared straight ahead, fingertips buzzing with frustration. What was Dowding's problem? Bullying knob! Beside her, Blu started coughing lightly and stopped when she looked at him. He signalled to the floor with his eyes at her pen, which was now by her foot.

She screwed up her face with confusion, and he shrugged in reply. It didn't make any sense. How was that possible? Bending down to retrieve the pen, she nodded and smiled quickly up at Blu who returned her gratitude with a lopsided grin. Jade sighed loudly behind them.

'Have you all signed the form for the school trip next week?' Mr Dowding hollered, even though the classroom was quiet. 'No, I don't know why it was deemed a good idea to go on a field trip ten days after the new term starts either, but then what do I know? I have only been teaching for thirty-four years. You two, the twins, were you told about the trip?'

'Yeah,' Jade said, her voice dripping in indifference. 'Our mam signed the papers and paid when we enrolled.'

A bubble of anticipation grew in Indie's stomach. Blu and Jade would be going on the school trip too.

The bell rang to signal the end of the lesson and she bundled over to the door with the rest of the class. Then she slowed down as she sensed Blu hover beside her. It was weird how she couldn't feel his emotions yet could still sense him like there was an invisible thread between them, something light yet strong tugging at her chest every time he was near. No, that was stupid.

'You going straight home after school?' he asked loud enough for the whole class to hear.

Indie tried not to visibly cringe as she nodded, spikes of curiosity from her classmates covering her skin like the feet of a thousand scuttling insects.

'Can we walk together again?' Blu asked, completely indifferent to the fact that his sister and Jesse were out in the corridor waiting, and now gaping at them open-mouthed.

Indie gave a noncommittal shrug and tried to ignore the swarm of butterflies dancing in the pit of her stomach. Blu grinned, his sister frowned, and Jesse's eyebrows shot up so high they almost flew off his face.

'…he's more myself than I am.'
~ Emily Brontë, *Wuthering Heights*

PART TWO

12

ELLA CLOSED HER laptop and rolled her shoulders, twisting her torso left to right in her swivel chair until the vertebrae in her back cracked back into place. She'd been editing photos for five hours, moving nothing but her fingertips. No wonder her back was sore. People thought that being a photographer was glamorous, that it was all about framing a shot and clicking a button. Little did they realise more time was spent in front of a computer than behind a camera.

The familiar crunch of the front door opening made Ella glance at the time in the corner of her screen—Indie was late home, and not for the first time. Taking a while to straighten up, Ella peered out her office window. That boy was out there again, grinning and nodding in the direction of her front door. Was he Indie's boyfriend? Was her little girl finally acting like a normal teenager?

'I'm up here,' she called out.

The front door slammed shut and feet thudded up the stairs until her daughter's silhouette was framed in the doorway.

'Hey! You look happy,' Ella said.

'What? Why? I'm not anything. I'm totally normal.' Indie sat at her mother's desk and twirled around in the chair. 'What you been working on?'

Ella pulled a face. 'That magazine shoot I did of that author. I'm done now.'

There was a stack of papers on Ella's desk, half of them covered in doodles. Ella always drew pictures when she was on the phone or thinking about a new project. She watched her daughter trace her fingers over the Biro-scribbled flowers, stars, and a strange shape that looked like a capital *I*. The symbol for the Indigo bar. Thinking of the place where she'd first met her late husband, the place they'd named their daughter after, always made her happy. It was why she often found herself scribbling its logo. Yet lately it was the face of Zac, not Josh, that worked its way into her daydreams. The time with the angel all those years ago was like remembering an old film; all those unbelievable things had happened such a long time ago she sometimes wondered if they'd happened at all. It had been just a handful of days, two decades ago, and still he haunted her.

'Who's the boy you keep walking home with?' Ella asked, trying to take her daughter's attention away from her scribbles. She didn't trust herself to explain the logo without getting upset. 'How come Jesse isn't with you?'

'The boy is called Blu and we're just friends. Jesse is still my best friend, but he's seriously obsessed with a football player right now so prefers to stare at him running up and down a field than walk home with me.'

Ella hid her smile and kissed the top of her daughter's head. It still smelled like it did when she was a baby. Her little girl. She spun her daughter around in the office chair and started to plait her hair, something she used to do years ago when they'd watch TV together on a Friday night. And by some kind of miracle, she was letting her. Indie hadn't let her mother get that close to her in a long time, which was why Ella stayed silent for fear of breaking the spell.

'Mum?'

'Hmm?'

'Does your neck hurt?'

How did she do that? How did she always know? Ella stopped playing with her daughter's hair and rubbed her shoulder.

'A little bit. I've been doing a lot of editing today.'

'I thought so. It's the way you're standing. Did you know the Bull and Bear are doing yoga nights? Thought it would be a good idea for you. They supply mats and everything.'

Ella swung the desk chair around until her daughter was facing her.

'A pub that does yoga nights? That's ridiculous.'

'Not really. They have that big room out the back, and afterwards they do healthy drinks and snacks at the bar. I always see their posters on the way home.'

'When is it?'

'Tuesdays and Thursdays. Seven o'clock. You should go tonight.'

Was Indie trying to get rid of her? Maybe she wanted to be alone with that new 'friend' of hers. Ella wasn't sure how she felt about that.

'OK, I might go. Want to come with me?'

She was met with an incredulous look. 'Who goes to yoga classes with their mum? No thanks, I've got a history essay to write.'

Ha, so she *did* want to be home alone. It was about time her sixteen-year-old daughter started acting like a normal teenager. Not that Ella was worried—Indie was more trustworthy than Ella had ever been. And maybe yoga *was* a good idea. Ella had been meaning to try it for a while, and Mai Li had mentioned that she wanted to start some kind of exercise class after having the baby. They could go together. There was no reason why they couldn't be healthy *and* have fun.

'Do they have a website?' Ella asked, while reaching for her phone. Her daughter shrugged, muttered something about Google, and sloped off to her room.

• • • • •

Yoga was a stupid idea. Ella was standing in the doorway of a pub, arms crossed and not enough clothes on for that time of year, or her time of life. It was freezing outside but it had seemed silly to drive to an exercise class in a thick winter coat, so she'd thrown on her zip-up hoodie and was now regretting it. Why wasn't Mai Li already there? She only lived down the road. Ella pulled at her T-shirt, but no matter how much she tried she couldn't get it to cover her backside. What had she been thinking? Evening exercise classes were for sporty, sprightly people.

Yet another twenty-something girl with a high ponytail and thigh gap brushed past her into the bar, forcing her to step aside. When did pubs get so healthy? When did it go from 'hair of the dog' to 'downward dog?' It was her own fault for living near such a pretentious area. She should have realised things were heading this way when the local launderette had been converted to a juice bar and the corner shop sold mainly coconut water and kale.

She checked the time on her phone. There was one missed call and three WhatsApp messages from Mai Li. She scanned them. Her friend's eldest child had nits, and Adam couldn't cope with de-licing four kids and managing bedtime without her help. Would Ella mind cancelling? And could they go next week instead?

Yes, Ella *would* mind cancelling! Her cheeks puffed out as she let out a long sigh, wishing she'd seen the message twenty minutes earlier before she'd left the house. Pizza in front of the TV would have been way more fun than freezing her arse off outside a poncey pub.

'Are you joining the class?' A tall man in cycling shorts had opened the pub door behind her and was beckoning her in. 'We're about to start. I need to lock the doors.'

She stepped into the warmth and looked around. It seemed like a normal pub, although it was empty and panpipe music was floating in from next door.

'My friend can't make it, and it's my first time. Maybe I should skip it this week,' she said.

'No, come in. You'll be fine. What's your name?'

'I'm Ella. But it's been a while since I....'

The man leaned over her, locked the door, then handed her a rolled-up yoga mat.

'Stay at the front with me, Ella. Don't worry, it's not Ashtanga, it's more of a meditative class. Just copy what I do. You'll be fine.'

With a flick of her foot, she kicked off her trainers, leaving them with the other shoes, and followed him into a room full of toned people with their backs to her. Everyone was sitting cross-legged on the floor, and as she sat down, she saw they had their eyes closed. Well, that was good; at least no one was staring at her tatty leggings that were older than most of the people in there. Copying everyone else, she faced the front of the room where a framed photo of a yogi had been placed on a shelf, alongside a pot spiky with burning incense. She kept her eyes on the front of the class—she didn't need to look around her to know she was the oldest and wobbliest one there.

• • • • •

By the time Ella was halfway through the class, following a long session of sitting on the floor and humming, she was feeling both virtuous and capable. One class a week, or every other week, sounded feasible enough. It was only a bit of deep breathing and stretching, after all.

The teacher talked them through the motions, Ella copying the girl next to her and stumbling a bit in places, but mostly doing OK.

'And relax into the downward dog,' the teacher cooed.

They all created a facedown arch with their bodies and looked between their legs. Ella's arms ached a little, and the backs of her legs weren't used to such a stretch, but it wasn't too bad.

Then she saw him. Two rows back a man, covered in tattoos with hair tied in a messy bun, was effortlessly flexing his bronzed arms. Enzo. She took in his broad shoulders, rippling under the strain of his pose, and the tips of his messy brown hair which had been bleached blonde, presumably by the sun in all those far-off places he'd visited. She couldn't see his face clearly, but it had to be him. Who else looked like that?

He was lifting one leg with ease and matching the movement with the opposite arm. Was that what Ella was supposed to be doing? She'd stopped listening to the teacher and could only focus on the upside-down image of a giant, tanned god between her legs.

Oh no, why was she thinking about him between her legs?

The room was getting hazy and little spots started appearing before her eyes. She blinked, shook her head, and was just about to right herself when the upside-down man behind her looked up. Enzo's eyes locked on hers and she lost her balance.

Fuck! Fuckety fuck fuck!

With a flump she collapsed into a heap on the yoga mat and curled up into a ball of shame. Maybe he hadn't seen her. Maybe she could stay like that for the rest of the class, or the rest of her life.

'That's good, Ella,' the teacher said. 'As soon as your body has had enough, get into the child's pose and rest. This applies to everyone. Do as much as you feel is comfortable and remain conscious of your breathing.'

She was more than aware of her breathing, because it was coming in fits and starts. Why hadn't she thought of bringing a bottle of water? An irritating tickle soon became a choking cough as she struggled to take in air, her throat too dry. *Not again!* Last time she'd seen Enzo she'd choked on her dinner, then got drunk and blubbered into his big, manly shoulders. And here she was again, curled up in a sweaty ball and coughing her guts up. How long had he been behind her, staring at her lumpy arse? Enzo wasn't the kind of guy who hung out with women who had coughing fits while working out. He probably did yoga all the time, and other cool young people exercises like capoeira and rock climbing and...

'Here,' came a low voice beside her. She glanced up, and there he was. His face, not red or sweaty like hers, smiling down at her. 'Have some water.'

She accepted the metallic sports bottle he was offering and gulped it down. Everyone in the class had stopped balancing on one leg and were now staring at them both.

'Asthma,' she lied. 'I overdo it sometimes. I'll be fine.'

Enzo narrowed his eyes and for the first time she noticed the scar cutting through his right eyebrow. Every inch of him was warrior-like. There was no way she could carry on working out now, not the way he was looking at her all intense and still like that.

'Come on,' Enzo said, helping her to her feet and leaning in closer. That wasn't helping, as if her legs weren't weak enough! 'Let's take a rest at the bar.'

A few people sighed irritably as she got to her feet, their cutting stares soon turning to envious glances as Enzo gently put his arm around her waist and led her out of the room.

• • • • •

'Well, that was embarrassing,' she muttered, clinking her glass of sparkling water against his and settling into a chair by the window. It was raining, the streets deserted. With everyone still in the yoga studio, the bar was silent except for the odd shuffle of the solitary barman and the swooshing sounds of the cars outside.

'Cheers for rescuing me,' she said. 'I'm not the sporty type.'

'You were doing fine from where I was standing. As soon as I saw you come in, I wanted to say hi. I couldn't focus on anything after that.'

Ella took a large gulp of her water, a sliver of ice making her shiver.

'You look different outside of a suit,' she said, nodding at his bare arms full of tattoos. His hair was no longer in a scruffy bun—instead mahogany locks with sun-bleached tips fell messily down his back. On anyone else it would have looked rough and unkept, but on Enzo it looked perfect. Savage. A man like that belonged outside doing adventurously crazy things. Clothes and walls and rules didn't apply to him. How many times had his job as a war photographer brought him close to death, she wondered.

'Yeah, I'm way more comfortable barefoot and in shorts.' He laughed. 'You look different too.'

She looked down at her old T-shirt and baggy leggings. Great, she didn't even have any makeup on. *Why?* Why had she left the house looking like this? It had been a long time since she'd worried about men taking notice of her, not since before Josh, but Enzo was… He was… different. She wanted him to like her.

'I like you,' he said, his eyes twinkling. 'You don't care what anyone thinks.'

'That's not true.'

He really had no idea.

'Do you live near here?' he asked.

She nodded. 'Not far, Muswell Hill, about ten minutes away. You?'

'No. I move around too much to have my own place. I'm staying at an Airbnb near Crouch End. I came to London for a small project, and the awards night of course, but I won't be here long. I don't get on with big cities. I prefer places a bit more deserted.'

She thought of all the dangerous, war-torn countries he'd been in. 'Like the desert?'

'No. Like the sea,' he said, flipping the beer mat off the table edge and catching it midair. 'I've spent a lot of time on the ocean. I feel hemmed in when my feet are on solid ground.'

'Wars and ships,' Ella said, pointing at his arm. 'That explains the ink.'

His laugh was quiet, wistful. 'A tattoo for every regret.'

Both of his arms and hands were covered in images. He was wearing a sleeveless cotton T-shirt and she itched to peak beneath, see if the tattoos spilled over to his shoulders and chest. 'That's a lot of mistakes.'

'Yes. I never seem to learn my lesson.'

Some of the markings looked old and faded, like the blue smudged ink found on the skin of old sailors and prisoners. Other images were brighter, more recent. Anchors and stars fought for space among feathers, ships, skulls, and beautiful women. One face stood out from them all.

'She's pretty,' Ella said, pointing at the picture on the inside of his left arm. A portrait of a woman with long dark hair and bright green eyes stared back at her, a purple-gemmed necklace at her throat and a lilac rose in her hair.

'She's my biggest regret,' he replied, a far-off look clouding his black eyes. 'I had her tattooed on a part of me where I could see her every day.'

'It's very good. Was it copied from a photo?'

'No, I have no photos of her, just a sketch from an old book. She's there to remind me of everything that's worth fighting for. Hopefully I'll find my way back to her one day.'

They both drank on in silence. Ella wished she hadn't mentioned the tattoo of the woman—it had clearly rattled him.

'Your job sounds interesting,' she said after a while.

'Interesting? I take photos of people dying and suffering. War is many things, Ella, but never interesting. Countries fighting one another is the same shit time and time again. The only part that changes is what the victims look like. Powerful men make the order, and defence-less children die. I guess I'm not the only one who never learns from his mistakes.'

Well, she wasn't expecting *that*. She ran her fingers over the watery rings the glasses had left on the wooded surface, wondering what she could say to lighten the mood.

'Do you have a family? Wife, kids?'

He shook his head. 'No. Everyone in my family is dead or lost.'

'My husband is also dead. It's just me and my daughter.'

He murmured his condolences. Ella had a vague recollection that it was Josh she'd been crying about at the awards night, so Enzo probably knew her story already.

Well, this was fucking jolly. What a great job she was doing keeping their chat lighthearted and fun. Maybe she should leave. She could pretend her phone was vibrating, check it, then say she had an urgent message from her daughter. Enzo seemed like a nice guy and was very easy to stare at, but if all they had in common was dead people it wasn't going to be the most thrilling of evenings.

The rain was falling harder now. Enzo dragged his gaze from over her shoulder and back to her face. There was a sparkle of interest back in his eyes, as if someone had flicked a switch from heavy to light.

'You said you have a daughter,' he said softly. 'She must be a baby.'

'Oh no, Indie's sixteen,' Ella replied, instinctively reaching for her phone on the table and scrolling through her picture gallery.

'You don't look old enough to be the mother of a teenager.'

Lots of people said that to her, but the way he said it didn't sound like a chat-up line, more like he was working out the maths and disappointed by the outcome.

She held up a photo of Indie. He shuffled closer to the screen, then snatched the phone off her and peered closer.

'Wow, she's…'

'Pretty, isn't she?'

'Yes. Of course, but… She reminds me of someone. What's she like?'

Ella shrugged and took her phone off him. There was an energy around Enzo that was unsettling, a stillness laced with lightning sparks like a storm that hasn't yet made a sound. She leaned back, her hands now on her lap along with her phone. 'Indie is like every teenage girl. Quiet, secretive, distant.'

Enzo's mouth opened and he took a breath, as if he was about to say something, then stopped.

'What?' she asked.

'Nothing, just that… She has brown eyes, like yours.'

'And?'

'And it was her father who passed away?'

'That's right. Josh.'

Ella wasn't going to name-drop and mention that he used to be a famous actor. It had been awkward enough while Josh was alive, let alone now he was dead. Anyway, Enzo didn't look like someone who watched action films in the cinema. He looked more like someone who did his own stunts just for fun.

'Your daughter looks nothing like her father.'

Ella frowned. So he *did* know who Josh de Silva was. How much had she told him at the awards night when she was blubbering like an idiot?

'Well, no. She looks more like me. My father's Spanish, so I guess she gets the dark hair from that side of the family.'

'And Josh was definitely her father?'

'Of course!' *Oh my god, could this man be any ruder?* Why was she still sitting there, listening to this crap? 'I think I'd remember if I'd been with anyone else.'

Enzo looked down at his empty glass, his cheeks tinged pink. *Good!*

He was right, Indie looked nothing like Josh, but that wasn't something you pointed out to someone you hardly knew. Ella thought back to the first time she'd held Indie in her arms and saw her thick shock of dark hair. Her first thought had been how little she looked like Josh and how much she looked like... No. She wasn't going there.

Maybe Enzo *was* simply curious. Josh had always said she let her emotions cloud her judgement when it came to their little girl. Mouth set in a straight line and her hand clenched around her phone, Ella told herself she'd stay a few more minutes.

'Please, forgive my lack of tact,' Enzo said. 'It's just that, since I spoke to you at dinner last Sunday, I've been convinced we've met before. That's why I'm asking so many questions. I think we have a friend in common. Someone I've been needing to get in touch with for some time.'

'Who?' she asked.

'Luci.'

Ella pretended to consider the name, although it didn't ring any bells. She gave Enzo a small smile and shook her head.

A shadow of disappointment swept over his face, then disappeared just as quickly. 'Doesn't matter. I thought perhaps you knew Luci's son, but clearly you don't.'

He'd leaned forward as he'd said the word 'son,' as if it was meant to trigger a response. The only friends she had were mums to very young boys and she was pretty sure that wasn't what he meant.

'Yoga's finished,' she said, pointing behind him and reaching for her handbag. 'They'll start handing out wheatgrass shots next and chatting about sugar-free diets. I'm not hanging about for that. Thanks for the drink, it was lovely to see you again.' She went to give him a peck on the cheek, but he held out his hand instead. OK, so it was like that. She shook his hand, gave him a tight smile, and headed for the exit.

'Ella,' he called out as she opened the pub door. She turned, icy wind whipping at her hair and down her thin top. 'I gave you my business card the other night, right? Do call me if you ever meet Luci. You'll know who she is when you do.'

She nodded and stepped out into the drizzle. That was the last time she was going to yoga, and the last time she'd be having a drink with Enzo. It was clear the only reason he was talking to her was because he thought she knew Luci, whoever that was. Perhaps she was the lady tattooed on his arm.

What kind of woman had such power over a man like Enzo that he'd have her image scratched into his skin forever?

13

THE GIRL PLAYED the violin, and Luci watched. She'd been standing unobserved outside the living room window for forty-five minutes now, and not once had the kid complained or slowed down. Eyes screwed shut in concentration, she sent sweet, liquid notes wafting through the slightly open window. She was talented, not that you would guess from the way her father was yelling at her.

'Violet! Lift your elbow and relax your shoulders. The recital is in two weeks and this time you need to get placed.'

The girl stopped and lowered the violin, staring intently at her slippered feet as they moved back and forth, carving lines into the plush carpet.

'I came second at the last recital out of thirty-eight people.'

'Exactly,' he shouted back, his chin wobbling with every command. 'Second may as well be last. With the amount of money I've invested in your lessons, the least you could do is make an effort. Your brother and sister were concert pianist level by fourteen and are both now doctors. What are your plans for the future? You can't even choose decent A Levels. At this rate I'll be dead before I see you make a success of your life.'

Violet jammed the violin firmly beneath her chin and continued to play. This time a furiously fast melody filled the room with spikes of anger and passion.

'Good. That's better,' the old man said. 'That's the kind of power you need behind every note. I have work to do—keep practising until I say you can stop.'

With a vigour rarely found in men his age, he marched to the living room door then stopped, backed up, and scowled into the shadows outside his window. He'd spotted her, and judging by the look on his reddening face he didn't like what he saw.

Luci didn't feel the cold, but she was still rather proud of her outfit: a fake fur coat, in shades of grey and black, and bright red lipstick. Beneath it she wore a little black dress and knee-high boots. Perhaps not the attire most people wore to stand in a stranger's flower bed during the evening while watching a girl play the violin—but Luci wasn't most people.

The old man yanked up the wooden sash and stuck his head out of the window, nostrils flaring. 'Who the hell are you?' he barked. 'And what are you doing in my garden?'

Green eyes, neon as a serpent's, stared intently into his milky pair. 'I'm here to talk to Violet,' she said slowly, enunciating every word. 'Open the front door, let me in, and forget I'm here. Also, stop being a nasty, bullying bastard.'

Scowling, he nodded curtly then left the room without a backward glance.

Violet's face was all angles. Her eyes large. Her sharp nose striking. Yet her features sat incongruously with the way she was staring out of the window—shoulders hunched, mouth agape, and violin hanging limply by her side.

In an instant, Luci was standing beside her.

'Who are you?' the girl stuttered.

'Stand on one leg.'

Violet's eyes widened in fear, the bow in her hand shaking as if she were conducting an orchestra, while the rest of her stayed deathly still. She appeared frail but Luci knew she was strong. She'd passed the first test. Another confirmed Nephilim.

'Sit down,' Luci said to the girl, shrugging off her thick coat. 'I have something important to tell you.'

Violet eyed Luci warily as she draped her coat over an antique chair and sat on the sofa. Luci leaned forward, her smile as sharp as a blade, making the girl inch closer to the door.

'Please,' Violet said, virtually a whisper. 'I don't have any money. Please don't hurt me.'

'I'm not here to hurt you. I'm here to save you.'

This wouldn't do at all. The girl had played the violin with such determination, such passion, and here she was quaking like an autumn leaf on a branch. Luci not only needed Nephilim, she also required them to be able to handle whatever was thrown at them. If Luci got as far as the spell, and every day it was looking more and more likely, then there were plenty of things that could go wrong. Any Nephilim involved needed to be capable.

Violet pointed her bow at Luci as if it were a sword, the shiny wooden violin held up like a shield. Although she stared intently at the stranger in her living room, there remained an air of curiosity behind her wide eyes. Luci shuffled back a little on the sofa, trying to appear as harmless as possible. Perhaps her outfit choice was a little too Cruella de Vil.

'I've been reading your secret blog,' she told the girl.

A flicker of fear passed over her face, then her jaw set tightly.

'What blog? I don't have...'

'I know what you are.'

Violet looked down at the carpet, shuffling from foot to foot, making more grooves appear in the plush pile.

'Oh, for fuck's sake, child. Put the violin down, you're not Boudicca!'

The girl swallowed and did as she was told, placing the instrument back in its case by her feet.

'Let's talk in your room,' Luci said, standing up.

Violet flinched. 'We can't. My dad will…'

With a swipe of Luci's hand, the living room door flew open. 'Your dad is a bully and the least of my concerns. Come on, lead the way.'

• • • • •

Tall, with twiglike limbs and long hair held back by a padded Alice band, Violet was every bit the unassuming private school girl. Therefore, her bedroom was not what Luci was expecting. Instead of a room filled with pretty pastels and tasteful furniture, every wall was plastered with bright flyers for DJ nights, raves, and clubs. A large rainbow flag hung above her bed and her bookshelf groaned under the weight of thick paperbacks, creased spines in shades of black and crimson. Dotted among the fantasy and paranormal tomes were figures of dragons and willowy fae.

'My parents haven't been in my room for years,' Violet said, noting Luci taking in her surroundings. 'They don't know me very well.'

With a flicker of a smile, Luci sat down on the girl's bed. 'I'm sorry I scared you,' she said. 'I've been searching for you for a very long time.'

Violet remained standing. 'That thing you did, when you opened the door without touching it…'

'Yes. You can do the same, I know. You've only just discovered your abilities, right? As I said, I've read your blog. I know what you are.'

Silence. The girl was very good at staring.

'Sit down, child. Let me explain.'

It was gone dinnertime, but the house was still. No noise of a TV or the girl's family preparing food or walking around. Was this what her evenings were like in the big house? Furious violin practise followed by a heavy, empty silence?

Violet shuffled over to her bed and perched on the corner.

'Am I ill?' she whispered. Her eyes darted to her bedroom door for the twentieth time in a minute. Luci sighed, then with a sweep of her hand she dragged Violet's chest of drawers across the room and blocked the exit.

'There. No one is going to come in. Talk to me. Tell me your story.'

The girl swallowed and closed her eyes. When she opened them again, something had shifted. A stillness settled over her.

'I feel like I'm going crazy sometimes. I'm really oversensitive to people's emotions. I can... This is going to sound silly, but...I can feel what others are feeling.'

'Can you feel me?'

She shook her head fast. 'That's why I was so scared when I saw you. You're the first person whose emotions I can't sense.'

Luci nodded. 'What else?'

'I can do what you just did. Move stuff...with my mind.'

From her bedroom window the cry of birds heading to their trees could be heard, while in the distance dark clouds were rolling in, casting a gloom over the garden and bathing the bedroom in shadows.

'What about your eyes? They look far too normal to me,' Luci said.

'My eyes are...' Violet screwed up her face and dropped her head in her hands.

'Show me.'

The girl disappeared into a small room which Luci presumed was a bathroom. In less than a minute she reappeared, her eyes shining a pale magenta and glistening with tears.

'I'm hideous! I look like a monster.'

With a quiet sigh, Luci walked over to her and rubbed the top of her trembling arm.

'I promise, you look nothing like a monster. I've seen all the monsters this world has to offer, and none look like you.'

'What's wrong with me then?' Violet cried. 'My eyes changed colour a few weeks ago and I totally freaked out. I was going to go to the doctors but when I went online it said it was the sign of turning into a zombie.' She glanced at all the books on her shelf. 'I was scared I'd get quarantined or tested on. So I bought coloured contact lenses. I thought maybe my eyes would change back on their own.'

She covered her face again, but Luci moved her hands away. 'Don't hide.'

Violet was so different to the street kid. Scar had *wanted* to be the Devil. As soon as Luci had driven him out of Redwood, he'd relished telling her how special he was, how his abilities and bright eyes were proof of his superhero status. Not Violet, though. The last thing she wanted was to be seen.

'What about your family? Have you spoken to them about this?' Luci asked.

She'd read her anonymous blog, she already knew the answer, but she wanted to hear it from the kid herself.

Violet shook her head from side to side. 'I'm so different to everyone else in my family. When I was a child, I used to tell my friends I was adopted. My brother and sister are much older than me. Mum had me at forty-two, said I was a big surprise. My dad was really shocked too. She loves me, I know she does, but he doesn't. He treats me differently than my brother and sister. They look like him—short, tanned, hair full of tight curls. But I'm tall and pale, and he hates it, like I'm doing it on purpose. He blames me for everything, says a man in his late sixties is too old to deal with teenagers and that I ruined his retirement plans. My mum acts like he's only joking but I can *feel* it. He hates me, but the way my mum feels about me is even worse.'

'What does *she* feel?'

'Shame. She wishes I never existed. I remind her of something, someone, but I don't know what. Whatever it is, she wants to forget it. That's why I've been at boarding school since I was seven. I come home weekends, but I don't know why, because I spend all my time in this room online or reading. No one knows the real me, not even my friends at school, which is why I wrote the blog. It's why I reached out, hoping someone would give me an explanation and...'

Before Luci had a chance to say anything the girl fell into her arms, her body shaking as she cried silent tears into her lap.

Luci put her arms around her—the act felt normal yet remarkably strange. When was the last time she'd held a child? The girl was seventeen, not exactly a baby, but the way she was sobbing, she was far from adult. Luci tightened her hold on her and thought of her own child. Had Zadkiel suffered like this when he'd discovered his powers? She'd been taken from him when he was so tiny and defenceless—just six years old. What had he done when his eyes had turned a vivid blue? Had he been scared when he realised he could move things with his mind? How had the people of Fiesole reacted to him? All the time Luci and Zadkiel had spent together after she'd wiped Ella's memory, all those years hunting for Nephilim, and not once had she thought to ask him.

It wasn't until her mouth began to fill with the sharp tang of iron that she realised how hard she'd been biting down on her lower lip. Why wouldn't the stubborn bastard call her back? There was a perfectly valid reason why she'd locked her son in that warehouse the day Ella died. If only he'd let her explain. Everything Luci did was for her boy, to protect him from others—and from himself. Everything she did was because she loved him.

'Can you make it go away?' The girl's voice was small, shaky, her breathing coming in ragged fits and starts. Her tears had left damp patches on Luci's black dress. 'I just want to be normal, like everyone else.'

Using the pad of her thumb, Luci wiped Violet's cheeks dry and looked at her properly. Such a pretty face, yet so striking and strong. If only she knew how special she was.

'I can't change what you are, Violet, but I *can* help you. I can show you how to use your gift. I can make you into one of the most powerful women in the world.'

Violet sniffed and rubbed her nose with the back of her sweatshirt. Then she laughed.

'Powerful? I can't imagine that—I never get what I want. I was going to get my hair cut short last month, but my parents wouldn't let me. They said proper ladies had long hair and that people would judge me if I chopped it off.'

It was a good job Violet couldn't read her mind right now, because Luci's thoughts were far from pretty. Here was a clever, sensitive, beautiful girl desperate to be listened to, and all her ungrateful parents cared about was her fucking hairstyle.

'I know about the hair,' Luci said, opening her large handbag. 'You wrote about it in your blog. You wanted it short and purple, right?'

The girl nodded and sniffed again, then gave a short intake of breath as Luci produced a pair of scissors and two boxes from her bag.

'I have many talents,' she told her. 'Want me to cut your hair? If you have to be different, then be your *own* kind of different.'

Violet grinned and studied the picture on the boxes of hair dye, squealing with delight.

'My parents will kill me!'

'No, they won't,' Luci said. 'You've seen what I can do. From now on, I'll make sure you're free to be yourself.'

With a curt nod, Luci made the chair in the corner of the room fly forward and land with a soft thud before Violet. The girl waved her hand and sent a towel flying out of the bathroom like a giant dove into her hand. She let out a squeal and Luci grinned back at her. She liked the kid—she was vulnerable but no pushover. This Nephilim may have been scared at first, but she knew what she wanted. So did Scar, the cocky little street rat, although there was still a lot of work to be done with him.

Running through the list of other leads in her mind, Luci felt hopeful. There was still a strong chance of finding more Nephilim. Luci never thought she'd end up heading a teen army, but things were shaping up well.

'Excuse me,' Violet said, twisting around in her seat as Luci applied dye to her hair. 'Earlier you said you knew *what* I am, not *who*. What did you mean by "what?"'

The tinting brush hovered over Violet's head as Luci considered how to phrase the next sentence. 'You're no monster, but you *do* know your father isn't your real father, right?'

Of course she knew, it was written all over her face. From the tremble in her chin to the way she shrugged lightly it was obvious she'd been waiting to hear those words for a very long time.

'I kinda guessed. Do you know who my real father is?'

Luci nodded. 'His name is Chamuel. You have his eyes. Looks like he met more than one woman seventeen years ago because… Never mind. I'll tell you later.'

Violet faced forward again but Luci could sense she wasn't finished with the questions.

'Luci,' she said again, quieter this time. 'I don't want to stay here. Can you help me?'

This wasn't the plan. Luci hadn't intended to wander around the country picking up kids like the pied piper. Over the top of the girl's wet purple head she could see her bony fingers twisting into knots in her lap. Then she thought of Scar, who she'd tucked away in the comfort of a fancy hotel. What difference would one more kid make?

'I'll talk to your parents. I'll be introducing you to others soon anyway, others like you.'

'There are more?'

'Yes,' Luci said, her chest filling with something thick and sturdy. Hope, like cement, setting resolutely in place.

Violet's gaze fell on her bookshelf, on hundreds of black and crimson spines. She looked up at Luci, her eyes shining like rose petals covered in dew.

'Am I… I know this sounds silly, but was my father a… What is my father, if he isn't like normal men?'

Luci smiled. 'Your father is one of the greatest beings there is. He's an angel. An archangel.'

'An *angel*?'

'Yes, and your purple hair is going to look fierce as fuck when you help me overthrow his leader.'

14

AS SOON AS he'd landed in Spain, Zac had called the parents of every one of his students and told them that due to a personal emergency all music lessons would be postponed until further notice. It was strange to hear Allegra's voice so curt and formal, no trace of the friendship they'd once shared. Releasing her had been the kindest thing to do, getting closer to her would only have led to more complications. There was only one woman Zac was interested in holding in his arms now, and he was just a day or two from seeing her.

'*Torre de los Angeles?*' the Spanish taxi driver asked, as they neared Tarifa. Out of the car window the curve of the ocean glided past, dotted with multicoloured specks of kite-surfers. 'I've not heard of the place. Is it new?'

Zac sat up and leaned forward.

'Seventeen years ago, when I was last here, it was a hotel converted from an old monastery. It had its own chapel. Do you know it?'

The taxi driver chuckled, his eyes fixed on the road ahead.

'Seventeen years is a long time. Things change, especially around here. You won't recognise Tarifa. It's very trendy now, new hotels, bars, fancy restaurants. The place you talk of was probably sold and part of a chain now. They'll have knocked down the old parts and added a water park; or put a wine bar where the chapel once was. You'll see. Can you direct me from here?'

Something hot and sharp twisted in Zac's stomach, squeezing tight over all that new hope he'd been focussing on during the flight over. He told the driver to take the next right and sat back in his seat. There was no plan B. He hadn't considered things may have changed, that Felicity and Leo may not be there. What if Ella had come back to run the hotel after Josh had died? Unlikely, seeing as the magazine article he'd safely folded away in his wallet spoke of a successful career in photography. But there was no guarantee that she hadn't sold the hotel, or that her parents were even together. Zac ran his hand over his face, mopping his brow with the sleeve of his shirt. Gabriel had been right, he wasn't prepared. He hadn't thought this through at all.

Another twist in his guts.

What would he do if Ella's family weren't there? He'd have to go back to the States and ask around in Santa Monica, see if anyone there knew where she lived now. That was ridiculous and a huge waste of time. He sat back and stared at the car's ceiling, and not for the first time wished he believed in God.

'Is this the entrance to the hotel you're looking for?' The taxi driver was pointing at a wooded area to his right.

Zac sat back up with a start, then sighed with relief. The gate was new, but other than that nothing had changed. He'd last visited in springtime, when a canopy of green had created dappled shade over the path leading up to the grand hotel entrance. Now, in January, the bare branches left eerie shadows instead, like spindly fingers pointing the way to his fate. They approached the gate and Zac squinted at a brass plaque on the wall beside it.

'*Los Tres Rios*,' he read out loud.

The driver let out an exasperated puff of air. 'There's no river here, let alone three. Very misleading. I sometimes wonder what goes through people's minds when they choose a name for a hotel. Makes no sense at all.'

Zac smiled to himself and sat back in his seat as the driver was buzzed through the gate and drove slowly through the wooded entrance toward the old monastery. The name made perfect sense. For the first time that morning hope flooded his chest.

The hotel came into view, and it hadn't changed a bit. Although Zac quickly wished it had as dozens of memories began to fight for attention. White lace. Whispers. Blood dripping from a giant crucifix. A scream so piercing it had changed the course of his life. Dusty books. Ella's smile. Ella's lips on his. Ella. Ella.

It was in this building's chapel where he'd first seen his mother after two thousand years. He looked up at the turret looming over him, it's yellowing stonework paling in the winter light and narrow stained glass windows running up its side like slashes in cloth. It was up there, in the old forgotten library, that Zac had last made love to Ella—then said goodbye to her forever.

Taking a deep breath, he paid the driver and picked up his bag. So intent on discovering Ella's whereabouts, Zac hadn't envisaged how difficult it would be to return. What it would feel like to revisit the building where his dreams had been shattered, where Ella had married the man fate had chosen for her.

What would his mother say if she could see him right now? Luci would be angry, of course she would. Angry he was acting so weak and needy, and angry he was doing something without her.

Well, Luci could piss off. She didn't know what love was; she only understood relentless obsession—obsession with her son and with her ridiculous plan to find more Nephilim and overthrow the realm. As if the success of a plan simply came down to how much passion she could pour into it. His mother had no idea of the sacrifices that needed to be made for those you loved—how impossible it had been for him to fight against destiny to take back the only person who had the power to complete him. Luci would argue that going into battle was proof of a person's strength, but Zac believed doing the right thing, even if it meant walking away, was even braver. He could have gone back to Ella at any moment during the eleven years she'd been married to Josh, but he'd told himself he hadn't because she was happy. And because it would keep them all safe.

But what had really been stopping him? His mother's jealousy? Trepidation? Fear that being with Ella for just those eleven years of her remaining life wouldn't have been enough, and then not being able to follow her in death would have destroyed him even more than this suffering had?

But he didn't have to worry about that now, because somehow Ella had evaded death. She was out there. He just had to find her…again.

Stepping into the welcome warmth of the foyer felt different to last time, when its tiled floor had been a cool relief from the heat outside. This time a fire crackled by the reception desk, but beside the odd painting or winter-themed touch, not much had changed.

'Can I help you, sir?' came a voice from behind the desk. A man in a navy suit and tie with a shiny name badge pinned to his lapel was smiling at him expectantly. Things had got a lot smarter around here.

'Are Leonardo and Felicity here, please?' he asked in Spanish.

'Are they guests? Do you know their surname or room number?' The receptionist tapped away at the computer as he waited for more information.

'No, I believe they are still the owners. Leonardo Santiago de los Rios?'

The man gave him a beaming smile. 'Of course, Lily and Leo. My apologies. They are on vacation. I'm afraid they won't be back until Wednesday.'

Today was Friday. Five nights. Too long.

'Do you know where their daughter Ella lives?' he asked.

'I couldn't possibly disclose that kind of information, sir.'

Zac leaned in closer, staring at the man until his pupils were fully dilated.

'Tell me where Ella lives.'

'I really don't know, sir.'

'Does anyone in this hotel know? Is her address written down anywhere?'

The receptionist shook his head so fast his neat, thick hair made a rustling sound.

'It's confidential, sir. That information isn't made public to staff.'

Maybe Zac could wait for Ella's parents. It would be nice to say hello to them after all this time. In fact, it would be nice to have a holiday of his own and gather his thoughts.

'That's not a problem. I'll wait for the owners to return. I'll stay here,' he said. 'What rooms do you have available?'

Snapping out of his trance, the receptionist made an apologetic face and turned his hands palms up.

'I'm sorry, sir, we're fully booked months in advance. There are no rooms until…' He tapped at the computer again. 'Two nights available in March and…'—he continued tapping—'…a week in September. Shall I make a reservation for you?'

It was nice to hear business was going well for Ella's family, but it wasn't helping his current predicament. Signalling to the man to lean forward, Zac locked eyes with him again.

'Is there anywhere in the hotel I can sleep for the next three nights?'

'No, sir. The only empty beds are in the staff quarters. Mr and Mrs Santiago de los Rios's apartment, or their daughter's suite.'

Zac's heart leapt. Of course, Ella's room. Was it creepy to sleep in her bed while she wasn't there? Would she mind? He doubted it.

'Give me the key to Ella's room and don't mention it to anyone. Don't let any staff near her apartment. Nobody must know I'm here. Unless I speak to you, simply ignore me.'

The receptionist nodded dumbly and handed over the key. Using his power of persuasion in such a forceful manner normally made Zac feel uneasy, but not today.

Ella's room key jangled in his pocket as he headed to the back of the hotel, his tread light and his heart lighter still.

• • • • •

Her room looked totally different to how he remembered it. Although that wasn't unexpected—few people's houses stayed the same over seventeen years. The suite was no longer white and blue, airy and beach-themed. Instead she'd decorated it in hot pinks and bright greens, with tropical-print wallpaper behind a single bed, which he presumed belonged to her child. The wall that had once displayed paintings, the largest space reserved for one of his huge white feathers pressed between two panes of glass, was now filled with family snaps. Ella and Josh on a beach, Ella and Josh at the top of a tall building, Ella and Josh on their wedding day.

The fact no photo existed of him and Ella together still pained him. Their relationship had only lasted a matter of weeks, granted, but it had also been impossible back then to capture him digitally or on film. Cameras liked him now. Would he ever get to see an image of the two of them together?

On the bedside table were more photos. He picked one up, tracing his fingers over the image of Ella and Josh cradling a dark-haired baby. Was that their child? Their son or daughter must have only been a few years old when Josh died. He hoped that was the case, because no child should have to remember the day they lost their parent.

The only thing that hadn't changed in the room was the large, wooden, four-poster bed on the other side of the room. Zac peered beneath it and breathed out sadly. He'd spent a lot of time hiding beneath that bed last time he was in her room, hiding and watching. Dust tickling his nose and his framed feather, which had been hidden under the bed too, digging into his ribs as he'd watched Ella get ready for her wedding day. Minutes dragged on like hours as he'd listened to her tell her friends how happy she was to be marrying Josh. It was all he'd needed to hear, and the only reason he'd remained hidden and let her go.

There was no room beneath the bed any longer; instead, there were a variety of transparent plastic crates filled with toys, colouring books, and children's clothes. Ella was a mother now, and her life was a lot fuller than it had been when Zac had last said goodbye.

He flicked off his shoes and lay back on her bed. When was the last time he'd had an entire week to himself to do nothing? Florence kept him busy. When he wasn't teaching or volunteering at the youth centre, Zac visited galleries and museums or took himself off to other parts of Tuscany for the day. Doing nothing wasn't an option. A still mind and body allowed thoughts and memories to trickle in—and that was to be avoided at all costs. For months, after he thought Ella had died, he'd stayed in bed without eating or sleeping. He could have gone his entire life without doing either had he wanted to, nothing could kill him, but after a while he began to look and feel like shit, so he had dragged himself back to the living.

But he could slow down now; it was finally safe to relax. No longer was it despair dancing along the fringes of his mind, but the possibility of hope—a faded glow that was growing brighter every day. Flickering, like a match trying to catch a flame, that tiny spark in the darkest corner of his soul was telling him that maybe, just maybe, things would work out after all.

With a final sigh he allowed sleep to take him. Ella was alive, Gabriel had told *him* and not his meddling mother, and in less than a week he would be back with the woman he loved.

Tomorrow was going to be a good day.

15

'ZADKIEL WON'T SPEAK to me.'

Luci ignored the look on Gabriel's face and took a bite of her pecan pastry. Vile. They were sitting in yet another homogenous coffee shop where everything looked and tasted of cardboard. The archangel took a sip from his tea and grimaced.

'Give it time,' he told her.

'That's the best you can do? Give it time?' The paper coffee cup beside her pastry had a picture of a horned devil drawn in purple pen on its side. She turned it around to face her. 'I spent two thousand years looking for my boy, Gabriel. Do you have any idea what that was like for me? Of course you don't, because you all thought I was dead. I wasn't. I was walking this godforsaken planet searching for my ethereal son. And what happened when I found him? Ella. She's all my stupid child can ever think about.'

The girl's name tasted as bitter on her tongue as the cheap coffee she was drinking. When would her boy realise that humans weren't important—that there were bigger things to worry about?

'Have you seen him lately? My Zadkiel?' she asked.

He didn't need to answer—the twitch in his cheek was all she needed to know that he'd spoken to her son.

'Is he keeping well?'

'Yes. He's happy.'

'Good. He's finally got over that bloody girl, then.'

'Not quite.'

The archangel took a tentative sip of his tea, his face still. Too still. He was hiding something from her, but it didn't matter. She'd get it out of him eventually. She always did.

'I'm worried about him,' she added.

Gabriel placed a hand over hers. Thousands of years and that look he was giving her still went shooting straight into the pit of her stomach…and lower. Jade eyes, crooked smile, sharp cheekbones, dark skin, and a history that went back millennia. He was doing it on purpose, the smooth bastard.

'Zadkiel is not a child, Luci.'

'I know, but he's *my* child. He may be centuries old, but he has the heart of a lovesick teenager. It's driving me mad. He's been obsessed with that Ella girl his entire existence. The boy needs a hobby.'

Gabriel laughed, a deep hollow sound that made everyone in the café turn and stare at them in the corner booth. Luci wondered what they saw. Lovers? Work colleagues? Best friends? Little did their fellow coffee-drinkers know that what they were actually witnessing was a meeting between the creators of the universe. A famous archangel and the infamous fallen one. Thankfully everyone was too busy snapping photos of their coffee foam for their Instagram stories to care.

'What's this?' Gabriel said, pointing at the sketch of the devil on Luci's paper cup.

It was her turn to smile.

'That, my dear friend, is a little joke between me and Felipe over there.'

A young man in an apron stood behind the bar pouring foamy milk into a silver jug. Messy hair framed a pale face, and a wooden disk stretched a large hole through his earlobe. Both arms were covered in ink—intricate tribal patterns—the kind middle-class white boys chose to prove they'd been backpacking to interesting places. He looked up, met Luci's eye, then went back to pouring his milk, a blush climbing up his tattooed neck.

'The barista?' Gabriel said, raising one eyebrow. 'Is that *your* latest hobby?'

'Maybe.' Luci stroked a loose curl of her hair across her lips, enjoying the way Gabriel's eyes followed it back and forth. 'Every morning when I order my putrid coffee he asks my name, and every morning I tell him it's Lucifer. That's why he draws this picture on my coffee cup. It's our little joke. Also, I'm fucking him.'

She studied Gabriel's face as she said the last line. He was resting his head on his fist, looking her straight in the eye as if he couldn't care less, but his right cheek was twitching again. He narrowed his jade eyes at the barista, who visibly swallowed and hurried to the other end of the bar. Gabriel was not a man, but he was still predictable.

'Hey,' Luci shouted with a laugh. 'Don't scare my toy away. He doesn't even know we've had sex. I made him forget.'

Gabriel shook his head slowly and leant forward. It was his turn to laugh.

'Go on, tell me.'

Of course he wanted to hear her game—he was an even bigger player than she was. Faces inches apart, she lowered her voice, relishing the look on his face.

'Every morning I order the same thing,' she whispered. 'We flirt, I keep it up for a few days, then we sleep together. But as you and I know, Gabriel, the fun part of any relationship is the chase. Just look at how many centuries my stupid son has wasted fawning over that girl. That's why I make Felipe forget each time we sleep together, so he keeps experiencing the exciting thrill of having conquered me over and over again. I'm a very giving person.' She bit her bottom lip. 'Don't look at me like that. It's just a bit of fun. I've done it twelve times now.'

'That's cruel, Luci.'

She flinched at his words. Gabriel crossed his arms and cocked his head to one side like she owed him an apology. So he was a saint now, was he? The famous Archangel Gabriel, always so calm, so controlled, and oh so cool. The one who never made mistakes or got spooked. The angel that couldn't be shocked.

She bit back a smile as an idea formed in her mind, something that might ruffle his feathers after all. It was a risk, but if she was right it would be totally worth it just to see the look on his face.

'Ella isn't dead, you know,' she said, leaning back in her chair with a grin. She'd had a hunch when she'd seen her son's blood around the girl's mouth that morning in the hotel library. It had only taken a few Google searches to confirm her suspicions. She was surprised her son hadn't thought to do the same after all these years. Probably too busy wallowing in his own self-indulgent puddle of pain.

Gabriel's eyes widened, but he wasn't as shocked as she'd expected him to be. So *that* was his secret he'd been keeping from her! Sneaky bastard.

'You already knew, didn't you?'

He mumbled something about having seen her photo in a magazine.

'Does Zadkiel know Ella's alive? Did you tell him?'

Gabriel looked down at the table then over her shoulder, anywhere but at her. Like every angel, Gabriel was unable to lie—but his silence spoke volumes. *Fuck!*

'He knows, but the realm doesn't. Mikhael still believes she's dead.'

Well, that was something at least. But her boy now knew, and Luci had no idea where Ella lived, which meant her son would find the girl, woman now, faster than *she* could. The taste of bitter coffee dregs mixed with the copper taint of her blood as she bit down on her lower lip.

Maybe it didn't matter anymore. Let Ella keep her boy—she had more important things to focus on. Every day that went by Luci was getting closer to forming her Nephilim army all by herself—she didn't need Zadkiel for that. Not until the end. Perhaps, once he was back with Ella, he'd change his mind about creating a descendant for the last part of the spell.

Silence settled over them as Gabriel fiddled with the string of his tea bag, failing to act disinterested as Luci shot coquettish glances at the flustered barista. She was already getting bored of the coffee shop boy, but her flirting was annoying Gabriel, so it was worth it.

'Where are you up to on your quest?' Gabriel asked eventually, voice flat and face still. He wanted her to know he was angry, but Luci knew he wouldn't stay that way for long. She usually won him over.

'Quest? Oh, I do miss that word,' she replied, stroking the angel's arm as she spoke. He flinched at her touch, but he didn't move his arm away. 'Remember the adventures we had, Gabriel? Back when we partied with Celts and dined with Pharaohs?'

There it was, that smile of his. He was thinking back to the thousands of years of excitement they'd enjoyed together before Mikhael had turned and the world stopped believing. All their shared history and it had culminated to this, an archangel and the devil in a coffee shop sipping insipid beverages out of paper cups and eating floppy pastries. Luci and Gabriel had witnessed the day coffee had been discovered. They'd joined the Mayans as they'd brewed the concoction for the first time, a powerful potion made to keep them awake long enough so the feathered gods could teach them to fly. How things had changed.

'Perhaps calling our challenge a "quest" is a little ambitious,' Luci said, pushing her pastry away. Gabriel picked it up and finished it in two bites, scattering a cloud of light flakes onto the tabletop. A crumb remained on his top lip which he caught with the tip of his tongue. Luci's stomach contracted.

'Without Zadkiel by my side, the last few years of my Nephilim *quest* has consisted of me sitting in front of my laptop researching sightings and unusual activity among sixteen to eighteen year olds. You wouldn't believe the things teens blog about and say on TikTok. Occasionally I hear from my whisperers too, when they have a lead, but it's hardly "Knights of the Round Table" stuff.'

Gabriel wiped his hands on the tiny napkin and nodded.

'What leads you got?'

'I met a kid on the streets. Scar. He's a little fuckwit, but I'm working on him. He thinks he's a tough crime lord with superpowers, like some Marvel hero, although he has no clue as to why he's different. Luckily I scared him enough to do what he's told…for now.'

Gabriel nodded, lost in his own thoughts. Was there more he wasn't telling her?

'Who else?'

'A girl. I found her through a blog she wrote about struggling with her Nephilim senses, although she had no idea that's what they were. She has potential. Why? You know of anyone else? I need four more.'

Gabriel's cheek was twitching again. What did he know? His jade eyes were restless as they scanned the room, his gaze finally settling over Luci's shoulder. He gave a curt nod and Luci swung around, hands out and fingers splayed, ready to use her magic if need be.

Three people she hadn't noticed earlier were seated behind her—a young man with long hair and two teenagers. No. It couldn't be. The man walked toward them, his footsteps beating in time to her hammering heart.

'What is this, Gabriel,' she hissed, her chair clattering to the ground as she got to her feet. 'I thought I could trust you!'

A few of the customers looked up, then just as quickly went back to staring at their phones. Felipe the barista hadn't even noticed the exchange.

'All is well, Luci,' Gabriel said softly. 'I invited him. He's on our side.'

The man with long hair picked up the chair and placed it back so Luci could sit down.

'Nice to see you again,' he said, taking the seat beside hers.

She couldn't stop staring at him, or that smile she'd once known so well. Lank brown hair hung past his shoulders, accompanied by a neat beard and eyes that shone like amber flames. Two thousand years was a long time, but she never forgot the face of one of her own.

'Rafael?'

'The one and only.' He extended his hand to be shaken but she ignored it, instead wrapping her arms around his neck and holding him close. It had taken two thousand years to find her son, but she never thought she'd get to see any of the other archangels too. Discovering Gabriel was on her side had been a big enough surprise seventeen years ago, but now another had joined her plight. She sniffed. After twenty centuries alone, she not only had allies now, but she also had her friends back.

'You look exactly the same,' she whispered into his neck.

They broke apart and he cupped her face in his hands, tucking a loose strand of hair behind her ear. 'I *can't* change, but you... You look more wondrous than I ever remember. Modern day suits you, Lucifer.'

She shrugged with one shoulder and gave him a watery smile. 'I got my ears pierced and discovered how flattering red lipstick can be.'

There was a titter of laughter behind Rafael. A delicate-looking girl with pale freckled skin, long brown hair, and golden eyes was giggling, her hand over her mouth. Beside her, a boy, so similar in features he had to be her older brother, was widening his own catlike eyes to stop the girl from laughing.

Luci's gaze flitted between the two teenagers then settled on the archangel before her.

'Yours?'

Back on his feet, with arms draped around their shoulders, Rafael squeezed the brother and sister closer to him. 'Sol and Amber. My pride and joy.'

They took it in turns to shake Luci's hand, staring at her with something akin to awe.

'My goodness, Rafael! You have children that survived to adulthood.' He grinned, and Luci couldn't help grinning back. She knew the power of a parent's love. 'And do they know...?'

'Yes. They know everything. They know who I am, what they are, and, most importantly, who *you* are, Lucifer. Gabriel came to me seventeen years ago and told me you'd survived. I can't tell you how happy I was. Sol was just a baby then and Rosaline, that's their mother, was expecting Amber. I didn't want to get your hopes up. I wanted to wait until my children were closer to adulthood before we came to you to express our allegiance. They now have all their powers and have given me their consent.'

Luci closed her eyes briefly, hoping the lump in her throat wouldn't turn to tears.

'And their mother? What's she like?'

Rafael's face lit up, and he grinned at his children.

'Rosaline is an exceptional woman. She knows all about our world and I love her deeply. I come and go, but she understands. She knows the love we share is...different. That the absence is the only way I can keep my family safe from Mikhael.'

Luci nodded. If she'd learned anything over the centuries it was that love could surpass all boundaries and norms.

'Has Gabriel explained to you about the spell?'

Rafael nodded. 'He has. Sol and Amber know their part in your plan, how they can help save us from our master's tyranny. They're ready.'

The brother and sister sat up, their faces solemn.

'Dad told us all the stories,' Amber whispered. 'We know about you losing your wings and…ow.' Her brother had elbowed her in the ribs, but she carried on regardless. 'Uncle Gabriel sometimes visits us too. He helped us when our powers came in.'

Luci shot the archangel a dark look, and he made an apologetic face.

'I didn't want to tell you until we knew they were ready,' he said, grimacing at the expression on Luci's face. 'Rafael wanted to do this face-to-face. I was only respecting his wishes.'

They were right. Had she known there were two Nephilim, children of a powerful archangel no less, ready and waiting to join her mission, perhaps she would have got involved in their upbringing, considered exploiting their powers too soon. This way they were almost adults; they had free will.

'Did I say something wrong?' the girl asked, her large orange eyes shining like topaz. She was the image of her father.

Luci stroked the girl's long hair, her throat aching at the thought of what her own granddaughter could have looked like, if only Zac would acquiesce to her wishes.

'My dear girl, do you have any idea how special you are?' Amber looked down, her pale face glowing from Luci's touch. 'You two are going to change the world, you know that? I just need to find two more like you. Two more wonderful, powerful, clever half-angels. Together we will unite our two worlds and we can finally stop hiding behind patriarchal rules and religious lies. That's all we need, just two more Nephilim.'

Rafael kissed the crown of his daughter's head. 'Gabriel may be able to help you with that,' he said, in his usual slow drawl.

What? How much was the angel keeping from her?

'You know more Nephilim, Gabriel?'

He had the decency to look sheepish.

'Maybe.'

'Who?'

'My own kids.'

Luci sat back down at their table. Gabriel didn't move. She took a swig of her coffee, remembered it was empty, then threw the cup at him. It hit him in the chest. She'd always been a good shot.

'*You* have kids?'

After what had happened to Jesus, Gabriel said he'd never father another Nephilim. What had changed? Rafael and his children looked on as Gabriel fiddled with the string of his tea bag again. Silence. She slapped his hand away.

'For fuck's sake, Gabriel. I didn't think you'd take that risk again.'

When he finally looked up his eyes were bloodshot.

'I watched Zadkiel die on that mountaintop in Spain. You have no idea what that was like, to see his wings and feathers scatter in the wind, his body lifeless, his eyes no longer blue. After that I…well, all of us… went a bit crazy. I told you. We spent an entire summer drinking and partying and… I was always careful, at least I thought I was, but clearly contraceptives don't always work with angels.'

'Who was she?'

'I don't know her name. She died. I'm not even sure if the kids survived.'

'Where did you meet her?'

For two thousand years Luci had tried to fall pregnant again, but mere humans were not strong enough to give her a child. Yet there was Gabriel, fucking anything that moved and producing offspring he didn't even want. That poor woman, who no doubt had died at the hands of Mikhael, had been so unimportant to the archangel he didn't even remember her name.

'There was a big music festival in Bristol. She was a Japanese student at the university there. She'd come to England with her twin sister. I sensed straight away that she was pregnant, so I kept an eye on her—I was looking out for her, planning to tell her everything as soon as the children were born. Then one day I couldn't feel her anymore. She'd been killed in a car accident.' He indicated quotation marks with his fingers on the word 'accident.' 'Probably Mikhael's handiwork. I presumed the kids were dead too. I never bothered to check, but now I'm not so sure.'

Luci probably should have offered platitudes about the death of the innocent woman or commented on the difficult lives these poor kids may have potentially had without having known either parents, but there was no time for niceties.

'Can you find out if your children survived?'

Gabriel shrugged. 'I could try. I thought I saw the woman's twin in Indigo just before her sister died. I might be able to find her.'

'Does Zadkiel know about this?'

Gabriel nodded and she ground her back teeth together.

'And does he know about Rafael's children?'

Gabriel nodded again, sending Luci's stomach into another spasm. *Motherfuckers.* She'd spent every day for eleven years with her son and he'd never mentioned these Nephilim—*archangel* Nephilim! Zadkiel had never known what was good for him. Fear governed him still, that had always been his undoing. Fear of change, of stepping away from what he knew. She'd stopped him from seeing Ella because she knew that to save the future the boy had to stop living in the past. But she'd been wrong—Zadkiel had never been interested in helping her. As soon as it was clear they wouldn't be able to perform the spell in time to save his true love, he'd lost interest. He didn't want what was best for his mother, or their kind. Her son just wanted his fairy-tale happy ending, and now he knew Ella was alive he certainly wouldn't be coming back to help his mother. He hadn't thought about her in two thousand years—why would he start caring about her now?

She ran her damp hands through her hair. *Bloody Zadkiel!* Why couldn't he ever put his family first? Love was a dangerous game and there were never any victors—just huge, gaping losses. Luci knew that, knew only too well what handing your heart to another meant, to watch it wither and die beside theirs. The only love you could depend on was family. Blood family.

'This is the closest I've ever got to completing the spell,' she said to the two archangels.

'Yet you don't look happy about it,' Rafael replied.

'He's right,' Gabriel added. 'What's wrong? If my children are alive, won't you have everyone you need?'

She shook her head. 'I have the three feathers—my son's, that I found in Ella's room back in Tarifa, plus mine and Mikhael's.' She stroked her necklace, the amethyst amulet that a Dutch witch had made for her back in 1613 to carry the remnants of those plumes. 'But even if we find the six Nephilim, I don't have the third descendant. Zadkiel never had a child, he's not even talking to me, and I have no other children that can provide me with an heir. I need three generations—me, my child, and a grandchild—to complete the spell. Without the blood of all three the ritual won't work.'

Gabriel leaned back and stretched out his arms over the back of the chair. A look passed between him and Rafael. The messenger archangel was grinning that grin again, the one that made Luci want to sit on his lap and do bad things. His job was to impart good news, something he'd been doing for eternity and was bloody good at. His face was glowing, jade eyes bright as leaves after a storm. What was he about to tell her?

'About that grandkid thing,' he said, his high cheekbones rising into a wide smile. 'I met a little dark-haired girl on a beach in Santa Monica six years ago. I have a theory.'

16

'I HAVE A theory.'

The woman sitting across from Indie peered over her glasses and crossed her legs, making her right ballet pump slip off her foot. It dangled precariously from her toes, swinging back and forth.

'I believe there is something you're not telling me, which is why we've made little progress over the last ten months. You need to speak to me, Indigo. Trust me and release your grief. What are you holding back?'

Indie stared straight ahead, boredom and disinterest pouring over her like thick paint, oozing globules dropping from the top of her head down to her toes. Warm, smooth, cloying boredom. It wasn't her emotion—it never was. It belonged to this woman, Dr Barbara Leproski, her eighth councillor in six years. Instead of going down the medical route as before, this time her mother had suggested getting psychological help with a spiritual twist. This therapist was medically trained but was also trying (and failing) to tap into the light of Indie's damaged soul.

Complaining to her mother about the futility of the sessions hadn't helped one bit.

'Grandpappy de Silva is paying for all the counselling we need,' Ella had insisted. 'It's the only thing he's ever done for you, so we should accept his kind offer and see if it will help you come to terms with your loss.'

'But I'm fine!'

'You can never have too much therapy, Indie,' Ella had replied. And that was that.

She didn't blame her mother for taking the only thing her grandfather had ever given them. Josh's father was a rich, famous, selfish arsehole. He spent his time dating young girl after young girl, leaving behind a trail of damaged ex-wives—Indie's grandmother having suffered the worst. Visiting Indie and Ella after his son's death was the least the old man could have done, but he hadn't. He'd been at his holiday home in the Seychelles, so had sent a bunch of flowers instead. A year later he'd been all over the news talking about how the trauma of Josh's death had inspired him to direct a film about the love between a father and son—even though it was a musical set in space, and the lead roles were both aliens. Ella and Indie hadn't spoken to him since, but he was still paying for this ridiculous charade.

Dr Leproski had her eyes closed and face tilted up to the heavens, silver rings on her delicate pale hands clinking together as she clasped them on her lap.

'Let us send positive vibes up to the merciful circle of angels who hover above us, healing our aura. Feel their holy light shine upon you. What would you like to say to our heavenly cherubim, Indigo?'

'Nothing.'

With a light pop, the therapist's suppressed irritation fizzled down Indie's arms and tingled at her fingertips.

'Your connection to your third eye is blocked, Indigo. Reach deep inside of yourself. Reach up through your crown chakra. We are all children of the light.'

Indie focused on the woman's energy, focused on her emotions like one might zoom in on a photo until it was nothing but a blurry collection of faded pixels. The woman's energy was low—she didn't want to be there either and she certainly didn't believe in the hippie-dippie nonsense she was spouting. Well, that made two of them.

'Right!' Barbara clapped her hands together and sat up quickly, making her dangly green earrings jingle excitedly. 'Let's try something new. Let's do some regression therapy. Perhaps if we can take you back to the day…'

'No.'

A thin smile appeared on the therapist's face, a smile that looked like it had been hurriedly drawn on her waxen face with a blunt crayon. Indie got a surge of satisfaction from having rattled her, her own feelings fighting through the foggy boredom and irritation the woman was experiencing.

'I know these things can be scary and daunting, but perhaps if we…'

'I'm not going back,' Indie muttered, attempting to keep her voice as steady as possible.

Barbara's irritation spluttered like a flame in Indie's gut, sharp and hot.

'Indigo, while you are under my care, I strongly suggest you remain open to my methods. We need to unlock the pain. Healing hurts, but strength lies in allowing vulnerability in. You need to allow yourself to feel!'

Feel? *Feel!* Indie knew all about feelings. She had experienced every single emotion possible, yet rarely were they her own. She knew her therapist disliked her, she sensed how irritated and disinterested she was, but something else was breaking through. Anger. Indie's grief was there, buried, scratching its way through the blanket of other people's emotions—ripping through the layers and hauling itself to the surface. And this time Indie let it through.

'You want me to go back to that day?' she said, her voice low, her words crumbling at the edges. 'Why on earth do you think I want to revisit the day I saw my mum and dad floating facedown in the ocean? Why would I revisit looking out of my bedroom window and seeing my dad's boat blow up? Have you ever seen a boat blow up, *doctor*? Have you? I never knew the sea could set on fire, or that bodies could burn like floating candles, or that the smell of charred flesh and singed wood would stay on my clothes, hair, and inside my nostrils for days. That kind of mess isn't easy to clear up, you know. The police don't come along and tidy it in a day like a road accident. Bodies were washing up outside my house for weeks. Well, *parts* of bodies.'

She could see it now. Clumps of hair caught on driftwood half-buried in the sand weeks later. The manicured finger the police found inside a shell, wedding ring still firmly in place. And the giant shard of metal, like a piece of torn paper, bobbing along the waves—one solitary shoe upon it shining like a bright red beacon.

Nobody had thought to send her away from the house while her mother recovered in hospital and the police investigated the destruction. She'd been left with staff, alone, waiting for her grandparents to arrive and rescue her. She saw a lot in those two days of waiting.

'Do you have any idea how an accident like that affects the mind of a ten year old, *doctor*? I remember it all just fine, thank you very much. I don't need to go back.'

Barbara nodded and silently jotted something down in her notebook, a practiced expression of patience and understanding masking her true feelings. Indie sighed, the shame of her outburst struggling to make itself felt through the therapist's thick unease. She never shouted. She should have kept all of that pain inside her where it was safely buried beneath everyone else's feelings.

After a few seconds of silence Barbara opened the window, mumbling something about it being stuffy in her office, but Indie was no longer listening. She was happy to sit in silence for the rest of the session, the two of them staring at one another until her allotted time was up. Nine minutes remained. That was doable. There was plenty she could think about in that time.

The day her father had been blown to pieces Indie had felt unwell. Their house had been full of movie people, strangers exuding exhausting flashes of excitement, their need to impress bubbling like champagne through her veins—but the general feeling had been light and fun. A fancy seafood buffet had been planned aboard the yacht, along with live music and games. Her dad was announcing news about his latest film, so a few journalists had also been invited.

'Want to join us, sweetheart?' her dad had said, squeezing her hand. 'You're a big girl now, you may even enjoy it.'

Although she'd desperately wanted to please him, prove she knew how to have fun like other normal children, below the surface of all the fizzing anticipation was a dark dread. A giant ball of foreboding swelled in her chest, telling her to stay away from the boat. No matter how much she tried to ignore it, it only grew bigger and darker.

'I'm going to stay home and read my book,' she said. 'Can you and Mum stay too? Please? Can you stay home with me?'

A look had passed between her mum and dad. She didn't need to guess what that look meant, she could feel it. Concern tinged with annoyance. There was something else too, the strongest of all feelings that had begun to emanate off her father lately like the glow of a light bulb.

I don't know you. You're not mine.

He loved her. She'd always felt that—he loved her so very much. Yet he knew something her mother didn't. He knew he couldn't possibly be her father, and Indie had no idea what that meant.

'Let's talk about more recent events,' Barbara said, bringing Indie back to the present. Opening the window had hardly made a difference; the room was still stuffy. 'What interesting things have been happening in your life lately?'

'Nothing.'

That wasn't exactly true. She'd been hanging out with Blu more, walking home with him and making small talk. Nothing worth mentioning, but it was nice. Jesse was still obsessed with watching Xavier at football practice every afternoon, so walking home with Blu had become their thing. She was cool with that. Being with him was like being alone, but with better company. Her head remained clear, which meant she finally had the space to think.

'How about school?' Barbara asked. 'Hold this crystal and tell me what you feel.'

The sharp pink stone bit into Indie's palm as she squeezed it tightly. She didn't believe in crystals, or magic, but it felt nice to take a deep breath and close her eyes for a moment.

Then the memories began to flood her brain, and she couldn't stop them. Snapshots of that day like a selection of still images, jumbled up and in the wrong order, as though a pile of photographs had been thrown at her feet. Her mum in a bright blue bikini and white floppy hat, asking their housekeeper Josefina to stay back and keep an eye on Indie. Her father kissing her forehead and calling her champ, a far-off look in his eye, then hugging her so hard it hurt her chest. There had been a dog, a ridiculous Chihuahua in a sparkly collar that a pouty-lipped woman had been carrying in a special handbag. The music coming from the boat was so loud Indie had been able to hear it from her bedroom. She'd shut the window. Then an explosion. Fireworks, she'd thought, as sparks of flaming red and orange shot through the sky. Bright yellow against a burning blue sky. Fireworks during the day?

Her brain hadn't understood what her eyes were seeing. People were floating, head down, in the water. The boat had disappeared and in its place was a giant bonfire. The ocean was burning.

That's when the tsunami of emotions engulfed her, literally knocking her off her bed and onto the bedroom floor. Arms flailing and legs shaking, she found herself curled into a ball, tears streaming down her cheeks. Shock. Fear. Pain. So much pain. Her bones were being prised open, cracking, splintering. Her chest was heavy, heaving. She couldn't breathe. Like a stranded fish she lay beside her bed, mouth gaping open, a silent cry forming at her lips. Her fingers grasped at her bedcovers as she hauled herself up, legs trembling and lungs clenched in an iron fist as she forced them to let in air.

Then she heard the screaming.

Not from the boat—the people in the water were silent—but from the crowds forming on the shore. Indie was back on her feet and fighting back the urge to vomit, hands shaking as she pulled up the blind at the window. The beach outside had frozen still, everybody standing like pegs in the sand staring out to sea. Holidaymakers. Neighbours. Josefina. Everyone had heard the explosion and, unlike Indie, they knew there were no fireworks in the day.

'We have five minutes left,' Dr Leproski said, holding her hand out for the pink crystal. Indigo had been gripping it so tightly it had left red lines on the inside of her hand. 'Can you think of a word that sums up how you are feeling today?'

Feeling? When she thought back to that day there had been nothing but feelings, but none of them hers or belonging to anyone she loved.

It had been difficult to open her bedroom window—the thin arms of a ten year old held little strength—yet she still managed to climb out and run to the beach. Adults ran to stop the barefoot girl racing to the shore, but she weaved through the throng and dodged their outstretched hands.

'Mum!' she'd screamed. She couldn't feel her parents. Why couldn't she feel them?

'Dad!' she'd yelled, wading out to the water.

They were there, they all were, floating facedown. The big-lipped woman with the bright yellow hair. A musician, his splintered guitar bobbing beside him. Waiters. Crew members, still wearing their white hats. A bright blue bikini. Her mother.

Indie was up to her neck now, salty water lapping at her chin, waves filled with floating detritus holding her back. A silver tray hit the side of her head and she pushed a charred piece of wood away, still hot to the touch as she tried to get closer to her mother's floating body. Then someone pulled her back, two strong hands lifting her out of the water.

'Come on, kid,' a deep voice said. 'You don't need to see this.'

Jade eyes stared down at her, bright against dark skin. The man deposited her back onto the sand without another word. She couldn't sense any fear radiating from him; in fact, she couldn't pick up any of his emotions at all. Perhaps it was the shock.

Indie hadn't thought of that man in a long time.

As everyone on the beach had swarmed into the sea and started pulling people out, the man had walked in the opposite direction and she'd never seen him again. The shore was a hive of activity after that, the air thick with panic and sounds. Sirens wailed in the distance as ambulances and police cars raced along the sand toward them.

Nobody noticed the little girl sitting on the sand, her feet in the sea, debris floating around her toes. Nobody noticed her reach out to a bundle of golden fur and drag it from the waves by its sparkly collar. The tiny Chihuahua was dead. Indie held him up to her face and cried into his cold matted fur, the dog's blood smearing her cheek with sticky warmth. She held the dog tightly, thinking of how the last person she'd hugged had been her father. Who was dragging him out of the waves? She couldn't see her mother's blue bikini any longer. Would she get to hold her parents one more time?

Then something moved against her face. The bundle was wriggling in her arms! The dog wasn't cold any longer, and he wasn't dead. He squirmed against her until she loosened her grip. More wet against her cheek. Blood? Tears? The dog's rough tongue was licking her face, and then it yapped. Barked. Broke free from her grip and bounded down the beach.

Had she brought the dog back to life? He'd been dead, he really had, and within seconds he was running through the legs of the rescue workers, sniffing and searching for his owner. Indie watched him disappear, his golden fur camouflaged against the yellow of the sand.

The paramedics had started lifting bodies onto gurneys and placing blankets over the faces of those fished out of the ocean.

'...de Silva...' she heard one of them gasp.

Indie raced toward a trolley where a tuft of sandy hair was peeking out from beneath a grey blanket.

'Dad!' she'd screamed.

The paramedics tried holding her back, but she pushed forward, throwing herself onto her father's cold, clammy body. His skin was puffy and grey, and a large gash on his forehead shone black, eyes staring up to an empty sky. All she had to do was hug him. If they would only let her hold him and make his cold body warm again, she could bring him back to life. *She could!* She had done it with the dog, she could do it with her own father. Her fingertips buzzed in readiness. She had powers that no one knew about. She felt things. She was special. Her dad had known. He had sensed that she wasn't like him, and now it was too late to tell him he was right.

Like a limpet she threw herself onto the trolley, attempted to wrap her skinny body around his, but the paramedics prised her off, talking softly in her ear.

'It's too late,' they were saying. 'He's gone. There's nothing you can do.'

'But there is!' she'd screamed. 'I'm special. You don't understand! I can help.'

Her father was dead, and it was all her fault.

'Tell me how you feel,' Barbara asked again, looking at the clock on the wall. 'Your feelings, Indigo. *Feelings.*'

Three minutes left. Indie matched her breaths with the passing seconds on the clock.

Tick, tick, tick.

She stared at the crystal vase of roses on the therapist's desk, droopy heads with brown sticky petals.

Tick, tick, tick.

How was she feeling? How was she *feeling*? She'd watched her parents get blown up. She'd saved a dog, but not her father. Her mother was pronounced dead at the scene but had come back to life at the hospital, with no intervention, hours later.

Tick, tick, tick.

Indie was different; she could feel things others couldn't. There was a chance the new twins at school were like her too. Maybe it was wishful thinking. The idea scared her, but she still wanted it to be true. She didn't want to be the only one anymore.

Tick, tick, tick.

Her mother was falling apart. The girls at school hated her. She hated herself.

Tick, tick, tick.

What was she feeling? What was *she* feeling?

The roses on the desk were dying, their sweet stench of death reaching her from the other side of the room. Petals curling, heads heavy, the water yellowing as their life ebbed away. She focused on them. Pushing past the doctor's thin crust of boredom and impatience covering her own emotions, Indie excavated deeper. So many questions, so much frustration, and pain. Lots and lots of pain.

Tick, tick, tick.

How was she feeling?

'Angry,' Indie said, her eyes still trained on the roses.

With an almighty crack and bang, the glass vase behind Dr Leproski exploded. Splinters of glass and wilting petals scattered across the room, the back of the therapist's head dripping wet from the putrid water.

'Goodness me!' Barbara exclaimed, jumping up as if she'd been shot. She hurried to the window, shut it, and surveyed the mess. 'The wind, it must have blown the flowers off my desk. How strange.'

Strange indeed, Indie thought. Because she knew the truth, and she knew that even nature wasn't as strong as she was. Perhaps her curse was really a gift, and perhaps she could do more than just feel.

Indie nodded at the clock, a smile tugging at her lips.

'Time's up,' she said. 'I'm done here.'

17

AS A YOUNG child, Indie's favourite book had been Roald Dahl's *Matilda*. She would beg her parents to read it to her night after night. Even then she'd understood how it felt to be different and an outsider, that desperate need to be left alone with nothing but books for company. Books and movies were Indie's sanctuary. They didn't have emotions of their own; instead, they helped her feel things in a safe way that she could control.

Before her father died, Indie's reoccurring dream had involved moving objects with the tip of her finger. Most of the time it was feathers she would guide through the air. With a slight flick of her wrist, she'd create magnificent flurries of downy white snow, forming patterns using nothing but the power of her mind. After her father died her dreams had turned to nightmares. Her visions were no longer filled with soaring plumes and magical scenes—instead she would spend her nights wading through seas of fire, silently screaming out the name of her father. And although Josh would often float past her, his face bloated blue and his sandy hair singed like tar to his scalp, it was never him she was searching for.

It was seven o'clock on Monday morning and Indie had already put her books in colour order—without leaving her bed. Three days earlier she had made a vase of flowers explode during her therapy session. She'd focused all her anger and frustration on those dying roses and sent the crystal vase shattering into a million glittering diamonds. She'd got home breathless, head spinning, and desperate to try again. On Saturday her mum had begged her to join her for a walk around Ally Pally with Mai Li and her kids, but Indie had feigned a headache. On Sunday Ella had wanted to have brunch with her in Muswell Hill and catch a film, but Indie had insisted she had to focus on her History essay. Of course she hadn't been ill or working. She'd spent forty-eight hours practising her telekinetic powers, and now she was a pro. While lying in bed, she nodded at her wardrobe and grinned as the doors flung open and her uniform, still on its hanger, glided out like a ghost and landed on her duvet.

This was a big deal. And exciting. And bloody terrifying.

• • • • •

'Hey, Windy Indie, you've been even quieter than normal today.'

It was lunchtime, and Jesse was in his usual place sitting beside her in the school canteen.

'You're doing your sullen Bella face again.'

He stuck two chips dunked in ketchup under his top lip and leered over her. 'Kiss me, virgin girl, and watch me sparkle in the sunlight.' His vampire accent was crap, but she still laughed as she pushed him away.

'Hi, Jesse.'

Xavier was heading for the bin near their table, carrying a plastic tray covered in pizza crusts. He nodded his head in their direction as he passed, causing Jesse to sit up straight and pop the chips into his mouth before waving back casually.

'Did the sexy Latino footballer actually say hello to you?' Indie said under her breath.

'Shut up.'

'He knows your name. Did you hear the way he said it, all husky and breathy?'

'Shut up.'

'Ha! Who's being quiet and sullen now?'

Jesse was the palest she'd ever seen him, so much so he could give Dracula a run for his money. She waited, but he didn't come back with a witty one-liner or break into song as per usual. In fact, tuning into his emotions, she could feel his crippling paralysis. Senses so heightened and full of shy longing there was no way those two were ever going to get together. Unless...

'Hey, Xavier,' Indie shouted.

The footballer was nearly out of the door but turned around at the sound of his name. Everyone in the canteen was now looking at Indie, but she hadn't thought much beyond calling out to him. She had to think fast.

'You dropped this,' she said, holding out a five pound note she had in her pocket.

'What the hell are you doing?' Jesse hissed.

Xavier walked back slowly, checking his own pockets in confusion. As he neared them Indie focused on his emotions. The guy was clearly trying not to look at Jesse, but she could feel his heart thundering so fast her own felt like it was going to explode out of her school shirt and send buttons flying across the room.

'Thanks, but that's not my money,' he said. 'I've only got a couple of pounds on me.'

Well, at least he was honest. Indie had never heard him say more than one or two words before. His accent was very sexy. She turned to Jesse, expecting him to give her a cheeky look, but he just sat there staring at his ketchup-smeared plate as if he'd been carved from white marble.

She slid the five pound note back into her pocket. 'My mistake.'

The pull between Jess and Xavier was so strong it was like sitting in the middle of an underwater current, trying not to be swept away. She had to do something. Then it came to her—she had powers now! Perhaps, by making something move, she could force these two cute losers together. It would have to be subtle though. She focused on Xavier's rucksack and twitched her index finger up a fraction. His bag slipped off his shoulder, sending books and papers tumbling at Jesse's feet.

'I'm so sorry,' the footballer said, scrambling to pick them up. 'Did my biology book fall on your foot, Jesse? It's so thick and hard.'

Indie stifled a laugh as a blotchy blush climbed up her friend's neck.

'I'm fine. Let me help you,' he croaked, joining Xavier on the floor.

Indie would have to do better than that in the future. The 'picking up books off the floor together' thing was such a cliché meet-cute and totally corny, the kind of crap she hated seeing in her favourite books, but it seemed to be working. Although she'd have to duck out of this threesome if the two of them were ever going to speak to one another.

Blu was sitting two tables along with his sister. She caught his eye and smiled with relief as he held his hand up to her in greeting.

'I need to speak to someone. Won't be long,' she said to the boys on the ground. It was as if she didn't exist.

'Oh my god,' Indie exhaled, throwing herself onto the seat beside Blu. 'I didn't think those two would ever speak to each other. It was killing me.'

Blu was grinning but Jade, as usual, was scowling as if Indie had interrupted their crucial work meeting.

'Good work,' Blu said. 'I like what you did there.'

'It was a cheesy move, but it seems to have worked.'

'Yeah, his bag falling was perfect timing,' Jade said, her words dripping in sarcasm. 'It's practically as if you willed it to happen.'

Indie stopped smiling and tried to arrange her face in a normal way. What did a normal face look like? Her mum had always said she was a crap liar, and now she was looking shifty when she had nothing to hide. No one would believe she had…abilities.

'She's only joking,' Blu said, cutting eyes at his sister. 'Not everyone makes voodoo dolls for fun, Jade. Some people believe in funny coincidences and chance encounters.'

She smirked at her brother, picked up her tray, and walked off without saying goodbye.

'Have I upset her?' Indie asked, watching Jade put her rubbish in the bin.

'No, you haven't upset Jade,' Blu shouted loud enough for his sister to hear. 'She's always been a miserable cow!'

Blu reached for his can of Fanta just as Jade swung round and fixed him with a stare. His drink wobbled then tipped over, soaking his white school shirt with splashes of orange.

'She's dead,' Blu muttered to himself. 'I'm going to fucking kill her.'

No one else had noticed the can wobble before falling, and no one else could hear Blu blaming his sister, but Indie could. She also knew impossible things were very possible indeed.

'Oops,' Blu said, pointing at his wet shirt. 'I'm so clumsy.' He patted himself down with a wad of napkins, although it wasn't really helping.

'So unlucky, it's practically as if Jade willed it to happen,' Indie said, repeating his sister's words back to him. He looked up sharply, his brows furrowed. Indie gave him a mysterious smile and his dark eyes widened, full of questions. Now he knew she knew—but which one of them was going to be the first to say it?

As soon as Indie had been unable to read Jade and Blu's emotions, she'd been convinced the twins were different. Yet until she'd managed to knock over her therapist's vase of flowers, she hadn't made the connection. Hadn't the map flown off the wall and smashed on the floor during her first history lesson with Blu? And hadn't he pointed at her pen when she'd dropped it, the pen that had somehow managed to make its way from her best friend's desk and back across the room to her?

She looked over at the table where she'd been sitting with Jesse. He was no longer picking up schoolbooks with Xavier—they were now engrossed in conversation. Blu followed her gaze.

'Looks like your mate has finally found the courage to speak to his crush,' Blu said.

'What makes you think they like each other?' she asked carefully.

One of the first things Blu had said to her was how obvious it was that Jesse and Xavier were crazy about each other, when it wasn't obvious to anyone who wasn't able to read their minds. Even now Indie could feel the chemistry between the boys from two tables away. She could practically see the air fizzing and popping around them, but no one else could. No one without her skills.

'Just a hunch,' Blu replied, shifting in his seat as if he'd said too much already.

Rolling up his wet shirtsleeves, he picked up the remains of his sandwich, now limp and soggy with Fanta. As he lifted it to his mouth Indie spotted something on his wrist, something she'd never noticed on him before. A small tattoo.

'What's that?' she asked, pointing at the symbol that looked like a navy blue capital letter *I*.

'A cheese and pickle sandwich,' he said with a smirk.

Indie hated smirks—who even did that outside of trash teen TV shows? But his always made her want to smile back.

'Your tattoo, smart-arse. What does it mean?'

Blu screwed up his nose at his soggy sandwich and put it back on his plate.

'It's an angelic symbol. Me mam had it in a sketchbook she keeps for her tattoo clients and when I told her I liked it she said it could be me sixteenth birthday present. She's pretty cool like that. Apparently it's the logo for the bar where she met me aunt.'

Indie stared at the tattoo. She'd seen it somewhere before, something to do with her own mother.

'Where did your mums meet?' she asked.

'Indigo.'

'Yes.'

'That's the name of the bar. Indigo, in Camden.'

Indie tried to swallow but her throat had turned to sandpaper. She breathed in for three and out for three, just like one of her many therapists had taught her. It wasn't working. She grabbed Blu's drink and took a swig from the tiny dribble left inside.

'That tattoo means Indigo?' she asked, her voice sounding small and tinny as if she were inside the Fanta can.

Blu nodded, giving her a look that said 'relax, it's just a tattoo.'

'That's my name,' she said. 'Indigo. That's what Indie stands for. I was named after the place my parents met. A bar…in Camden.'

His face was a picture, his eyes competing with his mouth to see which one could be the widest, then he burst into laughter.

'Fuck!' he breathed, making it sound ten syllables long. 'That's some crazy shit. What are the chances?'

'Yeah,' Indie said, the two of them staring at his inside wrist as if it were an exotic insect about to fly away. 'Weird coincidence.'

Except Indie knew coincidences didn't exist—it was one of the first things her mother had taught her as a young girl. She said everyone had a path to follow, and when unbelievable things like that happened it was a sign that you shouldn't ignore. Maybe Blu and his sister *were* like her. But what did that make them? And what did the bar have to do with it all?

'Have you been?' she asked him.

He was staring into the distance, his wet shirt and soggy sandwich long forgotten.

'Been where?'

'This Indigo bar.'

He shook his head.

'Let's go,' Indie said without thinking, then instantly regretting it.

She'd never been to a bar without an adult before, let alone one in Camden. Wasn't it meant to be a bit rough there? But maybe the symbol and the bar were a clue as to what her powers meant. She had to know if Blu and his sister were like her, if they could sense stuff and move stuff, if their bodies also felt too small to contain all that energy pushing to find its way out.

'What makes you think they'll let us in?' Blu asked.

His eyes shone mischievously, giving her the confidence to continue her recklessness. To tempt fate and see what happened.

'They probably won't. I'd just be happy to see it from the outside. It sounds like a weird place. I remember my mum telling me years ago it doesn't even have a website or anything. We should Google it, see if anyone's written about it online.'

'When do you want to go?'

Maybe it was the thrill of the strange coincidence, or her success in getting Jesse and Xavier speaking, or simply the knowledge she now had magical powers—but Indie was suddenly feeling wild and impulsive, and she didn't want to step down from the high.

'Tonight. You and me, straight after school. I'll need to go home first and change, get out of my uniform, but I can meet you at Camden station at six o'clock? Even if we don't get inside the club, it's still worth checking out. I'm curious, aren't you?'

One side of Blu's mouth twitched into a half-smile and he held her gaze, as if he were trying to work out why she had suddenly become so daring. He nodded and she revelled in the emptiness of being with him, of feeling nothing but her own emotions—excitement, trepidation, anticipation, curiosity, and something else. Something that she only felt when she was around him.

'I'm in,' he said.

18

GOING TO INDIGO was a bad idea. What the hell had she been thinking? For a start, Indie looked sixteen, because she *was* sixteen. And sixteen year olds weren't allowed into nightclubs!

Indie had walked home alone for a change. She'd looked for Jesse after school, but he wasn't on the field or answering his phone, and Blu had gone straight home to get changed. They were meeting in two hours at Camden station—their plan didn't get more detailed than that.

All was still and silent when she got home. It wasn't just emotions she was able to feel off others, she could also sense how many people were under the same roof as her—and thankfully, this afternoon, she was alone. She sent her mother a message saying she was revising at Jesse's house and she'd be home before eleven. Indie had no idea if she'd really be home by then, but if anything held them up, she could always lie some more. Being a good girl that never left the house had its advantages, because on the rare occasions she did misbehave her mother was beyond ecstatic that her weird daughter was acting her age. As if each rebellion was further proof that Indie was edging closer to normal. As predicted, Indie got a reply within a minute. Her mum would be home late and there was ten pounds on the mantelpiece if she wanted to order in pizza.

It had all been so easy. Too easy. Before she knew it Indie was at the entrance to Camden Town station, fifteen minutes early, and crapping herself.

For starters she had no idea if she was wearing the right outfit. What did women over the age of sixteen, who weren't breaking the law like she was, wear to a bar early evening? From the little she'd discovered about the bar online, Indigo was more of a chill-out place than a proper nightclub. Had it changed much since her own mum and dad met there twenty years ago? She hadn't wanted to wear anything too revealing—not that she had anything like that in her wardrobe anyway—but then she'd been worried if she dressed *too* casually there may be a dress code.

God, was this what all her nights out in the future were going to be like?

In the end she'd opted for tight black jeans, high heeled ankle boots that belonged to her mum and were a bit roomy around her toes, and a strappy top. Not that any of it mattered because her thick winter coat was covering it all up. Indie had also accessorised with hooped earrings, because she'd read somewhere that they made you look older. She'd even considered going on YouTube to see how to contour her face and make her apple cheeks look more angular, but she didn't want to end up looking like a panto dame.

Her appearance wasn't even her biggest concern. Finding the bar was. Because neither her nor Blu had managed to find out exactly *where* in Camden Indigo was.

She glanced at her phone. No messages. What if Blu didn't turn up? Should she call him? How long did people wait before sending a message? And what would she say?

'Boo!'

Indie jumped, then let out a quiet sigh of relief at the sight of her friend. She swatted him playfully. 'Don't scare me like that.'

'What's up?' Blu asked. 'You look nervous.'

Did she? She crossed her arms and shook her head.

'I'm fine. I got here early so I'm a bit cold.'

Looking over her shoulder, Blu steered Indie by the elbow to the side of the station as a large group of lads streamed out of the exit, shouting and jostling each other. It was as if he'd felt them coming before she'd heard them. No, she was being stupid. She had to stop reading into everything.

'Do you know where this bar is?' she asked.

'Along the canal, apparently. I was going to ask me mam, but I was worried she'd want to come too—she's a bit crazy like that—it wasn't worth the risk. I think her and me aunt went back once just after they met, but apparently the manager asked me aunt loads of weird questions about me mam dying. Put them off going back. They moved up to Liverpool soon after.'

Indie wasn't psychic, and she couldn't see into the future, but she had a bad feeling about this place. Then again, she reasoned with herself, if both their parents had met there then surely it couldn't be that bad. Could it?

They weaved their way along the high street, stepping over cans of discarded lager and takeaway cartons. It was already dark, but Camden was still teaming with shoppers hunting for bargains in the January sales. Paper bags with sharp edges banged into Indie's legs, and Blu's coat melted into the sea of a million other black-clad shoppers. With a quick glance over his shoulder, he slowed down and waited for Indie to catch up.

'There,' he said, pointing to a flight of steps leading down to an inky canal.

They were the only ones walking along the narrow strip that ran alongside the water. After the craziness of the high street, and the frenzied buzz of strangers still sticky on her skin, being alone with Blu felt like cool relief. A thick blanket dousing out flames. Indie couldn't imagine there was anything worth seeing down here, even the shadows were free of dubious bodies, but there were still a few dark buildings along the canals and one of them could be the bar. An icy wind whistled through her hooped earrings and the moon, reflected on the canal's rippling surface, looked like a series of pearlescent strips swaying to the beat of their echoing footsteps.

'Bit creepy,' she whispered.

Blu edged closer, his shoulder nearly touching hers. She didn't hate it, which was new. People getting too close to her normally made her dizzy, but this was nice. All her life she'd been desperate to block out what others were feeling, but right now she'd pay good money to know what was going through his mind.

What did he think of her? Probably nothing. Why would he think anything? There was no magical connection between them—this was simply what making a new friend felt like. Easy, fun, comfortable. So their mums had met their partners in the same bar years ago. Big deal. It wasn't some cosmic message from above sealing their fate and binding them together. Blu was new to London and had nothing better to do on a Monday night—that's all this was.

'There's a light through here,' he said, pointing at a building set back from the path and obscured by a cluster of spindly branches. How had he noticed the entrance? It was near impossible to see the club in the winter gloom. It would be even harder to find it in the summer too, with the leaves of the trees creating a thick wall along the canal.

'What do you think we should do?' he asked, as if she was meant to know.

There were no streetlights, and spiky tree branches were obscuring their view of the entrance. She switched on the torch on her phone and waved it around.

'I can see a guy holding a tablet by those big doors. Maybe he's a bouncer or doorman or something?'

'Turn the light out. We look like a couple of thieves,' he said, laughing quietly.

'Fine, but if I twist my ankle in these stupid shoes…'

'I'll catch you.'

Indie was thankful for the veil of darkness masking the heat on her cheeks. Unused to feeling her own emotions, blushing was rare, and now nerves and an icy sliver of fear were also snaking their way down her collar.

I'm safe. I'm safe. I'm safe, she sung to herself silently. Nothing could happen to her. She was strong now. She had powers stronger than she'd ever imagined—not that she had any idea how far she was prepared to go with them.

They pushed their way through the undergrowth until they reached the two men standing outside the building. There was no sign outside, or anything indicating it was a bar.

'Is this Indigo?' Indie asked the blond, skinny guy holding a tablet.

'You can't come in,' he said. 'You're too young.'

Blu held out what looked like an old-fashioned bus pass, flashing it like cops do in the movies. 'I have ID.' It was too dark to tell what he was holding up. A dodgy driving licence? A library card? He'd never told her about his fake ID! Anyway, how was that meant to help *her*.

The blond man didn't look at it. Instead, he stared at them, head at an angle, as if he were listening to far-off music. After a few seconds his eyes widened a fraction and he held up a finger, disappearing through the entrance door.

Blu was standing so close his chest brushed against Indie's arm. 'What do we do now?' he asked her again.

For such a cocky bugger he was asking a lot of questions tonight.

'I don't know. I guess we just stand here and wait until…'

'These two?' The owner of the deep voice had dark skin and high cheekbones, and he was following the blond guy out of the bar. His eyes flashed gold in the dark.

'What do you think?' the first man asked him, as if Indie and Blu weren't standing right there in front of them like a couple of idiots.

Blu held out his ID again, hand shaking, but the men ignored him. Eventually he put it back in his pocket, looked at his feet, and rubbed the back of his neck.

'Hey!' Blu cried out as the dark-skinned man grabbed his wrist.

'Where did you get that tattoo?' he said in his deep voice.

Indie stepped between them. 'Let go of him! We'll leave, OK? We just fancied a drink. We didn't even want alcohol.'

Blu cleared his throat. 'Well, actually…'

'We just wanted to come in and see what it's like inside. His aunt and her wife met here and so did my parents. This bar is special to us.'

The man let go of Blu's wrist as if he'd been scalded, then stared at them in the same intense way the blond man had—head cocked to one side, listening, even though neither of them were saying a word.

She pulled at her friend's sleeve, but the larger of the two men blocked their way. Now that he was closer, Indie could see that the larger man's eyes weren't gold but green, a bright turquoise. They reminded her of a beautiful jade bracelet her mother had bought in Thailand when she was little, which she'd accidentally dropped and smashed during a game of dress-up. Blu had noticed the man's eyes too, although he looked more afraid than impressed.

Suddenly, the bitter taste of smoke and seawater filled Indie's mouth. His eyes. She'd seen eyes like his once before, on the man who'd pulled her out of the water the day her father had died. It had been years since she'd thought of him, but he'd appeared in her memory four days ago during her therapy session, and now those same eyes were staring back at her. Throat stinging, chest tight, she swallowed down bile and panic.

'This is bullshit,' she shouted, pulling harder on Blu's coat. 'It's not worth it. Let's go home.'

The green-eyed man let out a sigh, loud like he was trying to blow them away. 'Fine. Get in. You can have one soft drink and stay for an hour.'

Blu looked at Indie and pulled a face. Her head hummed with the thud of her racing heartbeat, but curiosity won. She shrugged and they followed the man through the large doorway and down winding stone steps, lit by burning lanterns set in the wall.

'I'm not sure about this,' Blu whispered to her. 'There's something strange about these guys.'

Indie had been so used to the clear, easy sensation of walking along the empty canal with Blu earlier she hadn't noticed the clarity that had remained. He was right. The air was still free of emotions—the usual buzz of people's nerves, excitement, and insecurities was no longer there. Why hadn't she felt the doorman, and why couldn't she tune into the large guy beside them? Was Indie losing her abilities? All she could feel was her own uneasiness and the hammering of her heart.

They reached the base of the stairs, the man already waiting at the bottom, and were greeted by a woman standing before another set of double doors. Her hair was swept up in a sparkling scarf and her eyeliner was heavy, large dramatic flicks giving her a feline flare.

She stretched out her hands. 'I will need your bags and electronic devices.' Her voice was soft, like the purr of a cat.

Blu gave Indie a look she couldn't decipher and held up a finger to the gypsy-looking woman.

'Can I just send a quick message first?'

His thumbs flickered over his phone for a few seconds, then he turned off the screen and gave it to her. She took their coats too and went to hand them a silver bracelet, but the tall man shook his head.

'No need. They're with me,' he said.

They were? What did that mean?

Indie had never been out at night on her own, let alone to a bar, but she didn't think it was normally *this* dramatic. They were being totally reckless. They could be anywhere! What if it wasn't a bar but some kind of trap, a kidnapping ring, and they'd just handed over their mobile phones? She took a deep breath. She was being paranoid. Who would want to kidnap a pair of teenagers?

A pair of ornate doors loomed before them, giant golden handles shining like eyes against the dark wood. The black mahogany was carved with images of feathers and skulls woven through tangled vines. All was still and quiet. It didn't sound like there was a busy bar behind them.

After all this drama, if they got inside and it was a standard pub with a battered pool table and a shitty jukebox in the corner, Indie was going home.

'Welcome to Indigo,' the dark-skinned man said, opening the huge doors with a flourish. Blu take a sharp intake of breath as they stepped inside, and Indie knew exactly how he felt.

'Fuuuck,' he breathed. 'That ceiling.'

She looked up and her mouth dropped open. Thousands of tiny glowing orbs floated above them. They appeared to be glass balls filled with candles, thousands of them, hanging from the ceiling. Except there was no ceiling. It was glass and she could still see the inky sky and bare branches of the trees outside. This place must be even more amazing in the summer, at sunset, when the ceiling transformed into a riot of sky red and leaf green.

'I'll get your drinks. Join me at the bar when you're ready,' said the man in his booming voice. She may have imagined it, but there was a hint of amusement in his tone.

She turned a full circle. There were candles everywhere. Chandeliers, lamps, candelabras, torches, and chunky church-like candles dripping wax all over the bar—all vying for attention, fighting to see which one could give off the biggest glow.

'How the hell do they light them all?' Indie said.

Blu's dark eyes were growing wider by the second, the reflection of a thousand flames filling them with flickering copper.

'There's no electricity in here,' he whispered. 'Look around you. No lights, sockets, wires. They don't even have a till behind the bar. This place is...'

'Creepy?' she answered.

'No. It's magical.'

A couple behind them pushed past and Indie realised she was blocking the main door. She stepped aside, her gaze following the man and woman to an alcove gouged out of the dark walls. There weren't that many table areas; most people were sitting cross-legged on white cushions on the floor, drinks resting on low tables.

'I think this is what a bar in Ibiza would look like, if Ibiza was in fairyland.' Indie giggled. Why was she giggling? She never giggled!

Blu laughed. 'You heard the big man, let's go get our drinks.'

He put his arm around her shoulders and led her to the bar. His arm felt heavy, but she liked it. She'd never had a boy put his arm around her before, although Blu put his arm around everyone, so it didn't really count. She'd seen him do it with his friends in the school corridor, even his sister and Jesse. He was just one of those friendly, touchy-feely people. She didn't mind—unlike others where physical touch magnified their emotions, with Blu it was just the touch of skin on skin. It was OK—more than OK. She could get used to it.

The man with the green eyes raised an eyebrow as they approached. Blu let go of her. 'How much is a Coke?'

'Your one drink is on me, and I'll get you something better than a soda,' the man replied. He looked like he was on the verge of laughing again. What the hell was so funny?

He walked to the end of the bar and a few minutes later returned holding two glasses.

'Virgin Indigo Skies,' he said, setting down the tall purple drinks on the bar.

Indie frowned. What the hell had he just called her?

She must have been making a strange face because he looked like he was about to start laughing again.

'The drinks,' he said, sharp cheekbones twitching. 'They're called Indigo Sky, but these have no alcohol in them.'

Oh! Blu took a sip from the straw, made an appreciative humming noise, then took two huge gulps straight from the glass.

'My name's Gabriel,' the barman said. 'What's yours?'

'I'm Indie,' she answered. 'And this is Blu. Without an *e*.'

Gabriel's eyes flashed with amusement again. Indie was going to ask him why he found them so hilarious but took a sip from her drink instead. It tasted of creamy blueberry ice cream with a dash of vanilla and honey. She dropped the straw and drank straight from the glass.

'So, you two…' Gabriel moved his index finger from side to side, implying they were a couple. They both shook their heads fast. Really fast.

'Friends. Totally platonic, normal friends,' Indie said. 'Blu and his sister Jade are twins. They just started at Hillcrest.'

'What's Hillcrest?'

'Our school, in East Finchley. He's the new boy. My mum always says be nice to the newbies.'

What the hell was she blabbering on about? Was she drunk? Had the barman been lying about the drinks being nonalcoholic? She wanted to giggle again, and she couldn't stop smiling. *Jesus Christ, what was this place?* Why was she feeling so woozy and…happy? Why was she *feeling*? She gave a content smile and took another sip of her drink.

'Way to go, Indie,' Blu said, once the barman turned to serve someone else. 'Do you always go around telling strangers our names and where we go to school?'

He was grinning as he spoke, so he wasn't angry, but he was right. What if this Gabriel guy rang their headmaster and told them two of his underage pupils were hanging out in some weird bar in Camden?

'Sorry,' she squeaked.

'Doesn't matter. I feel fucking *high*,' Blu whispered, laughing into her shoulder. 'Shit, Indie. Have you ever smoked weed?'

She shook her head. She'd never smoked anything.

'It's like this.' He grinned again, his teeth looking neat and white in the glow of so much candlelight. 'It's like you're not properly inside your body. This place is crazy. Now wonder our parents used to hang out here. Staff are weird though.'

Indie nodded, tipping her drink back to get the last frothy drop from the bottom of her glass. 'I can totally see my dad loving it here. He'd have been chilling over in one of those fancy, white cushioned areas with all his mates, showing off. This isn't my mum's kind of place though. It's too fancy for her. I'm not surprised they fell in love here, though. I feel really…good.'

'Yeah?' Blu said, his gaze falling on her lips. Were they stained purple? She started to giggle again and nudged him.

'Hey! What'd you do that for?'

She nudged her shoulder against his again and made a face. 'You're weirding me out, Blu. I never know what you're thinking. I'm not sure I like it.'

He stopped grinning. 'Do you normally know what people are thinking, then?'

She put down her drink and wiped her mouth with the back of her hand. What did he mean? Did he know? Suddenly, she wanted to tell him all her secrets. So many secrets, all of which were on the verge of bubbling out of her like a fizzy drink that had been shaken.

I have powers! she wanted to shout. *I can heal, read emotions, and move stuff with my mind!*

All her life she'd kept these terrifying truths bottled up, unable to confide in anyone. Jesse would never understand, and her mum was a giant nope, but maybe Blu would listen. He might get it. He was different too. She was certain of it.

'Sometimes,' she said, her voice barely a whisper. He leaned in closer and she said it again. 'Sometimes I know what other people are feeling. I don't know why or how, maybe I'm a bit psychic or something, but I can feel their emotions.' She laughed—it sounded fake even to her. 'Except yours. I have no idea what's going through your mind, Blu. Maybe it's your eyes. They're so dark I can't read you.'

Blu was swirling the dregs of his empty drink around with a straw, his gaze fixed on the bottom of his glass. Why wasn't he saying anything? Why wasn't he taking the piss out of her mind-reading revelation?

'They aren't mine,' he muttered.

She frowned. 'What aren't?'

'My eyes. They aren't mine.'

Indie laughed, although a little too high to sound natural. He was either tripping for real or winding her up.

'OK, Robo-boy. You telling me you have x-ray vision and can see my underwear?'

Oh god, what was she doing? Was she flirting?

Blu wasn't rising to the bait though. In fact, he looked two shades paler.

'The colour. Of my eyes. They aren't… I mean, my eyes aren't this colour. Not anymore. They used to be, but I wear contact lenses.'

What was he talking about?

'Have you not noticed how weird all the staff look here?' he continued. 'Like hot models but with crazy-coloured eyes?'

Indie shrugged. 'Staff in these kinds of bars are *all* attractive, aren't they? I mean, I imagine so. I wouldn't know. It can't be *that* unusual. Can it?'

'The eyes, Indie. Didn't you see that guy's eyes? You think that's normal?'

'No,' she muttered. They *weren't* normal, but she *had* seen them somewhere before. 'I think they're really beautiful though.'

'Yeah?'

She nodded, and he straightened up.

'I'm going to the bathroom. Don't go anywhere. I want to show you something when I get back.'

He disappeared into the shadows, leaving her standing at the bar alone. What the hell was he doing? They'd finished their drinks—they should leave before this place completely messed with their heads. Indie leaned against the bar and squinted through the dim light. The club wasn't very full. About thirty or forty people were scattered around, lounging on cushions or sitting in the alcoves, and they all appeared to be paired off. Girls with girls, boys with boys, straight couples, and some groups where more than two people were holding hands or kissing. What was this place? It didn't feel sordid, not that she'd know what a sex club looked like. It had a nice vibe. The tendrils of emotion she was able to pick up from those nearby were mellow, chilled, and filled with nothing but pure love. Maybe that's why she was so floaty. Not the drinks, not the bar, but the rareness of positive emotion surrounding her like a light lilac mist.

There was a set of glass doors in the distance and occasionally someone would go in or a couple would exit. Beyond the glass partition she could make out a crowd of bodies moving. *Dancing!* Of course. The bar had no music, just weird forest sounds, but there was still a club section. Indie had never been dancing before, not outside of her own bedroom. What would dancing with Blu be like? Should she ask him?

He looked like the kind of guy who could make decent shapes on the dance floor.

'Don't freak out,' he said behind her.

She turned around, psyching herself up to ask him to dance, and found herself practically nose-to-nose with him. She stepped back until he was back in focus. Freak out about what? Why was he being so dramatic?

'*Shit!* Your eyes!'

He blinked three times, his face void of its usual smile. His eyes were… Indie couldn't think of a word to describe them. Shiny? Pretty? Glowing? Twinkly? Bright? Beautiful? Everything sounded corny and didn't even come close.

'I wear coloured contact lenses,' he said. 'My eyes used to be dark brown until I woke up one day, a few months ago, and they looked like this. I don't know why.'

They were green, light green like a tropical ocean. Indie stepped closer and peered into them. She clasped her hands together behind her back, fingers gripping fingers, anything to stop herself from stroking his face.

'That's, wow, I mean… Did you go to the doctors about it?'

He shook his head. 'Jade said not to. She said we had to figure it out ourselves because our mams would flip, they were already stressed about moving down to London, and they didn't need more to worry about. We thought they'd go back to normal.'

'Jade has them too?'

'Yeah, hers turned on the same day as mine. It sent her a bit crazy. She kept kicking off at school, which pissed our mams off even more. Don't tell Jade I said anything, though. *Please.* She'll kill me! I'm just so tired of keeping secrets. You know?'

Indie nodded. She knew.

'Wouldn't it be a good idea to be tested? There might be something wrong with you.'

His mouth turned down at the edges. 'There isn't, not in that way. I think it's linked to the other stuff we can do.'

Indie's skin prickled, her clammy hands gripping her fingers tighter. *She wasn't alone.* She wasn't the only weirdo in the world. This was it. Her one chance to say something.

'Stuff?' she said quietly. 'Like…' She took a deep breath. 'Like feeling the emotions of others, moving things with your mind, and healing people?'

Blu was staring at her, really staring. His hand shot out and gripped her arm, his strange eyes shining a bright turquoise jade. He was asking her a million questions without making a sound. She nodded her head.

'Yeah. Me too,' she whispered.

He pulled her to him and hugged her, arms tight around her back and his cheek pressed against hers. Holding her as if she were a raft in a vast ocean, and he were too afraid to let go. And Indie just stood there, rigid, too shocked to move.

'I knew it,' he murmured. 'I *knew* it. I felt it as soon as I met you. I told Jade, and she didn't believe me. I was right. I knew you were special.'

Special. She finally gave in to Blu's embrace and hugged him back, her body shaking against his. Somebody finally knew and they didn't think she was a freak—because they were the same. Blu and his sister were like her. She was no longer alone. She looked over his shoulder and noticed the barman, Gabriel, looking over at them while tapping away on his phone. He must think they were so pathetic, a couple of sixteen year olds hugging in a bar after one nonalcoholic smoothie.

Tears of relief pooled in her eyes and she blinked them back, not yet ready to let go of Blu. Not ever.

Then she froze.

Shit! A girl their age was marching toward them—and she looked really pissed off.

'Don't tell me you dragged me all the way over to this scuzzy north London hellhole to watch you two make out.'

Blu jumped back at the sound of his sister's voice.

'You came!' He reached out for her, but she pushed him off. 'Jade, chill, I thought we were going to be held hostage or something. I texted you where we were in case our bodies turned up.'

She rolled her eyes at her brother's stupidity then looked around at the bar, her face relaxing, obviously impressed. How could she not be? She turned to Blu and her features set hard again.

'Are you kidding me? You took your contacts out!' She shoved him in the chest. '*What is this?* You showing off to your latest girlfriend and telling her our business?'

'We're just friends,' Indie said, untangling herself from Blu. 'And keep your voice down.'

It wasn't right to shout in a bar like this—it was like having a fight in an ancient cathedral. Jade must have sensed it too because she lowered her voice to a hiss, pulling her brother to one side and completely ignoring Indie.

'Seriously, bro. What did you tell her?'

'She already knew.'

'How? Is she Buffy the Freak Hunter?'

'Indie's cool. She's one of us.'

'She can't be. She's lying.'

'I believe her. Come on, you said yourself it was strange we couldn't feel her.'

Indie had had enough of this. She'd gone from having a special moment, her first ever genuine moment with someone who completely understood her, to watching her new friend bicker with his bitch of a sister.

'It's true!' Blu whispered loudly.

'I'll believe it when I...'

Jade's hand shot up and slapped herself hard across the face. Even in the half-light of the bar Indie could see a dark pink mark blossom over her cheek. Jade stood stone-still, eyes wide, her hand still in midair.

'See. Told ya she had powers,' Blu shouted, doubled over in laughter.

Oh no, what had she done? Picking a fight with Jade was *not* the best way to prove her allegiance. Indie took a step back as the twins turned toward her, one of them furious and the other creasing over with laughter, then both their faces fell.

Blu swallowed. 'Um, Indie?'

'What?'

His sister inched closer, so close Indie could smell the faint minty scent of chewing gum on her breath as it warmed her cheek. What? What were they staring at?

'Fucking hell,' Jade said under her breath.

Was she going to hit her back?

'What?' Indie squeaked.

They were freaking her out. So was Gabriel, the barman with the crazy cheekbones, who was now standing with some guy with long hair. They were looking over, obviously talking about them.

'Your eyes, Indie,' Blu said. 'Your eyes! How did you do that?'

Jade spoke to her brother without taking her own eyes off Indie's. 'You were right. She's like us.'

Indie fumbled in her handbag for her phone, intent on using the camera function to check out her face, then realised they'd handed their phones in at the door. Her hand fell on a small makeup bag where she'd put a lip gloss and tube of mascara. It had a tiny mirror attached inside. She fished about, took it out, and stared into it.

'Oh my god!' she cried, her hand shooting up to her face. 'They're blue.'

'More than blue,' Jade said. 'They're bright as opals. Proper shiny and…'

'Beautiful,' Blu said quietly, then cleared his throat. 'And they keep changing from light to dark, a million shades of blue and indigo.' He lowered his head in embarrassment and rubbed the back of his neck, muttering something she couldn't make out.

Indie couldn't breathe. She reached for her glass, but it was empty. She needed a drink. She was going to start hyperventilating.

Jade passed her a glass of water—she had no idea where it had come from—and she gulped it down gratefully.

Was it this bar? Did this place give everyone crazy-coloured eyes? Or was it her powers, like the twins'? *What did it mean?* She had no time to untangle the mess in her mind before the two barmen started walking over to them, and they looked like they were in a hurry. She put the mirror back in her bag and pulled her hair over her eyes.

'You three,' Gabriel said. 'You need to get out.'

'We've done nothing wrong!' Jade shouted, pushing his hand away from her shoulder.

'You're not in trouble,' the other man said quietly. He looked like Jesus, a young, brooding Jesus, but with eyes the colour of yellow flames. Indie tried not to look at their eyes, but all five of them were doing a lot of staring at one another. Jade was the only one whose eyes weren't burning bright—and that was only because she still had her contact lenses in place.

'*Quick!*' Gabriel said again, ushering the trio toward the large double door from which they'd entered. He nodded to the gypsy girl, and she quickly handed him their belongings. With his arms full of coats and his hands holding their phones, Gabriel gave one last nervous glance at the bar and pushed them up the stairs. Once the cold night air hit their faces, the hipster Jesus man and the big guy appeared to relax.

Blu was far from chilled though. 'What the *hell!* You invite us in, then chuck us out?'

'Can we have our coats now, please?' Indie added, pulling hers from the bundle in Gabriel's arms. She was trembling, but it may have been from more than just the cold.

They were surrounded by nothing but dark trees and the silky black of the canal beyond. The silence was eerie and seemed to settle around them like a blanket. Indie had never felt so empty while being surrounded by so many people. She buttoned up her coat and pulled her collar up as an icy wind let out a low moan cutting through the branches above them. The two men were still looking furtive, even though there was no one else around.

'Go,' Gabriel hissed. 'And don't come back. It's not safe.'

'Who are you guys?' Jade shouted, as her brother tried to pull her back in the direction of the main road. 'And what the fuck *is* this place?'

Gabriel's face remained still, eyes glowing and mouth set in a hard line.

'You'll find out soon enough.'

19

THE FIRST THING Indie did when she woke up the next morning was rush to the mirror. The second thing she did was try not to have a panic attack. How was it even possible? How could her eyes have changed from not-even-that-exciting brown to a kaleidoscope of vibrant blues and sparkling lilacs?

She rubbed them, as if that was going to make any difference, then looked again. Were they getting brighter? It certainly appeared that way. She parted her curtains and stared outside. It was six thirty in the morning, raining and still dark—today was going to be shit on so many levels.

After being thrown out of the bar last night, Blu, Jade, and Indie had sought the safety of a crowd and headed to Camden market. It was only quarter past eight in the evening, and although the stalls and shops were now closed there were still plenty of bars and restaurants full of people. If the sudden onslaught of hundreds of shoppers' emotions affected them after the calm of the club, no one said anything. They bought their falafels from a rusty static caravan in the empty market, their order the only words they'd uttered in the last fifteen minutes, then sat at a brightly painted picnic table to eat.

Jade was the first to break the silence. 'So now there's three of us,' she said, her voice flat and tired.

'I told you,' Blu muttered through a mouthful of pitta.

'Well done, Blu. Seriously, is everything a fucking competition with you? So what? You worked out the girl you like at school has the same magical powers we do. Go write a poem about it.'

Indie looked down at her soggy wrap while the twins glared at one another. What did Jade mean by 'the girl you like?' And why the hell was Indie focussing on that when she was on the verge of joining the Avengers?

'Where can I get contact lenses like yours?' she asked quietly.

Jade curled her lip. 'Opticians, online, fancy dress shop. Wherever.'

'Don't be a dick,' Blu shouted at his sister. 'It's late, and we've got school tomorrow. She's hardly going to bunk off to go contact lens shopping with shiny blue eyes.' He smiled at Indie, a small smile full of solidarity and understanding, and the tightness in her chest loosened up a bit. 'We have loads at home—our mam sells them in the tattoo shop. Good job you used to have brown eyes like us. I'll bring you a pair tomorrow before school.'

Indie let out a long breath. OK, maybe this wasn't going to be so bad.

'Can we meet at, say, quarter to eight?' she asked him. 'School's open early for breakfast club. I can wait outside the library for you. Then I'll have enough time to put them in before class. Not that I know what I'm doing.'

The idea of touching her eyeballs made Indie want to be sick, especially those new eyes of hers that looked like something out of a horror movie.

'I'll help you.'

Both Indie and Blu's heads snapped up and turned to Jade.

'Did you just say something nice?' Blu said, giving Indie a flash of a grin.

'What? I'm not a monster!' his sister replied. 'I'll come to the school early with Blu and show you how to do it, Indie. If you don't centre them right the colour will show around the edges. I have a spare bottle of eye drops too. They'll stop your eyes from getting sore. It can feel a bit strange at first.'

Indie jumped up, ran around the table, and gave Jade a hug from behind.

'OK, now you're being weird. This doesn't make us besties,' she muttered, but her voice was light, and Blu was laughing.

Going undetected had been easy that evening too. Indie had got home before eleven, creeped past her mum asleep in front of the TV, locked the front door so it was clear she was back safe, then went straight to bed.

But now, back in her room at the crack of dawn, things no longer appeared so simple. For starters, where the hell were her sunglasses?

She'd searched inside every one of her tote bags and rucksacks, in every drawer, and on each bookshelf. No sunglasses. Why would she have sunglasses where they were easy to find when an English winter lasted twenty hundred years?

There was a knock at her bedroom door. All the banging around must have woken her mum up.

'You awake already, sweetheart?'

The handle was turning. Indie instinctively shot out her hand, making the door stay firmly shut.

'Indie. Your door's stuck.'

She ran and leant against it.

'I'm getting changed, Mum. Wait up.'

Crap, crap, crap. She was already fully dressed, hair done, and even her shoes on—but no way was she going to let her mum see her looking like an alien.

'I've seen you in your bra and pants before, Indie. Let me in. I just wondered if you had fun last night.'

'Give me some privacy, for god's sake!'

Her mother's mood plummeted the moment Indie shouted at her. The sharp scratch of barbed wire wound tight around her chest was a mix of Ella's upset and her own guilt. It wasn't fair; some girls had normal relationships with their parents. They could curl up with their mum on the sofa, tell them what was on their mind, share gossip from school, and actually enjoy being near them. But not her—the only way Indie could get through her day was by keeping her mum at arm's length. Her emotions were always so intense, way worse that anyone else's. If only Indie could learn how to tone them down or shut them out. If only she wasn't a bloody freak of nature!

'Fine,' Ella replied, her tone clipped. 'I'm going to have a shower. Come and say goodbye before you leave.'

Indie's body slumped with relief against the door, waiting for her mum's footsteps to retreat to the end of the hall before running back to her bed and pulling out the suitcase beneath it. The only place she hadn't looked was in the bag containing all her summer clothes.

She rummaged through bikinis, sarongs, and jean shorts until her hand closed around a hard case. Yes!

'Mum, I'm off!' she shouted through the bathroom door. She heard the shower pressure being turned down and a muffled voice telling her not to go yet as she had to talk to her. But Indie was too quick. She grabbed her coat, bag, and umbrella and slammed the front door before her mum could follow her.

The road they lived on had always been badly lit at night, but now, combined with the pouring rain, the sun still not up, and her huge shades on, Indie couldn't see a bloody thing. This was ridiculous, but she had glow-in-the-dark eyes now—so what choice did she have?

Her phone was vibrating in her trouser pocket. She fished it out. It was a video montage from Jesse. *Crap!* She'd forgotten to tell him she was going to school early. Good job he'd messaged her, or he'd have been waiting on the street corner all morning and she would never have heard the end of it. She clicked play and watched the one-minute clip.

It was the fairground scene from the movie *Love, Simon*, a full-on kissing scene from *Call Me by Your Name*, and various clips of hot footballers taking their shirts off. It was captioned *OMG! I HAVE SO MUCH TO TELL YOU!*

Indie grinned. So he'd finally scored with the footballer.

She began to type.

Eeeeeek! I'm so happy for you. This is the best news ever. I've gone to school early this morning as I left my history homework in the library and I need to make sure it's still there. I'll see you when you get to school and then you have to TELL ME EVERYTHING.

She signed it with five hearts in different colors.

She felt bad about lying to him—her history homework was in her bag—but there was no way she could tell him the truth. At least her trick in the canteen yesterday had worked. Maybe now Jesse could finally stop moping around after Xavier and calm down a bit.

Her phone beeped. He'd replied with a sad emoji and then a gazillion kisses. Oh god, he was hyper on a normal day. What on earth was he going to be like now he'd kissed his sexy Latino? Indie shuddered at the thought and marched on to school.

• • • • •

'Morning. I don't think the paparazzi followed you.'

Blu was leaning against the school wall with his coat hood up, which was now soaked through. A raindrop hung off his long lashes. It was strange to see him with brown eyes again, looking like a normal person. Except he *wasn't* normal, and he knew she wasn't either, and the truth crackled like electricity between them as they smiled shyly at one another.

'Come on, Holly Golightly. Let's get you back to boring before people wonder if you're hiding a black eye. Jade's inside because she refused to wait for you in the rain. She's getting on me tits, so good luck with her.'

He put his arm around Indie's shoulder, ducking under her umbrella, and they hurried into the school building.

Luck was on their side—the corridor was deserted. She left Blu outside the girls' toilets, shaking off the rain from his coat, and stepped inside.

Jade was waiting with her arms crossed. The look on her face made Indie want to turn around and go back home.

'Finally! You think I don't have better things to do than get up early and hang around toilets waiting for you?'

She whisked Indie's glasses off and gasped.

'Shit, girl. I forgot how bright they are. Your eye are way crazier than ours. They're not even staying the same colour. Look!' She pushed her head toward the mirror and Indie gasped. Her eyes were now dark purple, with cornflower blue swirls around the edges.

'Don't worry,' Jade said in a softer voice. She'd set everything up along the sink. 'These are really thin contacts. You won't feel them after a while.'

'Wait up.' Indie pointed at the toilet door and locked it with a flick of her finger.

'*No way!*' Jade looked like her brother when she grinned. 'I've never tried that. *Brilliant!* I still can't believe you're like us. How many more of us do you think there are? Do you go around trying to find other people you can't feel? I do.'

It was the most amount of words she'd ever heard Jade say.

'Yeah. Those two guys at the club last night were definitely like us.'

'I know, right? I mean, what the fuck was that about? I'm not going back to find out though. What did they mean it was *dangerous* to return? That's proper horror movie stuff. I'm all for avoiding *that* shit.'

Apparently, when Jade was excited, she spoke really fast and moved her hands around a lot. Indie wasn't sure if grumpy Jade or chummy Jade was scarier. She looked at the paraphernalia before her. Nope, sticking her finger in her alien eyes was definitely the scariest.

• • • • •

Indie couldn't stop blinking. The contacts weren't exactly painful, just uncomfortable and a bit scratchy. But what choice did she have?

'Good morning, good morning!' Jesse sang, as he bounded up to her at the beginning of lunch. She was putting some books in her locker and checking her eyes in a tiny mirror glued to the inside door. If her eyes looked any different with the lenses in, her best friend hadn't noticed yet. 'Yes, Windy Indie, you are still as pretty as ever. Soooo…want to know why I'm so happy, happy, *happy*?' he trilled.

Indie stepped back from Jesse and attempted to centre herself. The force was strong with this one today. Instead of the usual fizzing and popping, Indie's head felt like it was going to burst open and explode like a gaudy piñata filled with rainbow streamers and glitter confetti. Her blood had turned to champagne, and her heart was beating a saucy samba. How the hell did Jesse live with this much joy inside of him?

'I've no idea why you're so chirpy today,' she deadpanned. 'Did you get an A in maths?'

Jess was literally jumping on the spot and squealing.

'We went to the park after school, just me and Xavier, and he kissed me. *He* kissed *me*. I just stood there like a bloody lemon. I mean, I was in shock. I didn't even know he was gay—let alone that he fancied me. *He* fancies *me*! He was going on and on about how long he's liked me and…urgh. Anyway, then I kissed him back and…' He grabbed her wrist and squeezed. 'Oh. My. God. Indie, that boy is just… You want to feel his arms. No, actually, don't. He's mine. Argh, he actually said that. He actually asked if he and I should go out properly—like, be an item.

Be his proper boyfriend. *Already!* I'm literally going out with the school stud and I want to *dance!*'

Indie joined him jumping on the spot and squealing. She was so happy for him—at least she *presumed* she was happy for him, because there was no way she could feel her own emotions through the wild carnival of joy she was revelling in.

'What we celebrating?' Blu asked, appearing out of nowhere.

'You mean you can't guess?' Indie said with a smirk.

He smirked back, but Jesse was bouncing too happily on the spot to notice their major smirkathon. Blu nodded over at Jesse, then raised his eyebrows at Indie, as if to say 'wow, this is one full-on burst of happiness,' and Indie nodded, because it was wild and crazy and wonderful that the three of them were all feeling exactly the same thing.

Jesse suddenly stopped jumping and peered over Indie's shoulder. Xavier was at his locker.

'Go on!' she said, nudging him. 'Go say good morning to your new boyfriend!'

The tips of Jesse's ears turned pink, and his bubbling excitement turned down to a simmer. Xavier must have felt the weight of their stares because he looked up and winked at Jesse, beckoning him over with a nod of his head.

'Oh my god!' Jesse breathed out, turning to Blu and Indie and clutching his chest. 'He's killing me. Did you see that? He actually winked at me, at school, with people around us. My heart. Oh dear baby Jesus above, how the hell am I going to get through the day without snogging his face off?'

Jesse casually walked over, as if it was no big deal, and Indie had to grab on to Blu to stop herself laughing out loud.

'I can't take it,' she stage-whispered. 'It was bad enough when he just fancied him. What the hell is he going to put me through now? His emotions are out of control!'

'Not acceptable,' Blu said, faking a serious face. 'I guess you'll just have to hang out with me more. Self-preservation and all that.'

Indie made a serious face and nodded in agreement.

'*Or*…maybe Jesse's emotions will get diluted if we share them between us,' he added.

She let out a light laugh. 'I doubt it. Knowing my luck, they'll double. Shit, imagine *that*!'

Blu was grinning as he looked over at Jesse and Xavier talking.

'They're cute together,' he said. 'You did a good thing setting them up.'

'What can I say? I'm an angel in disguise.'

Blu gave her a crooked smile, and her tummy flipped. How much smiling could two people do? She'd smiled more in the last week than she had all her life—or at least more than she had in the last six years. If he made her grin any harder, she was going to end up with severe facial cramps.

Indie shut her locker and bit back a yelp as a face suddenly appeared beside her. Alyssa, her features contorted into a twisted sneer, and her two hangers-on Rochelle and Cassidy. She normally felt them creeping up on her, but between Jesse's joy-tsunami and Blu's cute grin, she'd been distracted. All the happy fizz she'd been feeling was quickly replaced by a tangle of sharp thorns catching beneath her skin.

'Is that your best chat-up line, Indie?' Alyssa said, loud enough for Blu to hear. 'Calling yourself an angel? Can't believe you're hitting on the new boy already. I bet you've already told Blu all about your famous dad and the glamorous life you used to have in LA. God, you're so *desperate*!'

Indie slung her bag over her shoulder, ignoring their forced laughter.

Blu, on the other hand, was narrowing his eyes at them as if in concentration. What was he picking up? Probably the same as her—

jealousy, insecurity, and plenty of self-loathing. Just being around them made her feel nauseous and itchy. Was he feeling it too?

'Are you Alyssa?' Blu asked, giving her a hundred-watt smile. 'I've heard about you.'

All three of them stared up at him through their lashes, and Alyssa fluttered hers for extra affect.

'You have?' she said coyly. 'Nice things, yeah? So how you finding Hillcrest? It's not too bad here, even though some people in our year are more interesting than others.'

'I like it,' he said, acting all casual as if the three cows hadn't just been abusing Indie in front of him. 'I'm learning a lot.'

The girls laughed like he was the most hilarious person ever.

'Yeah, like who to hang around with and who to avoid,' Alyssa purred, cutting her eyes at Indie.

'Absolutely,' Blu agreed. 'This place is pretty cool, actually. I was reading about the school curse yesterday. You heard of it?'

They shook their heads as one. What was he playing at? Indie wanted to head to the canteen—she hadn't eaten all day—but this was too interesting to miss.

'Oh yeah, Hillcrest is haunted,' he told them. 'Every year, one girl is singled out and real scary things start happening to her. I found some stuff online saying it's the poltergeist of a student who used to get bullied here years ago. She picks out the nasty girls. You know the kind, right? Always saying bitchy stuff and starting rumours? I'm sure you've come across people like that.'

They all nodded like puppets on a string, and Indie bit her lip to stop herself from laughing. He was good. She was already three steps ahead and was looking forward to seeing what Blu did next.

'What happens to the victims then?' Cassidy said, twirling her hair around her finger.

'Accidents,' he replied, face solemn. Indie bit her lips together even harder. 'I'm surprised you haven't heard about it. Although, of course, anyone who's enough of a bitch to be picked out by this…ghost thing…isn't going to admit it, right? Anyway, you three seem nice, so I'm sure you'll be fine. Indie was just telling me how friendly everyone in our year is.'

They smiled sweetly at her and she tried not to flinch at the sharp pain of millions of needles piercing her skin. Blu must have felt it too because he inched a little closer to her.

'Well, we'll see you around then, Blu,' Rochelle said.

All three waved at him, ignoring Indie, and headed for the lunch hall.

'Ready?' he whispered.

'Leave them,' she hissed back. 'They're just sad and pathetic. I feel a bit sorry for them.'

Blu lay a hand on her arm, the prickles from earlier ebbing away beneath his touch. 'We all have problems to deal with in our lives, Indie, but it's no excuse to treat people like shit. Sometimes you have to put yourself and your own feelings first. You never read *Matilda*?'

'It's my favourite book.'

'Good.'

He gave a small nod to the girls' backs. With a sharp squeal Alyssa tripped over, her arms flailing wildly, and landed face-first in the corridor in front of a large group of students queuing for lunch. A gang of year eight boys gathered around her, laughing and pointing as her friends tried to help her up.

'That's enough,' Indie whispered, trying not to laugh herself.

'No one fucks with me friends,' he whispered back. 'You're about the only decent thing in this school.'

He nodded again and a framed black-and-white photo of a class from the 1950s fell off the wall and shattered inches from Alyssa's face. Her friends yelped and looked around wildly, as if expecting a ghost to fly over their heads.

Rochelle whispered into Cassidy's ears, then backed away from Alyssa as she staggered to her feet. The crowd had thickened, and Blu's laughter was lost among the cries of 'shame' and 'how embarrassing' that rang out across the corridor. A teacher had seen the commotion and was now striding toward the broken glass and braying children, parting the crowds like Moses and the Red Sea. Someone else was watching too, at the far end of the hallway. A woman with long dark hair, a tight red dress, and bright lipstick. She was far too glamorous to be a teacher or anyone's mum.

'Who's that?' Indie said, nudging Blu and pointing to the other end of the corridor. But the woman was gone.

20

THE HALLWAY HAD cleared, and the school caretaker was already sweeping up the broken glass. Indie and Blu were the only pupils still standing by their lockers.

'That was a bit harsh,' she said under her breath. 'Alyssa was mortified.'

Perhaps Blu had been right to do what he did—that bully and her cronies had been giving her a hard time for years and she'd not done a thing to deserve it. Yet Alyssa's sticky film of shame and sadness still clung to Indie's arms and chest like slime. Once you'd felt the pain of another it was difficult to hate them completely.

'She deserved it,' he answered with a shrug. 'But if it bothers you, I won't take it further. Promise. Although it's tempting,' he added with a mischievous grin. 'People like her are the worst.'

'Yeah. They are. And thanks…you know…for sticking up for me.'

Blu's lips parted, as if he was going to answer, then he cocked his head to one side and gave her a half-smile. Looking at him was too difficult; it was making her stomach ache. She fiddled with the straps of her backpack instead.

'You hungry?' she asked.

'Always. Magic gives me an appetite.'

She laughed. This was crazy, standing in the school corridor talking about their abilities like it was nothing.

He put his arm around her shoulders, making her sway and lean into him.

'You OK?'

She nodded, holding her breath as he squeezed her closer.

'That *was* fun though, right?' he said. 'No one's going to fuck with you now!'

Indie rolled her eyes, but she liked it, the idea of being invincible. How did he do it? How did Blu make the one thing she'd always hated and feared feel like a superpower?

'Don't worry about Alyssa. I bet she'll lay off from now on. If not, you'll have to show her who's boss,' he added with a grin. His smile quickly faded as he turned to face her. 'You're worth a million of her.'

Indie swallowed. Would he judge her after what Alyssa said? She'd been spouting off about Indie's 'famous dad' and her old LA life, yet Blu hadn't asked her what she'd meant. Maybe he wouldn't. Maybe she'd have a chance to finally feel normal—well, as normal as she could be.

'I should ask Jesse if he wants to eat with us,' she said quietly, unable to think of anything but Blu's arm lying heavily over her shoulders as they headed toward the lunch hall.

She had no idea where Jesse was, probably in the canteen with Xavier holding hands under the table. Maybe she should message him. Who was she kidding? Jesse wasn't thinking of her right now and anyway, after her best friend's intense joy, followed by Alyssa and her gang's thorny attack, Indie was more than happy to chill somewhere quiet with Blu.

'Actually, forget Jesse,' she said, leaning further into him. 'Let's get something from the corner shop and eat outside. I need some fresh air.'

Blu's arm remained draped around her all the way down the road until they reached the shop. Other girls knew how to walk with a guy's arm around them, like it was the most natural thing in the world, but not Indie. Letting his continuous stream of chat wash over her, she focused on how not to walk like a robot, relieved he couldn't feel her own thundering heart beating within his.

They bought crisps, two chocolate bars, and a couple of ham sandwiches that had seen better days, then sat on a damp bench in the park nearby. Everyone called it 'the park' but it was more of an overgrown square with a couple of benches, a half-dead flower bed, and a crumbling wall at the back that had once belonged to a house long since demolished. The ruins were used as a graffiti canvass and somewhere for pupils to smoke behind in their lunch break.

'You all right?' Blu asked again. 'Your eyes not hurting or anything?'

She didn't know whether to nod or shake her head in reply to his two questions, so she chewed on her chocolate bar instead and replied with an 'uh-huh.'

The park was set back from the main road, and far enough away from the school that there was no noise at all—just the cold January wind whistling through the bare branches and the odd crow squawking. She blinked slowly and took a deep breath. Even though Blu did enough talking for the both of them, it was still peaceful. The air felt cleaner, her blood ran more liquid, and her head was clear. Time spent with Blu was like melting into a deep warm bath after a hard day.

'This is nice,' she said.

'Yeah.' He tipped back his head and stared up at the cloudy sky. 'You think this is what it's like for normal people, to be able to just… exist? You know, chill with a mate without always wondering if what you're feeling are your emotions or theirs?'

Indie popped a piece of chocolate in her mouth and chewed quickly so she could answer.

'Probably. I'm so glad I finally met someone I could share this with,' she said. Her cheeks prickled, and she rubbed them with her cold hands. Maybe he'd think they were red from the wind. 'I mean, the weirdness of our...condition. It was getting lonely dealing with it alone. I'm just glad I can talk to you about it. You've always had Jade, so I guess it's not been so bad for you.'

He nodded and bit into his limp sandwich, making a face but continuing anyway.

'True, except my sister hates me, so....'

She smiled, because it wasn't true, and he knew it. They sat in silence for a long time, occasionally looking over at one another and smiling as they picked at their lunch. The emptiness stretched between them—loose limbs, empty minds, a still nothing she wanted to lie back against and sleep upon.

Then something peculiar washed over her, a pang of something she hadn't felt before.

The sensation began in her chest, wet and warm, as if a thick liquid was being poured from her rib cage down onto her lap, heat spreading across the tops of her thighs and between her legs. She crossed them and focused on trying to open her packet of crisps. Her arm accidentally brushed Blu's, sending a million jolts through her body.

OK, this was strange. This wasn't an emotion she'd felt before, and whatever it was definitely didn't belong to Blu. Were they her own feelings?

Then, like a stampede of horses, her heartbeat gathered pace and her breath began to come in short bursts.

A quick glance at Blu confirmed he was looking at her, and he was frowning. Was he feeling what she was feeling? It wasn't exactly unpleasant, but it was making her dizzy, light-headed, and hot. Very hot. She looked around, but the park was still empty.

'Want a crisp?' she croaked, holding out the bag to Blu.

He took one and she did too, but her hands were shaking too much to eat it. She squeezed her legs together tighter, an ache forming between them. *What the hell?* She was only sitting next to her friend—what was happening?

'You feeling all right?' he asked, his voice sounding huskier than normal.

She nodded, suddenly wishing she could see his bright green eyes beneath his contact lenses. The *real* him. He sucked the salt from the crisps off his finger, making a million butterflies take flight in her guts. Her chest was refusing to let in any more air. Was this what fancying someone felt like? Didn't you need moonlight and cheesy music to feel this much… What was it? Passion? In the movies, characters felt like she did after a crazy car chase scene or impromptu dance number, all pent-up attraction leading to frenzied snogging. But Indie and Blu were just sitting on a damp bench in a freezing park eating Monster Munch—there was zero reason why her heart was fighting to climb out of her rib cage and throw itself into Blu's lap.

'Indie?' he said, the word barely a breath.

'Yes?'

His stare was so intense it made her shift in her seat, causing the ache in her centre to grow. Through Blu's dark contact lenses she could see his pupils dilating and drinking her in. Looking at him was too difficult; it was making whatever she was feeling worse. Or better.

'Can you…' He cleared his throat. 'Can you feel that?'

She nodded, her eyes darting around the park. Blu swivelled around on the bench too, looking for the source of emotion. Standing up, Bambi legs shaking beneath her, Indie took a few tentative steps to the back of the park. She peered behind trees and in the bushes. Then she saw them. Jesse and Xavier behind the crumbling wall, their tall lean bodies pressed against one another. They were kissing. Actually, judging by where their hands were, they were doing more than just kissing. And they were so wrapped up in one another they hadn't noticed that anyone else was in the park.

Blu appeared beside her and stifled a laugh.

'Fucking hell!' he whispered. 'If they go any further it's going to get proper pornographic.'

'Well, that explains that, then,' she said, a tight smile shaky on her lips.

The heat inside of her was building in intensity, hot lava threatening to erupt from her core. She turned around, brushed crumbs off her school jumper, and nodded in the direction of the school building.

'Let's go.'

Blu grabbed her coat sleeve. 'Come on. You not curious to feel how far they go? Let's sit on the bench again and see what happens. Don't tell me it doesn't feel good.'

'Perv,' she whispered loudly.

'Wimp.'

She laughed. Was the tightening knot in her stomach down to what the boys were doing, or the way Blu was looking at her?

She shook her head. 'We should go; this isn't right. It's proper weird.'

Leaving was the right thing to do, although Blu was right. She *was* enjoying the sensation—that hungry, ravenous need building inside of her. As if no matter how much she got of what she wanted, it wouldn't be enough. She ran her hands through her hair and walked slowly toward the school, struggling to wipe the grin off her face. After a few seconds Blu fell into step beside her.

'You know, I'd love to be that crazy about someone,' he said, so quietly she had to slow down to hear him better.

'You telling me you've never had a girlfriend? I find that hard to believe.'

He tutted. 'Of course I have, but...you don't feel your own feelings when you're with someone normal. At least people like us don't. I just want to know how I *really* feel about someone, you know? Experience only *my* emotions. That would be really special.'

'Yeah,' Indie said. 'Yeah, it would.'

They walked back to school in silence. Blu's shoulder was centimetres from hers, his fingertips occasionally brushing against hers as their hands swung by their sides. Once inside the school building it took a while for the bubbling heat from the park to stop simmering in the pit of her stomach. She missed it when it finally wore off.

21

THERE WAS ONLY one Hillcrest school in East Finchley, which meant Luci was in the right place. It also meant the remaining Nephilim were, right now, under the same roof as her. Was this it? Was this really the last step in her search? Scrolling through Gabriel's text message again, she noted the names and descriptions he's sent her. Jade. Blu. Indie.

Text messaging was a new thing. Luci had given the archangel a solar-powered phone after their coffee shop meeting and he'd been sending her the odd message. Sweet things. In-jokes. The odd comment that made her stomach twist in ways that concerned her. She'd been in bed with the tattooed barista when her phone had beeped that morning, and as soon as she'd seen the word 'Nephilim' she'd pushed the young man off her. Leaving him half-naked and wanting, she'd rushed straight back to her hotel without even bothering to erase his memory. It didn't matter anymore—she was already bored of that game.

The two Nephilim she'd already procured, Scar and Violet, had been enjoying the luxury of the same hotel as her over the last week, both unaware of the other's existence. Neither did they know Luci had created a force field around the building and filled the hotel with whisperers, her very own security team. The kids couldn't escape—she wasn't going to run the risk of losing her army again. She needn't have worried though, because Violet and Scar were more than happy filling their faces with room service and watching films on demand, not once asking to go back home or what the next step was.

Not long now until she needed them. If today went to plan, then all the Nephilim would meet very soon, and the day of reckoning would commence.

Luci closed her eyes and took a moment to compose herself. As soon as she'd arrived at the school, raucous jeering had erupted at the end of the hallway involving a girl facedown on the floor and a group of younger boys laughing at her. The noise was deafening, and Luci had to fight the urge to silence them all with a flick of her finger. Teenagers had never made much sense to her.

'Can I help you?' A squat woman in slacks and a cardigan was standing by Luci's shoulder. The lines on her brow were fixed in a perpetual scowl, and she had pearly pink lipstick smeared on her front tooth. 'Are you a parent or…?'

'I'm here to see the Head,' Luci replied. 'It's about three of your students.'

'Oh, goodness. I hope no one's in trouble!' the woman replied, placing her hand on her chest. 'Are you police, or social services or…?'

'Dressed like this?' Luci asked.

The woman pursed her lips, taking in Luci's curves, bright red dress, and towering heels, and nodded in the direction of the front office.

'Mr Barkwood is having his lunch at the moment, but if you could…'

Luci bent down so she was nose-to-nose with the woman.

'You will interrupt his lunch and tell him to come here—it's very urgent. Then you will forget we ever met.'

The woman nodded quickly and scuttled off, her kitten heels clacking along the tiled floor. Luci hated schools as much as she hated hospitals. So many people trying to do good for so many who rarely deserved it.

A middle-aged man in a tweed suit half jogged out of the front office, clutching a paper napkin and looking around the empty front desk. When he saw Luci he slowed down, wiping his mouth with a frown.

'May I help you? I was told it was an emergency.'

Luci looked deep into his eyes.

'Take me to your office. We need to talk.'

She followed him through two narrow hallways until they reached a wooden door with his name on a golden plaque. Inside the gloomy room everything was made of dark wood. The air smelled of musty books and the curtains were drawn. A pile of paperwork loomed precariously over an old computer, and pastry crumbs were scattered all over the keyboard from the half-eaten meat pie beside it. Mr Barkwood sat down behind his desk, and Luci perched on the edge of it, screwing her nose up at the stench of the man's lunch. The sooner she got this over with, the better.

'Tell me what lesson Jade, Blu, and Indie have together,' she demanded, making sure she maintained eye contact.

'I...I'm not familiar with all... This is a large school. I... We have over one thousand pupils. I will need surnames or at least a year group.'

Luci sighed. All Gabriel had told her was their first names, their school, and that the boy and one of the girls had Nephilim eyes. She smiled at the words Gabriel had used to describe his elation at finding his children, at finding himself face-to-face with a boy that had looked so much like the son he had lost. The archangel was eager to meet his children properly, but it was Luci's job to gather them together and keep them safe until the time was right.

'Jade and Blu are new. Twins. Either sixteen or seventeen years old. Their mother was Japanese, I believe.'

The headmaster's eyebrows shot up, and he tapped away on his filthy keyboard.

'Yes. Yes. I remember all the new sixth formers from this term—not as many of them as other years. Right, here they are. Bristol and Jade Usaki.'

'Bristol? What's his full name?'

'Bristol Levington Usaki, it says here. Oh dear, poor boy. Yes, some parents really don't think these things through.'

B. L. U. Ah, Blu. That made sense.

'And the girl? Indie? Is she in any of the same classes as them?'

The man's pupils remained dark and dilated as Luci probed him further.

'I don't have an Indie in their year, but perhaps... Oh yes, Indigo.'

Luci smiled. Violet, Scarlett, Sol, Amber, Jade, Blu, and Indigo. Exactly as the *Book of Light* had predicted. *The chosen Nephilim will complete the full spectrum of the soul,* the tome had read. Rainbows, chakras, light. Whichever way she looked at it—she had the full colour set of six and one to spare!

The headmaster turned the screen around to face Luci, showing a grid with pupils and lessons. 'One class. They all have history AS with Mr Dowding. See? There they are—the Usaki twins and Indigo de Silva.'

'What did you say?' Luci cried.

'History.'

'No, you stupid fool!' She grabbed him by the shoulders, her face inches from his. 'The girl. Indigo. What's her surname?'

'De Silva. Like the film director. That's her grandfather. Her father was an actor but unfortunately he was killed...'

'...in a boat accident six years ago,' she said to herself.

Luci's hands were shaking and clammy. Her hands never got clammy. She smoothed down her dress and took a deep breath. Indigo was Ella's child. Of course she was—she'd named her after the bloody bar, and Gabriel had said the brunette had bright blue eyes.

Her son's eyes. Zadkiel and Ella *had* fucking fucked in that fucking library! She *knew* it!

Tapping her fingers against her knee, she thought back to the day 350 years ago when she'd first seen the *Book of Light*. This was it. This was what she'd been searching for since the witch had shown her the spell—all the Nephilim in one place. If only she still had that battered book. She'd memorised every marking on every page, but now she was so close she was beginning to worry she hadn't remembered it all correctly.

The headmaster cleared his throat. 'Is everything all right, er, Miss…?'

'Shut up.'

So Indie was Zadkiel's daughter, but nobody knew. Gabriel had only just told Zac that Ella was alive, and Luci had wiped away Ella's memory right after she'd found her with her son in the library of that old Spanish monastery, so Ella would have no recollection of Zadkiel coming back for her. Let alone sleeping with him. Luci had to get to the girl before Zadkiel did, and before Gabriel figured out that the kid on the Santa Monica beach six years ago was the girl in the bar.

She took another deep breath. Well, well, well, everything had magically fallen into place. Nephilim had no life paths, so this wasn't destiny or fate at work. It was bigger than that. And to top it all off Gabriel and Zadkiel's children were friends? Neither of them knowing who their real fathers were—or that they were half-angels. This was just too delicious.

She swallowed down the lump rising in her throat and sniffed. She had a *granddaughter*. Somewhere in this very building was the key to the plan Luci had been plotting for over two thousand years. The descendant. She wiped a finger beneath her right eye, careful not to smudge her mascara, and turned to the bewildered headmaster.

The last time she'd seen one of Gabriel's offspring was the day she'd helped Mary Magdalene wash Jesus's feet, and now she was going to see two more in the same class as her granddaughter. Zadkiel's little girl. Her baby's baby.

'When's their next history class?' she asked, noting her voice had a slight wobble in it.

Mr Barkwood looked at his watch and gave a tiny smile. 'Five minutes. Would you like me to introduce you to their teacher?'

'No.'

Luci's smile, slow at first, grew wider and wider until her green eyes glowed catlike in the dim light of the office. 'I don't want to meet the history teacher. I *am* the new history teacher.'

22

INDIE AND BLU arrived at their next class together. The door to the history class was open but the room was empty. Strange. Mr Dowding was normally early so he could revel in his snide remarks about punctuality.

The class filed in, everyone fighting for the desks at the back. Indie sat at the front, by the wall, and Blu at the desk beside her. It was going to be like that now, was it? Turning her head to the left she pretended to look out the window so he wouldn't see her attempting not to smile. What was it Jade had said the night before, when they'd gone to Indigo? Blu liked her. *Liked.* She bit the inside of her cheek. She really had to stop all this grinning.

Everyone was already in their seats when the door flew open, banging against the wall, and Jesse fell into the classroom. He was out of breath.

'Sorry, Mr… Oh. Where's Dowding?'

Most people ignored him. Some shrugged.

'He's not here yet,' Indie called out.

Jesse scampered over to her. His face was flushed, and he had a small brown leaf in his hair. Indie picked it out and out of the corner of her eye caught Blu giving her one of his usual smirks.

'I couldn't find you at lunchtime,' she said to Jesse. 'Where were you?'

'Oh, nothing. There was…just…you know, this big thing I had to deal with…'

Blu laughed so loudly he had to clamp both hands over his mouth. Jesse's neck turned a deep maroon.

'OK, fine. I was with Xavier. In the park.' He looked behind him at Blu then leaned into Indie. 'Kissing.'

She picked another twig out of her best friend's hair and patted his red cheeks.

'Good. I'm glad one of us is getting some action.'

Blu spluttered at that then tried to style it out into a cough. Teasing him gave Indie a self-satisfied thrill. Of course she didn't want any "action" of her own—she wouldn't know where to start—but Blu was always so cocky it was fun to keep him on his toes.

With a sudden bang, the classroom door slammed open again and everyone fell silent. Jesse ran to his usual desk and sat down as twenty-two heads whipped up in unison to check out the stranger before them.

It was the same woman Indie had seen in the corridor before lunch. Like something out of an old-fashioned film, her bright red dress clung to her curves and revealed way more cleavage than was usually displayed at Hillcrest school. Hair thick and wavy, it tumbled over her shoulders, framing shiny green eyes that were exactly like… No, Indie was getting carried away. Not every new person she met with pretty eyes was, well, whatever her and the twins were.

'I'm Miss Luci, your new history teacher,' the woman said, her flawless face displaying no emotion at all. 'Mr Dowding won't be coming back.'

Hushed whispers floated around the classroom. The woman waited until everyone was quiet, then stared intently at each student. One by one the class trained their eyes on the teacher, until they were all transfixed in the same direction.

Indie glanced at Blu who was already looking at her, eyebrows raised. She gave a tiny shrug in response.

'Everyone, stand up,' Miss Luci said.

Like an obedient army, the class stood to attention. Indie and Blu reluctantly followed suit.

'Now take your right shoe off and place it on your head,' the teacher said.

Blu laughed out loud, but Indie noted he was the only one. No usual hum of incredulousness or amused titters her classmates usually revelled in. This was ridiculous. Wasn't anyone going to say anything? Fine, *she* would then.

'Sorry, Miss, could you please repeat what...' Indie stopped talking and looked around her. Every single one of her classmates, including Jesse, had done as instructed and were now balancing muddy school shoes on their heads.

Blu turned to her and mouthed 'what the fuck' and Indie made a face back. What was going on? Was it some elaborate prank?

'What the *hell*?' Jade was standing in the doorway, her arms folded and nose wrinkled in confusion. She looked Miss Luci up and down. 'Who are you? And where's Dowding?'

The teacher still wasn't smiling, her stance businesslike as if her strange shoe command had been part of her teacher training.

'I'm Miss Luci, your new history teacher. Please put your right shoe on top of your head.'

Jade's eyebrows arched even higher.

'I don't think so,' she said, walking past her and sitting behind Indie. 'Bloody nutcase,' she muttered, low enough that only Indie could hear.

Then Miss Luci smiled. A wide, crimson grin that lit up her entire face.

'You must be Jade,' she said, stepping forward until she was in front of the three of them. 'And you're Blu and…' As Miss Luci walked over to Indie's desk her bright green eyes began to shimmer. Were they tears? The woman blinked them away and tilted her head to one side.

'Indigo?'

Indie nodded. Their new teacher reached out her hand, as if she was about to stroke Indie's cheek, then lowered it again. With a little shake of her head, she composed herself and returned to the front of the class.

'OK, everyone. Shoes back on your feet, sit down, and forget that ever happened.'

'Miss,' Blu said, his hand high in the air. 'I'm a bit confused. Was the shoe thing some kind of test?'

Luci blinked slowly. 'Yes, it was, Blu. And the three of you passed. Now, who can tell me where the blackboard is?'

Their classmates, seemingly back to normal and no longer zombified, sniggered at the teacher's joke. Indie couldn't tell if Miss Luci was winding them up or not.

'Mr Dowding has a bunch of things saved on the whiteboard,' Jesse called out, pointing to the large screen on the wall. 'Yeah, just press that.'

Miss Luci tapped the screen, stepped back, and laughed at the image of an old galleon that appeared before her.

'I see. You're learning about the history of shipping and the Dutch East India Company. Is that right?'

Everyone nodded.

'That's interesting, because I happen to know a bit about that. What have you covered?'

'Trade routes and how it shaped commerce in the seventeenth century,' someone at the front called out.

Luci made a face. 'Well, that sounds fucking boring.'

Another snigger rippled through the class, but Indie wasn't laughing. First the twins started at her school, then there were those scary men at Indigo yesterday just before her eyes changed colour, and now *this*? Some unnaturally beautiful woman pretending to be their teacher and acting weird around them? Something wasn't right. What if they were all somehow connected?

Indie filtered the feelings of bewilderment, amusement, and curiosity emanating off her classmates and focused on the teacher. But all she picked up was…nothing. Miss Luci radiated nothing, not even a hint of emotion. Just like the staff at Indigo, her bright eyes were unreadable.

'Miss!' someone behind Indie called out. 'What about the school trip tomorrow? Is it still happening? Are you taking us instead?'

Luci frowned. 'Possibly. Tell me more about this excursion.'

While the boy told the teacher about the three-day trip planned for the historical sites of Bath and Bristol, Indie poked Blu's arm and beckoned him closer.

'I can't feel her,' she whispered.

Jade, sitting behind them, leaned forward too.

'Me neither,' she said.

Blu was biting his lower lip. 'You seen her eyes?'

They nodded at one another just as their new teacher swung around to face them.

'Everything OK?' she asked, a look of amusement passing over her face.

They mumbled a 'yes' and she smiled back, lips glossy, teeth white.

'It appears I'll be seeing you all tomorrow for our trip to the West Country. I have a feeling it will be more eye-opening for some than others.'

Indie could have sworn the teacher was looking at her when she said that.

'Right then, back to our lesson on seventeenth century trading routes.' She perched on the edge of an empty desk at the front, her tight dress riding up her thighs. 'Imagine a world where Europe ruled, and it got its power from violence and theft. It took land and riches, enslaved people, and wiped out cultures. It was a dark time, a filthy, shameful time that we've since packaged as a pioneering epoch of adventure and discovery. When we talk of progress and building nations, never forget that the riches of some were achieved through the suffering of many.

'Let us start with the Dutch East India Company. The company was founded in 1602 and was famed for trading in spices. But what many of you don't know is that in its time it was so powerful it had the ability to wage wars and imprison and execute convicts. They even created their own coins. In those days the seas were busier than motorways, with huge vessels carrying cargo of every kind.

'But it wasn't just the Dutch East India Company that successfully moved cargo. Many types of ships filled our oceans, trading in everything from sugar to porcelain, and carrying men from all over the world. Some of these men were wealthy, some of them criminals, and some of them gods.'

Luci closed her eyes and breathed in, her chest rising like a wave in a storm.

'And sometimes, those beautiful gods were pirates in disguise.'

'Nothing Ventured, Nothing Gained.'
~ Geoffrey Chaucer, *The Canterbury Tales*

PART THREE

SOMEWHERE
IN THE
ATLANTIC
OCEAN

1635

I.

THE LACE ALONG her collarbone was so itchy it was making her skin red, but Luci willed herself to ignore it as sweat pooled between her breasts. If her time on Earth had taught her anything, it was that uncomfortable clothing was strictly reserved for the rich. Those with no money were rarely affected by mere garments—life was restrictive enough.

She hitched up her skirts and took her first step onto the gangplank. The inside of her thighs were sticky from the morning heat, but she wouldn't be sustaining this charade for much longer. A little discomfort was a small price to pay for a free voyage across the Atlantic.

'Follow me,' she said to the two thick-necked men behind her, carrying a large trunk each. The cases only contained a few items of clean bedding, water, herbs, and her *Book of Light*—but no one had to know that. A wealthy lady, with servants in tow, got further in life than one who pushed and shoved her way to where she wanted to be. Life was nothing but a show, after all. People only saw what they wanted to see.

'You got the right ship, ma'am?'

A squat man with tufts of greying hair and few teeth, all brown, blocked her entrance to the deck. Eye to eye, she waited for his pupils to dilate before speaking.

'I'm boarding this ship. Move aside and bring me the captain.'

Running a finger along the inside of her lace neckline again, she ignored the curious glances of the men on board busy preparing the ship for her next voyage. The crown of her head stung under the glare of the sun. If she didn't get out of this ridiculous corset soon, she was going to faint.

Within a few minutes, a man appeared.

'I'm Captain Alexander Roberts,' he said, his English accent dripping in wealth and entitlement.

A dark blue velvet overcoat fitted snugly over his cream waistcoat, matching cream trousers tucked in to long boots. The sword at his side glinted, as did the multitude of brass buttons running down the edge of his coat. Luci squinted as the sun bounced off all the metal. A tiny pearl of sweat making its way down his temple was the only proof he was feeling as uncomfortable in this Caribbean heat as she was. Hands clasped behind his back, he squared his shoulders and lifted his chin.

'I wasn't expecting guests on board. Who are you with?' he asked.

Luci didn't have time for formalities. 'Look at me. Good. You will allow me aboard your ship, and you will tell your crew they are not to talk to me or go near me—although I will speak to them one by one in my own time. You won't take any notice of me either, unless I tell you to. I will sleep in your quarters and you will stay away. Is that understood?'

The man nodded, his pale eyes glazing over like frost on a lake.

'Show my servants to my new room,' she said.

The men with the trunks followed the captain to the back of the ship while Luci looked around her. It was a large vessel, and like many trading ships that made the journey from Jamaica to England, it was carrying barrels of molasses destined for the United Kingdom. Three months in the Americas had been enough for Luci to admit that the lead from one of her whisperers held no hope. Since finding Marisse in the Netherlands twenty-two years previously, she'd yet to discover another half-angel. Marisse had died old, but free, ten years after Luci saved her life in Roermond. After that, the fallen archangel and the witch's *Book of Light* had travelled the world in search of all the others the old woman claimed angel Azantiel had fathered. Marisse had been certain that there were entire groups of Nephilim in far-off exotic countries, and Luci only needed six. But Nephilim weren't immortal, so she was never going to find six of them at the same time. If only the witch had known a way of making people live forever so Luci had time to gather them up and perform the spell.

After months of sweaty, rainy days and whispers that led nowhere, Luci decided to return to Europe where she had a better chance of finding Azantiel's other offspring.

The main deck was a hive of activity, men running this way and that, carrying things and pulling ropes. Although busy, every single one of them was watching Luci out of the corner of their eye. Women were rarely seen on trading ships. Sailors were superstitious things and a woman on board was always bad luck.

'I am invisible to you,' she whispered to them, one by one. 'You can't see or hear me. I don't exist.'

Some crew members were high up in the rigging or inside the ship. She would leave them for later.

The boat began to rock as moorings were untied and cargo secured. Luci had never liked the water. She preferred her feet either firmly on the ground or, as was the case two thousand years ago, tucked up beneath her as she flew through the air. Wings and walking she could cope with, but a mermaid she was not. Unfortunately, she no longer had the ability to appear and disappear at will, flitting between continents in under a second, and she could no longer fly. Therefore, her only choice was to cross oceans on boats and drink her herbal concoctions to keep her nausea at bay.

Her belongings had been placed in the captain's cabin, her servants making their way across the deck toward her. She ushered them over as a few crew members looked on. They were probably confused as to who the two men were talking to, seeing as Luci was invisible to them.

'Did you stow my luggage away safely?' she asked.

'Yes, ma'am,' they answered as one.

Luci nodded. 'Very well. You must now leave the boat and forget you ever saw me or this ship. In fact, forget everything that's happened over the last three hours.'

They did as they were told, running along the gangplank just as the squat crew member with rotten teeth pulled it away.

'Where you off to?' he shouted out to them. 'You won't be able to get back on. We're sailing in a few minutes.'

The servants couldn't hear him. They'd already forgotten their part in the woman's master plan.

Luci stretched, then scowled up at the sun. Her time in Jamaica had been interesting, but not in a good way. She may not have found the Nephilim of which her whisperers had spoken, but she'd had the opportunity to visit a country that she hadn't been to in hundreds of years. Since she'd last visited the island the Spanish had invaded, killed off entire tribes, and fought bloody battles with pirates. African slaves were being forced to cut sugarcane and build up industries that would sustain undeserving European families for generations. There was even talk of the English wanting the island, although they were already in competition with the Dutch for prominence over the world's seas and trade. Luci was certain, in centuries to come, this time in history—a history written by the victors—would be revered for its growth and daring. But over the years she'd seen all the blood the history pages would never be stained with. "Progress" was the word white men used to excuse murder, theft, and cruelty. She'd punished plenty of these monsters during her time in Jamaica, but she was happy to be leaving the island before she wiped away every last white man on it.

'What you doing on board?'

The man before her had grey skin and was wearing a stained apron. He looked her up and down with one eye, the other presumably missing behind his crude eye patch—a piece of fabric wrapped diagonally across his head.

'I'm invisible,' Luci said, bored of having to repeat herself. Surely she'd spoken to most of the men by now? There were only a few left to talk to, namely those high up in the rigging checking the sails. 'You won't see, hear, nor notice me for the entire voyage. Or remember me afterwards.'

The man frowned, one bushy eyebrow wriggling along his forehead like a caterpillar, the other hidden behind the fabric.

'You're far from invisible, madam. In fact, you are going to be a distraction to our men. We leave in five minutes. Whose permission do you have to be on board?'

Luci closed her eyes slowly and took a deep breath. Of course, the missing eye. This had happened a few times in the past—she needed two seeing eyes to be focussing on her for her magic to work. This wouldn't do, it wouldn't do at all. All she wanted was a calm voyage and some peace and quiet.

'I'm with the captain,' she said. 'I'm his cousin.'

The man looked at her dubiously and was about to respond when he was called over by a man below deck.

'I'll be speaking to the captain myself,' he hollered as he backed away. 'Women on ships bring nothing but trouble.'

Luci smiled at him sweetly. Oh, how little he knew.

Gathering her skirts and welcoming the cool breeze on her legs, she marched to the back of the ship. Aft? Stern? It had a name, but she didn't care. She was a passenger only, and an invisible one at that.

Her servants had said the captain's room would be easy to find, and they were right. At the far end of the ship, with steps on either side leading to the poop deck, was a set of double doors with elaborate brass detailing and carved patterns of rope whittled into the wood. Of course they were locked, but that was no deterrent for a fallen angel. Placing the palm of her hand on the carved wood, she waited for the light click and pushed the door open. Six steps led down to a large room surrounded by a bank of curved, tiny lead windows. There even appeared to be a small balcony looking over the ocean. Inside was a wall lined with bookshelves, a desk on one side covered with rolled maps and strange instruments, and a mahogany table in the centre, on top of which sat a cut-glass decanter of whisky and matching glasses. There was also a short bed at the back of the room and a wash basin in the corner. This would do nicely.

Shutting the door behind her, she considered the whisky before deciding to do the one thing she'd been dreaming of all day. Reaching behind her she pointed her finger at the multitude of tiny mother-of-pearl buttons running down the length of her spine, releasing them from their holding. With every pop, the restrictive holds expanded inch by inch, enabling her rib cage to open, and allowing her to breathe properly again. No wonder women were so prone to fainting and swooning; it was impossible to do anything but sit quietly when no oxygen was permitted to enter your lungs.

She really couldn't understand the way fashion had evolved over the last two hundred years. When Luci had lived in the Roman times and amongst the ancient Greeks, they had been happy to wear flowing robes loosely tied up in the middle. Back when Luci was the greatest of archangels, women were revered, listened to, and worshipped as life-giving gods—now women were nothing but trussed-up onions, layer upon layer of fabric restricting all movement, breathing, and thinking. With every year that went by, waists got smaller and skirts got bigger. What was going to happen by the year 2000? Were women destined to be reduced to nothing more than a walking bundle of clothing, cinched in the middle like an hourglass made of frills and lace? Luci shuddered at the thought. They wouldn't if she had anything to do with it.

It was just as hot on board the ship as it was beneath the Caribbean sun. Yanking the dress by its itchy collar she ripped it off her body and kicked it into the corner. With each layer of clothing she peeled off her sticky, damp body, she felt herself return. Next were the thick white stockings, tight shoes, huge bustle, and the whalebone corset that had been leaving welts on her hip bones all day. Within seconds of removing the binding the red marks on her skin healed and she was finally free. Now barefoot and wearing nothing but a long white underskirt and loose smock, she pulled at the pins in her hair and let her curls tumble down her shoulders in a dark flurry. Free.

The trunks filled with her belongings had been placed at the foot of the bed. She padded over to them and reached inside for her book. That was all she cared about right now, her book and some pastries she'd taken from a stall on the way to the ship. Luckily Luci was immune to disease and hunger, which meant unlike most passengers on the ship she was guaranteed a healthy journey, but she'd need good food as a distraction if nothing else. The three-month voyage from Port Royal to Dover was bound to be nothing more than a boring test of patience. She had her book to study and plans to make—and a few sugary treats to keep her going. She'd manage.

Laying back on the bed, propped up by a multitude of brocade and tasselled cushions, Luci placed the *Book of Light* on her lap. The tome had been in her possession for over twenty years but there was still so much to learn. With a stomach-twisting lurch, the ship pulled away from the port accompanied by the shouts of men and feet running along the deck. She hated boats.

The pastries she'd bought had been wrapped in banana leaves. Perhaps eating something would settle her swirling guts. Peeling the wrapping away from its sticky contents, she was raising the sugary cake to her lips when the door clicked open. She put her food back down and licked her fingers.

A broad-shouldered crew member was creeping into the room. Silently, he locked the door behind him and headed straight for the captain's desk. Interesting. Luci's curious smile was hidden in the murky light of the room. He glanced furtively at the door, then quietly began to rummage through drawer after drawer, searching beneath piles of papers and maps.

'Can I help you?' she asked.

The man swung around so fast he hit his head on a shelf.

'Oh. I wasn't expecting anyone to be in here,' he replied in broken English. 'Least of all a woman.'

She recognised his accent, so spoke back to him in Portuguese.

'I can see that.'

She sat up, enjoying the look of surprise on his face. Not just at her language skills but the fact she was only partially dressed.

'I'm sorry, madam. I didn't realise the captain's wife was Portuguese. Nor that she was on board.'

'She isn't.'

'I see.'

One would think the man's sun-bronzed skin would be too dark to produce a blush, but nevertheless his cheeks flushed a few shades redder. Such bashfulness sat awkwardly against his hulking frame. He wore loose trousers that stopped at the knee, a white billowing shirt, and a navy cotton sash tied like a scarf along his middle. It was what most of the crew wore, but on him it looked less like a uniform and more like tattered clothing he'd grown out of. A sole survivor on a desert island.

The rest of him was pure pirate. Ears full of metal hoops, fingers covered in rings, and thick brown arms striped with dark patterns. He pushed his long hair away from his face and secured it with a ribbon he had tied around his wrist.

'What's your name?' Luci asked in Portuguese.

'I'm Lorenzo, madam.'

'Are you looking for anything in particular?'

'No, I...' He stopped and narrowed his eyes. Head tilted to one side, his brow creased into three deep lines as he failed to hear what he was listening for. 'Apologies for bothering you,' he said, bowing low and heading for the door.

'Lorenzo?'

'Yes?'

His gaze was fixed on her bare ankles, traveling up to her shoulder, which was peeking out from her loose top. Luci let him stare. It didn't matter; he wouldn't remember anything in a few minutes.

'You can't see me,' she said. 'You don't remember coming in here or talking to me. I will remain invisible to you. Understand?'

He narrowed his eyes again and nodded, then left the room.

What a shame. Out of all the men on board, he was certainly the most interesting. She should have kept him to play with.

II.

Holed up in the captain's cabin for days on end, Luci was getting restless. Patience had never been her strong point, no matter how many years she'd walked the Earth. She liked to keep busy, but there were only so many things one could do on a galleon ship unless it involved helping man the ship—which Luci had no intention of doing. The herbs had run out, and so had her pastries, although now that the ship had gathered speed her seasickness had abated sufficiently to make way for boredom.

She stretched and looked out of the tiny, blurry window. It was another blazingly hot day, making the sea glimmer a deep azure. It reminded her of her son's eyes, not that she'd ever got close enough to stare into them properly. In the distance, where the sea was shallower or met a reef, the colours melted into a deep turquoise with patches of jade. Gabriel. Now, *those* eyes Luci *had* got close enough to gaze into and she missed them. She often wondered what the archangel would do if he knew she were alive. Would he be happy, or had his allegiances moved over to Mikhael? Surely not. Was her dearest friend also friends with her son? She hoped so.

Fresh air and wind in her hair—that was what she needed.

The entire crew had been charmed into believing she was invisible, so Luci was free to walk about in whatever state she wished. Even if she were naked there would be no repercussions—but she chose to stay dressed. Not in her underskirt and tunic though—they were rank with stale sweat. She'd have to find something else to wear. Using the jug of water and basin in the corner, she freshened up, then turned her attention to the captain's wardrobe, because there was no way she was going to put her itchy, restrictive, and ridiculously hot dress back on.

Captain Roberts had plenty of outfits to choose from and Luci idly wondered what he was wearing right now, seeing as she'd forbidden him to enter his own quarters. She slipped on one of his frilly white shirts and a pair of loose cotton slacks that nearly reached her ankles, then secured the two in place with a thick brown belt around her middle. She still needed something to tie her hair back with.

Making her way to the desk she moved piles of paper and rolled up maps aside, searching for a piece of string or a ribbon. Pushing her hand to the back of one of the drawers, instead of finding some twine she felt a small metal lever. Ah. She'd seen these desks before, along with their hidden compartments. Was this what that rugged man, Lorenzo, had been searching for before she'd told him to forget she existed? She pressed the lever and a section at the front of the desk sprung open, revealing a hidden compartment. It was just big enough to fit her hand into. Reaching inside she pulled out a small drawstring leather pouch and emptied the contents into the palm of her hand. Rubies, lots of little rubies shining like bloody teardrops. So that's what Lorenzo had been after.

She put the gems back in the sack and threw the bag into one of her trunks, then pulled at a ribbon looped around a rolled-up map and tied her hair back.

Sea air, rubies, and clean clothes—the day was shaping up to be a glorious one.

The air outside was crisp and fresh, no longer scented with the fishy, sweaty smells of the port. She took a long deep breath and smiled.

The ship was its usual hubbub of noise, but it was mostly calm. So far, the waters had been tranquil and the weather fair, so many of the crew were below deck catching up with sleep or playing cards in the shade. Luci leaned over the wooden balustrade and gazed out at the endless expanse of blue in every direction. Restlessness tapped away beneath her skin. She should have kept at least one person on board to talk to—hidden one of the servants in her room or taken a crew member as one of her own. There were still at least six weeks of this voyage left; she needed entertainment.

'You, boy!' came a gruff voice behind her. 'No time to be idle. I have some barrels need moving below deck. You earn your keep on this ship, lad!'

Luci turned and sighed as a figure marched toward her. She'd forgotten all about him, the grey-skinned man with one eye. The only one she couldn't hide from.

'Goodness, it's you!' he exclaimed, looking her up and down in horror. 'I thought you'd left the ship.'

'No, I'm still here,' she said, her voice flat.

Should she kill him? It would be a lot easier to snap his neck and throw him overboard but judging by his grubby apron he was the ship's cook. He'd be missed. Plus having a murder on board would only throw the ship into chaos. Luci couldn't be bothered with the drama right now.

'You're… You're wearing the captain's garb. Bare legs? I can see… I can see your *ankles*. Dear lady, cover up! You can't walk around half-naked aboard a trading vessel!'

His shouting had alerted three other men nearby who were now running over to see why the cook was so upset.

'Whatever is the matter, Samuel?' one of them asked.

'This… This *woman* cavorting around on deck in men's clothing. Look at her!'

The three men stared in Luci's direction and she grinned back at them, knowing full well they couldn't see her.

'There's nothing there,' one of them said quietly.

'What? Yes, look. That's not a young lad—it's a *woman*! A lady wearing the captain's clothes!'

The three crew members passed worried glances to one another until one of them mumbled something about getting the captain.

'Yes, you do that,' Samuel, the cook, agreed. 'Go and tell him this woman is a thief and a harlot and…and…a *stowaway*, no doubt.'

One man rushed off while two remained, eyeing Samuel warily.

Luci smiled to herself. The poor man had just sealed his fate and made her life a lot easier. One less thing to take care of.

'They think you're crazy,' she whispered to him, inching closer.

He recoiled and pushed her away. 'Get away from me!'

The two men beside him looked at one another again. The younger of the two stepped forward.

'Samuel, there's no one there.'

'Are you blind, boy? She's standing right before us, practically naked with her legs and bare feet out for all to see.'

A crowd had begun to form and at the front was Lorenzo, so tall and wide that his shadow instantly cooled her. Everyone was staring at Samuel as he continued to point at what they believed was nothing at all.

'Out of the way!'

Crew scattered like ants as the captain strode over to the cook. He had a telescope in one hand and papers in another—he didn't look like he had time for any nonsense.

'Goodness, Samuel. What is all this commotion?'

'Her!' he said, pointing at Luci. 'Since when have we allowed women on board? Is she with you?'

'I don't understand.'

'That woman. Over there! She told me she was your cousin when she first boarded and I believed her. She was dressed in fine clothes and had servants carrying her belonging yet… Well…feast your eyes on her wantonness. She's wearing your clothes, sir—and not many of them at that.'

The captain gave a worried glance at the man who had gone to fetch him, and they nodded discreetly at one another.

'Possessed,' Luci whispered into the captain's ear.

'He's cursed,' he declared. 'It was the islanders, no doubt. He'll endanger everyone on board. Somebody take his other arm and help me get him below deck.'

'No! I'm not crazy. I may only have one eye, but I know what I'm seeing!'

His cries died away as three men dragged him down a flight of wooden steps and deep into the belly of the ship. A flock of birds overhead cawed and cried out, drowning out the cook's cries.

Luci smiled and waved up at the birds, who formed a perfect heart shape before spreading back out and flying away. Now that her only obstacle had been so easily taken care of, perhaps it was time for some further amusement.

She rested her elbows on the balustrade again and nodded at the sea below. A couple of dark specks on the horizon began to take shape. Dolphins. They were always so eager to entertain that it hardly took any magic at all. She waved her hands and suddenly a large pod appeared, swimming and jumping beside the ship. She waved her finger and five of them arched through the water in perfect formation before diving back in.

The crew soon stopped whispering about the crazy cook and returned to work with only a few remaining on deck milling about and looking worried. Someone had joined her at the balustrade. Lorenzo, the man who'd been searching for rubies in her room. He was leaning over the wooden banister, looking down at the dolphins.

Luci pointed at one of the creatures and clapped as it performed a majestic loop-the-loop in the air before entering the water without rippling the surface. She nodded and three more performed the same trick in perfect unison. This was much more fun than sitting in the cabin all day. She breathed the sea air deep into her lungs and smiled again, the hot sun stroking the back of her neck. Perhaps the next month or so would pass quickly after all.

'How are you doing that?' Lorenzo muttered in Portuguese.

Who was Lorenzo talking to? Surely not her. She'd charmed him into forgetting and he hadn't returned to the room since—it must have worked.

She ignored him and continued playing with the dolphins. They were chattering up at her now, asking for more instructions. She commanded them to dance along the water on their tails and they obeyed, five of them skittering along the water's surface.

'Who are you?' he asked, facing her.

She hadn't noticed his eyes when they'd first met in the cabin—it had been dark in there and their exchange had been hurried—but now, in the sunlight, she saw them for what they truly were. Black. Not dark brown like many eyes she'd seen on her travels where you could hardly make out the pupils, but a sparkling jet black the colour of precious onyx. She'd only ever seen eyes like that once before—on an angel.

Her breath caught in her throat, tightness blossoming along her chest. Lorenzo was a Nephilim. *That's* why he could see her.

'Stand on one leg,' she said.

He narrowed his eyes at her.

'Pardon?'

She was right, he was half-angel. Three months she'd spent in Jamaica searching for a man who her whisperers had heard could make things move and read minds. The locals had called him a god, a walking mountain, and here he was on the very ship she'd chosen to take her away from the island.

'I'm Lucinda, but you can call me Luci,' she said, holding out her hand and expecting him to take it and bow.

No reaction. He wasn't stupid—he wasn't going to be seen talking to a vision and risk being accused of the same madness the cook had.

'Why am I the only one that can see you?' he asked, looking out to sea and hardly moving his lips.

'Because you're not human. You know that, don't you?'

A look of panic passed over his rugged face. He looked up and down and behind him, as if some being from the sky was about to swoop down and ambush him.

'Leave me alone,' he muttered, before walking in the opposite direction.

'Hey!' She jogged after him, tugging at his sleeve. His arms were so thick and broad there was hardly any fabric to take hold of. 'I need to talk to you.'

For twenty years she'd been searching for Nephilim. Not since Roermond and Marisse had she come across a half-angel. She had to speak to him, explain who she was and what she needed from his kind.

'Please, Lorenzo. Come with me.'

He checked no one was looking then pulled her into the shadows. Bunching the cotton of her tunic collar in his fist, he pushed her against the wooden wall and towered over her.

'Whatever the hell you are, leave me alone,' he hissed. 'I saw the writing on the book you were reading in the captain's quarters. I feared what you were back then and now you have confirmed it. I want nothing to do with your kind.'

He stormed off, leaving her shirt crumpled and her mind reeling. He was a Nephilim and he feared her. No, he feared angels. Who did he think she was and what did he think she wanted? It could wait. He couldn't escape her until they reached their destination. She would make him talk one way or another.

In the meantime, she had to have a word with the captain. The ship was destined for England, but Luci needed to get to France. A tiny detour wouldn't hurt.

III.

Three days had passed since the cook had been deemed insane, and the crew were already grumbling that whoever had been tasked with the cooking was making an even crappier job of it than Samuel had. Luci didn't care. Although hunger was never comfortable, it couldn't kill nor weaken her.

It had started to rain, thick drops that fell like pebbles against the deck day and night, so she'd kept herself to herself and stayed in the cabin reading the *Book of Light*. There was still so much to learn about angelic power, her abilities, and how to take down the realm.

She also had to think about what she was going to do once the ship docked in Calais. Her initial plan was a simple one—find her son. Her whisperers had spoken of a girl with a scar on her leg. A servant who had befriended a beggar with piercing blue eyes. It could be nothing. Perhaps it wasn't Zadkiel and that girl, his soulmate, but it was worth a try. Except now she'd discovered a Nephilim. Lorenzo. If she could find five more, as well as Zadkiel and a third descendant, then she had a chance to bring down the realm.

Was it possible? Was Lorenzo worth changing her plans for? Perhaps he was, but he hadn't returned to her cabin again so it was up to her to pin him down and explain how he could be part of their salvation.

The rain had turned to a light drizzle, the deck wet and slippery. Although, after days in the stuffy confines of the sleeping quarters, she was thankful for the refreshing coolness on the soles of her feet. The wind had been blowing relentlessly, whistling through the cabin at night and keeping her awake. It may have been speeding them up, but it also meant more men were needed to adjust the sails and tighten the rigging.

Lorenzo was easy to spot, the largest of the men overhead, all reduced to dark smudges against the white billowing sails.

She had to get him down, and there was only one way to do it. He wouldn't like it, but she didn't care. Pointing at his dark silhouette, she used her power to manoeuvre him through the air, down the rope ladders, pulling him down until he was a foot above the deck. He cried out as he descended. To anyone watching it looked as if he'd missed his footing and fallen, but Lorenzo would know differently. She allowed him to stop a few inches from the wooden floor, where he clung to the rope, his entire frame shaking with relief.

'Did he hit the deck?' one man called out above their heads.

'I'm fine!' Lorenzo shouted. 'I'm not hurt.'

Then he noticed Luci beside him and flinched.

'It was you!' he said under his breath. 'You could have killed me.'

'I wouldn't do that.'

He looked her up and down again. She was wearing nothing more than loose pantaloons and a shirt with the sleeves ripped off. His lips parted as he took a long breath, then he lowered his gaze to his feet. She was naked beneath the loose garments, and he could tell. Clearly Lorenzo wasn't used to seeing a woman's breasts beneath a man's shirt, a round, soft body that wasn't tethered and trapped within a corset.

'Follow me,' she said. 'I need to talk to you.'

With a speed she wasn't expecting, he dashed past her, racing to the front of the ship and down a flight of stairs. Why, oh why, did he think he could escape her? Unless he was planning to jump into the ocean, he couldn't get away. And even then, she'd only drag him back.

Calmly, for Luci was in no rush, she followed him into the deepest depths of the ship. Through the galley, past a room full of hammocks, deeper still until she was surrounded by rows of cannons and ammunition. Down she followed him through stores filled with barrels, until they reached the lowest tier where there was nothing but more barrels and pools of rope.

Upon hearing her light tread Lorenzo spun around. Not only had she followed him, but he was cornered.

'Don't hurt me,' he said, his voice rushing out in one long breath. 'Please.'

'I don't want to hurt you. I just want to speak to you.'

'It was you that changed the direction of the ship, wasn't it?'

She nodded. 'I need to go to France.'

'Well, I need to go to England!' he shouted. 'I wouldn't have volunteered to work on this ship for such little pay if it wasn't going where I needed to go.'

'And the rubies,' she said nonchalantly.

Although it was dark four floors below deck, the space lit by nothing but the thin light through the cracks in the wooden ceiling, she saw Lorenzo's face blanch at the mention of the gemstones.

'I know it's what you want. Come to my cabin, listen to what I have to tell you, and you can have them.'

He opened his mouth to reply when a sudden cry of anger erupted from the corner of the room. Luci hadn't noticed the metal bars beside her. She'd been standing next to a cell, and inside the cage was Samuel, the one-eyed cook.

He grabbed her arm and pulled her backwards against the bars, taking both her wrists in his large hand.

'I knew I wasn't crazy!' he shouted in her ear. The fabric covering his missing eye was no longer there, leaving a gaping hole like a second mouth in his head. 'Run, Lorenzo. I have the witch. I'll kill her. Then everyone will be able to see I'm not mad.'

Luci didn't struggle, because she was in no real danger. In fact, this had turned into a very interesting predicament. What was the Nephilim going to do? Would he run away again, use the powers she knew he had to try and kill her, or would he protect her?

Right now, Lorenzo was doing nothing but staring in wide-eyed horror.

'The captain didn't know I had a knife in my apron pocket,' Samuel cried out, laughing maniacally. Luci felt the cold caress of a blade against her arm. 'No one thought to check me, did they? Me, mad? As if! I'm the only one she hasn't put under a spell. You and I, Lorenzo, are too strong for her evil powers.'

This was the Nephilim's chance to prove himself. Which way was he going to go?

Arms pulled tight behind her, the cold bars of the cage hard against her head, Luci jerked as she felt the blade dig into the flesh of her arm.

'No!' Lorenzo cried out. 'Don't hurt her!'

He thrust his own arm into the cell, but Samuel moved out of his reach, pulling Luci closer to him.

She cried out, not in fear or pain but in surprise. The motherfucker was slitting her wrist! She would give Lorenzo five more seconds before she snapped both their necks.

Then she saw it, the pool of rope beside her unfurling like a giant python. Lorenzo was staring at it and directing it into the cell. The cook was too intent on digging his rusty blade into Luci's wrists to notice the rope wind its way behind him, rising up, wrapping itself over his shoulders. By the time he felt the weight of it around his neck it was already strangling him, and Luci was free.

With one swift move Lorenzo pulled her toward him and clamped his mouth against her bloody wrist. Her first instinct was to pull away, but instead, she let him. She was curious, and the sensation of his warm lips against her sore wrist was surprisingly pleasant.

'What are you doing?' she asked.

'Stemming the flow of blood.'

'With your mouth?'

Keeping her wrist pressed to his open lips he fumbled with his top, ripping at the hem until he had a long strip of fabric. He let go of her arm and wound the ripped piece of shirt quickly around the wound.

'I thought you were one of them. You were reading their language, and you lifted me off the rigging,' he said, wiping his bloody mouth with the back of his arm. 'But when I saw you bleeding, I realised you couldn't be an angel. If you were, you would have defended yourself against Samuel, and you didn't.'

'Thank you,' she said, looking at the crumpled remains of the cook beneath a mound of thick rope. She hadn't needed saving, of course she didn't, but Lorenzo had done the right thing. He was also speaking of angels. Now was the time to talk.

'I feel a little peculiar,' he said, licking at the corner of his mouth still slick with her blood.

His eyes began to glow black, like a panther in the night. Perhaps it was the lack of light, but for the first time Luci noticed the contours of the Nephilim's body, how the muscles of his arms and legs strained against his clothes. He looked even bigger beneath the ship than he did aboveboard.

'Do you feel ill, Lorenzo? Drama can do that to a man.'

He gave a quiet chuckle. 'I can deal with drama, Luci. It's not sickness I feel, it's something…strange. Good. Although *you* won't be feeling very well if we stay here any longer. We need to look at your wound. Let me help you.'

'I'll be fine,' she said.

He nodded at the makeshift bandage on her arm and opened his mouth to say something, then stopped. No blood had seeped through the white cotton. Luci looked away, knowing what was coming next.

'I don't understand, you should be...' He began to unwrap the fabric slowly.

Oh no, this wasn't going to end well. Perhaps if she distracted him, she could buy more time. But what was the point? As soon as he saw that her skin had healed perfectly, the game was up. She had to tell him the truth.

The whites of his eyes glowed as they widened, staring at Luci's arm in shock. He rubbed it. Beneath the faint smudge of dry blood there was nothing. No more gaping wound.

'You... How... What are you?' He backed away, shaking his head from side to side slowly. 'I didn't save you, did I? It was a trap and I walked right into it. Keep away from me, you witch. I want nothing to do with you or your kind, *whatever the hell you are!*'

'Wait! Lorenzo, you can't hide from me.'

'You're invisible to everyone else, so you will be invisible to me too,' he shouted over his shoulder as he climbed up to the next level.

'Fine,' she shouted up at him. 'You really want to play this game? I can do that. You'll come looking for me eventually, though. You'll see.'

She rubbed the blood off her arm with the white strip of fabric, the corners of her mouth rising slowly into a half-smile. Lorenzo was smart, strong, and powerful. He also had a good heart. All Luci had to do was stop him from fearing her. It seemed she'd found her entertainment after all.

With a touch of her hand, she unlocked the cell door, put the rope back in its place, and sat the cook against the wall. He still had the knife in his clasped fist, so she ran it against his throat and let him slump to the ground.

That would do. No one was going to ask any questions about a madman killing himself.

Locking the cell door again, she climbed the ladders and stepped back into the sunlight.

She had one little task left to perform, and then she could change out of her blood-splattered clothes and wait for Lorenzo to come calling.

She made a bet with herself that he wouldn't last more than a day.

IV.

Luci woke with a start at the sound of the cabin doors flying open and smashing against the wall. Jumping out of bed, wearing nothing but a white undershirt as a nightdress, she only made it two steps until she was thrown against the wall by Lorenzo. Pushing himself flat against her, he banged his fist against the wall by the side of her head.

'Damn you to hell, Luci!' he hissed, his breath in her ear making the tiny hairs on the side of her neck stand on end. 'You made me invisible, didn't you? You petty, vengeful *bitch*. I had a plan and you're ruining it!'

She smiled, a slow smile that infuriated him further. His entire body stiffened with anger against hers. Was he growling? A low hum emanated from his throat, vibrating through his whole body, including his chest pressed against hers. It made her nipples ache. Interesting.

'You wouldn't talk to me,' she said.

'Because I know what you are, and I won't have anything to do with your world. You lost me my crew and destroyed my plans and now you want me to *talk* to you?'

'I need your help.'

'Why should I help you?'

Lorenzo's temper didn't scare her. Luci had the power to end his life in under a second. He knew it too but was clearly too angry to care. Wasn't this what she wanted though? Wasn't this why she'd been goading him, to get a reaction—any reaction?

'Are you enjoying all these emotions of yours?' she said quietly. 'Now you have no access to anyone else and can finally feel something?'

She'd taken him by surprise. His body softened against her and he stepped back, hands by his side.

'You know?'

'Of course. I know everything there is to know about Nephilim.'

Standing up straight, even at her tallest, Luci only reached Lorenzo's chest. His sleeves were rolled up and she trailed her hand over his biceps, hardly touching his skin. Her touch made his neck pink, his eyes following the path of her fingers as she outlined the dark markings on his skin. Tattoos were rare, generally reserved for Pacific Islanders and obscure tribes. Luci liked them.

'Is it strange to react to my touch, instead of focussing on my emotions?' Lorenzo looked away, but his jaw remained tense. 'Is it strange to be locked in a room with a woman yet not be able to sense her at all? To only be aware of your own feelings? Your body's reaction to mine?'

'You disgust me,' he said, shaking her off. 'Manipulative, demanding, arrogant, and wanton.'

His words slammed against her harder than his body had done, but she didn't allow the hurt to show. What did it matter what he thought of her? She didn't care about him. She only cared about how he and his kind could help her find Zadkiel and destroy Mikhael. That was all she wanted from this man.

'I'll pay you,' she said.

'To do what?'

'Listen to my story.'

'How much?'

'The captain's rubies. I told you, I have them.'

He looked at her from beneath his hooded eyes, darker than the deepest depths of the ocean. He didn't trust her. She didn't blame him. She'd not given him much of a reason to so far.

'Show them to me.'

She crossed the room and took out the pouch from her trunk, tipping the pea-sized gems into the palm of her hand.

His face was expressionless, but his eyes glimmered. Before she had a chance to react, he snatched them out of her hand, stuffed them in his mouth and swallowed. With a crooked smile he bowed and turned to leave the room.

Luci laughed silently to herself. He thought he was so clever—except he'd forgotten two things. One, she was stronger than him, and two, they were both invisible to all on board. No one was going to come to his rescue.

She allowed him to think he'd beaten her and chuckled to herself as he climbed up to the deck with a cocky swagger. Stupid boy.

Outside, men were swarming every which way, moving cargo and shouting at one another, but no one paid attention to their friend walking amongst them. With a flick of her finger, she pulled on Lorenzo's ankles and sent him flying facedown onto the deck, landing with such force a rush of air escaped from his chest with a grunt. He bared his teeth like a feral hound, his head swivelling from side to side searching for Luci, but no amount of flailing could reach her. She twirled her finger and he flipped onto his back, arms pinned to his sides.

'Two can play this game,' she purred.

Trapped on the ground, unable to move, he uttered every profanity under the sun in a variety of languages. Still no one could hear him.

'These emotions of yours,' she said, sitting astride him in nothing but one of the captain's old shirts. 'They're really intense now that you're finally paying attention to them, am I right? Tell me, how do I make you feel?'

'I hate you,' he said, his face contorted into a vicious snarl.

'I don't think you do. I think I scare you, which in turn excites you.'

'Don't flatter yourself,' he said, refusing to look her in the eye, his plump lips puckered in defiance.

She leaned closer to him. His torso felt cool against her soft cleavage, his heart beating faster and faster beneath hers. Little puffs of air tickled her cheek as his breath quickened. Perhaps Lorenzo *did* hate her, but his mind had forgotten to let his body know.

'Give the rubies back,' she said, her lips inches from his.

'Too late.'

'It's never too late.'

She placed her finger on his stomach and slowly followed the line of his taut abdominal muscles up to his broad chest. His eyes widened, head shaking side to side in tiny motions.

'No. Oh god, you can't,' he said.

She smiled. Oh god, she could.

Past his chest, she continued to stroke her finger up and over his throat until he began to choke. Men continued to walk around them, stepping over their friend's legs, oblivious to the drama unfolding before them. He thrashed against her, his strong body now powerless between her legs. Lorenzo was no match for her, and she wasn't going to let him go. His coughing got stronger until he was gagging.

She lowered her lips to his as the rubies finally worked their way up his throat and into his mouth. Her plan had been to suck them from his mouth, because when Luci made a point she liked it to be remembered. Except, as her mouth closed over his, something happened she'd never experienced before.

She made the mistake of looking at him, really looking at him, and he was staring back at her with such intensity that she momentarily lost her power over him. His eyes, hooded and cloudy with desire, held her gaze until she felt every part of her beginning to melt. Falling. Sinking. His hands, no longer held down by her magic, slowly slid over her waist and under the thin cotton of her shirt, revealing her thighs and bare behind. He pressed his fingers against the base of her spine, and she shuddered.

This wasn't right. What was he doing to her? Her powers were blocked. She couldn't think or do or... Her breaths shaky, her chest rising and falling, she was keenly aware that her shirt had gaped open, her breasts falling forward against his chest. He'd noticed, but only fleet-ingly. His gaze was still hooked on hers, sucking her in deeper. Then, so fast she had no time to stop him, he sat up and flipped her onto her back until she was pinned beneath him. Resting all his weight on his el-bows, his hands on either side of her face, he stroked his thumbs against her face, her neck, her collarbone in gentle circles. The light caress on her skin caused a light whimper to escape her lips. What was he doing to her? What magic was this?

Then suddenly he broke eye contact, turned his head to the side and spat out the rubies onto the deck. They skittered at the feet of the crew who looked at one another in bewilderment. They couldn't see their crewmate, nor the half-naked woman pinned beneath him. Not stopping to question from where the stones had come, they scrambled to the floor, scooping them up and holding them up to the sunlight.

Lorenzo ignored them. His body hovering over Luci's, his hands now cupping her face, he tilted his head to one side.

'I know you better than you think I do,' he said.

His body entirely covered hers, but they weren't touching. His weight was resting on his forearms, yet Luci's chest felt like it was be-neath a tonne of iron. Paralysed. She went to reply, but as her lips part-ed, he lowered his mouth to hers and kissed her.

She had no intention of kissing him back. She'd played these pow-er games before, although normally it was her who instigated them. Men would do anything for a woman when sex was involved. These sordid exchanges weren't something Luci took any pleasure in—but they were an effective means to an end.

Yet as the heat from Lorenzo's mouth ignited hers, her body re-sponded without waiting for her. His fingers were lost in her hair and she instinctively clasped her hands to the back of his head, pulling him to her. His tongue found hers and he groaned, that same primal growl that had vibrated through her in the cabin less than an hour earlier. The pull between them was deep, urgent, and hungry.

Teeth clashing and lips bruising, Lorenzo kissed her like he wanted to consume her very soul. Her entire body reacted to his touch, every inch of her skin alive and calling for him. She flipped him back over until they were rolling on the deck, their mouths fused together. When they finally stopped, she found herself on top and it was him clawing at her back, pushing her hard against him.

'Enough!' she shouted, clambering off and pulling down her shirt so it covered her thighs once more. The heat between her legs was dizzying. She closed her eyes and steadied her breath. 'This is not what I'm here for.'

Her voice was thick and hoarse and not convincing either of them. She had no idea what had just happened, but in the seventeen centuries she'd spent living as a woman she had never reacted like that to a man. Of course she'd kissed men before, and women—occasionally both at once. Seduction was, at times, a more powerful force than magic. She'd even allowed men to have sex with her, thinking maybe just maybe she'd carry a baby again, but no one had ever kissed her like that. It had never been about her own pleasure.

This wasn't going to end well. She didn't trust Lorenzo, and right now she didn't trust her own body. Luci was indestructible, but her soul was not. Luci was reckless, but she didn't take risks with her heart.

The crew continued to rush aboard the ship, exclaiming each time they discovered another ruby and pocketing them quickly. Lorenzo, stretched out on the deck and resting back on his elbows, appeared completely unfazed by the commotion of the crew or Luci's reaction. His hair had come out of its ribbon, falling over his face like that of a feral warrior, and his chest rose and fell as if he'd just been beaten in battle.

'I don't think either of us was expecting that,' he said, looking up at her in a way that made her feel naked.

She tugged at her shirt and pulled it closed at her neck. 'You lost the rubies.'

'Fuck the rubies. You wanted to talk, let's talk.'

No. Luci wasn't interested in this half-man anymore. To remain strong meant not getting attached to anything or anyone—it was how she'd survived for so long and stayed on top. Lorenzo could keep his shiny black eyes and lopsided smile and arms like tree-trunks and... With a flick of her wrist she sent him skidding on his backside along the polished deck until he crashed into the wooden balustrade behind him. Then she marched to the captain's quarters and slammed the large wooden door shut, ensuring it was locked in a way that no Nephilim magic could unlock.

She had to think. *Think!* Eyes screwed shut, a shake of her head, a series of heavy sighs. It was impossible. Every time she tried to focus on her plan, on all the Nephilim she was searching for, all she could think about was the feel of Lorenzo's lips against hers.

It was better to walk away from this before it went any further. She didn't need anyone in her life. Where there were people, there were complications. It didn't even matter that Lorenzo was half angelic, she was never going to get all the components in place at the same time anyway. So why bother recruiting him? It would be torturous to have someone like him around, making her mind crazy with anger and her body...

There was a pounding at the door.

'Luci!' Lorenzo bellowed. The mechanism in the door clicked unsuccessfully as he tried to unlock it. 'Let me in!' he shouted. 'We need to talk.'

She ignored him, just as all the crew on the ship were doing. He'd get bored eventually.

After a few minutes of pounding, he stopped. There was a light thud as he slid against the door on the other side and sat on the floor with a thump.

'That was new for me too,' he said quietly.

Luci moved to the wooden steps on her side of the door and sat down, ten inches of thick mahogany separating them. Lorenzo continued to talk, as if Luci listening or not made no difference to him either way.

'All my life I've been able to feel the emotions of others. I know you know this about us half-beings, but have you ever experienced it? Do you know what it's like to feel judged all your life? To feel what others think of you, yet never truly know your own mind or…heart?'

Silence. She waited, pressing her ear against the door. Was that his breathing she could hear, or the lapping of the ocean outside her window?

Perhaps he was waiting for her to reply, but what was the use? She was getting off this ship in five weeks and had no intention of seeing Lorenzo again. She had two goals in life, find her boy and destroy Mikhael—she wouldn't allow her energy or emotions to be directed elsewhere.

'You were right,' he said. 'You scare me. I'm terrified of you and I'm not used to it. I'm not a man who is easily rattled. Do you enjoy people fearing you, Luci?'

Hands in her lap, she twisted the amethyst rings on her fingers, thinking back to the day she'd terrorised an entire town and killed its residents by setting hundreds of crows upon them. Had she enjoyed listening to their fearful screams, watching them writhe in the icy mud as they were reduced to nothing more than a mass of bloodied rags? She had. That was who she was—the antithesis of good. Exactly what Mikhael had told the world she would be. But if Lorenzo feared her, why had he kissed her? He'd more than kissed her. He'd set her alight and ignited a dormant ember inside of her which was still glowing in the pit of her stomach. She also knew it would take but one tiny breath from his lips to turn that ember into a raging inferno. The thought was terrifying. Now they were both living in fear.

'You know why you scare me?' he continued. 'It's not what you are or your powers. I respect that. In fact, I'm in awe of it. I'm scared because I can't feel you and I want to. I really want to. As I said before…I know you.'

She rubbed her face in exasperation. 'What do you mean, you *know* me?'

She hadn't meant to say it out loud.

Now he knew she was listening his voice grew louder and more eager. 'I can see it in your eyes and the way you hold yourself. I don't need to be able to feel your emotions because I can see them written all over your face. You're sad and angry and hurt, and I want to know why. I've never had that—I've never wanted to know more about someone. But you, you're…'

Luci opened the door. He towered over her, a tanned, ferocious god carved from mighty oak and storm-weathered seas, eyes of starless skies and a body that shuddered with every laboured breath. Injured bears were often mistaken as helpless and approachable, but Luci knew animals at their most vulnerable were also at their most dangerous.

He followed her into the cabin, shutting the door quietly behind him and joining her on the floor where she sat with her back against the bed.

'Tell me your story,' he said gently.

'No.'

'Maybe I can help.'

She laughed. It sounded bitter and brittle. 'Nobody can help me.'

'Then let me listen.'

So she began at the beginning, in a world that didn't exist, a world where the first light was one of her own creation. Then she spoke of a perfect life filled with baby cuddles and fragrant flowers, and how she was brutally murdered and came back too late. And once she started to tell her tale she couldn't stop. It was a long, long story spanning epochs and lifetimes, a story filled with angels and demons, light and dark. She told him who she was, what she was, and what she wanted. He didn't flinch nor run away this time; he stayed and listened. As the words tumbled out and day turned to night, she heard her thoughts made real, and her shoulders slumped as she realised the futility of her life. As an angel she'd had her Choir, her friends, and as a mother she'd had her son, but as Luci she only had herself. The only one she could depend on. The only one that stayed.

Her story got easier to tell with every word. And as much as it physically hurt to tell, she comforted herself with the knowledge that it didn't matter that Lorenzo knew everything about her now. Words and people could be deleted from his memory; she had the power to make him forget. She was still safe.

At the mention of her time in Roermond and the *Book of Light* Lorenzo sat up.

'Azantiel was the Dutch witch's father?' he said. 'I've heard about her, and this book. He was my mother's father too.'

Over hundreds of years the rebel angel Azantiel had been responsible for bringing forth a number of Nephilim in the vain hope he could produce enough to assist with the downfall of the realm. But Mikhael had discovered his deceit and killed him. Her whisperers had told her about it just after she fled Spanish Holland. Mikhael eventually finished anyone who ever crossed him—including Luci.

'You descend from Azantiel?' she asked. 'Then you are only a quarter angel?'

Lorenzo smiled, a sad smile that made her chest fill with warm liquid.

'No, my father was an angel too. Zepar.'

Lorenzo was more angel than man! That explained a lot. It also explained his eyes, the ones she'd seen before in another. Zepar was a fighter, one of the realm's strongest warrior angels. She hadn't imagined him as a deserter—he'd appeared far too loyal to Mikhael in her time to ever lie with a human. Lorenzo must have guessed what she was thinking.

'He was avenging his friend, Azantiel. When my grandfather was murdered, Zepar vowed he would continue his work. Azantiel had schooled my mother in everything she needed to know about the realm. She could read angelic script and taught me and my siblings how to read and write in your language. She begged Zepar to give her children. She wanted to help bring an end to the tyranny.'

Luci grabbed the top of Lorenzo's arm. Her hand looked tiny against his flesh and hardly made a dent.

'Children? There are more of you?'

He swallowed and looked down.

'There were eight of us. Four girls and four boys. My mother called us the salvation of the world, the bringers of light. We all had Zepar's black eyes which got brighter with age, and she taught us how to use our powers. But…'

Luci didn't want to hear what happened after the 'but.' She could guess. She knew what Mikhael was capable of.

Her grip on his arm loosened and he gave a small nod.

'Archangel Michael found us in the end. Zepar could only protect us so far, but hiding was impossible. Mikhael killed my mother first. He wanted our father and all his children to watch her suffer.'

Luci covered her face with her hands. *Fucking bastard.* At least her own son had been spared from watching his mother being slain.

'Then he killed my baby brother. He was easy to dispose of; he was still in my mother's arms when she was slaughtered. One by one he murdered my brothers and sisters and then, when he thought we were all dead, he butchered the angel and set his wings on fire.'

No wonder Lorenzo had been fearful of her when he thought she was an angel. No wonder he'd despised her.

'How did you survive?' she asked, her voice so small it was hardly a whisper.

'My younger sister Rosa and I had been playing in a nearby field. When we arrived home and saw angels, huge wings we didn't recognise, we hid behind a cart. Mikhael was so sure of himself, so certain that he'd killed the six Nephilim that had been produced to aid his destruction, that he hadn't considered there may be more of us. Rosa and I watched our entire family die that day.'

Luci didn't cry often. She had seen more death and destruction than was humanly possible. She'd murdered, maimed, and tortured with pure abandonment, never giving it a second thought. Civilisations had been wiped out before her eyes as plagues and wars ravaged entire nations. Even Luci herself had died and risen countless times. She knew pain—and after spending lifetime after lifetime searching for her son, she also knew loss and failure. Yet the thought of a young Lorenzo and his little sister watching everybody they loved slaughtered by the one being she hated more than anything in this rotten world was too much. She let the tears fall, too exhausted by life's cruelty to wipe them away.

Without saying a word, Lorenzo leaned forward and brushed the back of his hand against her wet cheek. His touch scorched her damp skin.

'What did you do next?' she asked.

'What can a thirteen-year-old boy and his seven-year-old sister do? We survived, for a while. After the angels left, I ran back into the house. The floor was slippery with blood, and it took all my strength not to look at the faces of my dead family. I salvaged as many essentials from our home as I could carry, food and clothing, knowing we'd never be safe there again. Rosa and I lived in the woods for a few weeks, then we walked from village to village begging and stealing. I knew it wouldn't last long though. By the time we reached the port of Lisbon we were captured by a gang of men who'd heard about the family with magical children. They called us Sentients—mind readers. It wasn't entirely accurate, they knew nothing about the realm, but regardless of where our powers came from, they knew we were still a valuable asset they could sell. After striking us hard enough to knock us out, they carried us through the crowd of the harbour market over their shoulders like we were nothing but dead deer from a hunt. Rosa was concussed and hanging as limp as a doll, but I faked my injuries and kept watch instead. Although after a while it was clear where they were taking us. I'd seen these men in the market, trading in humans, and I'd also seen the cages on their cart where they kept their stock. Gathering all my strength I struggled, kicking and biting, and eventually released myself from the man's grip and fell to the floor. I was big for my age, but I was also fast. I ran to the nearest ship and hid aboard, watching the men bundle my sister onto their cart. My plan was to come back for her that night, to break her free before she was sold, except the ship sailed away before the sun set.'

Luci placed a hand on his arm, and he swallowed.

'I was hysterical. So scared, and so worried. I fought the crew like a wild beast, threatening to jump into the ocean and swim back to my Rosa. When they eventually calmed me down, they said I could stay, that a boy with my strength would be useful. So I did. And I've been on the high seas ever since.'

'And your sister?'

He shrugged. 'I don't know what happened to her, but I'm heading back to Europe to find out. I last heard she was in England. That's why I was so angry when you changed the direction of the ship.'

'I thought it was because you had plans for mutiny. To steal the captain's treasure.'

He bit down on his lower lip and gave her a lopsided smile. 'Perhaps that as well.'

'An orphaned rogue turned pirate.'

Lorenzo shrugged. 'You're no angel either, Luci.'

'Ah, but I was once.'

He laughed. It was the first time she'd heard him laugh and it washed over her like cool water on a hot day. It was a sound she wanted to hear every day.

Luci stood up and made her way to the large dining table in the centre of the room and poured two cut-glass goblets of whisky. It was dark outside. She had no idea if they were closer to sunset or sunrise. Lorenzo joined her and she handed him the drink.

'Stay,' she said.

He raised one eyebrow. 'So you like me now?'

'I didn't say that, but at least you trust me.'

'I didn't say that,' he replied with a smile.

'Well, I'm the only one that can see you on this ship, so you may as well take advantage of my company.'

He raised both eyebrows this time and she laughed.

'Not in that way.'

'Why not?'

'Because sex ruins everything.'

He took a sip of whisky while eyeing her over the rim of the glass. His gaze was melting her insides again, making the drink burn and churn inside her stomach.

'I'm sorry for the way I treated you before,' he said. 'I thought you were one of them. An angel, returning to finish me off.'

Luci shook her head slowly. 'I'm nothing like Mikhael. I hate that bastard as much as you do. There's nothing I won't do to get my revenge on him.'

'You must have loved him once, though,' Lorenzo said, taking another sip of whisky. 'He fathered your son, right?'

'I never loved him. I wanted a baby, and only an angel could give me one of those.'

'If you didn't like him, why not choose a different archangel?'

Luci thought of Gabriel and her chest swelled with longing. She missed him. She missed all her old friends, but especially him. She would never have asked that of her friends though, because she knew Mikhael would have put a stop to it. The only child he wouldn't harm was his own.

'Mikhael is the strongest of all angels, one of the first, and I knew I could seduce him. That part is never difficult with male bodies.'

Lorenzo frowned. 'Not just men's bodies. Surely all human bodies have needs,' he said.

'No. Not a woman's. This body I chose was not made for sexual pleasures.'

'That's not true.'

Luci laughed, clasping her hands over her mouth to keep the drink from flying out. She swallowed, ignoring the burn as the whisky slid down her throat.

'Excuse me? I've walked this Earth as a woman for seventeen hundred years and *you're* telling *me* that you, a young man in your late twenties, know what women feel better than I do?'

He shrugged. 'Yes. All my life I've felt nothing but the emotions of others. This is the first time I've been alone with a woman, not including my mother or sisters, where I haven't been engulfed by what she is feeling. I have felt women's emotions and I have lived them. I know.'

Luci put down her goblet and inched closer.

'Really? You know? Tell me how.'

Lorenzo put down his own glass, his bottom lip trapped between his teeth.

'I'd been sailing for a couple of years and I'd learned to speak quite a few languages well enough: English, French, Spanish, Italian, and I already spoke Portuguese, of course. Believe me, it's not easy being stuck aboard a ship full of men your entire adult life—especially if they come from all over the world and all you can feel is their needs—so languages help. But feeling their emotions *didn't* help. There's a lot of anger, irritation, boredom, and hunger on long voyages, but most of all trapped men get randy as hell.'

Luci grinned. 'I can imagine.'

'They say that women are bad omens on ships, but that's nonsense. They just aren't safe. Not because men *can't* control themselves, but because they choose not to. Anyway, I was fifteen, nearly sixteen, when we landed in the port of Southampton in England. It's an old, decaying place, far from pretty, but it was where the cheapest prostitutes could be found. My crewmates didn't care what these women looked like. After months of sailing, they just wanted to put their dicks somewhere warm and wet.'

Luci made a face and he laughed.

'Sorry, but there's nothing romantic about being a sailor. As you can imagine I was nervous about visiting one of these establishments, but I was also looking forward to discovering what all the fuss was about. Although I should have known better. A brothel is not somewhere a boy with sentient abilities should go if he doesn't want to be utterly overwhelmed by a variety of sensations—and not all of them lustful.'

'Was it awful?'

'No, just sad. The contrast between the emotions of the men and the women was so extreme I ran straight back out. A young girl my age chased me and pulled me back in, dragging me to a dark corner and rubbing her hands all over me. I couldn't tap into my own feelings though. All I could sense was how sad and bored she was.'

Luci thought back to all the men she'd slept with. Sex made things easier sometimes, and took little effort on her part, but she never did it for pleasure. No woman enjoyed carnal pursuits.

'Well, sex *is* sad and boring,' she said

'But a woman's body was created to be enjoyed.'

'By men,' she said.

'*No*. By *them*, enjoyed by the *woman*. You have a lot more ways of enjoying sex than we do.'

Luci rolled her eyes and stood up to fill her glass. The boy knew nothing.

'Let me guess, you had sex with this girl and she thanked you?' Luci said.

'No. I've never had intercourse, but I've spent a lot of time in brothels.'

She stopped pouring and turned around slowly.

'That makes no sense.'

Lorenzo joined her at the table and placed his empty glass beside hers.

'I never had sex with these women. I couldn't get aroused, because I was only feeling what they were. So instead I listened. Not to what they were saying, but what they were feeling. I spent more time in brothels when ashore than I did in taverns with my crewmates. They thought I was simply a randy kid who wanted to waste his meagre earnings on cheap whores. But it wasn't that. I desperately wanted to understand women. And I was a very attentive student.' Lorenzo glanced up at Luci and gave her a look that made her stomach lurch. 'My reasoning was that one day I would be married, and the least my wife deserved was a man who could make her happy in every way. I couldn't stand the thought of fulfilling my own physical desires with someone I loved knowing she didn't feel the same way. Anyway, I eventually got very good at satisfying a woman.'

Luci gave a sharp bark of a laugh. 'That's impossible.'

There was nothing satisfying about sex for a woman. It made children and it made men happy—that was it. Luci had chosen to have a young female body on Earth because it gave her power and it got her noticed, not because she would be able to get any pleasure from it.

Lorenzo was looking at her strangely, eyes dark slits of concentration.

'Are you telling me that in *seventeen hundred years* you have never been pleasured by a man?'

She thought of their kiss earlier, and how little control she'd had over her body and mind. She had no intention of losing herself like that again.

'What man is interested in pleasing a woman if he gains nothing himself?'

He shrugged. 'Me.'

Her stomach twisted like sharp metal, liquid heat pooling in her guts. Yet deep inside her chest something was buzzing.

'I wish I could feel what you're feeling right now,' he said quietly.

'Indifference and irritability.'

'You're lying. I may not be able to sense you, but I can tell what you want. Your pupils have dilated, and your hand has crept closer to mine on the tabletop.' Luci snatched her hand away, but he continued. 'You keep brushing your tongue against your bottom lip because your mouth has gone dry, and you're breathing shallower than normal. Am I right?'

She stood up straight and squared her shoulders. What was he playing at? She could pick him up with a flick of her finger and throw him out to sea. She could snap his neck with a blink of an eye. He was messing with the wrong woman.

'Not only can I not feel you, Luci, but this is my first time standing beside a woman where I'm acutely aware of my own emotions.'

Luci cleared her throat. 'And what are they?'

'Intense. Verging on painful.'

The cabin was bathed in dark hues of blues and greys and all was silent, save for the gentle lull of the sea against the hull as it rocked the ship like a cradle. She ignored his response and lit a number of large candles with a click of her finger until the room was ablaze in warm amber light. Immediately she wished she hadn't, because now she could see Lorenzo's face clearly, and it was filled with a need so strong she had to cross her legs beneath her flimsy shirt to steady herself.

'I'm not here for your amusement, Lorenzo. Don't fuck with me. I could kill you in an instant.'

'I know. Would you like me to leave?'

'No. Stay,' she said, for the second time that day.

His lips tugged up in the corners, slowly, so slowly that she had to lean against the table to steady herself. What was he doing to her? What magic was this?

'Prove it,' she said.

Lorenzo rubbed the back of his neck. 'Prove what?'

'That a woman's body is made for pleasure.'

He stepped closer to her, his towering frame making everything dark again. Tipping her chin up, he lightly stroked her lower lip with his thumb.

'Are you sure?' he whispered, leaning so close his own lips grazed the shell of her ear. She held her breath.

'I'm curious.'

'Curious is good,' he replied, planting a light kiss on her neck.

She felt herself weaken again. She reached out to support herself against the table, but he wrapped his arm around her waist and caught her. With a single swoop he picked her up and placed her gently on the bed.

'What do you need me to do?' she asked, trying to keep her voice from shaking.

'Nothing,' he replied. 'That's the whole point.'

V.

Luci and Lorenzo didn't leave her bed for a week.

For seventeen hundred years Luci had been avoiding love. She knew it existed, she'd loved her son passionately from the very first moment she felt him kick inside her, and she still loved him. But that was instinctive; a mother's love wasn't something you chose. But loving a lover was, and she'd been very good at avoiding it for a very long time.

She'd always believed that the love in fairy tales, the ones described in plays and song, was something created by humans to excuse outlandish behaviour and impulsive wonts. How could one person truly love another to the point where they would die for them? It went against every primal instinct that fragile humans required for survival.

Love was nonsense…yet it had finally caught up with her.

'We need food,' Lorenzo said, his naked chest flush against her back. They were a perfect fit, his body a shell that encased hers perfectly. He nuzzled the back of her neck and she moved against him, smiling as he groaned softly in her ear.

'I don't need to eat, remember.'

'Would you have me starve?' he teased, his fingers traveling lightly across her abdomen and down between her legs. She closed her eyes and sighed at his touch.

Was he the only man in the world who knew how to do this? The only one that had learned how a woman's body was capable of responding? How could she have lived for so long in human form without knowing that delicious secret, something she could even do to herself when alone? He'd been so proud of himself proving her wrong, and he'd been just as emotional when she'd pleased him back—his first time in bed with a woman where he was aware of his own pleasure. They'd been greedy with one another, ravenous, experiencing every single possible indulgence together. In the bed, on the table, against the window. They'd even ventured onto the small balcony along the back of the cabin and made love beneath the stars. The sea breeze had caressed their naked bodies and blown hair into each other's mouths as they'd kissed hungrily, making up for a lifetime of starvation. Plus, they both had powers and magic and were invisible to everyone on board, which made for some very interesting experiences.

'Are there no more biscuits left?' she said. 'I took some from the stores yesterday, along with the salted meat.'

'Maybe. It doesn't matter. I don't want to move,' he said, pulling her closer to him.

There had been a commotion outside the cabin a few days ago, cries of concern signalling the chef had been found dead below deck, but as instructed nobody had entered the captain's cabin. Luci and Lorenzo were living just outside of reality, safely tucked up in their own private cocoon. Death was common on galleon ships such as this one, and Luci imagined they'd probably thrown the chef overboard, relieved there was one less mouth to feed. No one seemed to be missing Lorenzo either, which suited her just fine.

'I've never felt this way about anyone,' Lorenzo whispered into her neck as his fingers slid further between her thighs and moved inside her. She closed her eyes and gave in to the wonder of his touch. Would it always be this good? Could it be? Was her mind clouded by passion, a basic physiological reaction that fooled her into thinking that these emotions meant something? Or was love real?

Her son was certainly besotted with that Arabella girl. He'd been fawning over her for centuries and Luci was sure they hadn't had a physical relationship like she was experiencing right now. Maybe angels *could* love humans—although what Lorenzo was doing to her now felt more godlike than human.

She gave in to his caresses and rode wave after delicious wave of pure, sweet desire.

'I love you,' he said, as he held her trembling body against his. 'I love you, Luci.'

Nobody had ever said that to her.

Zadkiel had told her as a child that he loved his Mummia; that was normal. Men had slept with her, telling her she was beautiful and that they were enamoured by her. But no man had ever truly known her and loved her and told her so as they lay together, warm, naked bodies intertwined.

Luci turned her head to the side and found Lorenzo's lips, kissing him with everything she had. She breathed in his breaths as she clasped the back of his damp head, deepening their kisses.

'Are you crying?' he asked, bringing his strong calloused hand to her cheek. 'Are you sad? Have I said something I shouldn't have?'

She shook her head, unable to speak.

'I meant it, Luci,' he continued. 'I don't want to live without you.'

Luci's shoulders shook as she gulped down more tears. She hadn't realised what was missing from her life until it was right there, holding her, telling her that it would never be absent again.

'Is that how you feel too?' he asked, his voice tinged with uncertainty.

Oh, Lorenzo, how little he knew. She tried to answer but couldn't. She nodded instead and he held her close as they lay in silence, both lost in their own thoughts.

'Tell me something I don't know about you,' she said after a while.

'I can paint.'

She turned her body to face him and rubbed her nose against his.

'You can? Will you paint a portrait of me?'

'Oh, my love, I will fill a hundred books with sketches of your beautiful face.'

She laughed. 'You could sketch in the *Book of Light*. That way we can keep your pictures forever.'

'Absolutely, and an oil painting. A small portrait showing off your jewellery. Our salvation.'

She rested her head on his chest and he planted a kiss on the crown of her head.

But it didn't last long. Their blissful bubble was shattered by a gruff voice shouting outside their door. A voice she hadn't heard before.

Lorenzo sat up abruptly. 'Did you hear that?'

She had. There was more shouting outside. Not the usual hollers they'd become accustomed to of angry men barking orders to one another, but something more urgent and terrifying—the sound of panic and danger. Lorenzo was out of bed and dressed before Luci had a chance to pull the curtain back and look out of the window. The deck was full of sailors, most of whom she didn't recognise.

'Pirates,' he whispered.

Luci threw on trousers and a top and joined Lorenzo outside. The ship's crew still couldn't see them, but the new men could, and they were visibly startled to see a beautiful woman tying back her hair and smiling at them.

'Good morning, boys,' Luci said, as something wet splashed onto her cheek.

The body of Captain Roberts was hanging by its neck from the rigging above their heads, his blood dripping onto the slain bodies on the ship below. Pirates had managed to slaughter half the ship's crew in the few minutes it had taken for Luci to throw on some clothes.

She may have initially surprised the new men on board, but they were no longer paying her any attention as they fought their way across the deck and continued their attack. She turned to Lorenzo, but he was no longer beside her. She scanned the deck and found him halfway up the rigging, knife between his teeth. The sight of him made Luci's heart skip a beat. Not just because he looked so rugged and dashing, but because someone she loved was in danger.

Luci sighed. She had been involved in many a bloody battle, but she'd never had to worry about the safety of another. Love definitely had its downside.

With a flick of her finger, she pulled him off the rigging until he landed beside her.

'What are you doing?' he cried.

'I want to keep you safe.'

'That's *my* line,' he replied with a grin.

'I'm indestructible; I can't die. Don't be foolhardy and get yourself killed, Lorenzo. I'm going to need you later.'

He gave her a cheeky wink and ran straight into the melee. Pirates and crew members clashed against swords and daggers, a thunderous tangle of limbs and metal and blood. A thick fog began to roll onto the ship, making it harder for Luci to see who was who. Anguished cries cut through the mist as bodies flew in the air, landing with sickening thuds on the deck, or into the water beside the pirate's galleon that had sneaked up on them in the night. Luci smiled as she spotted Lorenzo throwing unsuspecting men overboard using nothing but the power of his mind, but his crew were still outnumbered. The clang of weapons clashing and the cries of fallen men was deafening, their crimson blades dazzling Luci's vision. She snapped the necks of a couple of intruders, but all she cared about was Lorenzo's safety.

Then she saw him. He was staggering, pushing his way out of a group of armed men, stumbling toward her. And he was clutching his throat.

'*No!*' she cried as she helped him to the ground. 'No, no, no.'

A gash at his neck, dark and oozing, gaped open like a bloody yawn. His throat had been slit, turning his white shirt crimson. Lorenzo couldn't die! He'd promised to stay by her side forever. He was going to help her. He *loved* her.

Lorenzo's sticky red hands grasped at her face. 'I…' Blood bubbled up through his lips, his beautiful sparkling eyes turning a dim brown. 'Luci, I…'

How could this be happening? Ten minutes ago they were in bed together, those same hands on her body, his warm breath on the back of her neck. He'd told her he loved her—and now he was dying in her arms. With a crack, his head fell back onto the deck and his empty eyes stared up at a storm-filled sky.

The world stopped. Waves ceased to churn, the wind died, and Luci's heart went silent. The fire in her veins that Lorenzo had recently ignited erupted into a river of lava that wasn't going to cease flowing until it incinerated every being in its path. She released a cry so primal, so raw, even the crew stopped mid-fight to turn to the source of the invisible sound.

'Nobody is leaving this ship alive,' she screamed, pointing at each man in turn, the sound of their splintering bones echoing in the stunned silence.

She snapped the neck of every person standing, flinging them overboard with a deafening roar. She spared those she recognised, the original crew, although a red mist of pain obscured her vision to the point where she may have murdered a few innocents too. She didn't care—she only needed enough men to get this ship to France so she could bury her man. Then she could give up on love altogether. Hate had always been a much more dependable companion anyway.

She climbed the ship's rigging faster than any animal and jumped into the crow's nest. From her lofty vantage point she took down the remaining pirates, twisting their heads clean off their bodies with nothing but a flick of her wrists. These savage bastards had murdered the only man she'd ever dared to let in. She needed to see their heads roll. She wanted to stare into their faces frozen into masks of perpetual terror and pain.

Luci didn't stop even to breathe. She pushed her hair away from her face, chest rising and falling with exertion, then as the last pirate fell she jumped down from the top of the mast and landed on all fours like a cat.

'Bravo,' a voice called out, followed by a slow clap.

She spun around to face the owner of the voice, ready to decapitate whoever had the audacity to comment.

It was Lorenzo. He was on his feet, grinning, his shirt soaked in blood but his neck very much intact.

She ran at him and he caught her, her body shaking against his with relief.

'I thought you were dead. I thought they'd killed you,' she cried, trembling so hard he had to tighten his hold on her until her body stilled.

'They did. I remember dying.' He laughed, looking up at the heavens. 'Luci, I don't know what magic you did but you bought me back from the dead.'

'I don't have that ability,' she replied. 'It's not possible.'

The original crew were completely oblivious to the couple embracing beside them. They were rooted to the spot, their faces drained of colour as they stared around them, wondering how they'd managed to defeat so many men so quickly, and why most of the pirates appeared to have their heads on backwards.

'You looked exquisite up there,' Lorenzo said, his face buried in the crook of her neck. 'Killing men with magic while drenched in my blood. My warrior. My goddess.'

He'd seen her at her ugliest, her most evil, and he hadn't recoiled. In fact, he'd enjoyed it. She ran her hands up his back and her fingers through his long hair. 'You liked that?'

'Very much so.' He pulled away and took her face in his hands. 'I love you, Luci.'

'Still?'

'Always.'

He planted the sweetest of kisses on her mouth. The two of them were covered in blood, his and that of others, and their mouths hummed with the acrid tang of metal.

'The blood,' he said.

'I don't mind it.'

'No, yours. Your blood. The other day when I held your bleeding wrist to my mouth. Remember I told you I felt strange? Fortified? It's difficult to explain, but when your blood worked its way down my throat it tasted of more than iron. It tasted sweet and wondrous. I thought the shock of what happened to you had me imagining it. But perhaps it was that which gave me strength and power. Your blood saved me.'

He stepped back from her and pulled a dagger from the sheath of an unsuspecting crew member beside him. Nobody noticed him slice his arm, nobody heard Luci gasp, and nobody saw the delight on both their faces as the cut immediately sealed itself closed.

'You made me immortal, Luci,' he said, gathering her in his arms and swinging her around. Her foot caught the back of someone's head. The man looked around in confusion, making them laugh harder.

'You'll never die?' she asked.

'It seems that way. Things are working out rather well.'

'Indeed. And I got you a boat,' she said, pointing at the pirate's galleon beside them. If anyone had been left aboard, Luci could easily brainwash them to work for Lorenzo.

He laughed. 'One each,' he said, gesturing at the captain still hanging from the rigging.

'Our own fleet. All the better for finding your sister…if that's still the plan.'

He took her hand and held it up to his lips. 'I vow to you right here and now, my beautiful, powerful Luci, that I will remain by your side for eternity. We will find my sister, and your son, and every Nephilim on this planet, and we will avenge all those that Mikhael has hurt. I want to watch his feathers burn. I want to see you stand over his crumpled form as he begs at your perfect feet. For as long as you will have me, I will fight your foe. Will you have me? Will you be my wife and travel through life side by side. Forever?'

Luci swallowed. Forever?

Her forever was a very long time, and this wasn't part of her plan. She didn't need a man to complete her—it was…dangerous. Lorenzo had softened her edges—edges that needed to remain sharp, strong, deadly. Those edges protected her and helped to keep her going. Could she survive being part of a couple without losing herself? Could she be more…rounded? She wanted to. She truly wanted to be the woman he saw before him. A woman at peace, one capable of loving and receiving love. But maybe, with him by her side, her power wouldn't be shared or taken away—it would multiply. Plus there was something else he could do for her that no man had managed to do before him.

'Yes.'

'Really?' he cried, the light in his black eyes dancing.

'On one condition.'

'Anything.'

'I want a baby.'

That was the new plan. Luci and Lorenzo would find his sister, and then her son, and they would create their own family. The beginning of the end of Mikhael's realm.

'My pleasure,' he said, bringing his lips to hers and kissing her with so much longing her legs threatened to buckle beneath her. 'Shall we start now?'

She smiled. Family really was all that mattered.

23

ZAC LOOKED UP at the ceiling fan, its soft whir making him drowsy even though he'd already slept ten hours. He still had no idea where Ella was, but she was alive, which was enough to help him sleep peacefully for the first time in a long time.

Today he would be speaking to her parents and discovering her whereabouts. He wanted to punch the air, scream for joy, and shout it from the rooftops, but instead his stomach clenched in anticipation.

He'd done very little over the last five days but swim in Ella's private and heated pool, read her books, sleep in her bed, and occasionally venture upstairs and eat something from the restaurant. No one gave him a second glance.

Eventually he'd mustered the confidence to visit the tiny chapel. It was there he'd met his mother for the first time since she'd left him as a defenceless six year old in the Tuscan hills, two thousand years ago. He'd stared up at the giant crucifix that still hung over the altar—the cross that had impaled Ella's stepbrother Sebastian. Zac still had no idea what Luci had done with the man's body, and neither did he care. He attempted to push open the secret compartment below the altar, but it had been sealed shut. When he'd enquired at reception about the library in the turret the receptionist explained it had been transformed into a Penthouse Suite, which was only accessible from a door at the base of the tower. According to them, the secret entrance was nothing but an old story, a myth, and Zac had smiled indulgently and said that of course it was.

It was probably a good thing the library was no longer there. It would have been too much to bear to relive the last time he'd seen Ella. To remember how they'd made love on her wedding day, Ella perched upon a large window seat overlooking the hotel grounds, surrounded by hundreds of old, musty books. How stupid of him to have dared to believe it was the beginning of their new life together. For one precious hour he and Ella had been together again, before his mother and Gabriel had snatched it all away from him.

The clock on the bedside table told him he still had enough time for a few laps in the pool before facing the day. Felicity and Leonardo would be arriving soon, and he wanted to be the first thing they saw when they stepped into their hotel.

• • • • •

Zac had been sitting beside the fireplace in reception for over an hour. He'd told staff to ignore him unless he spoke to them, and that was what they were doing. He'd already completed the Sudoku puzzle in the local paper, flicked through various glossy magazines, and run through what he was going to say to Ella's parents, their first meeting in twenty years. How would they react when they saw him? Because like Ella, they too believed him dead.

Lots of scenarios had run through his head while waiting for them to return, but what he hadn't expected was for Felicity to spot him before he'd seen them. Her scream was so loud that half of the hotel's staff were by her side in an instant, leaving Leonardo free to glare at him.

'Good god, Zadkiel! You could have warned us,' Ella's father shouted as he marched toward him. 'Sitting there in an armchair like a bloody ghost. Lily, *por dios*, get a hold of yourself. We knew he'd be back eventually.'

Zac spoke calmly to each member of the staff until one by one they left, leaving him alone with Leo and Felicity.

'Please, join me,' he said, signalling to the chairs by the fireplace.

Felicity perched on the edge of an armchair and sipped from a glass of water someone had fetched for her. She was staring at Zac as if he were about to turn to smoke at any moment. Gabriel had been right—Zac really hadn't thought this through.

'*Padre*,' Zac said, stepping forward with his arms outstretched.

Leonardo's stern face softened a little, and he embraced the former angel.

'I haven't been a priest for a very long time, Zadkiel,' he said. 'Please, call me Leo. Lily, relax, he's as real as he ever was. Possibly even more so.'

Felicity put her drink down and gingerly stepped forward.

'Oh, Zac,' she said, suddenly crying into his shoulder. 'Oh, you poor, poor boy. How are you? Last time I saw you…you were…and Ella was…' Her body shuddered in his arms as he held her closer.

Why hadn't this occurred to him? Why hadn't he realised how fragile humans were? If this was their reaction, then what the hell was Ella going to say when he suddenly turned up on her doorstep like the living dead? None of them had any idea he'd come back for her seventeen years ago, or that his mother had interrupted their daughter's wedding. Everyone's minds had been swept clean and he'd kept away out of respect, allowing Ella to live her preordained life. What the hell was he doing, returning to pick at old wounds?

After he thought Ella had died, he'd toyed with the idea of paying his respects, visiting her parents and telling them everything—but he reasoned they would have suffered enough. Why add more drama to their lives? But perhaps he'd been fooling himself. Perhaps it was fear that had kept him away, fear of what they would say to him. Fear of this.

Ella's parents had aged, which was another thing Zac had forgotten to factor in. Leo was now grey and bearded, his face more weathered and lined, but still his chestnut eyes radiated nothing but kindness and love. Felicity, as elegant as ever, had let her blonde hair go white, and it was cut in a sharp bob. But apart from that, she was just as slim and composed as ever.

She stepped back from Zac's embrace and cupped his face in her hands.

'Look at you, still a young boy. I'm in my early sixties and you're still that guitar-playing gypsy boy I met on the beach as a teenager. Still Ella's boyfriend who sat at my dinner table and turned my world upside down. Still the boy who died so my little girl could…' She was crying again, huge sobs that made her crumple into a heap against her husband's shoulder this time. Perhaps she was not as composed as she once was.

'Let's go upstairs, Zadkiel,' Leo said. 'It's more private up there. We have a lot to talk about and I'm sure you came to see us for a very good reason.'

Zac nodded and followed them up a flight of marble stairs, through a security door, and into a private apartment.

'Would you like a drink?' Leo asked, pouring two glasses of red wine.

Zac shook his head, walked over to the living room, and sat in an armchair. Lily joined him on the sofa opposite and thanked her husband for the drink. She took a large swig, and Zac noticed her hand shaking.

'I'm sorry,' he said. 'It was wrong of me to turn up unannounced.'

'It's fine. It's fine. Although I'm curious as to how you found us,' Leo said, elbows on knees and face full of eagerness. 'Did you return with your former abilities or…? Pray, tell. I'm intrigued. I've been twenty years desperate to discover what happened to you. You know, none of your kind has visited me since that awful night at my cottage. None of the realm acknowledge me any longer. After you…left, it was as if my life's work had been nothing but make-believe. What happened to them all? When did you return? Please, tell us.'

So many questions, Zac had no idea where to begin. He wished he'd accepted that drink after all.

'Leo, I have a confession to make.'

Felicity looked up, her eyes wide with fear. What was he doing to them? He should make them forget he was there. He should extract Ella's whereabouts from them and leave. After all, wasn't that why he'd come?

Or perhaps he needed more than that. Redemption? Forgiveness?

He wanted to see them. It was as simple as that.

Few really knew Zac—what he was, what he had been—and it felt good to be welcomed back. Until now he hadn't realised how much he'd longed for someone he cared about to ask how he was. To have been missed.

'No need to be alarmed, Felicity,' Zac said with a smile. 'I don't bring bad news, but I *have* been a little deceitful.' This wasn't going to be easy. 'I returned seventeen years ago, the day of Ella's marriage to Josh. Their path was set, so I didn't get involved. You don't remember the interruption because you were made to forget, but I did come back. And I still love your daughter—that will never change. In fact, that's why I'm here, to ask where she is. I need to see her.'

Leo put his empty wineglass down, sat beside his wife on the sofa, and crossed his arms.

'No.'

'Pardon?'

'No, Zadkiel. That won't do. That won't do at all. What we witnessed on the mountain when you sliced off your wings, what your kind did to our daughter, to *us*, changed our lives forever. None of us have been the same since. You don't just breeze in here, tell us you've been lying for twenty years, then demand I tell you where Ella is. I won't.'

Felicity was staring at the former angel. Her face was grey with exhaustion, as if his very presence had drained her of all her energy. She reached up to her throat, then dropped her hand again, realising, and probably not for the first time, that she no longer owned the necklace that had led Zac to his mother.

'Go away,' she said.

Her words were a punch to Zac's guts. He'd expected tears, a lot of shock, maybe even an outpouring of relief and love to see that he'd survived—but not this.

'Please, let me explain...'

'You heard my wife,' Leo said, standing up quickly and looming over him. 'You brought us all nothing but pain. We've spent a lot of time and money on self-development courses, books, and healing retreats to help us come to terms with what we saw. But how the hell do you describe what we went through to a therapist? You dragged our only child into this dangerous world of yours, knowing she was destined to be happy with someone else. Then you left her, *chose to leave her*, to fend for herself not knowing if that *hijo de puta* Mikhael would be back for her. Do you have any idea the dark cloud we've lived under for the last twenty years?'

Leo's voice was getting louder and louder with every word, making Zac shrink further into himself. Maybe now was the time to force them to talk, then make them forget? Zac didn't need to hear this. This was not what he'd come here for.

'Josh died, do you know that?' Felicity said. Unlike her husband's voice, hers was barely above a whisper.

Zac nodded.

'Of course you do,' she replied, dabbing at her eyes. 'You know everything. You probably know the date we will die, and the date Ella dies, and who we will be next. Why did you let her marry him, Zac? If you knew she'd be a widow by the time she was thirty-four, why show her happiness for just a few brief years? No one deserves that. No little girl deserves to lose her daddy.'

Zac had been looking down as they spoke, studying the grooves in the wooden floor and hating himself more and more with every accusation they threw at him. They were right. It was all his fault. He was selfish, obsessed, and nothing but bad news. He never should have spoken to Ella at that bus stop in Highgate. All of this could have been avoided if only he'd kept away as planned. But at the mention of Ella's child his head whipped up. He wasn't going anywhere, not yet.

'Ella has a daughter?' he asked Felicity. The magazine had mentioned a child, and he'd seen photos of a tiny baby in Ella's room, but now that he was picturing an older, mini version of Ella his heart was swelling.

'Yes. You don't know? Her name is Indigo.'

Indigo. He smiled. Of course.

'Please,' he said to them both. 'Listen to me. I will tell you everything and answer all your questions. You deserve to know the truth. Then, if you still hate me and want me out of your lives, I will gladly go. I won't bother you any further.'

Felicity and Leo leaned back on the sofa and Zac breathed out a sigh of relief. There was still a chance they'd tell him to leave at the end of his story—but at least the option of extracting the information the other way still remained. He hoped it wouldn't come to that.

• • • • •

'Lucifer?' Leo said, for the fifth time. 'The fallen Archangel Lucifer is your mother?'

Zac nodded as Felicity handed him a bowl of crisps. He shook his head and popped an olive in his mouth instead. He couldn't eat olives without thinking of Ella and the pizza they'd shared in her room all those years ago.

Zac swallowed and spoke up. 'Yes, Leo. As I said, I had vague recollections of my mother in Fiesole two thousand years ago, when I was a child, but no idea of who she was. Mikhael had never attached a gender to Lucifer when he spoke of the Devil. He made out like he'd eradicated an inhuman beast from our realm and kept us all safe.'

'So your mother isn't…evil?' Felicity asked.

Zac laughed. Was his mother evil? She was hardly sugar and spice and all things nice. Well, maybe the spice part.

'She's complex,' he said. 'I don't doubt her intentions come from a good place, but she's driven and powerful. It isn't always the best combination when you harbour resentment spanning thousands of years. We no longer speak.'

Leo was still pacing, face screwed up in concentration. He would occasionally stop, raise a finger as if he was going to ask something, then continue pacing.

'You're avoiding Luci because she kept you away from Ella?' Felicity asked.

Zac nodded.

'She did the right thing.'

Zac wasn't expecting that. 'How was her erasing Ella's memory a good thing? How was stopping me from being with the love of my life right?'

Standing up, Felicity walked over to Zac, perched on the edge of his armchair, and put her hand on his shoulder.

'Zac, never underestimate the strength of a mother's love. She was protecting my daughter, and her own little boy. She knew Ella would be happy with Josh and that you were both under threat from Mikhael if you were found together. She knew Ella wouldn't enjoy her destined life knowing you were alive, pining for her. What I don't understand though is why, knowing Josh was going to die eleven years later, you still fought so hard for Ella against her own life path? Why weren't you happy to simply wait for him to die, then go to her?'

Zac had promised himself he'd be honest, that he'd tell them everything, but now he wasn't so sure. They were warming to him again. He needed them to trust him enough to tell them Ella's whereabouts. But how would they react if he told them the whole truth?

'I fell out with my mother because she stopped me seeing your daughter the day she was due to die.'

He closed his eyes and, sure enough, Leo and Felicity gasped and began asking questions at the same time.

'Ella?'

'What do you mean "die?"'

'When was this?'

'But she's alive!'

'Is she going to die soon? Is she in danger?'

Zac opened his eyes to find both of her parents standing over him, faces drained of colour. They both looked older than they had an hour ago. He'd done that to them.

'Ella was meant to die on that boat with Josh—that's why I didn't want them to marry. That's why I wanted her to myself—because I knew I wouldn't have much time with her.'

Felicity gave a tiny yelp and Zac instinctively reached out for her hand. She let him hold it and he squeezed it gently.

'She wasn't meant to live,' he said quietly. 'That's why I'm here. Gabriel told me she was alive, and that the angels can't feel her—they too think she died as she was meant to—but she survived death. I've never seen it happen before. It makes no sense. She's untethered and has no path any longer. She's free.'

Leo and Felicity looked at one another over Zac's head, then Leo let out a deep sigh.

'Why didn't you tell us when she was going to die?' Leo asked.

They were being ridiculous now. 'How could I!? I was an angel, one who had broken more than enough rules already. You don't go around giving people their death dates. I know the date you two will die too. I still remember it, but I'll never tell you.' Their faces had turned even paler. 'Don't worry, you have ages yet. Seriously, you live a long time.'

He rubbed his hands over his face and asked himself, for the millionth time, what the hell he was doing. He should have marched straight over to them, demanded Ella's address, erased the conversation from their memory, and marched back out. Yet, as difficult as this conversation was, it felt good to tell someone what he'd been up to the last seventeen years since his return. Back when he was a Path Keeper and angel, he'd spent many a long night talking to Leo, the priest, and sharing so much about the realm. And now, who did he have to talk to about angelic matters? Not Leo, not Luci, not his friend Gabriel…and definitely not Ella.

Leo's brow furrowed in concentration. 'Let me get this straight, Zadkiel. Your mother is on the hunt for Nephilim, but you won't help her. And Ella has no idea you're alive, she somehow survived her death, and you want us to tell you where to find her?'

'Please,' Zac said to them both, Felicity's hand still in his. '*Please.* Give me a chance to make it right. To explain everything to her. She has to know I came back for her as quickly as I could and tried to do the right thing. Is she happy? Are her and Indigo well?'

At the mention of her granddaughter, Felicity smiled and crossed the room to a bookshelf full of albums.

'I don't have many recent photos, but look,' she said, opening a book filled with printed pages of Ella, Josh, and a beautiful little girl with black curly hair and big brown eyes. She looked just like Ella, but darker. His chest ached as he flicked through the pages filled with happy family shots: blowing out candles on a cake with the number three on it, a little girl with pigtails riding a bike, Ella cradling a newborn while Josh planted a kiss on her cheek. How he wished it were him in that photo instead of Josh. Zac had often wondered whether he'd have been able to father a child after returning from the dead, and what that child would have looked like. Would his son have had his bright opal eyes? Would their daughter have had Ella's hair and smile?

Felicity said the photos were old, but how old? Was Indie nine years old now? Ten? He couldn't believe that Ella had a daughter. *Josh's* daughter. Indigo was probably traumatised enough having lost her father—how on earth was he going to waltz back into Ella's life and carry on where he left off so long ago? Ella wasn't nineteen anymore. She probably hadn't thought about him in years.

'I think I better go now,' he said, his voice shaky with emotion.

'No, don't go. I'll make us lunch,' Leo said.

Zac shook his head. 'I've already wasted enough of your day.'

He shook Leo's hand and pecked Felicity lightly on the cheek. Would they tell their daughter he'd visited them? Did he want them to? He had his hand on the door handle when Felicity spoke up.

'She talks about you all the time, you know.'

He turned around slowly. 'Ella remembers me?'

Leo laughed sadly. 'Remembers you? Considering you only spent a couple of weeks together, twenty years ago, she still manages to bring up your name in every conversation we ever have. Even Josh knew who you were. I mean, *what* you were.'

Ella had spoken about him to her husband?

'Go and see her,' Felicity said, even though it was clear it pained her to say it. 'As a mother, I worry that I'm making a mistake saying that. But as a woman, a woman who knows what it is to be in love with a man she doesn't think she can have…' She looked at Leo, who put his arm around her waist. 'Go and see her. Don't waste any more time. Death will catch up with us all soon enough.'

Zac clenched his jaw and nodded.

'Will you tell me where she lives?'

'345 Orchard Way, Muswell Hill, London N10. Do you want me to write it down?'

'I'll remember it. Thank you,' he said, hugging them both.

As they pulled away, he focused on their eyes. Leo's were just like Ella's, chocolate brown with long lashes, and Felicity had irises the colour of forget-me-nots. That's what he had to do—of course he did. His mother had been right all along; the life of a fallen angel meant leaving no trail and taking no risks.

'You'll forget I was here and forget everything I said,' he told them, looking deep into their eyes. 'If Ella and I don't work out, it's safer you know nothing. But...' He gave a hesitant smile, allowing himself a glimmer of hope. 'But, if things *do* work out and Ella *does* tell you about me going to see her, then you will remember this and explain that I stopped you from telling her. I *want* you to remember today. I want you to know I love you both, and how much I've always longed to be part of this family.'

They stood rooted to the spot, their eyes focused on nothing. How many times could you play with someone's mind? But it was safer this way. He was doing the right thing. With a roll of his shoulders and a deep breath, he opened the apartment door and closed it quietly behind him.

It was finally time for Ella to know he was back.

24

ELLA LEANED ON the banister as she shouted up the stairs.

'It's eight forty-five. Aren't you late for school?'

'No. It's the school trip today, remember?'

Ella hadn't remembered; she hadn't overseen her daughter's life for a while now. Maybe she should start.

'What time do you need to be there?'

'Not until ten. Coach leaves at ten thirty.'

Indie ran down the stairs and rushed past her mother, creating a light breeze that blew strands of Ella's hair into her mouth. She gathered it up in a ponytail, wondering if her hair was too long for nearly forty, and twisted it into a bun at the base of her neck. There was always a spare hair elastic on her wrist. God, when did she become so boring and sensible?

'Indie, you're making me dizzy. Why don't you take the bag back up to your room and check that you have what you need there, instead of going through it down here and running up and down the stairs a million times?'

Indie looked at her mother like she was talking in another language. It had always been like that—Ella filling the silences, and Indie appearing to be listening to something other than the continuous stream of words pouring out of Ella's mouth. And it had got worse lately. During the last week or two, since Indie had gone back to school, she'd been more distracted than ever. Prickly. Irritated.

'Why don't I drop you off?' Ella shouted up at Indie's retreating back as her daughter ran up the stairs again.

'I'm only taking my rucksack. It's not even heavy. Anyway, didn't you say the car is in the garage today?'

Ella had forgotten. She hardly used the car anyway. When she had work in town the bus was quicker. Actually, the Tube was quicker, but she couldn't get on the Underground without thinking of Zac—and too much time had gone by to be fixating on *that* ex.

'I can walk with you to school if you want,' she shouted up at her daughter.

'Mum, I can walk on my own.' Indie appeared at the top of the stairs, hairbrush in hand. 'Jesus! You'd think I was skipping the country. Stop fussing. I'm not a baby.'

Except she was to Ella. She was still that gap-toothed child with the wild hair and big round eyes who would ask her mummy strange questions like 'Why does the air change colour?' and 'How many different things does a smile mean?' Indie—her funny, quirky, serious baby girl who spent more time with characters from her books than real people.

'Who's going on this field trip? Jesse?'

'Yep,' Indie said, rummaging through her bag and counting how many pairs of socks she'd packed, then taking one ball out and chucking it on the sofa.

'And that new boy? What's his name again?'

'Blu,' Indie replied.

Her head was still buried inside her bag, but Ella spotted a light blush creeping up her daughter's neck. Something heavy thudded to the base of Ella's stomach. So that was it. That was the reason for her change in mood. Was this new boy her boyfriend? Or was he just an innocent crush?

At Indie's age, Ella certainly hadn't been all that innocent. She'd regularly got drunk with her friends in Spain, and although losing her virginity had been a horrific experience, it hadn't stopped her from having quite a few boyfriends afterwards.

But that wasn't the point. Indie wasn't Ella—thank god! Her daughter was…responsible. Plus, she'd always been a year younger than the rest of the kids in her class, which made Ella feel even more protective of her.

She supressed the sigh slowly building inside her. Was Indie having a boyfriend *really* such a big deal? Did her age make any difference? It was at moments like these Ella wished Josh was still around. He would have been so proud of their daughter; he would have been the last person to stress about Indie having male friends and going out. He was the kind of father every girl deserved—relaxed, supportive, and understanding. It wasn't fair! It wasn't fair that Indie was stuck with Ella, who struggled to be a mum at the best of times, let alone when trying to do the job of *two* parents.

'I know what you're thinking, Mum. And no, Blu isn't a boyfriend and it's not like that. His twin sister is going on the trip too. Loads of us are—the whole class, plus the geography class too. More than thirty students. Exactly how wild do you think two nights in Bath and Bristol are going to get visiting Roman ruins and the maritime museum?'

Indie had closed up again. Ella could see it on her face, like a shop pulling down its shutters. Done. No more to say.

Indie zipped up her rucksack, and Ella studied her closely. There was something different about her eyes lately too, a dullness. They no longer sparkled with life. Ella wasn't sure how much she could keep prodding and poking before her daughter snapped. Things between them had been like walking on a tightrope lately, constantly striving for that balance between being interested in Indie's life but not scaring her away.

'Is everything OK, sweetheart?'

Ella received a grunt in reply. *Great!* She'd fucked it up even more now.

'It's just that you seem…preoccupied, and you're going away. I worry.'

'Well don't, Mum. Mind out the way, please. You're standing in the middle of the hallway and slowing me down. I need to leave soon.'

Ella glanced at the clock on the mantlepiece.

'But you have loads of time. How about I make pancakes? Or pack you some snacks for the trip? You can tell me about your new friends, or who Jesse has his eye on now, or…'

Indie had already shrugged her backpack on.

'It's cool. I'll buy a muesli bar on the way to school. Bye!'

With a wave of her hand, her daughter was gone. No kiss, no hug, no 'I'll miss you.' Ella wanted to shout her name down the street, chase after her, and tell her how much she loved her. But that was silly. That wasn't something you did to your teenage daughter.

Ella locked the door and stared at the empty living room. The house seemed colder already. Two nights away wasn't that long, Indie would be back soon enough, and Ella had plenty of work to keep her busy until then.

She trudged up the stairs to her office, wondering whether a plate of chocolate biscuits was an acceptable breakfast.

25

INDIE ROUNDED THE corner of her school's road. It was empty. The coach wasn't due for at least half an hour but hanging about in the cold was still better than dealing with her mum's incessant questions and suffocating fog of concern.

'And today's Indie forecast is looking *hot, hot, hot!*'

Jesse was leaning against the school gate beside a couple of people in their year who were chatting to one another, the long handles of their mini suitcases in their hands. Indie's blood had begun fizzing well before she'd seen her friend. Jesse's emotions were so intense lately that colours had started to appear brighter around him. Even birdsong was shriller.

Indie rolled her eyes at him but couldn't help laughing as he sauntered over doing his best impression of a catwalk model.

'Look at you, hot stuff!'

'Oh my!' she cried, holding her hand up to her chest. 'He hath returned to me.'

Two pink patches appeared on his cheeks and Indie grinned at his unusual coyness. She gave him a light shove on the shoulder. 'You been too wrapped up in your new man to remember about your bestie?'

'You're still my favourite!'

Jesse threw his arms around her neck and hugged her so tight she nearly toppled backwards.

'Stop it! You're going to yank my earrings out.'

He stepped back and looked her up and down with a self-satisfied look on his face.

'Lip gloss? *Hooped* earrings?'

'What? I haven't made any more effort than usual.'

'Yeah, OK. You have perfectly applied eyeliner, Indie, like that takes no effort. Don't suppose you're doing this for anyone special? Maybe the hunky northerner who is proper hot for you and won't stop walking you home like some Victorian suitor?'

Indie rolled her eyes, but her cheeks were prickling. The thought of spending two nights in the same building as Blu filled her stomach with fluttery winged things.

'We're just friends,' she muttered. 'Oh my god, Jesse! Stop doing that with your tongue. You're disgusting. Anyway, what have *you* been up to the last few days? Is your crush boy still coming on this trip with us?'

Jesse grinned and nodded his head vigorously.

'And you and him are still…?'

Jesse squealed and jumped up and down. '…officially boyfriend and boyfriend. He gave me this!'

He held out his door keys and dangled a key ring in her face.

'A ferret?'

'No! It's a minx. That's what he calls me, his little…'

'I don't want to know. La la la.' Indie stuck her fingers in her ear and sang tunelessly, her eyes screwed shut. When she opened them again Blu was standing before her, giving her a lopsided smile.

'You feeling OK, Indie?' he asked.

Jesse was behind Blu, making a huge performance of silently laughing at her. Git.

'Yeah. My so-called best friend was being inappropriate as usual. Is Jade here?'

Blu nodded his head at his sister, who was talking to a group of people nearby, including Xavier. Spotting them, Jesse ran over and wrapped his arm around his boyfriend's shoulder, nearly knocking him over. That boy had no chill.

Indie and Blu looked at one another and burst out laughing.

'Want to sit next to me on the coach?' he asked.

She shrugged a yes, as if cute boys asked her to sit next to them every single day of the year, and he smiled at her like she'd just given him a shiny ferret key ring.

• • • • •

Sitting next to Blu had seemed like a great idea—except it wasn't.

He was seated beside the window, Indie in the aisle seat, and Jesse on the back row behind them with Xavier. The two boys were kissing, and not even quietly.

Over an hour had passed since the coach had left their school, and after a bit of small talk Indie was desperate to speak to Blu about important things, like their weird power things, but they couldn't risk being overheard by any of their classmates. Instead, they fell into a comfortable silence. Blu had his headphones in and was pretending to look out the window, while Indie pretended to read a book on her phone—yet neither of them were fooling the other. The emotions emanating from Jesse and Xavier behind them were nearly as X-rated as they'd been in the park. Why the hell had she sat next to Blu and so close to Jesse? She made a mental note not to be in a room next to her best friend tonight. It made her laugh that tonight they were expected to stick to their girl and boy dorms. As if *that* was going to stop Xavier and his 'little minx.'

She glanced over at Blu to gauge his reaction. But he wasn't looking out of the window—he was watching her in the reflection of the glass. Every one of her internal organs collided and all thoughts of Jesse and Xavier vanished, quickly replaced by a dry mouth and a head full of bees. She looked down at Blu's hand inches from hers on the seat. Her fingertips buzzed. She could practically feel the vibrations from his hand pulling hers closer. What would happen if she shifted in her seat and they touched?

'Attention, please!'

Mr Dowding was at the front of the coach, clapping his hands.

Blu took out his headphones and leaned into Indie. 'I thought he'd left. What's he doing on the trip?'

Indie widened her eyes and shrugged to demonstrate that she knew as little as he did, although she was relieved the weird Ms Luci wasn't heading the trip like she'd said she would. There was something not quite right about that woman, and Indie wasn't up for finding out what.

'Right, if everyone could stop talking and…what on earth are you two doing at the back?'

Indie's seat shook as Jesse and Xavier straightened themselves up. The heat that had been permeating her chest and thighs for the last hour suddenly cooled to an icy chill. She bit back a smile as Blu covered his mouth, his shoulders shaking. He must have felt their scorching ardour sizzle to a stop too.

'Right!' the teacher continued, as the bus turned into the forecourt of a service station and pulled into a parking space. 'We will be stopping here for ten minutes. During that time, you are permitted to use the facilities, and by that, I mean the toilets and maybe buy a snack—not the arcade machines—and then we'll split into our groups.'

A wave of murmurs filled the coach. Groups? Did he mean history and geography classes would be splitting up? Indie could hear Jesse anxiously whispering to Xavier.

'I haven't finished yet!' Mr Dowding shouted, signalling to the kids that had already stood up to sit back down. 'Ms Luci has an announcement.'

Indie sunk lower into her chair and felt Blu bristle beside her. His sister Jade was three rows up, and she too swivelled around and made a face at Indie. This wasn't good. That woman wasn't normal.

Luci stood at the front of the coach, her long hair in serpentine tendrils around her bare shoulders. Was she wearing a strapless dress? In January?

'Look at me, everyone,' she purred. She had hardly raised her voice, yet the entire coach fell silent and every head turned her way. How did she do that? She waited until there was complete silence, then looked at every student in turn.

'Three pupils will be leaving this trip and joining me instead. You won't notice them go, you will not mention it to anyone else, and you won't remember me being here or talking to you. Once they, and I, have left this vehicle, you will continue to your destination as planned and none of you, including the teachers, will notice them missing. Is that understood?'

Everybody's heads nodded in unison. Everybody's except Indie's, Blu's, and his sister's. Blu tapped Indie's knee with his own and she shook her head, once again confirming she knew as much as he did.

'Good,' Luci said. 'Indie de Silva and Blu and Jade Usaki—collect your bags and follow me.'

Their classmates continued looking straight on like freeze-framed robots. Indie twisted back in her seat, but Jesse wouldn't even look at her. It was as if she were invisible.

Jade was on her feet. 'Excuse me,' she shouted out, waving her hand to get their new history teacher's attention. 'Where exactly are the three of us going?'

Luci looked at her and blinked twice, as if Jade was the most boring person she had ever spoken to.

'Pick up your bags. When we get there, I'll answer all your questions. Even the ones about why you're different.'

Different? Blu stood up next and Indie joined him, the two of then shuffling into the aisle.

'We're not going anywhere until you tell us who you really are!' he said, squaring his shoulders. 'How did you do that? How did you make everyone into a zombie?'

Blu pointed at the driver and Mr Dowding, who were also staring straight ahead, but Luci ignored him.

'Are those yours?' she asked, signalling to the luggage rack above their heads. He nodded, and immediately two bags fell to their feet with a thud. Had she done that? Was Miss Luci also like them?

With a resigned sigh Jade plucked her own bag from the overhead storage and joined the woman at the front. Indie and Blu followed. Everyone else continued to stare straight ahead, a coach filled with row after row of mannequins.

The doors flapped open at the nod of Luci's head and she strode across the service station forecourt in her impossibly high heels. She didn't have a handbag or coat, let alone an overnight bag.

'Jade, wait!' Blu hissed, once Luci was out of earshot. 'This is dead weird. I don't like it. Why do you think she's chosen us?'

Jade slowed down, and they huddled together.

'No idea, but wherever we're going will be more interesting than spending three days with Mr Dowding at the Roman Baths.'

'Hold up, is that… Is that our car?' Indie muttered, nodding her head sideways, in what she hoped was a subtle way.

Luci was standing beside a gleaming black limo. The door was open, revealing a plush interior with tiny blue lights. It was like something from an American high school prom movie—corny as hell, but expensive.

Blu's eyes widened. 'What the fuck?'

Jade lay a hand on both their shoulders and leaned in closer. 'Listen, I agree this is weird but it's not like anything can happen to the three of us if we stick together. Right? I mean, we can do magic!' She laughed quietly at her own lame joke, but Indie struggled to join in. They *could* do magic, but she had a feeling that so could the mysterious Miss Luci. And she was about to take them somewhere that may answer the questions they'd been asking themselves all their lives.

'Get in the bloody car!' Luci shouted.

The three of them looked at one another, waiting for someone to make the first move. Indie cleared her throat, but her mouth was so dry it made her want to cough. She tightened the straps on her backpack and wiped her damp hands on her jeans, willing herself to walk.

'We have no choice now anyway,' Blu said, straightening up and slinging his bag over his shoulder. 'The coach has just left without us.'

26

MISS LUCI DIDN'T say a word as she drove the three of them in the ridiculous limo further into the countryside. The car windows were tinted, transforming the outside to a dull grey. Jade was scrolling through her phone and Blu had his headphones back in, bobbing his head up and down to whatever music he was listening to. Weren't they scared? Weren't they even worried as to where this strange woman was taking them?

After fifteen minutes of silence Luci drove them through a set of wrought iron gates and pulled alongside a large house. She turned around in the driver's seat, pointed through the back window, and with a click of her fingers shut the gate behind them.

'Looks like everyone is already here,' she said, getting out of the car. Her heels crunched on the gravel as she opened the car door for them like an overdressed chauffeur.

'You have no idea how many centuries I've waited to unite my Nephilim and have you all under one roof,' she said, signalling to the front door where two girls and two boys roughly their age were standing. What did she mean by 'centuries?' The other teenagers looked as uncertain and confused as Indie felt.

'These are your people. The seven of you are going to change the world. But first, let's eat.'

It was obvious Blu and Jade had no idea what Luci was talking about either, but they followed her into the large country house, giving a shy smile to the four people standing in the entrance hall. And they, in turn, eyed them suspiciously. The girl with purple hair visibly relaxed as soon as she saw Luci, although the boy in the beanie hat beside her sneered and kissed his teeth when Luci winked at him. His sneer changed into a smirk as soon as he set eyes on Jade and Indie.

'Nice,' he said, nodding in approval as they passed him.

Blu shot him a dark look. Jade's was even darker.

The other two teenagers looked like twins, a girl and boy, although there was something about the way he had his hand on his sister's shoulder that made Indie think the boy was a year or two older. Their identical long brown hair fell to their chests, and their smiles lit up their fiery eyes. *Their eyes!* Indie looked back at the other girl and boy, noticing her eyes were pink and his closer to a deep red.

'Fuck,' she heard Blu say under his breath. He'd noticed too. Luci was right, they *were* with their own kind—but what did it mean? What the hell *were* they?

'You must all be very hungry,' Luci said, ignoring the wary stares they were all giving one another and heading straight to the kitchen.

'I made bread and some vegan dips,' the girl with the long hair said. When she talked the light smattering of freckles over her nose danced like dappled sunlight. 'I also prepared some crudités. Violet and Scar got here literally five minutes before you did, so we've not had a chance to explain anything to them yet.'

She had a slight twang to her voice. Indie wasn't great at English accents, but she'd been to St Ives once on holiday with her parents and the girl sounded like they had. Like a soft-spoken pirate.

'Great work, Amber,' Luci said. The girl physically glowed from the compliment.

How did these teenagers already know Luci? Was she their teacher too?

'You got any crisps or chips or something?' the boy in the beanie said, screwing his face up at the assortment of chopped-up vegetables on the table. Indie presumed he was Scar. 'Why don't we order tacos, yeah? I ain't eating this rabbit shit. You get me?' he said, turning to Blu.

Blu shrugged. 'I'm not fussed.'

This was what everyone was going to talk about? Seven teenagers in her history teacher's kitchen chatting about vegan dips. Wasn't anyone going to ask why they were all there?

'Excuse me.' Indie put her hand up, and seven pairs of eyes turned in her direction, most of them glistening like precious stones in a jewellery shop window. 'Why are we all here? Are you all on the history trip too?'

The boy in the beanie guffawed and waved his arms in amusement.

'You for real? You think that bitch is a teacher?'

Luci raised her eyebrows at him, and he stared back at her, daring her to do something about his outburst.

The long-haired boy stepped forward. He looked like he should be holding a skateboard under one arm. It was the first time Indie had heard him speak, and his accent was even stronger than his sister's.

'We need to show Luci some respect. She's our leader, and as such we should listen to her patiently and with an open mind. She is not a teacher, although we could all learn a lot from her.'

Jade and Blu glanced at Indie, Scar curled his lip, and Violet, her bright hair matching her name, kept her gaze fixed firmly at her feet.

'Thank you, Sol. My brother is right,' Amber said. 'There's a lot to talk about. I'll bring the snacks out to the living room, shall I?'

Indie shrugged her bag off her back and left it in a corner beside Blu and Jade's. This was getting weirder by the minute, but she was hungry—and the bread smelled nice. She went to text her mother, let her know there had been a change of plans, but Luci was already beside her.

'No phones,' she said. 'I'll give them back to you afterwards.'

'After what?' Indie asked, but Luci had already plucked the phone from her hand. She then entered the living room and demanded the same off Blu and Jade. They were already sitting on a large doughy sofa, the coffee table before them laden with plates of colourful vegetables, dips, and bread. Before they had a chance to argue, Luci had magically snatched the phones from their hands. Hanging, suspended in mid- air, Luci grabbed at them like she was catching butterflies in a net before walking away, returning empty-handed a few seconds later.

'Hey,' Jade shouted. 'You can't just…'

Luci tilted her head to one side. 'I *can* just. No one else has a phone with them either. Now, tuck in everyone. Then we'll do the intros.'

Indie half-heartedly picked at the sliced cucumber and smiled a small thanks to Amber for making it. The girl beamed back. She seemed constantly happy, and it made Indie think of Jesse. Except, unlike with her best friend, Indie couldn't feel any emotion emanating off the girl. In fact, she couldn't feel *anyone's* thoughts. It was strange, but it also allowed her the space and silence to think. Were they safe? Would Jesse be worried about her? Would Luci's hypnosis, or whatever it was she'd done on the bus, really make everyone forget about them?

Scar didn't eat anything, clearly holding out for the tacos that weren't coming, and Jade and Violet were sharing a plate of red peppers between them.

Luci poured them all a glass of water then straightened up, looking out over her mini congregation like a vicar at mass. What was it that Sol had said about Luci being their leader?

'Isn't this wonderful?' she said.

Blu's leg made tiny jerky motions beside Indie's, but his eyes were fixed on Luci.

'Right then,' the teacher continued. 'Let us start. Jade, Blu, and Indie—take out your contact lenses, please.'

'I'd prefer not to,' Jade said. 'Me hands are all dirty and…ow!'

Luci pointed at them and plucked the contact lenses out of their eyes in one swift motion, discarding the tiny plastic ovals on the carpet and flicking them away with her foot.

'You won't be needing them anymore,' she said.

The four others stared at Indie, Jade, and her brother, two with bright jade eyes and Indie with azure irises, a mix of calm seas and summer skies. It was clear they were all comparing colours and trying to work out who was who.

'After tomorrow we shall no longer need to hide who we are. In fact, we will be celebrating our powers,' Luci said. She crouched beside Indie and cupped her face in her hands, moving her head back and forth as she studied her eyes closely.

'Beautiful. Just like your father's. Your grandfather's are icy, like the monster he is, but your eyes have a stunning depth to them. They match your name perfectly, Indigo.'

Scar laughed at the mention of her name.

'Something amusing?' Luci asked him.

He shook his head while leering at Indie. She felt Blu move closer to her on the sofa, his leg now pressed firmly against hers. He was watching her out of the corner of his eye, his stare like a hot brand on her skin.

Luci cleared her throat. 'Right then, introductions. Amber, please start.'

Amber jumped up and Indie sunk lower into her seat. Group introductions? Really?

'My name is Amber and I'm sixteen,' she chirruped. 'This is Sol, my brother. He's just turned eighteen. I'm a Pisces and I love horses, and he's Sagittarius and loves reading. We live in Glastonbury and are homeschooled by our mum. Oh, and our father is Archangel Rafael.'

She sat down with a flourish, her smile only slightly faltering when everyone remained silent.

'Any questions for Amber?' Luci said, still standing.

'Yeah,' Jade shouted out. 'What the fuck is this hippy bullshit cult you've brought us to? I'm not taking part in this nonsense!' She jumped up and headed for the door, which shut by itself and locked as soon as she reached for the handle.

'You can't leave this house until I say so,' Luci said.

Blu pulled Indie up by her sleeve and they joined his sister. 'You can't keep us prisoners!' he shouted.

Scar was laughing so hard he was practically curled up in a ball in the armchair, and Violet was staring down at her empty plate. Sol and Amber were still smiling, although more patronising than welcoming this time. The Earth-loving brother and sister were giving Indie the creeps.

'I told you this would happen,' Sol said to Luci, who was trying to rearrange her features into something resembling calm and patience.

'Please, the three of you, sit down. This is not a cult, and everything Amber said was true. It's why I brought you all together. The seven of you have a very special gift, some more so than others, so if you could please *sit and be quiet*'—she said the last few words through gritted teeth—'I can answer questions afterwards. The house is sealed by my own forces—no one can get in or out. It's for your own protection. No one inside this house is going to hurt you and after tomorrow you are all free to get on with your pathetic, mundane lives. Although once you've heard what I have to say, I have a feeling you may not want to.'

Jade's face was set hard, but she did as instructed, and the three of them sat back down.

'Right, if that's the end of the histrionics let's carry on. Violet?'

The girl with the purple hair and big round eyes stood up, gripping the edge of the sofa to steady herself. Her hands trembled and she clasped them in front of her as if they were about to fly off the ends of her arms.

'I'm Violet. I'm seventeen and from Kent. I don't really know what else to say, except that I never felt like I fit in until I met Luci and she explained that I'm like this because of who my real dad is. I mean, I've always had a dad, but he never felt like my dad. You know?'

Indie found herself nodding and stopped.

'Anyway, it's nice to meet you all.' Her gaze met Jade's as she said this. She flickered a quick smile in her direction then sat back down quickly.

Luci sighed through her nose.

'OK, this is taking too long, and I'm bored. Honestly, I was expecting my Nephilim to have more personality than you bunch of wet flannels. I'll do the intros. To my right is Scarlet…'

'Bitch, please. I ain't no Scarlet. My name is Scar and you know it.'

'Shut up, you tiresome boy. Your name is Scarlet. Your mother called you that because of your eyes, which were tinged with red from birth. She met your father when she was selling T-shirts at a music festival eighteen years ago. I doubt you know this, so stop spouting your pathetic vitriol and listen. She got pregnant after a quick fumble in a tent, had you but struggled on her own. She started taking drugs, died on a piss-stained mattress somewhere in Hoxton, and from the age of three you were brought up in foster homes. Correct me if I'm wrong.'

Scar narrowed his eyes at her then looked down at his trainers. He blinked a few times but didn't say anything.

'I found Scar on the streets. Where else? He mistook me for a prostitute, such a pleasant boy. Anyway, that's all behind us now because he's been in a fancy hotel for the last week being treated like a little prince and he's learned the error of his ways. Am I right, Scarlet?'

He bit down on both lips at once and gave a curt nod.

'He also likes watching cookery programmes and reading autobiographies.'

'For real?' he shouted. 'I got street cred, man.'

'No, Scarlet. You do not. You're a boy, and you will soon be greater than any of that crap you were doing in the backstreets of Redwood. It's not your fault, your father is a bit of an arsehole too. No doubt you'll meet him soon.'

Scar sat up at the mention of his father, glancing briefly at the door.

'Tomorrow,' she said, placing a hand on his shoulder.

'Is he an angel too?' Jade said, her voice dripping with sarcasm.

'Yes,' Luci replied. 'Archangel Chamuel. He's down in history as a peacekeeper, although we used to call him the Viking King. He rarely questions Mikhael. It will be interesting to see what his master makes of his sordid encounters on Earth. Mikhael isn't too fond of Nephilim.'

Scar looked at Luci like she was speaking in tongues. 'What?'

She rubbed her temples and went to speak, but Amber cut in first.

'We're all half-angels. Our fathers are from the Angelic Realm. In fact, they're from the highest order—archangels. That makes us the strongest kind of Nephilim. That's why our eyes look like this and we have certain…abilities.'

Scar was still frowning. 'What about them two, then?' he said, pointing at Jade and Blu. 'Their eyes are crazy green. Mint colour. What's their story?'

Luci's face lit up in a way Indie hadn't seen so far. It was as if someone had struck a match inside of her, her skin glowing like a paper-thin lantern full of light.

'Their father will certainly join us tomorrow,' Luci replied, looking at the twins. 'He's very famous and very special. I take it you've all heard of Archangel Gabriel?'

Jade let out a deep sigh but stayed silent.

'Of course,' Blu said. 'He's in the Bible. Everyone knows the Christmas nativity story.'

'Not me,' Violet said. 'I'm Muslim.'

'You don't look Muslim,' Scar said.

'What's that supposed to mean?' Violet shot back. 'Because my head isn't covered? Or because I speak English and have short purple hair?'

Scar shrugged. 'Just saying.'

Luci shot him a warning look and continued to speak. 'Gabriel is in the Quran too, and the Torah. In fact, he's mentioned in nearly every holy book and scripture there is. He's more than just an angelic messenger. He was the father of Jesus, and he's a very good friend of mine.'

Jade burst out laughing and looked around the room, as if searching for something.

'OK. You got us. Where are the cameras?' Blu remained still beside Indie, while his sister spun around in a full circle. 'The prank was clever. Opening and shutting doors and chatting about angels, but you took it too far. Jesus is not my half brother.'

'He is. Well, he was.'

'This is stupid. Come on, Blu, this is stupid, right?' She turned to her brother, her voice rising a couple of octaves. 'Our mam was a student at Bristol uni when she got pregnant. She wasn't getting it on with some angel.'

'She chose your names before you were born. You, Jade, are named after the colour of her lover's eyes,' Luci said quietly. 'She was murdered because of you both.'

'Me mam died in a car accident!' Jade spat, tears pooling in her eyes.

'She was murdered because you are all dangerous. You are the children of shadows. The key to joining our two realms so we can finally rise against their tyrannical leader and stop hiding.'

Scar was now staring at Luci, his mouth a perfect O-shape.

'You saying all our mums fucked angels?'

Indie squirmed in her seat. No one had mentioned her yet, and she wanted to keep it that way. What a load of nonsense. Yes, everyone in that living room had bright eyes and a confusing past, but her mother loved her father—she would never have cheated on him. Or lied to him. Indie would have sensed it. But all she'd felt emanating from her parents was genuine love and respect. None of these far-fetched stories applied to her.

'That's right, Scar,' Luci said. She didn't look so luminous anymore. Her eyes had dulled and were rimmed with shadows. 'You are the chosen Nephilim who, as legend has it, will complete the full spectrum of the soul.'

Amber and Sol nodded knowingly, although Violet was looking puzzled.

'Excuse me? What do you mean "spectrum"—is that spectrum as in abilities, mental health issues, or colour? You know, because of our names?'

Everyone turned to her. Their names?

Luci nodded. 'Well observed, Violet. It's in the *Book of Light*, an ancient spell book I lost back in the seventeenth century.' Indie thought she heard Scar mutter something about craziness, but it may have been Jade. 'It explained that the Nephilim would be linked. And you are, by your names. Sol is yellow, Amber is orange, Scarlet, Violet, Jade, Blu, and Indigo. The full spectrum.'

Scar began to laugh again, this time joined by Jade and Blu. Even Violet had her hand over her mouth.

'Seriously, Luci. You're trippin'. You saying we're special because we're named after the rainbow? That's just some crazy coincidence.' He shook his head in amusement. 'I ain't no Care Bear.'

'No, you're not.'

With one sudden movement Luci threw her hands in the air and sent the dining table at the other end of the room hurtling toward them. Without hesitating for a second, the seven of them raised their hands in defence and the table smashed into thousands of tiny pieces. Splintered shards of wood rained down upon them like confetti, settling in their hair and on their clothes. The food on the table was covered in sawdust and wood shavings, and the carpet sprinkled with nails and tiny pieces of wood. Luci picked one out of her cleavage, looked at it, and dropped it on the floor.

'You aren't Care Bears. You are my powerful, unstoppable army. My six invincible Nephilim.'

They were all too stunned to move, snatching quick glances at one another to see who would be the first to say anything. Angelic fathers? Jewellike eyes? A table that seated ten, now turned into nothing more than lining for a guinea pig cage?

'There are seven of us,' Blu muttered. 'You said six Nephilim, but there are seven of us.'

Luci walked over to him, blew a wood chip off his shoulder, and gave him a wicked smile.

'I could make a bad joke about that,' she said, smiling wider at his confused face. 'And yes, you are right, I have my six Nephilim and one extra.'

She turned to Indie beside him and lay a cool hand on her arm. Indie froze beneath her touch. What did the crazy woman want with *her*?

'Because one of you is more special than the others. Indie here isn't like the rest of you. Indie is the third descendant.'

Blu locked his eyes on Indie. She may not have been able to feel his emotions, but she knew what his face was telling her—*stay calm, don't panic, I won't let the crazy woman hurt you.*

'Descendant?' Indie stuttered. 'What does that mean?'

'It means I've waited for you for over two thousand years, and now you're going to help me take the power away from Mikhael.'

'Who?'

'Archangel Michael, the leader of all angels. Your father's father.'

Indie swallowed. Luci's grip on her arm was tightening.

'If…if I'm related to the…the king of angels,' Indie said, hardly believing the absurdity of her words, 'then who are you?'

Luci let go of her arm and stroked her cheek. She stared into Indie's eyes, like she'd done a few minutes earlier, although this time her own shone an even brighter emerald green. The others had gathered behind Luci, staring at Indie too, making her feel even more of a weirdo than she already did.

'Who am *I*?' Luci laughed softly. 'I, my precious, powerful child, am Lucifer. The bringer of light, the creator of all things, and the first angel to fall. Which makes you my boy's little girl. The granddaughter of the witch they couldn't burn.'

'You're…the Devil?'

'Yes, Indie. And I'm also your grandmother.'

27

AFTER LUCI'S ANGELIC revelations, then collectively making a dining table explode by sheer magic, the seven Nephilim were put into teams. It was like being on a school trip after all, if your school was Hogwarts and your headmistress was Beelzebub.

Luci was sitting on the breakfast bar dishing out orders.

'Boys, stay here with Sol. He's your team leader. Indie, join Violet and Jade over there. Amber will be instructing you on how to perfect your kinetic abilities and protect yourselves from the feelings of others. You will need a clear head tomorrow. You can't afford for any human's emotions to cloud your judgement.'

Indie dragged her feet over to the others in the dining area. There was now a large space where the table had been, before they had obliterated it.

Luci had already tidied up the wood splinters with a simple wave of her arm, every last shaving now in a bin bag by the back door. Indie wondered whether the crazy woman owned a vacuum cleaner, or if she did her cleaning by wiggling a few fingers.

'Why are we learning this?' Blu asked, moving begrudgingly beside Scar.

'To fight,' Luci said, ignoring the collective looks of horror on their faces. 'Tomorrow we are going face-to-face with the most powerful being there is. I need you to be ready.'

Jade stared at Luci, wide-eyed. 'We're fighting?'

'Hopefully not in the physical sense. But maybe.'

'You said you're the Devil. Lucifer, yeah?' Scar said, tilting his chin at Luci. 'Can't you kill him on your own?'

Luci shook her head. 'The real Devil doesn't exist. And no, I can't kill him alone. He has a sword.'

Scar took a step toward her, his shoulders swaying with swagger. 'That ain't nothing. I can get you a gun. Need backup?'

She sighed and took her phone out of her pocket, making him jump back. Blu's eyes met with Indie's and they stifled a giggle. So much for Scar's hard-man act.

'No, we don't need guns for this war, Scarlet,' Luci said, scrolling through her phone. She put it back in her pocket. 'We need power, your collective power. Amber and Sol will explain what will happen at the site tomorrow morning. You need to protect your minds and have your wits about you. Mikhael is mean and dangerous.'

'Meaner than kidnapping children and keeping them imprisoned?' Jade shouted out, ignoring her brother mouthing 'shut up' from across the room.

'Believe me, you have no idea what being imprisoned is really like,' Luci replied. 'You came of your own free will, remember? After tomorrow you may leave, do what you want. You'll be helping me rid the world of tyranny at the highest level, and in exchange I'm guiding you on how to use your gifts better. Anything you're not happy with, say now.'

Scar put his hand up. Luci nodded at him.

'What do you want?'

'Can we get tacos for dinner?'

Everyone laughed, and Scar revelled in the attention, waving his hands about and nodding.

'And to think I wanted more children of my own,' Luci muttered.

• • • • •

For three hours Amber taught the girls about mind shielding and long-distance tuning. They sat beside the large bay window at the front of the house and she showed them how to tune in to emotions at a distance as people walked by, then they practised blocking out the feelings of others. Indie hoped the neighbours weren't watching the house, wondering what four strange girls were doing staring out of the window all afternoon.

'Is this Luci's house?' she whispered to Amber, looking at the framed photos on the mantlepiece. A regular family, a child hugging a Labrador, and two people standing in front of the Eiffel tower. There was no way Luci was anyone's grandmother, let alone Indie's. The idea was ridiculous. She didn't even look old enough to be her *mother*, but perhaps they were related. Did that mean the people in the photo were also related to her? 'I hope she's not angry we smashed up her table.'

'She threw it at us, so she only has herself to blame,' Jade spat.

'Don't worry,' Amber replied. 'Luci doesn't live here. She probably mind-controlled the cottage off someone.'

'No, I didn't,' came a voice from the breakfast bar. Luci hadn't moved from the kitchen all afternoon, furiously texting and scrolling through her phone instead.

Amber blushed. 'I didn't mean…'

'I rented the house from Airbnb.' She raised her eyebrows at the expression on Amber's face. 'With *money*. The proper, boring, legal way.'

She nodded at the fireplace, making large flames appear out of nowhere. They licked up the side of the mantelpiece, instantly turning the white surround a sooty grey. 'And if things like this happen'—she waved her finger and a reading lamp flew into the fireplace, its bulb exploding loudly as soon as it hit the flames—'then it doesn't matter. We can get away with it.'

'What you do that for?' Scar shouted.

'The lamp was ugly. It's been bothering me all day.'

With a blink of her eyes the fire went out and she carried on scrolling through her phone.

Violet looked at Jade in panic, and Jade lay a hand on her wrist. 'Don't worry. I think she likes us.'

'Don't joke. She's very powerful,' Violet whispered, glancing at Luci to check she hadn't heard. 'She totally brainwashed my parents into thinking I'd gone back to boarding school, then had me locked up in a hotel all week.'

'Locked up?' Jade replied, moving closer to her. Indie and Amber stopped talking too and listened. 'Are you OK? Did she hurt you?'

'Oh, no. It was great. Five-star luxury, all the food and movies I wanted. She bought me books, clothes, and she did this.' She pointed at her head.

'She coloured your hair?' Jade said.

'Yeah. It used to be really long and black and I said how I'd always wanted short purple hair, so she made it happen.'

'Luci's a hairdresser, too?' Indie said quietly, edging into their conversation.

'There's nothing that woman can't do,' Violet replied. 'She's been really nice to me. Kept saying it wouldn't be long until I met my own people, you know—you guys.' She smiled shily at Amber and Indie, although her eyes settled on Jade's the longest.

'Luci isn't lying,' Amber said. 'I know it sounds crazy, that we got our powers because we all come from angels, but it's true. Unlike you, I know my father, and I've seen him appear and reappear. I've seen his wings.'

Jade didn't look convinced, but Violet was hooked on every word the girl was saying.

'Do you think we'll meet our real fathers tomorrow?' Violet asked.

Amber nodded. 'Luci's very famous in their realm, the original fallen angel—Lucifer.' She turned to Indie, who shrunk back from her stare. 'Sorry, Indie, it's also true you're related to Satan herself. But she's not evil, I promise, she's just really pissed off.'

Jade rolled her eyes so only Indie could see. She didn't know what to think. Of course it was silly and far-fetched, but then so was seven magical children in one room smashing tables in midair.

As soon as it turned dark outside everyone lost interest in practising mind games, so instead they started passing pieces of furniture and ornaments to one another using nothing but the power of their minds. After a while they tried blocking each other's magic, and even attempted to lift one another off the ground. Indie had never pushed her abilities this far and was surprised to find herself the most powerful. She wanted to ask Luci so many questions, about her father and her abilities, but the woman had hardly spoken to them the entire afternoon, and Indie was too nervous to approach her. All she'd learned was that tomorrow morning, at some ungodly hour, they were going to head to a field and hold hands in a circle. And they weren't to run if the shit hit the fan—whatever that meant.

'Hey,' Blu said, sidling up to her. 'You look a bit freaked out.'

Indie slumped to the floor, her back against the wall, and Blu joined her. Everyone else was too busy playing catch with an airborne armchair to notice.

'Yeah, of course I'm freaked out. The Devil's my grandmother, my dead father isn't my father, and apparently tomorrow we're fighting the king of angels.'

Blu chuckled and elbowed her playfully.

'Could be worse.'

'How?'

'You could be here alone.'

She leaned into him. She wanted to rest her head on his shoulder, but that would be weird, so they just sat in silence instead.

'Jade thinks it's all bullshit,' Indie said.

'Jade thinks everything's bullshit. She's worried.'

'How can you tell? She looks fine to me.'

They looked over at his sister who was laughing at something Violet was saying to her.

'She gets extra friendly with people when she's worried. It overcompensates for her nerves. Jade hates anyone knowing how she really feels.'

'And you? Are *you* worried?'

'Nah,' he said, leaning so close his cheek was nearly touching hers. 'How can I be worried when you're here with me? You're me favourite distraction.'

Her stomach filled with warm liquid. 'Yeah?'

'Me absolute favourite.'

The moment was shattered as Luci entered the room, holding her phone in the air.

'Gather round, my magical children. It's time for a group photo.'

'Yeah, man. Selfie time with the angel crew,' Scar shouted, dropping the armchair that was hovering in midair. It bounced three times on the carpet, then toppled over.

'This isn't a crew, Scar,' Sol said, his face deadly serious.

'Yeah, it is. We're like the X-Men.'

'And women,' Jade shouted out as she joined him next to Luci.

Blu helped Indie up off the floor and they reluctantly joined the others.

'Yeah, whatever,' Scar said. 'This is our squad and ain't no one more powerful than us. Right, Luci? Angel Crew is coming for you!' he said, pointing at the phone as Luci pouted and took a selfie of them all.

The doorbell rang, and they all broke apart with a jolt.

Luci laughed. 'Most powerful crew? I've seen mice hold their ground better than you lot. I'll answer it.'

Indie looked at Blu, who looked over at his sister, who looked at Violet, who looked at the door. Did anyone know they were there? Police? Their parents? An angel?

Luci walked back in and they all looked at her expectantly.

'Tacos!' she cried, holding two paper bags up in the air. The relief in the room was palpable. 'Now lay the table for dinner.'

Amber was the first to giggle, followed by Violet, until in the end all of them were laughing.

'Um, Luci, we blew up the table,' Blu pointed out.

A ghost of a smile passed over her lips.

'Sit on the floor then. Plates are in the kitchen.'

It didn't take long, between the eight of them, to bring everything they needed from the kitchen into the living room, where they sat on cushions and passed around bags of fries, onion rings, and tacos. A few minutes into the meal Luci stood up and tapped her glass of water with a knife.

'Quiet, please. I have something important to say.'

Everyone fell silent and Indie noticed Sol give his sister a reassuring look. God, those two were so smug! Like class prefects who always knew what the teacher was about to say.

'I'm proud of you,' Luci said, smiling down at them as if they were her own children. 'Today is the first time you've met, and you've got on relatively well. Violet. Scar. You two especially, as you came here alone. Keep this camaraderie up, because tomorrow you will need to work as a team and have each other's backs. I don't know what Mikhael will do, or even if the spell will work, but thanks to my granddaughter'—she smiled at Indie, who looked down at her lap—'I finally have all the elements required to bring down the realm.'

'Excuse me.' Jade had her hand up. 'What happens after? I mean, if you kill this leader of angels, aren't we complicit in murder? I'm not going to prison because you hold a grudge against some guy I've never met.'

Everyone, except Sol and Amber, murmured their agreement.

'Nothing can happen to you while you're with me,' Luci said. 'And it won't technically be murder. He can't die. I'll just be punishing him in a different way.'

She disappeared into the kitchen and returned with a jug of something resembling red wine.

'You can't serve them alcohol, Luci. They're minors,' Sol said in his clipped tones.

Luci frowned and gave him a look that made his neck a mottled pink.

'Calm down, fun sponge, it's blackcurrant juice.'

She poured seven glasses and handed them out.

'Cheers, everyone,' she said, clinking her water glass against their juice.

'You not got a beer?' Scar asked.

'Drink it.'

'Or WKD. I don't mind…'

'Drink it!' Luci roared. 'Just drink the fucking juice. All of it. All of you!'

They did as they were told, leaving red rings around their mouths. Luci kept pouring the juice into their glasses until there wasn't a drop left. Indie swallowed it down, its sweetness making her want to gag. She'd lost her appetite now.

'Good,' Luci said, taking a deep breath. 'Now bedtime.'

'Come on!' Blu said beside Indie. 'It's not even nine o'clock yet.'

Luci stared at him, making him shrink back against the edge of the sofa. 'We're getting up before dawn tomorrow. Believe me, you need to rest. Sol and Amber, you take the twin room at the front of the house. Blu and Jade, you take the one at the back. Violet and Indie, there's another room next to the bathroom. I'll be on the top floor.'

'What about me?' Scar asked, stuffing a third taco into his mouth. 'I'm quite happy to snuggle up between Indie and Lavender, or whatever she's called. Or I can swap with you, Blu. I'm sure me and your sister could get cosy.'

Blu was on top of Scar before Indie and Jade could stop him, fries squashed beneath his trainers and taco sauce ground into the carpet. Jade was pulling at his top and Sol had a hold of Scar, but the boys were strong. Luci looked on, partly amused and partly exasperated.

'Stop them!' Indie cried, looking at her. 'If you need them healthy tomorrow, then stop them beating the crap out of each other.'

Luci sighed, then waved her hands in the air like she was conducting an orchestra. Scar went flying one way and Blu the other, both crashing into the wall at opposite ends of the room.

'Scar, you're sleeping down here on the sofa,' Luci said. 'If I hear you so much as attempt to speak to any of these girls, I will rip your balls off and make you wear them as earrings. Is that understood?'

He nodded, wiping at the blood around his mouth. Indie could have sworn Blu split Scar's eye socket with the first punch, but beside the food all over his clothes Scar looked untouched. Everyone turned to Blu, who was already on his feet and dusting himself off. He too had sauce stains on his sleeves, but no cuts or bruises.

'Blu, you better watch your temper tomorrow. A move like that could get us all killed. Understood?' Luci said.

He nodded too, then sat back beside Indie and took a swig of his cola.

'Good. That's enough testosterone for one night. And Scar?' He looked up at her, the dim light of the room making his angular face look more demonic than usual. 'You may want to get to know Violet a little better.'

Violet made a choking noise on her taco and put it down, her face full of revulsion. 'I'm good, thanks. I don't need to get to know him any more than I do already.'

'Yeah,' Scar said, kissing his teeth. 'She ain't my type anyway.'

Luci looked at them, nonplussed. 'No, Scar, she's *not* your type. She's your sister. Have you not noticed you a similar eye colour? That's because you have the same father. Archangel Chamuel. You are children of a celestial warrior.'

Violet looked from Luci to Scar, then ran out of the room crying, with Jade chasing after her. The room was silent, save for the thumping of feet on the stairs and the distant sound of sobbing.

'Tonight's going to be fun,' Indie whispered to Blu. 'I have to share a room with that girl.'

28

A BLACK CAT dashed in front of Zac, nearly tripping him up, as he made his way down Orchard Way. He'd forgotten what winter nights in England were like—dark, cold, and wet. Curtains were drawn, a soft glow highlighting their edges, and bin bags rustled at the end of people's drives as the wind blew his hair into his face. It wasn't raining, but it wasn't far off.

He glanced at his watch for the fourth time since he'd alighted from the bus at Muswell Hill. It said twenty to nine, but he couldn't remember whether he'd adjusted his watch on the plane or not. Was it Spanish time or English?

What would he do if Ella wasn't home? He'd wait on her doorstep, that's what he'd do. It wouldn't be the first time he'd huddled in a doorway all night just to catch a glimpse of her.

Zac raised the hood of his top beneath his coat, although it did nothing to keep away the bite of the January wind. He was a fool. Huddle in her doorway? What was he thinking? He had to stop acting like a stalking chancer and get a grip! He was there to tell her they were both free, off the angelic grid, and that he loved her. His days of lurking in shadows were over.

House numbers to his right were odd and in ascending order. 341... 343...and finally...345 Orchard Way. He was outside Ella's house and the upstairs light was on. She was home.

This was it.

The gate creaked as he pushed it open and headed for the front door. He took a deep breath, then turned around again. No, he couldn't do it. Maybe he'd sit on her garden wall instead, keep his back to the house, and take a few minutes to think this through.

As far as Ella was concerned, this was the first time she was seeing Zac since she was nineteen years old. The last time she'd seen him he'd just sliced his own wings off in front of her and died at her feet. He couldn't just knock on her door and say hi like he'd been away for a long weekend!

'Oi!' A woman was shouting at him. 'Get off my garden wall. I've told you lot before. Go smoke somewhere else.'

Zac smiled at the sound of the voice. Ella's voice. He didn't move—he wanted to hear it again.

'I mean it,' she shouted. 'When will you boys stop sitting on my wall? I'm not shutting this door until you piss off!'

Zac stood slowly and, keeping in the shadows, turned around to face her. The street was dimly lit, and he knew she wouldn't be able to see his face under his hood. He thought back to that day at the back of the bus, how he'd hidden from Ella just like this before rescuing her from Josh. Rescuing—ha! Ridiculous. Who had he been fooling? Josh had become her husband, her true love. Zac should have kept his hood up that day and saved everyone the pain.

Ella was still standing on her doorstep, hands on hips. This wasn't how he'd imagined seeing her after all this time. On the plane over he'd practised a special speech about fate and the universe and taking chances, but it seemed futile and silly now he was standing before her.

Though she couldn't see his face, he could see hers perfectly, the light of the hallway highlighting her curls and soft skin. She was wearing tartan pyjamas, her feet bare, and in her right hand she held a glass of orange juice. She hadn't changed a bit; she looked exactly like she did in the photo Gabriel had shown him in Florence. Even without makeup, with her hair tied back, and wearing shapeless bedclothes she was still a picture of utter perfection.

'Don't you dare walk down my path, you little sod. One more step and I'm calling the…'

'Rivers?' he said, lowering his hood. 'It's me.'

Ella stopped talking. In fact, she looked like she'd stopped breathing. She took a step closer, her hand trembling so violently the juice from her glass spilled over the edge and onto her hand.

'No,' she said. 'No. It's not you. I don't believe it.'

'I came back.'

He stepped into the light and she gasped, dropping her drink on the stone path. The glass smashed, a piece of glass grazing her bare toe. Zac thought back to the time they'd met when he was working at Indigo. Fate certainly had a sense of humour, and history a predictable tendency to repeat itself.

'Zac?'

He went to kneel down, to lay his hand on her foot and stem the bleeding, but before he had a chance to move she swung around and threw up over her lavender bush. Vomit dripped off the tiny purple flowers as the night air filled with the sound of her retching.

This wasn't panning out as he'd imagined. He'd made the girl he loved vomit from the shock of seeing him! He watched on helplessly. Would rubbing her back help, or would it piss her off further? He decided to heal her. Crouching down, he ran his finger along her foot until the cut closed. Her flesh reacted to his touch, a line of goose bumps pushing against his fingertips, making his own skin pucker. While he was on the ground, he picked up the broken glass and placed it on the side of the path, then stood and put his arm around her.

'Are you OK?' he said. 'I'm sorry. I didn't mean to scare you.'

'Get off me!' she cried, straightening up slowly and wiping her mouth with her sleeve. 'You've got to be kidding me! Now? *Now*, after twenty bloody years? You know it's been twenty years, right?'

The curtains at the window next door twitched.

'Can I come inside, please?' he said quietly. 'I can explain everything somewhere more private.'

'Go away, Zac. *Go!*

'Really?' he said, his voice catching in his throat.

'Yes.'

'You want me to leave?'

'Yes. No. I *never* wanted you to leave, *remember*? That was the whole fucking point. You weren't meant to leave me!'

He closed his eyes. Well, what did he expect? Tears of gratitude? Frenzied kissing? A warm dinner by the fire and a night of reminiscing?

'Just get inside,' she said, hobbling down the path to her front door. 'I can't stand here all night, covered in blood and sick.'

Zac followed her into the house and shut the door behind him. Well, that hadn't exactly gone to plan. But then, when it came to Ella, nothing ever did.

29

HE WAS IN her house. Zac. The angel who'd died for her on a rain-soaked Spanish mountain when she was a teenager. The guy who'd saved her life more times than she could count. Her first love. And the one who'd left her when she'd needed him most.

What the hell was he doing back, and why now after so long?

She told him to take a seat in her living room then ran upstairs to the bathroom to brush her teeth. Was she imagining it? What if it was just someone that *looked* like Zac, and she'd invited some random hoodie into her home by accident? She stuck the toothbrush into her mouth far too roughly, gagged, then ran back to the landing and looked over the banister. It was definitely Zac. Her Zac from twenty years ago looking the same as he had back then. Well, of course he did, because he was an angel. A dead angel zombie ex-boyfriend. *Fuck!*

She washed her hands and changed into the first set of clean pyjamas she could find, all the while checking her eyes weren't playing tricks on her. Pyjamas? Why didn't she put proper clothes on? Too late, she wasn't wasting any more time. He was still there, sitting on her sofa, head in his hands and mumbling to himself. What was he saying? Something about a speech.

She checked her face in the mirror—old—and took her hair out of its ponytail. That was pointless too. Her hair was too greasy and remained flat at the front, with a weird lump in the middle and then frizz. Jesus! Why was she bothering? She was a nearly forty-year-old widow with a twenty-something/two-thousand-year-old ghost of an old flame downstairs. What she looked like was the least of her problems. Still, at least she no longer smelled of sick.

Zac looked up as she descended the stairs, but she wasn't prepared for his eyes. The full force of blue hit her, a kaleidoscope of colour and emotion shining brighter than any precious stone. A fresh wave of nausea washed over her, and she gripped on to the banister to stop herself from stumbling.

'Can I get you a drink?' she asked.

She didn't wait for an answer as she turned right into the kitchen and poured gin onto ice, then added tonic, but not a lot. She drank half of it before topping it up with more tonic. The ice cubes clinked together as she walked back into the living room. Zac hadn't moved.

'Are you OK?' he asked.

She nodded, then her phone rang. She considered ignoring it then remembered Indie was on a school trip. She glanced at the screen. It was Enzo. She'd added his number to her phone after their weird yoga encounter, and he must have found her number on her website. What the hell did he want this time of night? It didn't matter, now was not the time for a chat. She ended the call.

'Don't mind me. If you need to speak to someone I can wait outside or...'

'It was just some guy. Enzo. He's a photographer, like me.'

'You're dating?'

'No.'

'I can…' Zac went to stand but Ella held her hands out in front of her.

'Please…just…just sit down.'

She chose the armchair across from him and looked at the fallen angel properly. He wore a grey hoodie under a leather jacket. Was it the same top he'd worn the day they'd first met? Surely not. Jeans. Trainers. Long wavy hair. The bluest of blue eyes. How did they do that? The blues were merging into one another like marbling on paper—swirls of aquamarine into cobalt, then running to navy and indigo. *Indigo!*

Did Zac know she had a daughter? Did he know she'd married Josh, and that he'd then died? How had Zac found her? Oh crap, he was probably reading her mind right now and picking up on all her jumbled emotions.

'I've missed you,' he said, his voice a cracked whisper.

Every cell in her body lit up and her eyes pooled with tears. How long had she longed to hear him say that? But not now. Too much had happened to allow herself to be swept up in him like she'd been at nineteen. Life wasn't that simple anymore.

She didn't trust herself to speak, so she stayed silent.

'There's so much to tell you,' he said. 'Starting with the fact that I came back for you, three years after I died. The moment I awoke in a tomb in Highgate cemetery I went looking for you. You need to know that you were the first thing on my mind.'

Ella took another sip of her gin and tonic, but she couldn't taste it. Her head was swimming. What did he mean he'd come back for her? She took a deep breath, but that didn't help either. He glanced at her hand gripping the arm of the armchair.

Opening her mouth to speak she discovered her tongue had disappeared, and in its place was a mouth full of sawdust and bitterness.

'I went to your hotel. In Tarifa,' Zac continued, looking down at his trainers. Why wouldn't he look at her? Perhaps it was best he didn't—she might be sick again.

'The day I found you was…'

He stopped talking. Silence hung between them, heavy and loaded. Her lips parted again, but no sound came out.

'It was your wedding day,' he said eventually. 'I saw how happy you were, how fate had brought you and Josh together as planned, so I walked away.'

Ella couldn't move. Her hand burned with the cold from her icy drink, the other hand still grasping the armrest, fingertips digging into its soft fabric. She couldn't see his face, just a mop of soft curls as he stared down at his feet. There was something warm on her cheeks. Tears, leaving wet tracks along her face, down her neck, and into the collar of her pyjama top. She didn't move to wipe them away. She didn't make a sound. She couldn't.

Perhaps because of the silence, or the stillness that vibrated between them, Zac slowly looked up. When his eyes met hers, she felt the ground shift.

'You came back?' she whispered, her voice soft as a sigh.

He nodded.

'And you let me marry Josh anyway?'

Zac blinked twice, not taking his eyes off her. Her tears were falling heavier now, his silhouette nothing but a watery blur. She thought she saw his hand reach out for her, she blinked, and it was back on his lap.

'It's more complicated than that.'

'How, Zac? How is it more complicated? You came back for me—but you walked away without even saying hello? *I thought you were dead!*'

Her voice came out a high, warbled squeak. She sniffed, her mouth filling with snot and saliva. Blood, sick, tears, and now mucus. Lovely. She ran into the kitchen, put her empty glass down, grabbed a wad of kitchen towel, and blew her nose. Her head was pounding, her eyes stinging. Passing the mirror in the hallway she caught sight of her reflection and grimaced.

Back in the living room Zac had his face in his hands. His eyes were bloodshot and his skin paler than she remembered. She leaned against the doorway, her legs too shaky to take her back to the armchair.

'Ella, I did say hello. We even… You said you wouldn't marry Josh, that you wanted to be with me, but then we agreed it was too dangerous.'

'Don't lie to me!' she shouted, shocking them both. She marched back into the room until she was standing before him. 'Don't tell me you spoke to me. I think I'd remember if we spoke!'

He sighed, a long, heavy sigh filled with so much pain Ella thought he was going to start crying. He appeared to be collapsing in on himself, getting smaller and smaller, his face sunken, his shoulders hunched.

'My mother erased your memory. Mikhael heard you were marrying Josh and we couldn't risk him finding me or her…or killing you. I didn't want to leave you, but Luci and Gabriel were right—it was too dangerous for me to stay.'

Ella's breaths were coming in short bursts. 'Your mother? I met your mother? And Archangel Gabriel was there? Who else attended my wedding without me knowing?'

'Sebastian.'

Ella's eyes widened, her head shaking in small jerky movements. Her stepbrother?

'It's OK. My mother killed him,' Zac continued. 'It's a long story, but she did it for you. She killed Sebastian for you.'

Ella swayed and Zac caught her, gently manoeuvring her onto the sofa beside him. She lowered her head between her legs, resting her elbows on her knees, and tried to remember how to breathe. No way. No, this wasn't happening. None of it made sense, yet it explained so much. The shadows in the gallery watching her get married. The blood on her dress and the altar. No one being able to track her stepbrother down since he'd gone on the run twenty years ago. Her headache and that awful feeling of unease on her wedding day. Zac didn't lie, he *couldn't* lie, which meant everything he was saying was true.

'You found your mother?'

'Yes.'

'Your plan worked, then? She came back from the dead and so did you?'

He nodded.

'Is she nice?'

His mouth set in a straight line. His silence spoke volumes.

'You know Josh is dead, right?'

He nodded again.

'And that Josh and I had a daughter together?'

He gave a small smile, and their eyes met for a second, or perhaps it was a lifetime. Ella pointed at the mantelpiece where there was a photo of her with her arms around Indie. It was taken by Josh the day before he died, on the same beach where his body had washed up. Indie was ten in the photo, but Ella couldn't bear to update it knowing it was the last photo Josh ever took of his family.

'She looks like you,' Zac said, smiling.

What did he want from her? Why was he here?

'My mind is bursting with questions, Zac. I don't know where to start. But I guess you already know how I feel.'

'No. I no longer have that ability,' he said quietly.

'Oh.'

'Were you going to ask what I'm doing here after all this time?'

'Yes.'

Zac bit down on his lower lip. He looked so young—had he always looked so young? She remembered thinking he was so big and powerful when she first met him, but now he looked like a very confused and sad boy.

'I'm glad you're sitting down, because it's about to get even weirder,' he said. 'I didn't learn that you were still alive until last week.'

'What do you mean "alive?"' A shiver ran up Ella's spine. Was she in danger?

'You were meant to have died with Josh. I've known your death date since before you were born. When I heard about the boat accident, I knew you'd followed your path and were dead. I grieved for you, Ella. For years after your death, I was a mess. I no longer wanted to live, but I don't have that choice—I can't die. I didn't even bother to double-check whether you were truly gone because no one has ever escaped their destiny; even Gabriel said he could no longer feel you. My life ended that day. I stopped speaking to my mother, and I cut myself off from the world.' He rubbed his face again and let out a long breath. 'I knew I wouldn't see you again, that I wouldn't be able to find you in your next life, because of who I am now. I missed my chance to say goodbye to you, and that was it… I'd lost you forever.'

A single tear ran down Zac's cheek, and he brushed it away quickly. When he continued speaking, his voice was raw and husky.

'I saw Gabriel last week and he said he read a recent interview with you in a magazine. *You were alive.* I didn't believe him. I had to see it with my own eyes.'

His shaky hand hovered over hers, but he thought twice and pulled away, returning it to his lap.

'I did die.'

Zac looked up, his eyes puffy and pink.

'You did?'

'Yes, I was officially dead for fifty-seven seconds. I was dead, then I came back. The doctors said it was very unusual for me to have returned without any form of resuscitation, that they must have missed my pulse, or the machines were faulty. But I know I died. I remember.'

Zac pressed the heel of his hands into his eyes, his head moving slowly from side to side. 'I'm so sorry. I should have been there. You should never have suffered alone. I've let so many years go by. I had no idea.'

'Hey, it's not your fault,' Ella said with a wavering smile. 'You're here now, and neither of us are dead anymore. So that's a good start.'

He returned her smile, such a sad one it made her heart crack a little.

'Can I hug you?' he asked.

Did she dare? For the last six years, since Josh had died, she'd held herself together by nothing more than tangled gossamer threads of uncertainty and a sticky resolve made from the knowledge that everything in her life was happening for a reason. She'd dealt with Zac's death, and her husband's, and she'd survived—because she'd believed it was all part of a bigger plan. Except it hadn't been. The last six years had not been her destiny. She'd learned how to live alone, to be the strong one that held everything together. If Zac touched her after all this time, would she crumble and collapse? Would her resolve come tumbling down?

She nodded her head slowly, and he took her in his arms. The moment his hands slid around her waist and up her back she felt it, every single one of her emotions crashing like a tidal wave. She buried her face into the crook of his neck and breathed him in. She was nineteen again, and her angel was making the world a safer place for her.

This time the tears appeared with no warning. She wrapped her arms around his neck and her entire body shook. Like the barriers of a dam bursting, she released a deluge of pain upon the fallen angel—and in turn, he cried his own river of relief.

'I have so much I need to tell you,' he said. 'I don't know where to start. Perhaps I can come back tomorrow. We can meet for a coffee, maybe?'

'No. Don't go,' she sobbed into his shoulder. 'I couldn't bear to see you go again. Can you stay? My daughter is away tonight. I have a spare room. Would you mind?'

She felt him smile against her cheek and he held her tighter.

'Of course. I'm not going anywhere. Not now.'

30

INDIE HAD BEEN standing in the hallway, outside her bedroom door, for ten minutes. She had four options.

1. Tell Jade to get out of her room so she could go to sleep. Except Violet had started crying again and Jade had insisted on them talking in private.

2. Go downstairs and watch TV, but Scar was on the sofa and who wanted to be anywhere near *that* creep right now?

3. Sit in the hallway all night.

4. Knock on Blu's bedroom door and ask him if she could chill out with him.

It wasn't much of a contest. She knocked on his door and, upon hearing his voice, stepped into the room. He was sitting up in a single bed, his knees raised beneath the duvet and a comic balanced upon them. On the other side of the room was a sofa with Jade's clothes on it. He looked amused to see her. As he placed the magazine facedown beside him Indie realised he'd been reading manga, and that the cover was emblazoned in Japanese letters. She had no idea he spoke another language, let alone read it.

'Sorry to barge in. I had nowhere else to go.'

Blu narrowed his eyes and looked at her in that special way of his—head tilted to one side and top lip curled like he was secretly laughing at her. But in a nice way.

'What's wrong with your own room? Does Violet snore?'

'Violet is still upset that she's related to a street rat, and your sister is in my room. They said I had to get out for an hour or so, that they needed to talk in private. I don't want to go downstairs in case Scar is still skulking about, and I don't want Miss Luci...I mean, Luci...'

Blu laughed quietly under his breath. 'I don't blame you. Come join me,' he said, patting the bed.

Did he really expect her to sit on his bed? At night?

'I'll sit on the sofa, it's OK.'

'I wouldn't. We tried turning it into a sofa bed and now it's all twisted up inside. You might get jabbed by a bedspring.'

Indie had never been in a boy's bedroom this late before—in fact the only boy's room she'd ever been in was Jesse's, and he didn't count. She crossed her arms over her flannel pyjamas and perched on the edge of the bed.

'I'll go back once Jade and Violet have stopped talking.'

'You might have a long wait,' Blu said with a smirk.

'I'm so tired,' she mumbled. 'Today has been beyond weird and I really need to lie in the dark and process it, not pace the hallway waiting for them to finish their private chat.'

She had her back to Blu, partly out of respect—she had no idea what he was wearing under the covers—but mainly because if she looked at him, she'd want to sit closer. And if she sat closer, she'd get too relaxed. And she couldn't risk falling asleep in his bed and making things awkward between them.

'I don't think my sister is coming back tonight,' Blu said.

Indie swung around.

'Why are you finding this so funny? I need to get to sleep. What is so important that Jade and Violet need to…'

Oh! She was so stupid.

Blu must have seen the penny drop because he wiggled his eyebrows, making Indie laugh.

'Yeah, Jade likes girls—and she's not shy about letting them know. And Violet, with her purple hair and big, round, pink eyes like some anime character? Totally her type. I don't think you'll be sleeping in your room tonight.'

Indie made a face, and Blu laughed. He patted his duvet again.

'It's only a single bed but it's quite big, and I'm not starkers under here. I'm wearing me Batman PJs.'

She shuffled up and sat beside him, on top of the duvet.

'Batman pyjamas?'

He grinned and lowered the covers. His T-shirt was bright yellow with a Batman logo on the front, and his trousers were cotton and covered with cartoon strips. She laughed out loud again. Blu was a geek! So much for the cool, tattooed boy that won her over with his witty charm and charisma.

'I never had you down as a Marvel fan.'

'DC. Batman is DC Comics. Spider-Man is Marvel. Don't be getting those two mixed up—they don't like it.'

'Have you always been a superhero fan?'

Blu turned to her, head resting on his bent arm.

'Yeah. Me and Jade used to dress up when we were little. We used to tell our mams we had magical powers, and of course they'd play along. Took us a while to realise our parents thought we were pretending. Hey!' He gave her leg a nudge. 'Why you looking at me like that?'

She'd been thinking about baby Blu. How cute a tiny version of him running about in a mask would have looked, and how nice it must be to have a sibling to share secrets with.

'You're a dork,' she said, tracing the lines of the Batman logo on his chest. His breath caught at her touch, and she snatched her hand away. Had *she* made him do that? Was he squirming because of her? She shivered at the thought.

'You cold?' he asked, tugging at the duvet beneath her. 'Get in. I won't bite. The caped crusader is quite valiant, you know.'

She shuffled under the covers, letting him tuck them around her. Her eyes were already getting heavy.

'Warmer now?'

'Yeah. Thanks.'

Blu went back to reading his magazine and Indie lay rigid, staring up at the ceiling, so close to the edge of the bed she was practically falling off. After a while he put down the comic and turned to her.

'You tired? Want me to turn the light out?'

She shook her head.

'What's up?' he asked, inching closer. Warmth radiated off him.

'I'm scared.'

She hadn't realised how frightened she was until she heard herself say it out loud. She was more than scared though—she was terrified. Was Luci really who she said she was, or one very disturbed, dangerous woman? And what the hell was she going to make them do tomorrow?

'You don't trust Luci?' Blu asked.

He shuffled closer still, making her stomach plummet right through the mattress and spill out over the floor. She was overreacting. They sat a lot closer than this at lunchtime, and when they walked home together their shoulders nearly touched. Yet being alone in a bed, his body inches from hers—well, that was different. She shivered again. Blu must have noticed her discomfort because he moved away a little but then lay a hand over hers on top of the duvet, making her feel even more light-headed.

'Hey, Indie,' he said, shaking her hand until she looked at him. His eyes shone minty green like a cat's in the sunshine. She'd never seen them up close like this before. 'Try not to stress, yeah? Luci's cool. She's here to help us. She said tomorrow we're going to meet our fathers.'

'My father's dead,' Indie said quickly, her voice barely a whisper.

Blu made an apologetic face, then squeezed her hand tighter.

'Sorry. I didn't mean… It's just that, Luci said…'

'She said we come from angels!' Indie spat, louder this time. She held his gaze. 'Angels, Blu. Fucking angels! The woman's crazy.'

She sniffed. She hated how she always got teary when she was scared. It was easier around other people, focussing on their emotions meant she didn't notice her own until she was alone hours later. But with Blu, her emotions were always there, raw and on the surface, begging to be noticed.

'Hey, don't get upset. Come here,' he said, pulling her toward him so her head was on his shoulder. His arm was trapped behind her back, but he didn't seem to mind. She let him, her left hand squashed between them and her head in the hollow beneath his arm. She tried not to read too much into it. He probably hugged his sister and other girls all the time, the same way he put his arm around everyone. He was just one of those guys.

'I think it's ridiculous,' she continued, talking into his chest. 'Everyone knows angels don't exist.'

'And mind-reading kids with neon eyes and supernatural abilities *do*?' He laughed. 'We're a bunch of freaks, Indie. All of us. She's brought us together because she has a higher purpose for us. I'm curious about tomorrow. And don't forget…' He gripped her shoulder tighter. 'Jesus is my half brother.'

'And the Devil is my grandmother.'

'OK, you win.'

Indie melted into his chest and closed her eyes. She didn't know whether to laugh, cry, or scream with frustration. It was so quiet. Not outside—the wind was still blowing and the rhythmic swoosh of cars on the wet road outside was making her sleepy—but inside her head there was a wonderful expanse of silence. She couldn't remember the last time she'd been in a house full of people with her mind full of nothing but her own thoughts. Why were she and these other kids different? And how on earth had Luci managed to find so many others like her?

'Blu? Do you really think our fathers are angels?'

He breathed in deeply, making her head wobble on his chest.

'Who knows? Me birth mam, before she died, told me aunt that she knew nothing about me dad except he had crazy green eyes and looked like a model. Then he just disappeared. Maybe he was different, like us. Think about it; you don't look anything like your dad.'

'You don't know anything about my…'

'Yeah, I do. I know he was the actor Josh de Silva,' Blu said, squeezing her closer to him. She could feel his warm breath on the crown of her head. 'Jesse told me the first time I met him. I never mentioned it because you never talk about him, so I figured it was private. I didn't want you to think that's why I wanted to be your friend. Anyway, you don't look like him.'

Indie swallowed down the lump in her throat. She was too tired and too confused to be angry at Jesse for being such a gossip. Also, Blu was right, she looked nothing like her dad. Memories came flooding back of the way her father used to look at her, how strong she'd felt his emotions. He'd always known she wasn't his, although Indie had no idea how he knew. He still adored her though. The fierce love he had for his family radiated off him stronger than anything else. Maybe that was why she had no siblings. Perhaps her dad wasn't able to have kids, and he knew it, but kept quiet when Ella got pregnant because he'd wanted a family. Or maybe he just felt it, deep down, that Indie wasn't his. She'd never know.

'Who do I look like, then?' Indie asked Blu, looking up at him until their faces were inches apart.

'You really want to know?'

She nodded.

'You look exactly like her,' Blu said. 'Like Luci.'

Indie closed her eyes, wincing as the knots in her stomach grew tighter.

'I know.'

'So you believe she's the Devil and you're her granddaughter?' he asked.

Indie shrugged, which wasn't easy to do clamped as tightly as she was against his side.

'I don't know. She's deranged and she's powerful, yes, but maybe all our abilities get stronger with age. No way is she immortal though, with a son old enough to be my father. That's crazy. And no way would my mum have cheated on my dad. Those two were madly in love. I felt it. There was nothing fake about that.'

Everything Indie was saying was true—except for one thing. That constant lilac mist. The heavy cloud that always descended over her mother when she spoke of destiny, religion, or her teen life in London. There was something there, something half-forgotten and too painful to confront.

Blu was still looking at her. 'You're right, Luci sounds like a loon—even if those hippy kids, Sol and Amber, are totally convinced. As soon as we get the chance tomorrow, we'll make a run for it and get out of here. OK?' He placed his thumb under her chin and tipped her face up, so he was looking straight at her. 'I won't let anything happen to you, Indie. I promise.'

'Really?' she said, not daring to look away from his turquoise-speckled eyes. 'You think you can hold your own against a woman with powers so strong she's trapped us in a big house in the middle of nowhere, taken our phones, and thinks she's Lucifer? You'd fight that?'

Blu laughed softly into her hair. 'Yeah. For you I would.'

Indie tried to take a breath but had forgotten how, so she drank in the sight of him instead. What would happen if she put her hand on his chest again? Did she dare? She placed her right hand back on the Batman logo and he took a sharp breath.

'I wish we weren't here,' she said, her voice sounding far away and hollow.

'Where would you prefer to be?'

His voice was different too, deep and raspy as if he needed to clear his throat. He was still looking at her, the pupils of his eyes so dark they left nothing but a light green ring around them.

'I'd prefer to be in my room. Or yours. Together, like this, just not in the same house as a bunch of supernatural teenagers we've never met before.'

His full lips twitched at the edges. Once upon a time, even just a few weeks ago, the idea of being in this situation would have terrified her. She wasn't like this. Boys didn't like her like this. But after everything she'd experienced since she'd met Blu and his sister, and now being in a strange house surrounded by strange people, this was the most natural thing she could think of doing. She couldn't feel Blu, but she knew what he wanted. This was what it must be like to be normal. To just know. To trust your instincts.

'And what would you do, if it was just us. Like this. Alone?' he asked, his voice barely a whisper.

Indie angled her face higher, close enough to smell the soap on his skin.

'I'd let you kiss me.'

He parted his lips, moving a fraction closer without taking his eyes off hers. She gave a tiny nod of her head and he closed the distance between them, brushing his lips against hers. Indie closed her eyes and focused on every inch of her body popping like tiny bubbles. This wasn't the same feeling she experienced when she walked past couples kissing, or when she soaked up the attraction others found toward her. And it was a lot sweeter than the hunger she'd felt between Jesse and Xavier.

This was tender and soft. These were her *own* emotions, just hers, and they were dissolving her from the inside out.

Blu was kissing her, *actually kissing her*. Indie's very first kiss. But it only lasted a couple of seconds.

'Like that?' Blu said, out of breath.

Indie shook her head slightly and swallowed.

'No. I would let you kiss me properly.'

This time his smile split his face in half, all shiny white teeth and dimples. She shuffled up to sitting, releasing her left arm and draping them both around his neck.

'Properly?' he said, stroking her hair slowly until his fingers came to rest on her collarbone.

'Properly. Like this.'

She didn't know if it was her newfound powers, or learning who she really was, or being this close to Blu—but she suddenly felt emboldened. Invincible. Brave. She pressed her lips against his and his tongue moved against hers as they leaned into one another's embrace. He lay her back on the bed and turned into her, his mouth urgent but tender against hers. They kissed forever. Days and nights passed. Planets collided. New stars exploded into being and nothing was left of the universe but tiny little bubbles popping inside of her and his soft lips on hers.

When they finally came up for air, Blu was the first to speak.

'Fuck.'

Indie smoothed her hair down and cleared her throat.

'Yeah. So…'

'Fuck. Indie, I… Fuck.'

'You OK?'

'Yeah. No.' He sat up and straightened his T-shirt. Then opened his mouth to say something, frowned, shook his head, and attempted to speak again. 'That's the first time I've kissed like that.'

She blinked. Once. Twice.

'You must have kissed other girls before.'

'Yeah. Course. But not like that. I mean, that was... Didn't you think that was different?'

Her cheeks prickled. 'I don't know. That was my first kiss.'

Blu's face softened, and he tucked a stray hair behind her ear.

'Well, lucky you, because it was perfect. Come here.' He pulled her toward him and held her tight. She held him back, breathing him in and running her hands over the back of his head. His chest rose and fell in time with hers.

'You know I'm crazy about you, right?' he murmured into her shoulder. He planted a kiss where his words had been. 'Since the first day we spoke at school I needed to be with you. It's like, until I met you, I wasn't properly alive. You know? Like everything was noise and darkness, but with you I can see clearly. I can breathe properly. It's wild.'

He pulled away quickly, his hands resting on her shoulders.

'Listen. I have no idea what's going to happen tomorrow. Today has been mad, surreal, but you... You and me... This is real. Right? I mean, that kiss, us. You didn't do that just because you were scared. I mean, you like me too, right?'

Indie stroked his cheek, smiling at the panic in his bright eyes.

'Of course I like you, Blu. A lot. I want this, just like you do. Although, you should be aware that making this official will mean more kissing. You think you can handle that?'

Blu didn't smile. Instead he cupped her face in his hands and kissed her so long and hard that she fell back against the bed, his body pressed against hers. So many emotions fought for attention, but all she could do was kiss him back and enjoy the feeling. Every one of her own wonderful, precious feelings. Whatever happened tomorrow, this had happened tonight. Her and Blu. That's all that mattered right now.

'We need to get up early tomorrow,' he mumbled, kissing her neck and making her squirm.

Indie sat up and jumped out of bed.

'OK. You're right. I better get back to my room and get some sleep.'

'Whoa. Wait. If you want to go that's cool, but Jade is in your room. Want me to get her out?'

Indie shook her head. 'Shit, I forgot. No, leave her. I can stay in this room with you, but...'

Blu held up his hands. 'I'll stick to my side of the bed, I promise. No touching. Or I can try and sleep on that.'

They both looked over at the broken sofa and laughed. She threw a pillow at him.

'I *want* touching, you dork. Lots of touching.'

'Really? Because I think it would be better to take our time and...'

'Cuddling! I meant touching of the hugging kind.'

He grinned. 'Oh. Good. That's my favourite kind.'

He lifted up the covers again and she slipped under, pecking him on the lips.

'Good night, Blu. And thank you.'

'For what?'

'For being you. For understanding me.'

'Same,' he said, turning out the light.

She turned her back to him and sighed as she felt his arms slip around her waist.

'I could get used to this, de Silva,' he murmured into her neck.

She smiled into the darkness. So could she.

31

AFTER SHOWING ZAC to the spare room, Ella had padded quietly to her bedroom where she'd spent an hour staring at the ceiling.

It hadn't been easy saying good night. She'd done it quickly with an air of indifference, thankful he could no longer feel her true emotions. But what was she feeling anyway? She could no longer tell.

She'd wanted to stay up all night asking question after question, but her head was about to explode. Him being in her house was surreal enough, let alone everything he'd said about his mother still being alive, interrupting her wedding day, and then her memories being deleted.

How could she believe anything she didn't remember? And what did he want from her?

All the years she'd imagined Zac's return, even after marrying Josh, she'd always seen it as dramatic and sexy, but it wasn't. It was raw and confusing. After their hug she'd made him a cup of tea and, after a few minutes of polite small talk, they'd both agreed they were tired and needed to get some sleep. That was it. Now she was in bed tossing and turning, trying desperately to pick apart the memories of her wedding day for any glimmer of the truth she'd been forced to forget.

It was no use.

She silently opened her bedroom door and tiptoed down the hallway until she was standing outside the spare room. Zac was on the other side. Was he asleep, or was he too lying in bed thinking about her? She placed the palm of her hand on the wood, imagining it soaking up his energy and sending it through her body. He said he could no longer feel her. Even if he couldn't sense her standing there, surely her heart was beating loud enough for him to hear.

She opened the door a crack, not wanting to knock in case he was asleep. He wasn't. He was sitting up in bed reading an old copy of *National Geographic* she kept on the nightstand. Zac was completely oblivious to her standing there, giving her flashbacks of the last time he'd stayed the night at her house. She could see him in her mind's eye sprawled out on her sofa, the dull light of the winter sun highlighting the undulations of his chest and the muscles in his shoulders. Nothing had changed; he looked exactly the same. Unlike Ella. Back then she'd been a gorgeous nineteen year old. He hadn't said anything about wanting her back, but even if Ella *was* interested, she was sure he wouldn't want what she had become. He carried on reading and turning the pages, the golden light of the bedside lamp making his bare torso glow.

'Zac?'

He jumped and shut the magazine quickly.

'Ella! I didn't know you were there. Can't sleep either?'

She shook her head and smiled shyly. This was silly. She was a grown woman, and this was her house. What did she have to be embarrassed about?

'Come in,' he said, beckoning her over with a nod of his head. He pulled the duvet up until it covered his chest.

Ella shut the door and perched on the end of the bed. 'Are you warm enough? Can I get you anything? I forgot to ask if you needed a toothbrush. I have some spare ones in…'

'I'm fine. Thank you.'

Ella picked at her thumbnail, willing herself to say something. Anything. This was Zac, for goodness' sake; her problem used to be speaking *too* much around him. There was still so much she wanted to ask, yet here they were looking at their hands like awkward teenagers. He'd noticed her picking at her thumb and was smiling, probably wondering why she hadn't ditched the habit years ago.

'This is strange,' she said. 'You. In my house. In my spare room. I never…'

'You look like you're going to fall off the end of the bed,' he said, motioning with his head for her to move up.

She shuffled closer. It had been fine downstairs, when they were sitting in the living room and she was still in shock, but now the air between them felt charged. Something about the early hours of the morning, the house so still and the streets outside so silent, that made whatever this was feel illicit. She did up the top button of her pyjama top, but it wouldn't stay closed. Her hands were clammy. She surreptitiously wiped them on her pyjama bottoms, wondering why the hell she'd changed into those tatty PJs with purple and green stars, plus one of the sleeves had a hole in it.

She twisted her wedding and engagement rings around, thinking of something to say. Zac had always been comfortable with silence and appeared happy to sit there quietly. Nothing had changed. His eyes were trained on her fingers, on the large pink diamond Josh had presented her with on her birthday seventeen years ago. The day they'd got married felt like yesterday, yet also like a million lifetimes ago. Indie had been telling her mother to take the rings off, that it wouldn't upset her if she chose to date again and start afresh. But Ella felt naked without them. Exposed. Except for now. Although she was nervous and apprehensive, she still felt safe. That was the one thing Zac had always made her feel.

'I was thinking…' she started.

Zac's eyes darted from her hands to her face, trapping her breath in her throat. As he'd lay dying on that stormy Spanish mountain, his eyes had faded from a brilliant blue to a washed-out grey. She thought she'd never see them shine again. Yet here they were, boring into her soul as deeply as they'd always done.

'I was thinking that it's all a bit unfair.'

Zac frowned and sat up, the duvet falling from his chest to his waist. Ella looked away and focused on the wall behind him.

'A lot about our situation has been unfair over the years,' he said carefully. Pain flickered behind his eyes, a hurt so naked Ella flinched. All those memories of his, spanning back thousands of years. 'What exactly are you referring to, Ella?'

She moved a little closer, her back brushing against his raised leg under the covers. She wanted to lean back on it but didn't. Instead she fiddled with her top button, but it wouldn't stay closed.

'It's just that… For years after you left, I imagined you coming back and me jumping straight into your arms and carrying on where we left off.' She gave a little laugh and his face broke into a huge grin. Was that how he'd imagined it too? 'But it's been twenty years since I last saw you, Zac. I was young when we met but I'm forty years old in April. *Forty!* I know that's nothing to you, but I'm more than double the age I was back then. I'm a mother, a widow.' She bit her lips together and gathered herself. 'I run my own business, I have a home and responsibilities, and what we had, it was…it was a fling. We had a love affair that lasted a couple of months on and off. In fact, we didn't even date. We only saw each other…'

'Nine days,' he said. 'I spent nine days with you in total.'

'Exactly, nine days. We had an amazing time twenty years ago, when I was just a kid, and it lasted *nine days*. What does that even mean? How do I know what we had was true love? What does a nine-teen year old know about real, serious love that lasts forever? I was married for eleven years, Zac. Josh was exactly what you told me he would be. He was perfect. We were so happy.'

A muscle twitched in Zac's jaw. It pained her to upset him, but she had to hear herself say these words out loud. Zac was back. Seeing him was all she'd wanted at the beginning—but too much time had passed. It was unrealistic to think they could be anything but friends now. If that.

'What exactly do you think is unfair?' he asked. He was trying to keep his face neutral, but she could see his eyes were full of hope. Hope for what?

She breathed out a big puff of air and attempted to do up the top button of her pyjamas again. Her hands shook, her fingers clumsy. The bloody thing wasn't staying put.

'Let me,' he said.

She moved her hands away, waiting for him to lean over and do it up—but instead he simply looked at her throat until her top moved on its own, the button popping into the slit and staying closed. Ella swallowed, the fabric against her throat like a caress from his fingertips. She had no idea he could still make things move without touching them.

This situation wasn't making her emotions any easier to deal with, him lying there half-naked and perfect, dressing her with only his eyes.

'Your memories of me are over two thousand years old,' she continued. 'So, the way we feel about one another is incomparable. It's not…balanced. You fell in love with me twenty centuries ago, knew me as all these different women and have hundreds of memories of our time together and I…I have nine days,' she added quietly.

His hand was inches from hers, and she willed him to take it. She needed to touch him, feel his skin against hers. She'd got used to the constant gnawing pain of missing her husband, yet until now she hadn't realised that she'd missed Zac just as much…for even longer. But it was futile to wish for his hand in hers—he couldn't sense her anymore, and she wasn't brave enough to take the lead and reach out to him.

'You want to remember me coming back for you?' he said.

She nodded. 'You said you have a new ability now, that you can make people forget. Isn't that what your mother did to me? So maybe you can help me regain all my memories?'

Zac rubbed his face. 'I don't know, Ella. It will change the way you remember your wedding day. I don't want to ruin that for you.'

'But I need to know everything that's happened in my life, Zac. *My* life. You owe me that much and more.'

He raised his eyebrows. 'More?'

'Yes, I want to remember everything.'

'That's all there is, Ella. I only had that one day with you, your wedding day, before I had to let you live your life. There *isn't* any more.'

'Yes, there is. What about the other girls?' She looked down and picked at her thumb again. 'Evie during the war, Arabella when we first met, plus the others you mentioned. You said there were many others.'

Zac lifted her chin with the tip of his finger. Her face hummed under his touch.

'Ella, look at me. You really want to do this?'

She nodded. Their eyes were fixed on one another the same way they had been at Highgate Tube station all those years ago, the first time she felt herself fall into that warm, enveloping blue.

'You want me to bring back every memory your soul has experienced on Earth?' he said. 'In every single lifetime?'

She nodded again, but Zac didn't look convinced.

'I can try, but I'll only let you remember our moments together. Your lives haven't all been easy, Ella, and your deaths definitely weren't. There's no need for you to relive every grisly detail. But one question first…'

She waited, but he went silent, as if searching for the right words.

'What do you think it will achieve?' he asked after a while. 'Why put yourself through this?'

She smiled, finally finding the courage to place her hand on his.

'Because I want to have the same advantage as you, Zac. A level playing field. I need to remember our history together, in order to consider my future.'

32

'SO HOW DOES it work?' Ella asked.

'I don't know. I've never done it before.'

'That's reassuring. Where do you want me?'

Where do you want me? Why was she so incapable of talking normally around him? This was a stupid idea—she should just go back to her own bed. Zac had been back in her life one night and already she was playing with magic and making a fool of herself.

His lips were twitching. Was he laughing at her? Ella rolled her eyes and smiled, and the smile he returned made her nerves wash away.

He patted the bed. 'Get a bit closer. Sit next to me, so I can look into your eyes properly.'

'That's all I have to do? Stare into your eyes?'

'That's what I do when I make people forget, so I guess so.'

She shuffled up until she was sitting cross-legged in front of him on the bed.

'Will it hurt?' she asked, wiping her sweaty hands on her pyjama bottoms again. Classy.

With a slow shake of his head, he placed a hand on either side of her face. It took all her willpower not to lean into his touch. Her stomach was churning like it had been when she'd seen him on her garden path that evening. Throwing up on him would be a terrible idea right now.

'Look at me and relax.'

His face was inches from hers, close enough to kiss him. It would be so easy to lean in right now and press her lips against his, to forget all the complicated obstacles she was placing in their way. Her daughter wasn't home, and she had a semi-naked, young, handsome ex-angel in her spare room. She was practically in bed with him. Why was she going through this charade? She was sure Zac still liked her. Of course he did—he was hardly going to go off her after two thousand years.

Zac started speaking in hushed tones and her own thoughts slowly melted away. At first her mind was blank and bright white, like an empty canvas. Then suddenly it was filling with vivid images. Pictures flickered before her eyes as if someone was thumbing through a colourful picture book.

It had begun.

'Remember our time together since our very first life, but *only* the parts where I feature. Remember your life as Arabella...' He began to reel off a list of names, and with each one a series of images flashed through her mind like a carousel of people and places on fast-forward. After a few minutes he ended with '...then Evie, and finally Ella. Remember our time together in this lifetime, even the moments that were stolen from you. Remember me, Ella. Remember all of me.'

He let go of her face and she blinked in quick succession.

'Well?' he asked.

Ella focused on Zac's face, the lines of concern etched on his forehead and the muscle twitching in his jaw. Her vision was obscured by the millions of scenes fighting for attention in her mind.

'I'm fine,' she muttered. 'I just need to lie down.'

Zac moved out of the way, and she lay back on the pillow and closed her eyes. Tuscan hills, lavender, goats, a little cottage, a river, a healed hand, a kiss, the sweet syrup of figs. The lush green of an island, running, a mountain, jumping, flying. A big house, dark hair, tight petticoats, an inn, two women holding hands. She tried to get the memories in order, understand what belonged to whom, slow down the pictures. After a few breaths she was able to watch the memories in sequence. Nearly one hundred women, some lives short, some long, some decadent and others full of pain. Each existence was condensed, showing just the highlights—a film trailer for each lifetime. Arabella in Roman Fiesole, Ebrah in Islamic Cordoba, Aria in Renaissance Florence, Elien in Dutch Roermond, Isabella in Victorian England, Evie in war-torn London, and a library in a Spanish turret… Her eyes snapped open.

'Zac?'

He was by her side in an instant.

'How are you feeling? Are you in pain? Did it work?'

She sat up, shuffling her bottom back so she was sitting straight against the pillows.

'Did we…' She looked up at the ceiling. 'Turn around.'

He did as instructed, and there it was, the tattoo of wings on his back. Inky feathers spread out from his spine to the backs of his arms. She hadn't noticed it when he was sitting up in bed, but now she could see the way his tattoos peeked over his shoulders and down his arms. She ran her finger over them, ink wings appearing to flutter as his back muscles twitched at her touch.

'I remember. I hit you with a stool, you were bleeding, I saw your tattoo, and then we…'

He was facing her again. Sapphire eyes turning a deep shade of purple.

'We what?' he whispered.

'In the *library*! Above my hotel's *chapel*!'

He shrugged, and she didn't know whether to laugh or cry. That had been her wedding day. She'd remembered getting ready with Mai Li and Kerry, walking down the aisle to Josh who had looked so handsome in that suit and… No… Her old memory ended there and had started again as they'd married but that wasn't how it went. Two hours had passed between walking down the aisle and saying 'I do.' And in that time, she'd somehow ended up in the library with Zac. He'd mentioned his mother had killed Sebastian. Had she murdered him in the chapel? On her wedding day? She could see a woman in a red dress, and Sebastian flying through the air, and Jesus on the… No, that wasn't Jesus on the cross, it was her stepbrother. Luci had impaled him on a giant crucifix. She remembered it all now, how she'd used the secret tunnel to escape to the library and Zac had followed. Had they really made love up there? She couldn't believe she'd so readily given herself over to him, as if Josh had meant nothing to her. But then she'd only known Josh a week before marrying him. Back then he wasn't the person he was to her now. Tiny fragments were flitting through her mind and she struggled to fit them together.

Ella scrambled off the bed, but Zac grabbed her hand.

'Wait, where are you going? Stay seated. You might get dizzy.'

'No, get off! You were right, this changes everything. For so many years I was happily married to Josh, oblivious to the awful things I did. I had no idea that you… That we… This makes a mockery of my marriage!'

Zac let go of her hand. 'Listen, as soon as I realised you were back on your path, I walked away. I never intended to come between you and him. If I hadn't heard you screaming in the chapel when Luci murdered Sebastian, I would never have gone back. All I've ever wanted was for you to be happy.'

She moved toward the bedroom door, but her mind was still processing millions of scenes that kept flooding her mind. Lifetime after lifetime, like a computer downloading a file of images. She shook her head, but she still couldn't see clearly. The room began to swim, and she stumbled. Zac caught her and led her back to the bed.

'I have no idea if the human brain can deal with this many memories,' he said, watching her as if she may explode any minute.

Ella picked at her nails. She couldn't bear to look at his face anymore. Zac was no longer a magical, intense fling she'd had as a teenager—her spiritual awakening—he was now a being that had featured in every single one of her lives. Her memories of him were no longer limited to rainy days in London and forty-eight hours in a little mountain village in Spain. They now spanned continents and millennia.

'What are you thinking?' he asked. She wasn't used to hearing him say that. He'd never had to ask before.

'That my life is a lie.'

He shook his head slowly, his face crumpling with regret. 'My mother should never have taken your memory away. I've hated her for what she did for a very long time, but she did it to save your life. Both of our lives. Your love for Josh was real, and you lived your path exactly as planned. I only came back because I heard you were still alive. You were meant to die six years ago.'

'With Josh.'

He nodded, and Ella bit the inside of her lip to stop her chin from trembling.

'I remember everything now, you know. Not just what happened between us and the time we spent together, but so much more. You may have always had the ability to feel my emotions, Zac, but I bet you had no idea what I was thinking in every lifetime.'

'Thinking?' he said, inching closer to her.

'Yes. You do realise that what a woman feels and says may not be the same thing as what she's thinking.'

He frowned. He clearly did not.

'Give me an example.'

Ella gave a tiny smile, because for the first time they were truly equal. He no longer knew her better than she knew him.

'My memories aren't only of the times we spent together,' she said. 'But also of every time I thought of you. Which was a lot.'

His cheeks tinged a light pink. He looked up, then looked down just as quickly.

'Yeah?'

'It appears so. Did you know, as Dutch Elien, that after having visited the healer's house for herbs I returned home to my husband and had really amazing sex with him—because I was thinking of you?'

His eyes widened, and Ella laughed.

'Ha, so who's the all-seeing, all-knowing god now?'

'I never said I was a god,' he replied.

'No. But you were to me. In Fiesole, you were my secret miracle.'

They sat in silence, both of them finally sharing the same memories of those dusty days in Italy and all that followed.

Ella sighed. 'So many things have happened in my lives where five minutes, or a slightly different decision, could have changed everything. In Fiesole, if I'd gone to your cottage via a different route, my brother and I would have been safe from my mother and that awful soldier. You and I would have had a family and the life we always dreamed of. Not just that life. Even as Aria, I already regret not telling you how I felt.'

Zac screwed up his face in confusion. 'I hardly spoke to you in Florence during the 1470s.'

'I was madly in love with you!' Ella said, grinning at the memories. She was enjoying herself, for once telling the former angel something about their time together that he didn't know.

'But I could feel you. You were nervous and jumpy around me. I made you uncomfortable.'

Ella let out a light laugh. 'Yes! You had me near to fainting. I would have these wild fantasies that you would whisk me off my feet and carry me out of the artist's studio, into the woods where he'd set us in that painting, and we'd make passionate love under the stars.'

'You're making this up,' he said, although his eyes were shining with delight.

'As if I could. And, this may sound stupid, but was the painter called Botticelli? As in *the* Botticelli? Are we actually in a famous painting together?'

Zac nodded. 'Botticelli's Primavera. You're the one…'

'Who's looking at you like she's crazy about you? I know the painting. Sexy boots, by the way.' She laughed, covering her face with her hands. 'This is totally fucking crazy. You know that, right? Normally, when a woman my age gets in touch with an ex, it's via Facebook and they share amusing photos of when they were at school together. But not us, we're talking about the time we appeared together in a Renaissance painting.'

Judging by Zac's face, he didn't think it was strange. Well, he wouldn't. He'd experienced stranger things than this, no doubt.

'Did you do that a lot then?' he asked her.

'What?'

'Imagine what making love to me would be like, even the times when we hardly spoke?'

She shrugged. 'Not always. In the late 1800s, when I was rich Isabella, I was gay. I never looked at any man in that way, not even you.'

'So what did you think of me then?' Zac asked.

'Are you fishing for more compliments?'

'Maybe.'

'I loved you deeply, Zac, like I would a brother. More so than the brother I already had.'

He bowed his head. 'I loved you deeply too, and I have done in every lifetime. I can't tell you how many times I've wanted to be able to go back in time and tell you things would be OK. That the things you fought for as a woman years ago would be better now. Not perfect, but better.'

Ella thought of her stepbrother Sebastian. No, not perfect at all. How many more lifetimes would she have to live until she felt entirely free and safe?

The shyness she felt around Zac earlier had gone. How could it not? Zac was no longer someone ancient who looked younger than her, a fleeting fling she'd had in her teen years. He was a presence that had been beside her in every lifetime. Sometimes as a friend, or a lover, other times as a face in the crowd or a man she would fantasise about. But what was he to her now? What did he want to be?

His eyes appeared to be asking her the same question.

'You must be tired,' he said hesitantly.

'As if I can sleep now! My head is still filling up with memories. It's buzzing with activity in here,' she said, tapping her temple. '*You* must be tired, though.'

He shrugged. 'I'm immortal. Sleep is a habit, not a necessity.'

'Well, either way, I should leave you alone.'

'Why?'

His gaze was so familiar now. It was the same look he'd given her as they'd bathed together in the Fiesole stream two thousand years ago, the same intense stare she'd remembered in every lifetime—but never more so than when he'd sat her on the library window seat on her wedding day and made love to her. He wanted her. All of her. Her preoccupation earlier with her age, how she looked compared to when they'd first met, was farcical now she could remember the dozens of faces she'd owned and bodies she'd lived in during every lifetime.

Zac loved her soul, she understood that now. He didn't notice her hairstyle, the shape of her eyes, the colour of her skin, or curvature of her waist. He didn't care. When he looked at her, the way he was looking at her now, all he was seeing was the real her: the pure light that was left each time she died and shed her physical form.

And now that she knew who she really was, and all the different versions of herself, everything seemed so ridiculously simple. All the lovers and husbands, friends and family that had featured in her lives had merely drifted in like fallen leaves and left just as quickly. Only Zac remained. The thread that bound her lives together, like beads on a string, was him. Her one constant. Her everything.

And the one truth she was certain of was that she loved him.

She loved him so certainly, so purely, that those four letters weren't big enough to hold all that power. She finally felt what he'd been feeling all the time they'd been together, how their feeble human bodies, insubstantial sacks of thin skin and hair, were not enough to hold all that light. The only way their energy could be contained was to be united, to make a whole from two separate halves.

He was waiting to see what she did, and she knew he would accept whatever decision she made. She didn't consider Indie in that moment, or her life and how Zac being in it would change everything. She didn't have to think about love—she just had to feel it. And the only way she could feel it was to let herself.

His question hung in the air between them. Why should she leave him alone? She had no answer, because there wasn't one.

'Everything is so much bigger now,' she whispered.

'What do you mean?'

'I'm nervous. Since all I can remember are lifetimes where we couldn't be together, I can hardly believe we ever can be. These new, but old, memories of us together are so real—yet the present feels like a dream. I'm afraid if you touch me my body is going to shatter into a million glittering particles and I'm going to float away, forever pining for you.'

Zac took a shaky breath, his eyes never leaving hers.

'I won't touch you, then,' he said.

Ella was about to protest when she felt the fabric of her collar move, and the top button became undone. Had Zac done that? She tilted her head in question and he raised one eyebrow in response. Lighting shot up her spine, fizzing inside veins that no longer carried blood around her body but sparks, eternal light that could never be dimmed.

Zac's eyes focused on her pyjama top and the second button came loose. Ella gave him a ghost of a smile and bit down on her bottom lip. He shifted, his eyes turning from aquamarine to dark navy.

'Want me to stop?'

She shook her head. She wanted him; she always had.

All the different versions of herself in every lifetime, that had never felt his touch or lips against hers, were now reaching out to him. It wasn't one person wanting another, it was dozens of Arabellas wanting one glorious him. She moved closer, her leg above the duvet brushing against his beneath. He was close enough to reach out to her, to hold her and kiss her, but he didn't. Instead, he moved his eyes over her chest and undid the third button.

Now her cleavage was exposed but she didn't move a muscle as slowly, so slowly, Zac inched both sides of her top apart with his mind, forcing the fourth button to pop open.

The cool air hit her bare skin and she took a sharp intake of breath, her chest reacting to his gaze as it would to his warm touch and soft fingertips. She stole a glance at him and at the sight of his eyes boring into hers a light whimper escaped her parted lips.

'More?' he mouthed soundlessly, and she gave a short nod in response. She didn't dare speak.

As the fifth and final button slid open, she arched her back and closed her eyes, listening to Zac's breathing getting faster and shallower, feeling the fabric of her top slide down her shoulders and arms until he'd removed her top completely. He hadn't touched her, he hadn't said a word, yet she was already grasping the duvet cover in bunched fists.

He moved closer and her eyes flickered open, waiting for his kiss, but instead he moved his face to the side of her neck and inhaled the scent of her hair. The faint stubble of his cheeks grazed her earlobe, and his hair tickled her collarbone, stroking her breasts like a feather.

'Ella.' His breath was hot in her hair and she shivered, tilting her head to one side as his lips barely brushed the surface of her skin.

She was going to shatter. She knew as soon as he touched her she would unravel like the string of beads that she was. Every single version of her coming undone.

Another whimper escaped her throat as he used his eyes to send a light caress up her arm, across her shoulders and between her rib cage, down further until it reached the waistband of her pyjama bottoms.

His eyes looked up at hers, and she gave a light nod. The small, crooked smile he gave her in return made her heart swell.

She sat up, still on her knees, holding her breath as she felt her trousers slowly being inched down her thighs. His eyes were dark now, nearly black, his lips slightly parted. She wanted to kiss him, throw herself at him, while at the same time wanting to enjoy every intense second of his eyes on her bare skin. He'd fully undressed her now and she remained beside him, kneeling, naked.

'Are you done, Zac?'

'I've barely started,' he said, moving a strand of hair back off her face without touching her.

She peeled back the bed covers and smiled, the sight of his naked body sending her straight back to the nights they'd shared together twenty years ago.

'Am I allowed to kiss you yet?' he asked.

She shook her head and he smiled again, enjoying the game.

Ella had no idea what this meant for them both. Was Zac back in her life for good?

She couldn't think about that right now because the heat of Zac's stare was making the flames in her veins hiss and spit. Every inch of her was reaching out for him. Even if this was just one night, it would be worth it. Her and Zac, their light united one more time. He loved her. She loved him. That couldn't change. Whatever happened to them, their souls would keep finding each other.

Sitting back against the headboard, Ella could see he was visibly restraining himself from placing his hands on her waist as she slowly sat astride his thighs. His chest was rising and falling even quicker now, each shallow breath making his body twitch between her legs.

'Can I kiss you now?' he asked again.

She shook her head, and he laughed.

Ella was on the pill, not that she'd slept with anyone since Josh, but she still had to ask.

'Do we need protection?' she asked.

Zac's face softened. 'That's your choice, but I've only ever been with you, Ella. One woman, just you. I haven't, and I wouldn't, ever go with another.'

She didn't need to hear any more. In one swift motion she lowered herself on him, and Zac cried out with pleasure. His hands on the back of her head, he brought her face to his and he kissed her with two thousand years of longing. Their lips locked, souls fused, bodies become one as he moved inside her.

Ella had forgotten. She'd had sex with plenty of men since the first time with Zac, and she'd made love to her husband countless times since her and Zac's encounter in the hotel library, but she'd forgotten what this was. Until now.

This was more than sex. This was more than lust, or need, or even love. What Zac and Ella had shared in every lifetime, albeit briefly, was her lifeline. He was her oxygen, her blood, the beat of her heart. This could never be a one-night thing. Their love wasn't even a one-*lifetime* thing. What they had was forever, and forever wasn't ending for a very long time.

Ella had been right, she *did* shatter into a million tiny specks of glorious light. And it was for this very moment that her soul had returned to him over and over again.

'*The wheel is come full circle; I am here*'
~ Shakespeare, *King Lear*

PART FOUR

FROM FRANCE
TO
ENGLAND

1649

<u>VI.</u>

LORENZO HELD LUCI'S hand on one side and his sister's on the other as they raced along the deserted beach.

'The boat is this way,' he shouted.

Luci cupped the base of her stomach for support, occasionally glancing behind her at the men chasing them. She accidentally kicked a seagull pecking at the sand. With a flick of her finger, she raised it and threw it behind her. The cries of the two men battling with a faceful of wings and a sharp beak made her laugh out loud.

Their beautiful ship was in the distance, anchored in deep water. It was a majestic sight, with its wooden bust of a beautiful dark-haired woman and woodwork painted in rich blues and gold. Lorenzo had named the ship *Anjo Rosa*—Angel Rose—after the two most important women in his life. His wife and his sister.

On board was their crew—the Ghosts. Made up of twenty-three young men and women, they served as both their teammates and Luci's whisperers. They were all saved souls given a second chance by angels. Luci's Ghosts. She'd had whisperers before, but these ones would live forever. Aboard the ship, they knew to keep out of the way of their two captains and only do as instructed. But when they were safely in port, their job was to talk and listen and gather clues that might lead them to Nephilim and Zadkiel.

That's how Luci and Lorenzo had found themselves back in France fourteen years after they first met, rescuing his sister from a traveling showman who made money from the rich and the curious, promising them the world's only mind reader. They'd found Rosa in a cage, hands tied behind her back and blindfolded, her captors having realised the only way she could use her powers against them was with her eyes and hands.

Two hours later they were running toward the little rowing boat waiting for them on a secluded beach in La Rochelle.

'How are you fairing, my love?' Enzo shouted out to Luci.

'Fine. We're nearly there.'

It wasn't easy to run while seven months pregnant. In fact, she wasn't entirely sure she hadn't wet herself, but she wasn't going to say that. It would only take twenty minutes to row to the galleon, and from there they would be safe.

Their crew were not only competent fighters but also immortals. Luci had been eager to test out Lorenzo's blood theory the first opportunity they got. The Ghosts had been handpicked by her and her husband—fighters, pirates, thieves, and murderers. Every single one of them had been saved from the noose and chopping block, and every single one innocent of their accused crimes. There was no doubt about that—it was impossible to lie to a fallen angel.

Luci had never forgiven herself for failing to recue Elien from the gallows the day she'd run burning through the Dutch field, screaming out her son's name. She'd made up for it since though, saving the lives of other poor and innocent people and giving them a purpose greater than any other. For that the Ghosts owed her their life, an eternal life. It also made them the most loyal crew there was.

Two of them were standing beside a small rowing boat and had already spotted them. They held their swords aloft, while Rosa helped Luci into the raft. The men chasing them slowed down as soon as they realised they were outnumbered.

'Want us to finish them off?' one of the swordsmen asked.

Enzo was panting as he clambered on board behind the two women. He shook his head.

'Too late,' Luci said, snapping her fingers and watching the men collapse on the sand.

'Why didn't you do that earlier?' Rosa asked, her face still puce from running.

'I fancied some exercise. Fresh air is good for the baby.'

Rosa looked at her brother in horror, but he only had eyes for his wife and was grinning like a madman.

As the crew rowed the boat toward their blue-and-gold galleon, Luci breathed a sigh of relief—they'd found Rosa just in time. Now they could relax and be a real family. She rubbed her stomach and smiled as the baby wriggled in response. If only Zadkiel knew his mother was still alive, that he was about to have a new baby brother or sister. There was still time. Time was all Luci had ever been able to rely on.

For fourteen years her and Lorenzo had tried and failed to perform a miracle, but finally it had arrived. So many babies had been lost in the first few months of pregnancy, but this one was different. This one was a fighter.

She turned to her husband, her chest aching at the sight of him hugging his long-lost sister. She hoped one day both her children would have a moment like this.

Lorenzo asked all his questions at once, while Rosa kept stroking his face and marvelling at his beard and strong arms.

'Did they hurt you?' he asked. 'How long have you been with them? Do you still have your powers? Have you met anyone else like us?'

'I'm unhurt,' she replied. 'It's been awful, in so many ways, but I always knew you'd come for me.'

Her brother grinned. 'I didn't think you'd know who I was. You were so young, I thought you'd forgotten about me,' he said.

'How could I? I remember every second of our family being murdered by those angels. And I remember my big brother looking after me, practising the angelic script with me, and explaining how we were special. Although I nearly didn't recognise you. Had it not been for your voice and your eyes, the exact shade as Mother's before she…'

Enzo looked down and Rosa lay a hand on his arm. He hugged her again, and she kissed his cheek.

'Now tell me, brother. How on earth do you look so young and sprightly when you're six years older than me? By my calculations you turned forty this year, but you don't look a day older than twenty-five.'

'I have my beautiful, clever, and ever-so-deadly wife to thank for that.' He patted Luci's stomach. 'Look at how radiant she looks. I can't believe our baby boy will be arriving in two months.'

'It might be a girl,' Luci said.

'It's a boy,' he replied with a cheery nod. 'And he will be named after me!'

Luci swatted him playfully and he laughed. She turned to his sister. 'Rosa, I can't tell you how much I've longed to meet you. Lorenzo speaks of you often.'

Rosa hugged her in return. She was exactly as Lorenzo had described. Thick dark hair, tanned skin, and large eyes as dark as his—although hers sparkled a lot less. It would take more than a hug to banish the years of horror she had endured.

'I have so many questions,' she said in French. She hadn't spoken a word of Portuguese since she'd been kidnapped and taken to France aged seven. 'Thank goodness you can both understand me.'

'Rest,' Luci said, placing her hand on hers. 'When we reach the ship you will have your own room and can enjoy a peaceful night. We'll tell you our story in the morning, after we set sail,' Luci promised. 'We are heading to a cottage in Cornwall, southern England. We'll be safe in our new home. The voyage should take no more than three days, should the winds be favourable. The house is not far from the beach.'

Lorenzo put his arm around his wife and squeezed her to him.

'Luci is going to make a wonderful mother. She has a son, too, but like us she was separated from him when he was very young. As soon as our baby is old enough to join us on the high seas, we will continue our mission to find his big brother.'

Rosa gave them both a watery smile. 'I love babies. I've helped many, many women deliver theirs. It helps, if you have our ability, to be able to sense when a child is in distress. I can assist you, should you wish. Except, of course…' She stared at Luci and shook her head, as if trying to dislodge a thought. 'I can't feel you or the baby. I take it Luci is one of us, Enzo?'

'Kind of,' he said. 'Oh, what joy it is to hear you call me Enzo after all these years. I'd forgotten your nickname for me. I've missed you so much, Rosa.'

Luci looked at the brother and sister beaming at one another and realised, for the first time since she'd held Zadkiel in her arms all those years ago, that she finally had a family.

VII.

A baby has little say in what happens to it in life, but it *does* have the power to decide when that life is going to begin. Luci went into labour two months early, and no amount of witchcraft or magic was going to change that.

It was the dead of night when Rosa was awoken by shouts coming from the deck.

'What are you doing out here?' she cried, finding Luci leaning over one of the ship's canons, her face twisted in pain. 'Where's the crew?'

'I sent them away. I wanted some fresh air because my back hurt, but now I can't walk.'

She rushed to Luci's side. 'Where's my brother?'

Luci pointed up at one of the sails. 'He's up there. He can't hear me.'

'Are you in pain?' Rosa asked.

Luci shook her head, then nodded.

'I think the baby's coming.'

They'd been sailing for two days and were only a further day and night away from England. In that time Luci had told Rosa her story: who she was, about the search for her son, and how she'd fallen in love with Lorenzo. Rosa had seen enough in her short life to no longer be surprised by anything the world threw at her. The two women had become good friends, which was fortunate as Luci didn't have many of them.

'Don't worry. I've done this before,' Luci gasped. 'It was a long time ago, but Zadkiel was also early, and I managed to birth him alone. I can do this, but perhaps you will help me?'

Rosa nodded vigorously. 'Of course. I know what I'm doing. Let me fetch some bedding and make you comfortable.'

By the time Rosa returned, Luci had staggered to the centre of the ship where Lorenzo was now on deck using his powers to adjust the sails further.

'Lower the sails and drop the anchor,' Luci said, leaning on his shoulder and doubling over at the waist. 'We're not going anywhere.'

Lorenzo let go of the rope and put his arm around her.

'Are you feeling unwell? Is it the baby?'

Clean sheets in hand, Rosa ran up to them and brushed Luci's hair away from her face.

'You will be more comfortable below deck. I can make you up a bed.'

Luci shoved her away and stood up straight again.

'You want me to give birth in a hammock? I'm fine. A baby will be born wherever the mother lays. I'll stay up here; the sea air will do me good.'

With that she slumped to the ground, leaning against the side of the ship, and took a deep breath. Then another. After a while she was taking long and steady breaths in, then hissing through her teeth as she exhaled.

Lorenzo looked at Rosa over Luci's head, but they didn't need words to communicate what they were thinking. The baby was coming and there was nothing any of them could do, except follow Luci's orders.

Lorenzo busied himself gathering up the sails and dropping anchor. Luckily, they were alone—the crew knew better than to leave their rooms unless commanded.

Luci allowed Rosa to sit her on clean sheets, and she loosened her nightdress.

'What can I do?' Lorenzo asked. Although he was making every effort to keep his face still and calm, his voice was trembling—as were his hands.

'Don't fret,' his wife assured him, with her own shaky smile. 'I can't die, and our child is made of eighty-eight percent angelic blood. This one will make it. I can feel it.'

'But you were not due for seven more weeks. We were meant to be settled in our cottage by then. I had it all organised and...'

She threaded her fingers through his.

'Just stay beside me, as you have always done.'

● ● ● ● ●

It was a long night. The swollen moon mocked Luci with her full and vibrant figure. Wisps of cloud caused the light to dim intermittently, then shine like a thousand candles upon the deserted deck of the galleon. Where twenty-six people should have been working, sleeping, and keeping watch, just three remained: a devil, a pirate, and a half-angel.

An entire night and day passed and nothing, but everything, happened. While Lorenzo paced the deck and Rosa rubbed Luci's back, the fallen archangel travelled deep within herself. She was back at the beginning. Before the stars were created, the seas, the skies, or the Earth had formed. She was in the centre of silence, a cavernous hollow gorged from the tiniest speck of existence. Two heartbeats —one body—two souls. All she could hear were her own breaths, and all she could see was the vast universe that resides within us all.

The gentle murmurs of her husband were nothing but lapping waves gently stroking her periphery. Rosa's rhythmic circles upon her back was the pulsating beat of life coursing through her veins. It was just her and the baby, tucked away in their own private cocoon—but not for long. The child was about to enter the world, whether Luci was ready or not.

Sensing the quickening of the contractions, she scrambled on all fours and Lorenzo rushed to support her. He kneeled before her and she rested her arms on his shoulders, her sweaty forehead pressed against his.

'Our baby...will do great things,' she said, panting.

He closed his eyes and smiled, their noses nearly touching. She could tell he wanted to kiss her, to hold her, to show her how much he loved her, but this was not the time. This was the time for stillness.

Luci had hardly made a sound all night and day, although Rosa kept rubbing her back and peering between her legs.

'I can see the head,' she said excitedly. 'I think you're but a push away.'

Lorenzo took the weight of his wife, and she tensed against him. She clenched her teeth, as her fingers grasped his thighs, and she buried her head into his shoulder. With one deep growl, a primal cry like nothing he'd ever heard before, she pushed back. Rosa exclaimed with delight as the baby slipped into her waiting arms.

Then silence.

Luci raised her leg, careful of the cord that was still attached to the baby and toppled back. Lorenzo caught her and lowered her down gently.

More silence.

Kneeling between Luci's parted legs, Rosa rubbed the baby with the clean sheet now rusty with blood.

'Is it breathing?' Luci asked, her voice hoarse.

Lorenzo leaned over her shoulder and pulled the sheet away to reveal a tiny, yet perfect, face. The eyes were closed, lips puckered in a miniscule bud and cheeks a sallow blue.

'Is it alive?' Luci asked again, this time her voice so quiet it was hardly audible over the cries of the gulls above. For a moment she imagined the squawks were that of her child, but nothing that small could produce such a sound.

She held out her arms and Rosa quickly handed her the baby, pushing up her nightdress further so she was able to bring the baby to her chest with the umbilical cord still attached. Lorenzo stroked its downy hair, his giant hand nearly big enough to cradle his child entirely.

Nobody said a word. No physician nor nurse was required to utter the words they were all thinking.

'Unlace Lorenzo's boots,' Luci instructed Rosa.

She kept her stare fixed on the horizon. She daren't look down at the child nor up at the eyes of her husband; both would split her heart in half.

Rosa and her brother didn't question her. She held out his boot in one hand and the lace in the other. Luci took the lace.

'Lorenzo, pass your sister your knife.'

She felt him take a sharp intake of breath behind her, his chest shuddering against her back.

'My love, please don't do anything…'

'The knife.'

He did as instructed, and Rosa took the cutlass off him. The sun was setting low in the sky, making the knife glint menacingly in the dusky light.

'I'm releasing our child into the world,' Luci said quietly. 'It's time to let go.'

She tied the shoelace around the umbilical cord close to the child's stomach, then nodded at Rosa who proceeded to sever the ropelike cord with Lorenzo's knife.

Luci felt nothing. No pain, no emotion, nothing. After so many years living life as a human, she thought she'd experienced every high and low a woman could feel, but this was new. It wasn't even an emotion; it was the opposite of feeling—it was a void. She was hollowed out; the very last vestige of her soul had exited her body along with the baby. Luci was done pretending to be human, thinking she deserved a normal life. This was her punishment, retribution for all the wrongs she had committed.

For centuries she'd tried to conceive, convinced it was the age of her body letting her down. Other men had been useless, but with Lorenzo she'd discovered the ease in which she could conceive. But the trouble lay in carrying the child—her husband was clearly not angel enough. Unlike Mikhael, the most powerful of archangels and the father of her only child, Lorenzo was still a Nephilim. An angelic father and Nephilim mother made Lorenzo three-quarters angel, but it still wasn't enough to create a being that could survive the womb of the Devil.

She no longer cared about death. She no longer cared for living, either.

'Luci?' Rosa said, trying to get her attention.

The fallen angel continued to stare at the horizon, as if the endless expanse of sea held all the answers. But the sea was ignoring its creator.

Rosa wiped the back of her hand against Luci's wet cheek and looked up at her brother, whose eyes hadn't left the face of the sleeping baby.

'What are we to do with your child?'

He shrugged, his own eyes glassy with tears.

'Should we not at least find out if it's a girl or boy?' she said to him, her voice a half-whisper.

'No!' Luci roared, snapping out of her trance. 'It's dead. The first child my body has created in two thousand years and I failed. Who cares if this poor soul is a girl or boy? What does that matter if it never got to take a breath in this world?'

Rosa's eyes widened but she didn't say a word.

'What do you wish to do?' Lorenzo said gently to his wife.

'We carry on.'

Luci shrugged off her shawl and wrapped it carefully around the wrinkled babe. Its head fell back, the body like that of an old rag doll. Luci wiped its face clean with the edge of the fabric, then screwed up her own eyes. Blocking out the sight of the child wasn't enough to keep away the pain that was speeding toward the void. The baby looked just like Zadkiel as a newborn: thick dark hair and pink rosebud lips—except Lorenzo's strength was also there, in the baby's clenched fists and determined face. Even in death, their child had come out fighting.

Her husband was beside her now, brushing her damp hair away from her sweaty brow.

'I love you,' he whispered in her ear. 'I love you so much. I'll do anything you want me to. What can I do?'

She twisted around, but his face was no longer that of a god. He was a fallible, grieving man—nothing more than a human whose heart had been ripped into shreds, then screwed up into a bundle of lifeless perfection wrapped up in an old shawl. Luci was empty, and Lorenzo was filled to the brim with all the agony in the world.

'Go,' Luci said. 'Take the child and bury it on land. I will follow shortly.'

He shook his head, his brow furrowing in confusion.

'Leave you? Never! You've just given birth, Luci. What if something happens?'

She looked over his shoulder. The sun was a glowing orb hovering over the English Channel, bleeding a pink gleam upon its tranquil waves. Death wasn't done yet.

'It already has,' she said.

He and Rosa turned to look in the direction of her gaze, and Lorenzo swore under his breath. On the horizon was a ship bearing the flag of the British army, and it was heading their way. Had the law finally caught up with them? Or had the army been watching their stationary galleon, wondering why it hadn't moved for twenty-four hours so close to shore? It didn't matter. The baby had arrived early, and their plan had failed.

'Go!' Luci shouted again, thrusting the tiny bundle into Rosa's arms.

The brother and sister stared at her, neither of them moving.

Luci staggered to her feet, holding her sagging stomach in two hands. The cord swung between her legs as she slipped on the slick deck. Lorenzo tried to help her, but she pushed him away.

'Take the small boat. I'll stay and protect the ship and crew. I can push the waves in your favour, create a strong tide to guide you to land quicker.'

'The crew doesn't need you. They can fight and survive.'

'They don't have our powers and they can still get arrested. We need them.'

'We'll find others to work for us, other ships. None of it matters.'

'Lorenzo, I *want* to fight. I need to. Take Rosa. She's the only one who can die.'

'Please, come with us, Luci,' he pleaded, his black eyes glistening like pebbles in a stream. Those same eyes she'd planned to wake up to every morning.

'I can't. I'm not done yet,' she gasped, gripping the side of the ship as another contraction hit her.

Women spoke of giving birth as if it were all about the baby, but few mentioned the passing of the mass which gives the baby life during those nine months. Another birth of sorts; not as painful but just as vital. The placenta had to come out. Luci couldn't die, unlike many women before her receiving inadequate care, but neither would she attempt to move until she knew her body was empty.

She groaned as another wave of contractions hit her. Her stomach spasmed in sharp pulses as her husband looked on, his face as grey and troubled as the sea. She had never seen him look so lost.

'What's happening? Is another baby coming?' he cried.

Luci shook her head, the convulsions robbing her of words.

'Get…on…the…'

She clutched her abdomen with one hand, and with the other waved in the direction of an overturned wooden rowing boat behind them. The ropes anchoring it in place unravelled slowly, like snakes dancing to their master's tune.

Lorenzo's eyes flitted between the small vessel and his wife, who was now bent double, her face screwed tight in concentration. There was a loud, wet thud as something hit the deck and Luci kicked it away.

'Take the fucking boat, and my child, and get off this godforsaken ship!' she roared.

'How do we…?' Rosa faltered.

'Get inside and I'll lower it down to sea level on the other side. The approaching ship won't see you. I'll come and look for you on land.'

Lorenzo didn't believe her. It was written all over his face.

'Take the *Book of Light*,' she shouted, signalling to the back of the ship. 'Protect the spell book in case I don't have time to retrieve it once

I've finished with the army. I'll get the crew to shore then come and find you.'

Rosa, the tiny bundle still clutched to her chest, ran inside the ship and returned holding Luci's treasured book and a small oil painting.

'I didn't think you'd want to lose this,' she said, holding up a portrait of Luci Lorenzo had painted. It was Luci's favourite, her hands as if in prayer displaying her beautiful jewellery. The key to their salvation that would never be realised now.

Rosa stepped inside the small wooden boat, which was now the right side up, but her brother remained on deck.

'Luci,' he said, attempting to put his arms around his wife. 'My love, please. I can't leave you. What if the soldiers board the ship and you're too weak to defend yourself?'

'Weak?' she cried, her bloody hand holding his chin in a tight grasp. 'You think giving birth has made me *weak*, Lorenzo? It's a woman's bloodiest battle. It makes warriors of us!'

She kissed him deeply then flung her hands in the air, sending the Nephilim flying into the boat with a crash. He winced at the blow then tried to stand, but the force of her outstretched arm stopped him moving any further.

He took the baby off his sister and gazed down at its angelic face. Luci wanted to see what he could see, take one last look, but why torture herself any further?

'I don't want to fight you, Luci. I'm begging you to think this through. Think of me and our child,' he pleaded. 'I can help you.'

Luci kept her hands outstretched, eyes blazing a violent green. She didn't need his help—she didn't need anyone anymore. She loved Lorenzo, more than she thought she was capable of loving any man, yet what good was he if he couldn't give her the child she so desperately wanted? She'd lost Zadkiel, and now this one. She was done losing the ones she loved—it was better he left now than to await the inevitable horrors of the future. She would return to him in her own time—he wasn't going anywhere. Her and Lorenzo were both going to live forever, which right now was nothing but a mocking curse.

She looked at the precious book in Rosa's lap, picturing its pages filled with spells, sketches Lorenzo had drawn of her, and decades' worth of dashed hope. Luci knew for certain now that only an archangel could give her a descendant, which meant there was no chance of her ever completing the spell. Luci had only insisted they take the book so Lorenzo would believe she would return to them—but she didn't really need it. She'd memorised every passage of that great tome. Spell 666 was the only one she cared about, and her only chance of completing it now lay bundled up, dead, in the arms of her husband.

Lifting the wooden boat so it hovered above the ship, Luci gently lowered it down onto the waves. The two Nephilim were now hidden from view from the approaching army. Her stomach was still pulsing, although it was now empty, barren, hopeless.

She leaned over the side of the galleon, the sight of her baby clutched in the strong arms of the man she loved making her engorged breasts ache and leak. The inside of her thighs were sticky with blood, her nightshirt sour with milk, and her heart a twisted mass of raw agony the likes of which she hadn't experienced in seventeen hundred years. Not since she'd seen her first child murdered, then stolen up to the heavens by his winged father, had she felt so alone.

She willed the waves to carry the vessel away to shore, and the boat began its course, but Lorenzo hadn't given up.

With an almighty leap he threw himself at the rope ladder on the side of the galleon and began his ascent.

'I promised to never leave you, Luci,' he cried. 'I promised to fight for you for all eternity. That was our deal. Fight or die.'

Luci bit her bottom lip, the tang of blood permeating her mouth and mixing with the briny scent of the sea. Why was Lorenzo doing this? Couldn't he see she was a failure? That she had nothing left to give him but a life filled with disappointment? His duty lay with his sister now, not her.

He was climbing the ladder fast, the wooden lifeboat drifting further and further away, and the army's ship so close on the other side that Luci could count the men on board. The rage inside of her was old and bloody, and the unsuspecting men aboard that ship were about to feel her full wrath. Luci didn't want Lorenzo to see her pain unleashed on so many. He thought she was a goddess; through his eyes she had been something worth loving—but she knew the truth. Mikhael was right; she was a monster. The mother of destruction. Death, shadow, and pain. A woman who couldn't hold on to her own children.

With a flick of her finger, she plucked Lorenzo off the ladder and threw him with all her might back into the small boat. It rocked from side to side as his head smashed against the edge. Rosa struggled to reach out to him as she clung to the baby as well as the book and painting in her hand, the small boat tipping against the waves. The woman's eyes were wide with terror as she stared at her lifeless brother and the icy water collecting at her feet.

Lorenzo didn't move. Perhaps Luci had broken her husband's back, or neck, or his skull, but he would survive. She had given him eternal life, the first person to live forever through her magic, so she was certain he'd come around once they reached land. He'd be angry with her at first, but Luci could deal with anger—she knew all about that.

She stared intently at the waves, making them swell and carry the wooden boat to safety, accompanied by the faint cry of gulls in the distance. She covered her ears, blocking out the sound so similar to that of a newborn's wail. A sound her baby was never going to make.

Once she put away her grief, she'd find her way back to Rosa, her baby's grave, and the only man she'd ever loved. Her family. She knew life paths and fate didn't apply to her, but she still believed in hope and second chances—otherwise what the fuck had she been doing for two millennia?

The galleon lurched as the army drew alongside it, tiny boats approaching its side as men climbed the rigging and spilled onto the deck. Luci would ensure they remained unaware of the crew below deck, there was no need to put anyone else in danger.

Luci was ready. She was always ready.

The first soldiers to board the ship halted with a start. Swords brandished, and faces set with intent, they froze at the sight of an empty vessel with no one on board but a dishevelled woman in a bloody gown.

'Hello, boys,' she said, her teeth gleaming and the sky a claret-red behind her. 'Are you ready to die?'

VIII.

The following day, a ship drenched in the blood of the British army finally made its way to the English coast. Fourteen hours after one of its captains, his sister, and a dead baby had vacated the ship, a crew member died. This was only worrying because the victim was meant to be immortal. The cause of death had been a silly accident involving Luci slipping on the bloody deck, falling on the man and causing him to hit his head against a canon. He died a quick, albeit ridiculous, death. It was also an impossible one.

It was at that moment Luci realised that not only did she have the power to give eternal life, but that she alone could take it away.

It was also when she realised that there was a strong chance she'd murdered the only man she'd ever loved. Perhaps Lorenzo had never awoken after she'd thrown his crumpled body into the boat. She never did return to their idyllic cottage in Cornwall to find out; neither did she learn where her baby was buried.

She didn't need to face the pain.

Luci put her soiled notions of love aside and returned to being Luci—the Devil, the witch, the woman who didn't care. She reasoned if Lorenzo *was* out there, he wouldn't search for her. And if he ever did, it would not be out of love but to seek his revenge.

33

ELLA SAT UP in bed, sweat trickling between her breasts. She reached out in the darkness and felt an arm. A chest. Zac.

She'd had a vivid dream, a vision, but at least the part about Zac having returned was real. Ella went to slither back beneath the duvet, but Zac was already awake. He kissed her forehead.

'What's the matter?'

She stared into his blue eyes. It was a lifetime ago since they'd last been in bed together that winter's night in Spain, yet it felt like only yesterday.

'Strange dream,' she said, her heartbeat slowly returning to normal.

'Tell me.'

'It's not that interesting, but maybe it will make sense to you. I was a girl from London, but it was a long time ago. Maybe the 1930s or '40s. I was walking with my friend along a river. There were so many boats, so many different kinds and sizes. Some for fishing, some with cargo on board, but all of them filled with men.'

Ella could still see it now, like a memory. So real she could even smell the pungent stench of shellfish mixed with diesel that tainted the air. The men on the boats were rough and strong, with arms like boulders, tattoos, wrists as thick as rope.

'I was returning from school. I wore shiny leather shoes and long white socks, pulled up to my knees. It was a windy day. I know that because the fishermen were swearing as they gathered up their sails. My friend, a blonde girl, was giggling at something one of the dockers said to her. Then the wind lifted my pinafore and she laughed. One of the men saw too and ran over.'

Zac sat up in bed, yawning. 'Could be a past-life memory. Sounds like Evie and Dolly, your last incarnation. Did the man hurt you? I wouldn't be surprised if you remember past traumas; cells can carry them inside of us as much as our own DNA. Try not to dwell. I don't want you to get upset.'

Ella shook her head. 'It was fine. Nothing like that happened. But this man, the sailor, he kept glancing at my thigh as I tried to push my school skirt down. I had the same birthmark on my leg back then, the curved one I have now.'

'Yes, you've had it in every one of your lifetimes. It's quite common for birthmarks to correlate to past injuries or how a person died. You got that mark when you hurt yourself escaping Sabinus in Fiesole, back in 5 BC.'

Ella frowned, pulling her leg out from under the bedsheets and rubbing her thumb over the light red mark. She remembered now, the tree trunk and the agonising escape to Zac and the cottage.

A loud beep came from the bedside table and Zac sighed impatiently. He reached for his phone, looked at it, and slammed it back down.

'Who's that texting at this time of night?' Ella asked.

'My mother. She's been messaging me all day, winding me up. I'll turn the volume off. Sorry. Please, go back to your story.'

Ella sat up further, plumped her pillows and shrugged. Zac was just being polite. She knew full well other people's dreams were boring.

'The man that ran up to me, he didn't look like the others. He had tanned skin and really dark eyes, strange tattoos everywhere, and long hair tied back. He asked if I knew you.'

'Me?' Zac said. 'Why would he ask after me?'

'No idea. He asked if I knew a Luci and Zadkiel. I shook my head and he looked really disappointed.'

'Strange. Do you remember who he was?'

She did, but it was silly—a stupid coincidence. It made no sense.

'This is why it was probably a dream. The man, I…I think it was Enzo.'

'Enzo? Your photographer friend?'

'Yes. It's weird because when I met him a few weeks back, he asked me if I had a friend called Luci. I didn't think anything of it. Yet here I am now, remembering him from nearly one hundred years ago and he was asking me the same question then too. The man I remember looked the same as him, perhaps less tattoos. How is that possible? Or did I dream it?'

Zac's face was blank.

'For that to be possible, for him to be immortal, he'd have to be an angel….'

'He's not. He can use electricity. He plugged in my phone to charge it. He's human.' Ella wasn't going to mention that she'd been testing him because he'd looked too beautiful, too perfect, to be a normal person. 'But he does have really sparkly eyes.'

Great. Now Zac was smirking at her as if she'd just admitted to having a crush on the heroic-looking photographer. Which she kind of did. Correction—she'd *had* a crush, before Zac had appeared back from the dead and she'd had a flashback of Enzo being a docker one hundred years ago. God, she needed to get some sleep.

Zac's phone beeped again, and he swore under his breath. He turned down the volume, then frowned at the screen.

'What is it?' Ella asked.

'Luci. She says she has them all.'

'All what?'

'Nephilim. She says she's going to perform the spell at dawn and bring down the realm. She's even sent a photo.'

Ella turned Zac's phone toward her.

'It's a selfie. Your mum has taken a selfie with a bunch of kids. She's crazy.'

Zac went to delete the message, but Ella grabbed the phone off him.

'Wait!'

She enlarged the image, until a pixelated face filled the tiny screen.

'What's the matter?' Zac said.

'Message her back. Ask her where she is.'

'No. I'll just ignore her. She's been sending coded messages all day. She's goading me, and I don't have time for her nonsense.'

'Message her right now!' Ella shouted, making Zac sit up. Ella's hands trembled as she pointed at the phone screen. Zac peered closer.

'That's my daughter. That's Indie. Why does your bitch of a mother have my little girl?'

'But that's a teenager. I thought Indie was a young child.'

'What? She's not a kid. She's sixteen.'

'I'm confused. The photo you showed me, she was young. I thought she was ten or eleven.'

'Zac! What the fuck are you on about? Your mother has my daughter. Call her and find out where the hell she is and why she's holding her captive!'

Ella was already up, pulling on her underwear and yanking her hair into a ponytail. Zac tapped the screen on his phone and held it up to his ear.

'She's not answering. Maybe she's gone to bed. It's gone one in the morning.'

'She just fucking texted you, Zac. Of *course* she's not asleep. Where is she?'

Ella had her jeans and jumper on and was pacing the room.

'Why would she have my daughter? I've been back with you *one* day and already something's gone wrong. Always the bloody same. Is this some kind of revenge? I know you fell out with her, but I swear to God if she lays a hand on…'

Zac's face had turned deathly pale. He ran his fingers through his hair, his eyes darting back and forth.

'Ella. Sit down a minute, please. Luci won't hurt her, I'm sure of it. I need you to answer a few questions for me. Try and stay calm.'

'Calm? *I'll* calm down if *you* stop looking so petrified. What the hell is going on?'

'Indie is sixteen, you say?'

'Yes.'

'What colour eyes does she have?'

'Oh, for fuck's sake, Zac. Brown, like mine. Why does it matter?'

His face relaxed a little, but he was still thinking.

'What's Indie like? Is she quiet, thoughtful, pensive?'

What was he playing at? Why was he stalling when her daughter was in danger?

'Yeah, she's quiet. A bit, I don't know, socially awkward—like lots of teenage girls. Look, Zac, I don't have time for this. You'll get to meet her, I promise, but right now we have to do something. We need to call the police so they can track down the text message.'

Ella looked for her phone. Where the hell had she put it? She reached for his, but he pulled it away.

'Stop! Ella, there's only one reason why my mother would be interested in Indie. Listen to me. When did you find out you were pregnant?'

Ella's face crumpled. This was too much. She should never have opened the door to him. Why was it that every time she saw Zac, there was a drama? She'd had years of normality with Josh, but one night with the fallen angel and her daughter...

She rubbed her face and sighed. 'I found out I was pregnant six weeks after Josh and I got married. Indie was a honeymoon baby.'

'But you didn't have any other children?'

Ella shook her head. 'I don't even know how I got pregnant the first time, because we used protection. We tried again years later but I couldn't conceive, no idea why. We had so many tests. She was our little miracle. What? Why are you looking at me like that?'

'It wasn't a miracle,' Zac whispered.

'What do you mean?'

'The library.'

Ella stared at him. He wasn't making any sense. He was wasting time. They needed to call the police and the school, report Indie missing.

'You and me, Ella. In the library of the hotel tower, seventeen years ago. Remember?'

The images returned. Crawling through a hidden golden door in the altar, avoiding the glassy stare of her dead stepbrother hanging above her head. And the blood, so much blood. Then Zac at the library door, his face bloody too. Kissing him, blood in her mouth. The stone window seat, dusty cushions, pulling up her wedding dress, feather tattoo. Sex. She and Zac had slept together the morning of her wedding day, just before Luci had wiped away her memory. They'd had sex six weeks before she discovered she...

'Oh no,' Ella said faintly, sitting down on the bed. 'Oh god. Oh fucking god. It all makes sense now. The way Indie is and looks and... Zac... I think...'

He was staring at her, his eyes shiny with tears.

'Indie's my daughter, isn't she? My mother worked it out before we did. She's finally found the missing piece of her puzzle.'

Ella held his face in her hands.

'We have a child together,' she said, resting her forehead on his. 'All this time I thought you were dead, and we had a little girl.'

Zac closed his eyes, tears falling down his cheeks.

'I didn't know. I didn't know,' he kept repeating under his breath. 'I would have come back, for the both of you had I known. I thought you and Josh were happy; I didn't want to make your lives worse. I had no idea. I would have helped her. Ella.' His eyes met hers. 'You have no idea the struggles she's been having. The abilities she has. I know, because two thousand years ago I battled with the same powers. It was a scary time. All these years she's kept them to herself, and it's all my fault. She's not only a Nephilim, Ella, Indie's the third descendant. She's the one person my mother needs in order to destroy the angelic kingdom. Tomorrow Indie is going to face, and possibly help kill, Mikhael—her own grandfather.'

Ella was shaking so violently she couldn't breathe. Large rasping sobs burned her throat as she fought for air. Poor Josh, he'd loved Indie so much. And poor Indie, scared and confused, suffering in silence. As a child, when Indie had stared at her mother, it wasn't because she was empathetic or peculiar—it was because she was reading her mind. Could her daughter heal too? Could she move things with magic, like Zac could? Were her eyes going to turn a million shades of blue like her father's? And Josh, Josh had died never knowing the truth.

'We need... We need to...' Ella struggled to speak as Zac tried to call his mother again, his own hand trembling at his ear.

'I don't know where they are!' he shouted. 'My malicious mother and her scheming plans! She has our little girl, Ella. She has her and she'll make those kids do whatever it takes to bring my bastard father down.' He rubbed his bloodshot eyes. 'We need to get to them before daybreak. Luci's taunting me, Ella. She knows we'll figure it out, but she won't want me there because she knows I won't let her do it. I won't let her use innocent children like pawns in her game.'

Ella was still trying to breathe, her chest shuddering as she attempted to form words.

'Is it possible? Does Luci have everything she needs to complete the spell?'

Zac was pulling on his jeans and shaking his head.

'She thinks she has. I gave her a vial of my blood years ago, except it's not really mine—it's goat's blood. I've never trusted her, Ella.'

His words were bouncing off her. All she could see was what Luci had done to Sebastian all those years ago. What the witch was capable of.

'That's good, isn't it?' Ella said, picking at the skin of her fingers. 'It's good. She can't perform her magic, which means she can't put all those kids in danger. Zac, you don't look convinced. What is it?'

'This is what scares me. If she goes ahead with the spell, and it backfires because it's not my blood, then she puts the children in danger. What if Mikhael retaliates when he realises she doesn't have the power to finish him? He could kill them all.'

Ella had been at the receiving end of the warrior angel's wrath. She never wanted to see Mikhael's sword again, least of all anywhere near her daughter.

'Find your fucking mother!' she screamed at Zac, who was now standing by her dressing table. 'We need to get to them. Where the hell are they?'

'I should have listened to her. She was always blabbering on about ley lines and magnetic Earth centres, the best places to perform the spell, and I didn't listen. All I cared about was you.' He shook his head. 'There are hundreds of places around the world that hold enough energy to conduct the ceremony. Mexico, Egypt, Scotland, the bloody Bermuda Triangle.' He looked at his phone again. 'I can't tell by the photo. They're in a house. They could be anywhere. There's no one I can think of that would know where to find her.'

He put his phone down on the dressing table, beside a business card Ella didn't recognise at first. It was black with simple silver writing. Then relief flooded through her.

'There might be one person that wants to find Luci as much as we do. Someone who might know where to find her,' she said, picking up the card.

'Who?'

'Enzo.'

34

THE WIND HOWLED through the trees, bending their branches and whipping them against the pale moonlit sky. It was as if the night itself was anxious. Did it know something they didn't? Ella tucked her scarf inside her coat.

'Want to wait inside?' Zac asked, running his fingers through his hair to stop it from blowing in his face.

She shook her head. 'Enzo's never been to my house before. I said I'd wait outside.'

'How long did he say he would be?'

The faint pool of light from the streetlamps picked out the sharp edges of Zac's face. He looked tired and worried. Ella stroked his cheek and his eyes flashed in the semidarkness, sending a flurry of flutters to her chest. Zac, her Zac, was right there beside her exactly when she needed him. Although it was because of his bloody mother that Indie was in trouble in the first place. Indie. Zac's daughter. *Their* daughter. How was any of this real?

'Enzo's staying in Crouch End. It's not far. He'll be here in a minute,' she said, her voice fighting against the roaring wind.

This was all her fault. If she hadn't taken the car to the mechanics, they could be on their way. Wiltshire was only two hours away, less at this time in the morning, although Enzo hadn't said where in Wiltshire Luci would be or what she was doing there. In fact, he'd insisted on driving there himself.

'Did you mention I was with you?' Zac asked.

Ella shook her head. She hadn't known how to describe Zac. Her lover? Her boyfriend? Her soul mate? Although, if she were honest with herself, she was worried mentioning him might have made Enzo less willing to help.

Zac took her hand. 'So, you and this Enzo.' He looked down at their intertwined fingers. 'Are you…?'

'No! I've only met him a couple of times. I'm not sure we'd even be classified as friends. He's just someone I know.'

Zac nodded, his face solemn.

'Hey.' She knocked him with her shoulder, and he looked up. 'You don't get to come back from the dead and start demanding who I'm with or what someone means to me. You know that, right?' He nodded, his face still. 'I mean it, Zac. You've been gone for twenty years. I'm not nineteen anymore. I, well, it's going to take some time to adjust. You know?'

His jaw twitched. Ella had seen that look before.

'I didn't know!' he said, his cobalt eyes fixing on hers. 'I promise you, Ella. If I'd known I had a daughter—' His voice caught on the last word, and he swallowed. 'You have no idea how much I wanted a family with you. A chance to have a normal life. To think that Indie has been struggling with what she is, alone, with no guidance. That the last six years, when you should have been dead, we could have been together and…'

Ella wrapped her arms around his neck and made the same shushing noise she used to make to Indie after Josh died, back when her daughter would wake night after night plagued by nightmares. Zac relaxed in her arms, his head leaning on top of hers.

'I couldn't come for you earlier. Please believe me, Ella. Mikhael would have killed you, and our daughter. He'd have figured out who she was in a heartbeat.'

'And now?' she asked, her voice muffled against his shoulder.

'You're no longer on the grid.'

'The what?'

'Their radar, the map of life, whatever you want to call it. I told you, the archangels can't feel you—Gabriel confirmed it. That's why I came back now, once I knew it was safe. I can't believe my mother worked it out before we did!'

Ella pulled away.

'Will Indie be OK?'

She looked up at his taut face, filled with night shadows and centuries of pain. She imagined she could read his eyes, as if the shifting colours were a code for what he was thinking, but all she saw in them was love. Raw love for the three women his life now revolved around.

'My mother won't hurt her, Ella. All she's ever wanted was a grandchild.'

'But, Zac, I remember everything now. I remember what Luci did to Sebastian, impaling him on a cross like he was a pig on a butcher's hook! In the Netherlands, over four hundred years ago, she let me hang when I was accused of witchcraft, after telling me she wouldn't. She doesn't care about people. She only cares about getting what she wants.'

'Luci also saved your life. More than once. She won't hurt Indie.'

They stood in silence, hands clasped together, lost in their own thoughts.

'Do you trust him?' Zac asked her after a few minutes.

'Who?'

'Enzo.'

'Yes. I don't know why, but I do. I told you, I think he's one of them. Not an angel but… I don't know. He's connected somehow.'

'That's what I'm worried about,' Zac said, more to himself than her. 'Exactly how does he know my mother?'

Ella had her theories, but before she had a chance to voice them a bright light swung around the corner and Enzo's car came into view. It was a tiny two-seater Smart car. The photographer looked ridiculous driving it, like an ancient tribesman who had got trapped inside a child's plastic Little Tikes' car.

He wound down his window as he pulled over, and Ella walked up to him.

'Thank you so much for doing this.'

'Of course, I wouldn't leave you stranded.' He looked over Ella's shoulder as Zac stepped out of the shadows. Enzo's expression was unflinching, but his eyebrows twitched up in mild surprise.

'I'm glad you weren't waiting out here alone,' he said to her, although his eyes stayed trained on Zac beside her. The two men looked at one another, Enzo tilting his head to one side and narrowing his eyes as if listening for something.

'Let's go!' she said, startling them both. She had no time for their antler-locking bullshit. 'I'll squeeze in the back. Is this even a seat back here?'

'I wasn't expecting anyone else,' Enzo muttered.

'It's fine. Zac, you go in the front.'

At the mention of Zac's name, Enzo frowned. Not an expression of anger or frustration but of confusion, like he was trying to work out a complicated equation. Ella squeezed into the back seat, angling herself so her legs wouldn't be squashed as Zac adjusted the front seat. It gave her flashbacks of the time she'd shared a car with him and her father all those years ago in Spain, the day he'd died. He swivelled around to look at her and gave her a tiny smile, clearly remembering the same thing.

Enzo pulled off with more power than Ella thought the tiny car could muster as she struggled to find the seat belt clasp in the dark.

'Where are we going?' she asked.

'Stonehenge,' Enzo replied.

· · · · ·

The only time Ella had seen the roads out of London so clear was when she'd been on her way to the airport, which was the only time she was in a car at five o'clock in the morning. Her eyes itched with the need to sleep, but her brain was racing too much to rest. Enzo had put the radio on after a tense ten minutes of silence and the three had been lost in their own thoughts for most of the journey.

It was interesting sitting in the back and comparing the two men before her. She'd always thought of Zac as tall and strong—he'd always been more powerful than Josh in build and strength—but now beside Enzo he looked like a teenager. No matter where Ella saw Enzo, he always looked out of place—too big, too imposing, too wild. He belonged in a desert, in the middle of a storm at sea, or climbing a mountain with his bare hands, long hair flying in the wind. He belonged in the wilderness of the past.

Ella stared at the faces of the two men. They actually looked a little similar—she hadn't realised before, but now they were side by side it was clear. Both olive-skinned with dark hair (Enzo's longer than Zac's) and sharp jaws. Did Ella have a type? Not that she felt anything toward Enzo now that Zac was back. Would she ever feel anything toward anyone ever again? She doubted it.

'Thank you for the lift,' she said.

Enzo nodded. He wasn't his usual relaxed self. Was it because she'd got him out of bed at the crack of dawn, or because of Zac? They'd glanced at one another a few times, but neither of them had said much beyond polite small talk. She thought back to her dream and the questions Enzo had asked her last time they'd met. She had to say something.

'Enzo, a funny thing happened.'

OK, perhaps it wasn't going to be that easy.

He looked at her reflection in his rearview mirror.

'I had a dream. Well, more of a memory, really.'

'Probably just a dream,' Zac said. She ignored him.

'Remember how you asked, after that yoga class, if I knew anyone called Luci?' she continued. 'And I said I didn't? Well, I wasn't lying.'

'Right,' he said, not taking his eyes off the road.

'Zac turned up and that's when I discovered my daughter is with this woman. This Luci. That's why I was hoping you'd know where she was. Which you do. So that's good.'

'And what does this have to do with your dream?'

'You asked me about Luci and Zac before. Eighty years ago, when I was Evie.'

The car swerved slightly, and Enzo straightened the wheel. He looked at Zac, then at the rearview mirror again, then back at the road.

'You remember that?' he asked slowly.

'Yes. I was at the docks with my friend Dolly. You were on a boat and, well, you looked exactly the same as you do now.'

Zac was staring at Enzo, waiting. The photographer didn't say anything for a long time, although from where Ella was sitting, she could see his jaw tighten the way Zac's did when he was stressed.

They sat in silence for a few minutes, until Zac spoke. 'Why are you searching for my mother?'

'So you *are* Zadkiel,' Enzo said quietly. 'I wasn't sure at first. I thought, if you were her son, you'd know where she was.'

Zac shook his head. 'It's not that easy anymore. Now answer my question; what do you want with her?'

Ella had heard him use that voice before, and it normally preceded violence. Although she couldn't imagine Zac being able to inflict much harm upon a guy the size of Enzo, inside a car as small as this one.

Enzo remained unfazed—instead he pointed at Zac's feet. Ella sat up and looked to where he was signalling. A brown canvas bag lay in the footwell.

'I'm returning that to her,' he said.

Zac picked up the bag and lifted a large leather-bound book from inside. Its yellowing pages were worn and torn around the edges, and the golden writing on the front was faded—although the markings weren't any alphabet Ella recognised. Zac removed the elastic band holding the old book together and carefully opened it.

Ella couldn't see his face from the back seat but heard an unmistakeable sharp intake of breath.

'Is this…?' He didn't finish his sentence, instead gently turning each page and poring over the strange symbols on the aged paper. Some of the words were illegible, nothing but light smudges. There were also diagrams and pictures drawn inside, along with notes scrawled in the margin in different coloured ink. Not everything had been written in the same hand.

A memory was resurfacing. Ella screwed up her face, trying to place the book. She'd seen it before, in a house. An old house by a canal, where Luci had lived with an old woman. A witch? Did this book have something to do with the grand spell and her daughter?

Zac turned to Enzo, his face ghostly pale, the lights from the motorway making his eyes black.

'This is the *Book of Light*, isn't it?'

Enzo nodded.

'There are drawings of my mother in the back,' he said.

Enzo nodded again but didn't say anything.

'Have you read it?'

'I know it word for word.'

'You can read angelic script?'

'Yes.'

Ella sat up. Angelic? She shuffled forward, until her head was wedged between them. Had she been wrong all along? Was Enzo one of them?

'I don't recognise you,' Zac said. 'You aren't from our realm. Why is this book in your possession? My mother said she lost it over three hundred years ago.'

'Luci left it with me. She has no idea I've been searching for her.'

'Who the hell are you, Enzo?' Zac shouted.

The photographer shrugged, unperturbed by Zac's outburst.

'Maybe it's best Luci tells you herself. We're nearly there.'

35

'TIME TO GO!'

Indie woke with a start. Someone switched a light on, and she shielded her eyes. Blinking at the glare, a silhouette of a woman was framed in the doorway of her bedroom. No, not her bedroom. A different room. Blu's room, and he was in bed beside her.

'Fuck off, Jade,' Blu mumbled, burying his head under the pillow and turning over.

'Get up!' Luci shouted.

She threw her arms into the air, making the bed wobble precariously. Slowly it began to rise. Indie grasped the covers as the bed suddenly tilted to one side, tipping Blu out first with Indie quickly following. She landed on top of him in a tangle of bedcovers and limbs before the bed fell back in place with a thud.

'There's breakfast downstairs,' Luci said. 'We leave in fifteen minutes. Don't be late or I will drag you out as you are.'

With that she marched down the hallway, leaving the bedroom door wide open.

Indie looked down at Blu beneath her, her hands on either side of his head and her hair in his mouth.

'Morning,' he said, giving her a lazy smile.

She scrambled off him, but he took her hand.

'Wait, I've got something for you.' He opened her hand and kissed her palm, then closed it again with a squeeze. 'For later.'

Indie laughed and rolled her eyes, keeping her fist closed as if she could lose his kiss. Blu was lying on the wooden floor with pillows and sheets scattered around him, Indie sitting beside him, like it was the most normal thing in the world. He looked so happy. Last night he'd told her he liked her. Now he'd kissed her palm like it was something they did every day, like she was his girlfriend.

'Hi,' she said.

'Hi.'

He stayed on his back, looking up at her like they were in no rush at all. Except they were. They had fifteen minutes until they left for… She had no idea what was going on, but Luci didn't look like she was in the mood to be argued with.

From her place on the floor, she reached up to the curtains and pulled them to one side. It was still dark outside, not even a smudge of daylight on the horizon.

Blu sat up and rested on his elbows.

'I guess we better get ready,' he said, his voice still thick with sleep. He didn't move though—he was still staring at Indie. 'Was I dreaming, or did Luci magically lift the bed up and throw us out of it?'

'That's exactly what she did.'

'And, tell me if I imagined this, but was she wearing a black halter-neck leather catsuit. In the middle of January?'

'Yes.'

'And was there some kind of utility belt thing around her middle?'

'Yes.'

'Fuck.'

Indie stifled a laugh then kissed him, giggling as his hands grasped the back of her head and pulled her deeper into him.

'Someone got lucky last night,' came a voice from the doorway.

Indie and Blu sprang apart. Scrambling to his feet, Blu glared at Scar who was already dressed and sneering down at them.

'Nah. My bad. No one gets laid wearing Batman PJs.'

'Out the way, creep,' Jade said, appearing behind Scar and pushing him to one side.

She glanced at her brother and Indie, standing side by side surrounded by bedclothes, and handed Blu a piece of buttered toast. He ripped it in half and shared it with Indie.

'Oh, you two are cute. Real cute,' Jade said, rolling her eyes. 'But we need to get going. Scar, fuck off. Indie, go to your room and put some clothes on. Bro, I need to talk to you.'

Blu grinned at Indie as she pushed past Scar and ran barefoot back to her bedroom. She looked over her shoulder at him, but Jade had already slammed the bedroom door shut without touching it.

• • • • •

'It's pissing down.' Scar closed the front door again and shook himself like a dog. 'It's not even morning yet and you want us to go out in that?'

The rest of the Nephilim grumbled in agreement. Indie hoped whatever Luci had planned for them would be called off and they could all go back to bed. The way Blu kept looking over at her he was clearly thinking the same thing. When would they get a chance to kiss again? Maybe focussing on that would help her stop worrying about all this angel nonsense.

Luci peered out of the window and sighed.

'What we are doing today is going to change the world. It may also be very difficult and very dangerous. If you're going to start whinging about a drop of rain, then you're not strong enough for me. You may even be dead by the end of the day.'

The Nephilim turned to one another, trying to gauge if she was serious.

'What are you all good at?' she asked.

'I ain't going to say here, but it involves my tongue,' Scar said with a laugh. No one joined in.

Amber put her hand up and Luci nodded, a resigned expression on her face.

'We can move things with the power of our mind?'

'Yes. Well done.'

Scar made a face behind her back and Sol pushed him.

'So,' Luci continued, looking like she wanted to be anywhere but with them. 'If we can move things, and it's raining, what can we do about it?'

'Move the clouds?' Violet mumbled.

'Yes, move the fucking clouds!' Luci shouted, opening the door again. 'Well, go on then. Move them over together, just make sure you do it in the right direction. Move them west, toward the sea, give the locals a sunny day.'

Blu sidled closer to Indie so their fingertips were touching.

'She's crazy,' he whispered. 'But I'll try if you will.'

She held his hand and he squeezed it back. She could get used to this. They joined the others at the door and held one hand up to the sky. She felt like an idiot, and it was clear the others did too.

'Do we say something?' Jade called out.

'Like what?' Luci asked. 'Abracadabra? No, just will the clouds away and then let's get going. Sun will be up in half an hour and we can't waste any more time. The spell needs to take place at sunrise.'

The rain kept falling and Indie's arm was getting wet. Water streamed down her sleeve, but she kept it raised. Something was happening. Slowly at first, then in a sudden rush, the sky cleared, the stars shone, and the rain stopped. Everyone looked around at one another and cheered. Violet and Jade hugged, Blu kissed Indie on her forehead, and Sol even high-fived Scar. Luci rolled her eyes, but Indie could see she was happy. Her magical Nephilim gang had worked as a team and changed the weather without bitching and arguing.

'Can we make the sun come out now?' Scar said, stepping outside and tilting his head up at the clear sky.

'If you think you are powerful enough to move a star, then be my guest,' Luci said. 'But I created the sun, and even I can't control it.'

No one said a word. Luci's random comments weren't scary or surprising any longer. Indie figured they'd find out soon enough whether she really was the great being she claimed to be.

They crossed the road and headed across the first field. It was still inky dark outside, the spindly trees creating crisscross patterns against the fading moon. Indie caught up with Luci.

'Where are we heading?'

'The next field,' she said, pointing to what appeared to be a crumbling building in the distance. 'It's a ten-minute walk, or twenty if these kids don't hurry up.' She raised her voice, so everyone could hear. 'This isn't a geography field trip. Look lively!'

Luci was still wearing nothing but a leather, backless catsuit and high-heeled boots. All she needed was a mask and whip to complete the look. Indie had no idea how she wasn't dying from hypothermia. Her school trip to Bath was suddenly the most appealing thing ever. She wondered what Jesse was up to, and whether he'd realised they were missing yet.

She slowed down so Blu could catch up and he immediately took her hand. 'What's the time?' she whispered.

'Just gone six.'

'Do you think anyone has told the school we're missing?'

He shook his head and rubbed his eyes. No one had slept much the night before.

'She made them all zombified, remember? I bet no one even noticed we left.'

Indie shuddered at the thought and shuffled closer to him.

'Blu?'

'Yeah.'

'I'm cold.'

'Come here.'

He let go of her hand and put his arm around her, holding her so close she could smell the cool fabric conditioner scent of his scarf. She breathed him in and closed her eyes, letting him lead. He stopped suddenly, and she opened her eyes again.

Luci was standing beneath a large oak tree, gathering them together.

'Listen. This is important. When we get to the location, we will need to get into position right away. You remember what we practised last night?'

Everyone nodded, although no one looked convinced except Sol and Amber—who were, as usual, taking it all very seriously.

'Once you're in place, you don't move. I don't care what happens, even if someone gets hurt, you never leave your spot. The force between you will be strong—never let go. You got that?'

They nodded again, but Luci was already striding ahead across the field.

'Hey,' Blu whispered in Indie's ear. 'For as long as you want me, *I'll* never let go. Promise.'

Indie smiled up at him and he kissed her on the lips, slow and tender. It was already the best day and the worst day of her life. Then she walked straight into a giant rock.

'What the hell!'

The boulder was white and jagged and came up to her shoulder. She looked around her. There were dozens of them in a semicircle.

'Whoa! Check that out!'

Blu hadn't seen her walk into the rock as he was too busy pointing across the field. A large collection of dark shapes loomed through the dusky light of predawn. They stopped walking, the others quickly catching up with them.

'Are they stones?' Jade asked, under her breath.

Indie had been wrong, it wasn't a crumbling building she'd seen in the distance.

'They're massive and in some kind of circle,' Violet added.

Sol stepped forward and turned to face the gang, his arms stretched wide. '*This* is Stonehenge.'

Scar was staring into the distance, his face screwed up in confusion. 'What the fuck you on about?'

'There are more than nine hundred stone circles in the UK, and this one links them all via underground ley lines. It's one of England's most powerful energy centres and older than the pyramids of Egypt. It was built over five thousand years ago.'

'Why?' Blu asked, squinting at the huge rectangular stones, some even balanced on top of one another like doorways for giants.

'Humans don't know, but angels do,' Amber said, smiling broadly as she joined her brother. 'This is where the spell is going to take place as soon as the sun rises. It's where we are at our most powerful. Any other questions?'

Luci was now in the centre of the stone circle, staring up at one of the taller structures as high as a two-storey building. It looked like a house a child had made from wooden blocks, two vertical rocks rising out of the ground and a horizontal block balancing on top of them both.

'Yeah, I have a question,' Scar said. 'What are those two dudes doing sitting on top of the stones? And how the fuck did they get up there?'

36

'HELLO, BOYS,' LUCI called up at the two men, smiling.

The sky was slowly lightening to a dull grey. The men were out-lined against the early dawn, their faces in darkness. They both stood up. Then, as if they were simply descending a flight of stairs, they stepped off the rock into thin air, landing on the ground without so much as bending their knees.

'Looking good, Lucifer. Perfectly dressed for the occasion,' said the first man, his eyes travelling over Luci's leather-clad body. He had dark skin and eyes glowing a minty green. 'A catsuit and high-heeled boots for a winter's walk at dawn?'

Luci ran her tongue over her bottom lip.

'We spent the first few thousand years on Earth completely naked. I never heard you complain then.'

His eyes sparkled, and Luci twirled a lock of her hair.

'I told you I'd find more Nephilim, Rafael,' she said to the second man.

'Clever girl,' he replied, high cheekbones lifting as he smiled. His eyes burned gold like flames as he looked past Indie at someone behind her. He raised his hand, making dozens of leather and silver bracelets twinkle at his wrist.

Sol and Amber pushed past Indie and ran toward Rafael.

'Daddy!' Amber cried, flinging herself into his open arms. Sol hesitated for a second then also leaned into his father's embrace. All three of them had identical long, straight brown hair and looked more like siblings than a father and his children. Judging by the look Jade and Violet were giving one another, they weren't buying it either.

'I'm Rafael,' said the man, giving the group a warm smile. 'I see you've already met my precious children.' He planted a kiss on the crown of their heads, and they beamed back up at him. 'Gabriel and I have been waiting a long time to meet you all.'

The other guy was Gabriel? *Archangel* Gabriel?

'I know you,' Jade said, her voice strained and arms crossed. 'You're the barman from Indigo. And the Jesus-looking dude, you were both there.'

Indie's eyebrows shot up and she felt Blu stiffen beside her. How had they not realised?

'You must be Jade,' Gabriel said. 'Hello again, Blu.'

He opened his arms out as if they too would run into his embrace, but Jade remained with her arms crossed. Blu held out his hand which Gabriel shook with a nod.

'Why didn't you tell us all of this when we saw you at the bar?' Blu said. Indie already knew Blu well enough to see that he was doing his best to look unperturbed, when it was exactly the opposite of what he was feeling.

'It was too dangerous to tell you who and what I was then. I wouldn't have been able to protect you from the others. Everyone at Indigo works for Mikhael.' He looked over at Jade. 'I'd like to get to know you both better, if you'll let me. I've waited a long time to meet you.'

Jade gave an indignant huff. Gabriel looked completely unruffled and turned to Indie.

'And you must be Zadkiel's daughter.'

Indie frowned. Luci hadn't mentioned her father's name and she hadn't thought to ask. She'd never heard of an angel called Zadkiel. She shrugged, and Gabriel laughed, a booming hollow laugh that reverberated off the giant stones surrounding them.

'Oh, I've seen that face on your father many times before. And your eyes! Luci, they look just like his.'

The fallen angel put her arm around Indie and squeezed her tight, as if they were the closest of friends. Indie tried to keep her face straight—she couldn't let them know how freaked out she was by this whole situation.

'My beautiful granddaughter. She's powerful, Gabriel. And smart. She's our key.'

Indie glanced at Blu. Sensing her panic, he reached for her hand and threaded his fingers through hers. Gabriel noticed, and Indie noted a small flicker of amusement on the man's face.

'So, who else do we have?' Gabriel asked, looking past her.

'Violet and Scar,' Luci said with a sweep of her hand. Violet edged closer to Jade, but Scar stepped forward with a swagger until he was right in front of the two men.

'Luci told us stuff about you both, but we haven't decided if it's all a load of bollocks yet or not. She said I would meet my dad today, but I don't see no bloke that looks like me.'

Gabriel laughed again, shaking his head.

'Chamuel?' he asked.

Luci nodded and Gabriel smiled at Scar and Violet again, still shaking his head. 'I never thought my man Chamuel would defy Mikhael enough to father *two* kids. I can see the apple hasn't fallen far from the tree with this one though. You have the warrior spirit, boy,' he said, looking down at Scar. 'Use it wisely.'

Scar kissed his teeth and opened his arms wide.

'Show us then. Luci's had us locked up, talking about angels and shit. Prove it. You want us to fight some battle, then get your feathers out.'

Jade uncrossed her arms and stepped forward. 'He's right. If you want us to take part in this nonsense, we need proof.'

Luci stood between Gabriel and Rafael and ran her hands down their arms.

'The Nephilim have spoken. Get your kit off, boys.'

Gabriel looked at her incredulously, but Rafael was laughing softly.

'My dad has the prettiest wings out of all of them!' Amber said, grinning at the others. Sol put his hand on her shoulder to quieten her, but she was jumping on the spot with excitement. 'Show them, Daddy. We still have time until the sun comes up.'

Gabriel pulled at his jumper while Rafael began to peel away the layers he wore: a patterned waistcoat, a thin scarf, a billowing shirt.

'This isn't right,' Violet said, the first thing she'd uttered since they'd arrived at the stones. 'I don't feel comfortable in the middle of a field, in the dark, with two strange men taking their clothes off.'

'Just their tops,' Luci said.

'This isn't something we enjoy doing in the winter either,' Gabriel added. 'But I guess I can't keep tearing holes through the back of my jumpers. There's a reason why, back in the day, we used to only wear flowing robes around our middle.'

Luci smirked, and Gabriel gave her a look that made her giggle even more. Blu squeezed Indie's hand and she squeezed it back in return, trying not to laugh herself. Were his alleged dad and her alleged grandmother *flirting*?

The men were now topless, looking like a couple of underwear models. The wind was flattening the grass around them and humming as it swept through the stone boulders, but Gabriel and Rafael didn't seem bothered by the cold. They looked at one another, nodded, then rolled their shoulders and arched their backs.

There was a faint sound of rustling, like the crunch of dry leaves in autumn. Then slowly, in the light of a dim golden glow that seemed to emanate from behind the two men, shapes began to appear slowly from their backs like plants growing in slow motion. Glowing in the dusky predawn light, long broad feathers blossomed over their shoulders like soft, downy starbursts. It wasn't long before Gabriel and Rafael were adorned with a giant set of wings each.

Gabriel stepped to his right to make room his growing plumes. Each feather was long and bright white, the tips edged with gold as if they had been dipped in sunshine one by one. The brightness of his wings contrasted with his mahogany skin, making him look like he'd been carved from wood and precious metals.

The Nephilim fell silent, mouths open and eyes wide, heads turning from one set of wings to the other. Rafael's were nothing like the other archangel's. His were bronze in colour, flecked with splashes of fiery orange and topaz. He stood there playing with a strand of his hair, nonchalant, as if he were waiting for a bus.

'So, my cynical Nephilim,' Luci said, running her finger along the edge of one of Gabriel's feathers. He shivered but stared straight ahead. It was clear by the look on her face she knew exactly what having your wings stroked felt like, and she was enjoying making him feel uncomfortable. 'Are you all still non-believers?'

'Nah, man. This is *wild*!' Scar shouted, running up to the two angels and inspecting them from behind. 'Look!' he shouted. 'They proper come out of their shoulder blades. This ain't no joke. Check it out.'

One by one the rest followed, peering at the men's backs and tentatively touching the wings, then jumping back with nervous laughter as the angels twitched their shoulders and made their wings flap.

'This is real,' Indie whispered to Blu and Jade. 'Luci wasn't lying. Amber and her weird brother aren't mad. They are real angels.'

Jade had gone very still. It was the first time Indie had seen her look anything but fierce.

'You think he's our dad?' she said to Blu, quietly. He nodded, making a hard ball form in Indie's chest. If Gabriel was really their father, and he was really an angel, then where was Indie's biological, celestial father?

'OK. Enough fun for one day,' Luci said. 'We have three minutes until sunrise. Into position please.'

Rafael kissed the top of Amber and Sol's heads again and followed Gabriel to the next stone tower. The Nephilim looked at one another.

'Luci?' Jade said. 'What do we do now?'

'There are six round stones, like paving slabs, set into the ground. You see them? They are your markers. Each one of you stand on one. Not you, Indie—you can join me at the front. Whatever happens, no matter how scary things get, stay on your markers. If you step off them the energy loop will break, and we will lose power. Is that understood?'

Everyone nodded, although no one looked like they fully understood.

'Stay safe,' Blu said quietly in Indie's ear as he walked past. She grabbed his hand and he turned around.

'You forgot something,' she whispered, reaching up on her tiptoes and kissing him.

'You're amazing,' he said, squeezing her hand and joining the others.

One by one, the Nephilim stood on the round stones that were half hidden by the grass. Luci looked up at the sky, streaked in hues of peach and terra-cotta.

'It's time.'

She nodded at Gabriel and Rafael positioned beneath the stone arches, wings splayed out like magnificent halos. They nodded back, faces as still as the rocks surrounding them. Indie noticed Gabriel was clenching his fists, which didn't bode well. She turned her head at Blu who was already looking at her.

'It's OK,' he mouthed.

Archangel Gabriel was a few meters from them both and had seen the exchange. He nodded slowly at them both, and she immediately felt it—he was ancient, and good, and wouldn't let anything bad happen to them.

Sol was the last to get into position, and as soon as he stood on the stone marker the ground began to shake. Not like an earthquake, but a vibration that travelled up Indie's legs to her chest. Opening her mouth a little to stop her teeth from chattering, she turned to Luci beside her, whose eyes were now shining like spring leaves after a storm—except *she* was the storm. And she was muttering words that Indie didn't understand. A language she'd never heard before.

The Nephilim stood transfixed, nervously glancing at one another, but the archangels remained still as statues—wings open, feathers gently blowing in the breeze. The sky was now an angry red, like the world was burning and reaching up to the heavens for help. A speck of molten orange sun slowly climbed over the treetops. Luci continued muttering incoherently, eyes closed, and hands palms-up. As the sun rose higher so did her arms, until the first ray hit the stones and then exploded into six magnificent beams that bounced from Nephilim to Nephilim. There was a collective gasp, but nobody moved. They didn't dare.

As each Nephilim glowed, strange markings began to appear on the side of the rocks behind them. Indie recognised one as the logo of bar Indigo, the same symbol Blu had tattooed on his wrist. The others were similar—an alphabet of a language she'd never seen before. The markings shone white against the rock, like they were made from neon light.

The earth beneath their feet continued to vibrate, then suddenly mud and grass parted, making way for another giant rock that rose out of the ground and stopped waist-high before Indie and Luci. It too was covered in glowing symbols, although the top wasn't flat like the other boulders but sunken like a bowl. It was an altar. An altar? What were they expected to sacrifice?

Stonehenge was lit up like a carousel, each symbol, stone, and Ne-philim glowing, their light forming an intricately starred pattern. Luci smiled down at Indie and whispered, 'This is it, my darling girl. It's time to meet your maker.'

She pulled the rings off her fingers and placed them in the bowl-like dip in the boulder, then unclasped her necklace and added it. The centre of the bowl glowed red and in an instant the jewellery was reduced to a pool of liquid metal studded with a sprinkling of amethyst stones.

Luci unclipped one of the pockets of her utility belt and pulled out a long feather. It looked old and tatty, but Indie could see how it had once been magnificent and bright white. Was it an angel feather? If so, whose? It didn't look anything like the ones Gabriel and Rafael were currently displaying.

'It used to belong to your father,' Luci said, as if she could read In-die's mind. 'Before he fell. He killed himself for your mother, did she tell you? I doubt it. I've no idea if she even knows he survived.'

The wind was howling through the rocks and Indie's hand trembled as she tucked her hair behind her ears. Angel father who killed himself for her mother? It didn't make sense. She tried to swallow, but her mouth was too dry. Surely her mother would have had emotions linked to the memory of this. Indie would have felt it! Except…maybe she had. The lilac mist. That hidden something her mother was always trying not to think about, that must have been about Zadkiel. Ella's an-gelic lover. Indie's father. Her heart was beating so fast she was scared it was going to climb straight out of her mouth and sacrifice itself upon the stone altar.

She turned to Luci, who was staring straight ahead. Her eyes were focused on those of Gabriel who was standing like a soldier, legs apart and shoulders squared, as if bracing himself for battle. The ground still vibrated beneath their feet and the air crackled with energy. Gabriel gave a quick nod to Luci and she dropped the feather into the bowl, the molten metal swallowing it whole.

The sky, that had seconds earlier been lit with shades of orange and buttery yellow, turned grey. Thick, dark clouds billowed above them, making the stones and their strange symbols grow brighter. Indie and the Nephilim looked up, heads swivelling back and forth. Was it going to rain? Were they expected to move the clouds away again?

Then something began to flicker before them. In the centre of the ring a shape was forming. It was large and round and white. As the image became clearer, Indie could see it was a mound of sharp, red-tipped feathers, and beneath them was a man. An angel.

The figure unfurled his giant wings—they were bigger than the ones belonging to Gabriel and Rafael, white feathers dipped in crimson. He stood up, a large sword as tall as a child clasped in his hands. His long blond hair blew in the wind, his body naked save for a white cloth wrapped around his middle, and his eyes a cold, pale blue. They were fixed on Luci and wide with either shock or fear. Perhaps both.

'Mikhael,' she purred, stepping in front of the altar. 'So kind of you to join us.'

The angel looked frantically around him, his eyes widening further when he saw Gabriel and Rafael.

'How...?' he stuttered, then stopped.

He was counting the Nephilim, his gaze finally falling on Indie.

'Six, six, six.'

'Yes, the spell,' Luci said, giving him a smile that made Indie shudder.

Was this the Archangel Michael that Luci had been telling them about? What was she going to do to him? Every part of Indie's body was telling her to run, to get away from whatever was about to happen, but she remained rooted to the spot, as did the others. Although judging by the looks on Amber and Sol's faces, this guy was scarier than any other angel.

'How are you alive?' Mikhael breathed. 'I killed you, thousands of years ago.'

Luci raised one eyebrow. 'Well, you didn't do a very good job of it. You always did think you were more powerful than me, you narcissistic cunt. You didn't kill me, Mikhael, you grounded me. You took my wings, but not my life.'

His eyes darted around him. 'And Zadkiel?'

'Ah,' she said, her mouth curled up in a sneer. '*Now* you ask after your son? You could have protected him, made him the great being he was destined to be—but you didn't. You dampened his power to retain your own. So weak. No, you didn't kill him either. In fact, you enabled him to create the most powerful descendant there is.'

Luci beckoned Indie over with a crook of her finger, but Indie didn't move.

'See, Mikhael,' Luci said with a vicious laugh. 'Your reputation precedes you. Even your own granddaughter knows you're a piece of shit.'

Mikhael flinched at the word 'granddaughter' then looked around at the other Nephilim, their eyes glowing in the grey light.

'Gabriel?' he said, looking at Blu and Jade. He turned to Sol and Amber. 'Rafael? And…no, not…'

'Chamuel defied you too,' Gabriel called out. 'Most of us did. You lost us a long time ago.'

Mikhael roared, his wings flaring behind him, their tips flaming red. Blood on fallen snow.

'No, I forbid this!' he shouted, attempting to run toward the other angels but being thrown back by an invisible force. He was trapped, quickly realising it was the energy running through the Nephilim which was keeping him in place.

'How does it feel to have no power?' Luci snarled. 'To shout and shout and not be heard? For no one to care about your pain and turmoil? Feel it, Mikhael, because this has been my truth for an eternity.'

The archangel brandished his sword and held it aloft.

'You think a group of children is going to finish me? Some pathetic spell from your witchy handbook? I've been the ruler of all, forever, and while I have the sword, I'm untouchable.'

Luci opened another of the pockets in her belt and took out a small dagger. The sky was still dark and heavy with foreboding, but the glow from the altar's symbols shone off the blade's silver handle, making it glimmer.

'You think your tiny knife is any match for *this*?' cried Mikhael, pointing his sword at her. Then lowering it, he strained against whatever powerful magic was holding him back. His face was inches from Luci's, spit collecting at the edges of his perfect mouth. 'You don't scare me. These children aren't going to stand here all day and night. As soon as one of them moves I'll kill the lot of you, the way I should have killed her mother twenty years ago.'

He pointed at Indie and she gasped, stumbling back from his glare. Her mother?

Gabriel growled, his face contorted in anger. 'Your time has come,' he said to his master slowly. 'Your tyranny over our world and theirs is over.'

A look passed between him and Luci as she stepped back behind the altar and grabbed Indie's wrist.

'It's time to say goodbye,' she said quietly, looking at Mikhael and holding the knife aloft. 'The blood of the descendant will complete the spell.'

Was Luci going to kill her? Sacrifice her at the altar? Indie pulled against Luci's fierce grip, the knife glinting in the half-light, but the fallen angel was too strong. Indie opened her mouth, ready to cry out, but someone else was already screaming. A long piercing wail that reverberated over the rocks, causing all the Nephilim to turn their heads at once.

'Get your fucking hands off my daughter!'

37

ELLA'S FEET HARDLY touched the ground as she raced across the field toward Indie and Luci. Although the sky had suddenly turned from the deep reds of a pretty sunrise to thick, dark clouds, the stone circle was clearly visible, looming out of the semidarkness. When Enzo had stopped the car and Ella jumped out, Stonehenge had looked empty, just as it always did. But as she ran toward it the image shifted to a surreal reality. Strange markings were shining out of the rocks like neon lights. Angelic symbols, she'd seen them before—on her mother's amethyst jewellery, in the book they'd been poring over in the car, and over a number of lifetimes in different scenarios. How many hundreds of years had she lived beside angels and never known?

Enzo had explained everything to them on the journey over. Who the children were in the photo Luci sent Zac, their special gifts, and their connection to the Angelic Realm. He'd told Ella what Luci wanted to do, and how all the secrets and spells in the book had been passed down from an angel who'd managed to father enough Nephilim to keep the truth alive before dying at the hands of Mikhael and his wrath. The only thing Enzo hadn't told them was who he was.

Ella was running so fast she'd stopped breathing. In an instant Zac was beside her, using his powers to help her virtually glide over the grass. Jaw clenched, eyes trained on Luci, they raced toward the woman standing in the centre of the circle and holding a knife to their daughter's wrist.

'Don't you dare fucking touch her,' Ella shouted again as she reached the clearing. She stopped and doubled over, fighting for breath.

Then she saw the wings. So many wings.

Gabriel and Rafael were positioned under two stone arches with Mikhael in the centre, sword held aloft in a warrior stance. Last time she'd seen him he'd worn a cape and armour—this time he looked like the famed archangel from all the old paintings. Giant blood-tipped wings, flowing hair, brandishing that vicious sword and wearing nothing but a scrap of white gossamer fabric around his middle. A living biblical depiction of a warrior angel. His eyes burned a cool blue, but it wasn't him Ella was interested in.

'Mum!' Indie cried, struggling against Luci's grip.

Zac's mother held their daughter by the wrist, and at the sight of Ella yanked the girl back.

'Impeccable timing as always, Zadkiel.'

'Let her go!' he shouted.

'I'm not going to hurt her. Look.'

She turned Indie's hand over and began to peel her fingers back from her clenched fist one by one. Indie struggled but it was no use. Luci was stronger. Of course she was. With the tip of her blade, she made a deep incision on the palm of the girl's hand and held it over the stone altar.

'I only need a little bit,' she purred.

Three drops of blood fell into the bowl, making a hissing sound upon contact. The cut on her hand gaped open like a smile, then just as quickly sealed shut. With a lick of her index finger Indie rubbed at her wound, but beneath the drying blood there was nothing there.

Luci let her go and she ran straight into her mother's arms.

'My baby, my baby,' Ella kept whispering into her hair. 'Are you hurt? Did she hurt you?'

Indie trembled against her but shook her head.

'Enough, Luci!' Zac shouted. 'I'm taking Indie home now.'

'Zadkiel, we're not finished yet.' Gabriel, his best friend, cut a striking figure, his dark skin glowing against the white of his golden-tipped feathers.

Zac shook his head slowly. 'I expected more from you, Gabe.' He turned to Rafael. 'And you. You're making a mistake siding with her, and I want no part of it. As for you'—he turned to Mikhael, who was standing a few meters from him—'whatever fate befalls you, I hope it hurts.'

With a tentative hand on the back of Indie's head, Zac guided Ella and his daughter away from the stones.

'You're meant to be dead,' Mikhael shouted, his voice low and gravelly. 'All of you. Ella, Zadkiel, Luci. *You are all meant to be dead.*'

Zac turned around, slowing, eyes narrowed to black slivers of hate.

'I died to escape *you*,' he spat. 'Yet here I am, back in a world where my mother haunts my every step. You can both destroy one another for all of eternity, I don't care, just don't involve my family.'

'But you *are* involved, son,' Luci said.

She cut a line down the inside of her wrist and smiled as a stream of blood hit the bowl with another hiss, thin plumes of purple smoke snaking skyward.

'I have just one step left to complete the spell. Stay, watch the show.' She opened a compartment in her belt and took out a small vial. 'This is your blood, Zadkiel. Remember? You gave it to me years ago, back when we were on the hunt for Nephilim. Once I add this, it's all over. Your father will lose his power and we'll both finally get our revenge. Surely that's worth waiting a few minutes to see?'

Zac gave her a pitying look and Luci shrugged, pouring the blood into the mixture in the stone bowl.

'You can't do this,' Mikhael screamed, throwing himself at her and yet again bouncing off the invisible barrier. He thrashed and made swiping motions with his sword, but he was trapped.

Zac gave a short laugh, making his mother look up with a start.

'You think I'd give you my blood, knowing what you would do with it? You think I want to start a war with our realm? That's not my blood you just poured in there,' he said. 'That's goat's blood. So good luck with that.'

Ella held her daughter close as Zac put his arm around them both, leading them away from the stone circle. There was a lot of explaining to do, and Ella had no idea where to start—although judging by the way Indie was looking at Zac, her daughter already knew most of the story.

'You're lying,' Luci shouted at her son, mouth set in a straight line of defiance.

The stones rung with silence as everyone held their breath, waiting to see whether the last vial of blood would complete the spell. Nothing happened. Zac never lied.

'Is that it? It didn't work?' A boy in baggy trousers, one of the children positioned around the stone circle, stepped forward. 'Can we go home now? It's not fair that Indie gets to be picked up by her parents, but we're left standing here like a bunch of knobs!'

The ground shook.

'Scar! Get back in position!' Luci screamed, but she was too late. In a flash, Mikhael took the opportunity to free himself from the broken energy field and was running toward Luci, hate and vengeance carving deep lines across his face. She turned to run but wasn't fast enough; the archangel's hands were already closing around her neck.

'I should have known you wouldn't die,' he hissed, mouth curling at the edges and eyes so pale they shone like opals. 'Bad women never do.'

She pushed him away with such force he flew back into one of the stones, feathers coming lose from his wings and littering the ground like giant scraps of bloody paper. He scrambled to his feet but was knocked back again by a kick to the guts from Gabriel, who was now towering over him.

'I've wanted to do that for such a long time,' he growled. 'I never understood what she saw in you.'

Mikhael laughed. 'You're pathetic, Gabriel. Your adulation for the Devil only got you as far as being the father to a dead prophet. You can't take away my power, none of you can.'

With that he shot into the air, landing on the top of one of the giant stones.

'Give up, Lucifer. Without your precious Nephilim, you are nothing!' he cried, sweeping his hand in an arc.

There was a loud crack, like lightning hitting a tree in a storm, and Blu crumpled to the ground, followed by Scar.

'No!' screamed Indie, freeing herself from her mother's hold.

Rafael and Gabriel were already wrestling the archangel on top of the stone as the Nephilim gathered around the fallen boys.

'He's broken every bone in their body. Look at their necks and their backs,' Indie cried, wildly looking around her. 'Luci! Zadkiel! Do something.'

Jade was beside her in an instant, cradling her brother's lifeless body in her arms. His head was twisted all the way around, looking over his shoulder.

Ella surveyed the carnage, unable to move. It was happening again. Angels in an open field killing and torturing. How had she allowed this to happen? How had her daughter got caught up in this world as Ella herself had done when she was just a few years older than her? It was all her fault for talking to Zac at a bus stop twenty years ago. For sleeping with him on her wedding day. For never being able to walk away from the angel that had loved her forever.

Indie was crying, cradling the broken body of the injured boy who looked around her age. Ella tried to pull her away—they had to get away from this mess—but her daughter wouldn't move. Then she realised who the dead child was. Indie's friend, Blu, the one who'd walked her home every night. He was staring blankly up at the dark grey sky, eyes shining like jade. Eyes just like Gabriel's. Her daughter had been dating Gabriel's son? They were *both* half-angels?

'Back to your places. All of you,' Luci shouted. She hadn't moved from her place at the stone altar, and she was smiling.

'No!' Jade screamed, tears soaking her face. 'You did this, Luci. *You* dragged us out here, told us we were saving the world, and now my brother is dead.'

'Dead?' came a mumbled voice from Jade's arms. She staggered back as Blu sat up and rubbed his neck. 'I'm all right, just got a bit of a headache.'

Indie threw her arms around him and peppered his face with kisses as his sister slumped over his chest. Beside them, Scar came to life too, looking even angrier than usual.

'What the fuck just happened?' he said.

Luci nodded at him. 'You're OK, Scar. Don't worry. Mikhael thought he was being clever by trying to kill my Nephilim, but as usual I was one step ahead. You can't die. None of you can. Immortality—my little thank you gift to you all.'

A growl rumbled from the tall rock above them, where Gabriel and Rafael were holding Mikhael down, face flat against the rock.

'I don't get it,' Scar said, rolling his shoulders and wincing. 'How did we survive?'

'A special drink.'

'You created a magic potion and forced them to drink it?' Zac shouted.

The Nephilim had now gathered around Luci, Blu leaning on Indie as he shakily took a step. Their expressions ranged from fear and revulsion to excitement and confusion. Luci was in her element, all eyes on her.

'I didn't force anyone to drink anything, Zadkiel. It was in the blackcurrant juice, which they drank willingly. You're welcome, kids. Now get back to your markers. Time to stop this bastard once and for all.'

The Nephilim ran back to their original positions, Indie joining her mother as the ground began to shake once more.

'We need to go,' Zac said, looking down at his daughter in a way that made Ella's chest ache.

Indie shook her head. 'I'm not going anywhere until I know my friends are safe,' she whispered back.

'Zadkiel?' Luci's face was no longer filled with sharp determination, her eyes glassy at the sight of her son with his hand in Ella's, their daughter by his side. 'My boy, please. All we need is your blood and we can finally stop this. Remember our plan? The one where we're finally free to be with the ones we love?'

Zac shook his head. 'I *am* with the ones I love. I have a daughter, Luci, and I owe it to her to end this perpetual feud. Indie.' He looked down at her. 'I let you down, you *and* your mother. I only found out I was a father a few hours ago. Had I known sooner I would have been at your side in an instant. I'm so sorry.'

Ella looked at Indie staring up at Zac, her daughter's eyes puffy and jaw set hard. How had she never realised she was his? They both had the same thick dark hair, Luci's hair, the same curve to their lips, the same eyes. She couldn't get used to seeing Zac's eyes shine out of her daughter's face. No one would believe he was her father, there was barely ten years between them, but the way he was looking at her no one would ever doubt his love for her.

'Do it,' Indie said quietly, the first words she'd said to him. 'Finish Mikhael. He just tried to kill Blu, and I know he nearly killed Mum. *End him!*'

Zac looked at Ella and swallowed.

'I can't… This isn't my war, Indie. Believe me, I hate Mikhael as much as you do, but I don't want to see any more suffering.'

'That's a shame. Because I do,' came a gravelly voice behind them.

Ella had forgotten about Enzo.

38

SPELLBOOK IN ONE hand, eyes fixed on Luci, Enzo stepped out of the shadows of a giant rock. Had he been there the whole time? Watching and doing nothing?

Memories came flooding back into Ella's mind, images of lives that had long been lived. Luci, always fearless, always strong—being attacked by a Roman soldier, as a witch engulfed in flames and running through a field of black feathers and death, in a chapel impaling Ella's stepbrother to a giant golden crucifix. Ella had shared many lives with Luci, and in every one of them the woman's face had been filled with nothing but angry intent and determination. In all those lifetimes Ella had never seen her look like this.

Luci was staring at Enzo, mouth opening and closing like a fish gasping for its last breath. Her face was chalky white, contrasting wildly against glossy raven hair. With shaking hands, she steadied herself against the stone altar.

'Lorenzo?' she breathed. 'You're alive?'

Enzo remained silent, as still and unmoving as the rocks surrounding him.

'My darling, I feared I'd killed you,' Luci continued, tears soaking her face and leaving black tracks of mascara in their wake. 'I had no idea, after I made you immortal, that I was the only one who could bring about your demise. You were the first. I didn't know. Forgive me, my love. Please.'

Blinking slowly, face showing no emotion, Enzo walked up to her. Immediately Luci began to run her hands over his face, checking he was real, whispering his name over and over again.

'I'm not Lorenzo,' he said gently, picking up the silver knife that lay beside the bowl. Droplets of Luci's blood still glimmered on its blade. 'I'm Enzo.'

'I don't understand.'

Nobody moved. The Nephilim were rooted in position, Zac held Ella and Indie closer to him, and the archangels clenched their jaws as Mikhael continued to push against them, but they all wanted to hear. They all needed to know who this man was, and what part he played in their celestial battle.

'You *did* kill Lorenzo. The pirate was my father, and I am your son.'

Luci shook her head in tiny motions, her lips mouthing the words 'no, no, no.'

'You thought I was dead when I was born, but I wasn't. I was made from his immortal blood and yours. I *can't* die. Although after what I've just witnessed, it appears I'm not the only one. We're all pretty bad at dying around here.'

Nobody laughed.

'But… How did you know about me?' she said.

He held up the old book. 'This. And my aunt Rosa. She raised me and taught me everything about the realm. As a child I used to look at the sketches at the back of the book, pictures my father drew of you, and vowed one day I'd find you. One day I'd play my part in bringing down *that*.'

Enzo pointed at Mikhael, his onyx eyes shining with hatred. 'He slaughtered my father's family, and many before him. Angels, Nephilim, and humans—anyone who has stood in his way for thousands of years. I've fathered many a Nephilim in my time, intent on helping with the spell, but sadly they've all lived and died in the time it took for me to find you. Then I met her.'

He looked up and Ella recoiled, leaning into Zac's chest. So that's why Enzo had been so interested in her scar, her name, and her connection to Luci.

'I'd heard all the stories about your son and his eternal love—you'd told my aunt your whole life story. For over three hundred years I've looked for Ella, hoping she could lead me to you somehow. And this time she did.'

Ella had been wrong. Enzo wasn't an angel, but he *was* an immortal Nephilim. Zac's brother. And more importantly...a second descendant.

'My baby?' Luci mouthed.

She pulled him to her, and Enzo's face crumpled as his mother's arms wrapped around him. Ella couldn't help but smile at the exchange. She turned to Zac, but he wasn't smiling—his eyes were trained on the silver dagger in his brother's hand.

'I'm here to complete the spell, Mother. I'm here to end what my brother never had the guts to do.'

Dragging the tip of the thin blade along his wrist, Enzo pulled down sharply, releasing a river of blood into the dip in the stone altar. A roar filled the air as Mikhael fought against the archangels, face twisted in horror. Luci's hands were clamped over her mouth, eyes still glistening with tears.

As the bowl filled with blood, the skies cleared, and a beam of light shone down like a spotlight on Mikhael. He screamed, a sound so brutal, so raw, that Ella wrapped her arms around her daughter's head to shield her from his cries.

Gabriel and Rafael let go of their leader as he tumbled off the great rock to the ground, feathers scattering to the wind. His cries continued, screams of agony that ripped through the core of the archangels, the fallen angels, and the Nephilim. They all staggered, hands over their ears, faces screwed up in distress at the sound—the onslaught of his agony.

Then, with a thunderous crack, Mikhael went up in flames. Wings, like the bellowing sails of a galleon ship about to sink, burned so bright the others had to shield their eyes. Two shining beacons signalling the end of the world.

Finally, silently, he collapsed to the ground. The leader of the Angelic Realm had been reduced to no more than a writhing pyre of burning feathers.

39

MORNING HAD BROKEN, and tourists had begun to gather at Stonehenge, one of the county's most popular historical monuments. Cars parked, coaches pulled over, people took photos—but no one could see the drama playing out amongst the ancient rocks.

Zac shook his head in disbelief. His mother's powers had no limit. If she could lock him in a warehouse for four days, then she could easily create a mirage to hide the massacre of an angel in plain sight.

Very little was left of his father, who'd been reduced to nothing more than a trembling, naked man curled up on a scorched patch of grass. His scalp was burned and what little hair remained was plastered to his crown like melted plastic. His back was a blistering crater of peeling skin, and his body was naked, save for a strip of singed rags around his middle and two twiglike shards protruding from his shoulder blades. The archangel's magnificent wings were no more.

'Please,' he mouthed at Zac, his icy eyes the only part of him that hadn't been damaged. 'Help me.'

Zac looked away.

'Only you would have the audacity to beg your son for help after the way you treated him!' Luci roared, kicking Mikhael in the ribs and causing him to crumple at her feet. His sword was impaled in the ground beside him and she snatched it up, inspecting its gleaming edges for any sign of damage. There was none. 'You left our son without a mother when he was only six years old. You refused to tell him who he was, hiding his powers from him so he would answer only to you for eternity. You even lied to your own kind. You told them I was crazy, I was bad, I was evil. *You told the whole fucking world that Lucifer was the Devil!* Her breaths came in short, sharp bursts. 'When you could no longer control me, you made sure you controlled how others saw me instead, you gaslighting bastard! You distorted history and my legacy. You turned everyone against me. *I'm not the evil one, Mikhael.*'

Crouching down so her twisted face was inches from his, she lowered her voice. It was empty and hollow yet filled to the brim with lifetimes of hurt. 'Do you have any idea how long it has taken me to get my boy back? To win back the affection of my friends? To trust...' She swallowed. 'To trust men again? It took seventeen *hundred* years to meet a man I could love, who truly loved and understood me in return. But I killed him, because I'm a monster. A monster *you* created.'

Enzo placed a hand on his mother's shoulder and Luci closed her eyes for a moment, collecting herself. When she opened them again and looked up, the smile she gave Enzo made Zac's stomach lurch.

But Luci hadn't finished yet. She pushed the archangel so he rolled over and had to look up at her, his charred body flat against the grass. 'You filled me with a rage that lasted thousands of years, Mikhael. But rage doesn't make a woman reckless, it makes us shine. It turns our blood to lightning beneath our skin. I passed that rage on. I passed on the light to every woman who's hurting inside, and there's a lot of us out there.

'People don't like it when women get angry, did you know that? Of course you do. You've done everything in your power to keep us in the dark. You were behind the witch hunts, and you helped write the rules men used to control us via their fictitious gods. Well, your gods aren't real, and neither are your demons. It took me a long time to catch up with you, Mikhael, but I knew the day would come when I watched you cower at my feet. Because when you spend a lifetime with lightning in your veins, you don't stop until you set the world on fire.'

Luci's entire body shook as she gripped the hilt of the archangel's sword tightly, using it to pull herself up to her feet. Her eyes glimmered with tears of frustration, but her jaw remained clamped tight.

'Typical woman, all emotion and no sense,' Mikhael snarled. His voice was as burned around the edges as the singed skin clinging to his skeletal face. 'If I couldn't kill you, then you can't kill me.'

'Maybe I can't,' Luci replied, tilting her chin up and blinking back the tears. 'But I *can* watch you suffer in eternal agony.'

Gabriel and Rafael joined her side. 'And we'll make sure you do.'

This was Zac's cue, his chance to show his allegiance to his mother and friends, but he didn't move. He hated his father, but he wasn't a torturer. He took no joy in watching the suffering of others, no matter how much they'd made him suffer too.

Then Enzo stepped forward, looking every bit the warrior that Luci had always longed for in a son.

'Whatever you do, make him suffer,' he spat.

Mikhael groaned as he attempted to sit up, but even lifting his head was impossible. Luci didn't look at him as she kicked what was left of his ribs, the sharp tip of her boots causing him to keel over and roll up into a charred ball at her feet.

'We've only just got started!' she shouted out to her Nephilim with a smile. They were still at their assigned position, faces ashen and too scared to move. 'Come, my angels. Gather round. You no longer have to hide in the shadows.'

Indie went to step forward, but her mother held her back.

'Let me go,' she hissed.

'Stay with us. This is dangerous.'

'Maybe for you,' she muttered. 'But not for me. I'm one of them, and I'm sick of having to hide it.'

Pushing her mother away, Indie marched to the altar and joined her friends. Ella reached out to her, but Zac pulled her back. What was the point of holding their daughter back? Indie was right, she was safer with Luci than against her.

The boy with the green eyes grinned at Indie and enveloped her in a warm hug, planting a kiss on her forehead. Zac frowned at Gabriel, who shrugged and made a face. He'd talk to him later.

As for his mother, she was exactly where she'd always wanted to be—standing before her two favourite archangels, her new son Enzo, and the seven Nephilim as if she were on stage performing to adoring fans. But Zac refused to be one of her sycophants. With his arm around Ella, he remained on the periphery, too aware that the woman beside him was the only pure human among them. The only vulnerable one. The way Ella leaned into him it was clear she was thinking the same thing.

'You are my army,' Luci cried. An icy wind whistled through the stones, blowing back her hair and exposing her bare shoulders, but the fallen angel was too infallible to let something as trivial as weather affect her. 'Today is the first day of the new world. Mikhael is no more and I have his sword, which means we are no longer governed by tyranny or the Angelic Realm. As of today, the two worlds will unite, and we can freely be who we've always been.'

A cheer rang out from the Nephilim, a couple of them hugging and the rest high-fiving. Zac didn't know what Luci meant by a new world, but it didn't sound good. Back in the Uffizi Gallery he and Gabriel had reminisced about the old days, back when angels weren't forced to live in secret but were revered and worshipped instead. Could the world go back to that? He doubted it, not now that money was more important than faith. With power came corruption and, looking at his mother standing before them wearing a ridiculous leather catsuit, stiletto heeled boots, and a hungry look in her eye, he couldn't imagine she was envisaging a world filled with Renaissance romance. What was she going to do now her quest was over? Slip away quietly? He doubted it.

'This freedom you speak of,' Gabriel shouted out. 'You saying Raf and I can finally retire from guiding stupid humans toward their best lives?' He winked at Luci, whose lips twitched into a lascivious smile. 'Because I'm more than ready for a long holiday.'

'I'll see you on the beach, my friend. Mine's a mojito,' Rafael added with a laugh, hugging his children to him.

'It means more than that,' Enzo said. He pushed himself to the front so everyone could see him, clearly enjoying the attention as much as his mother.

There was something about Enzo that made Zac feel uneasy, and it wasn't just because he'd suddenly found out he had a brother seventeen hundred years younger than him.

'She hasn't told you, has she?' Enzo shouted out to the crowd.

Zac rubbed his face. Here we go. He'd been right. Because when it came to his mother, it was always safest to expect the worst. Luci gave him a quick glance then looked away again, her chin jutting out and her eyes steely. He recognised that look. It said 'you didn't need all the information. Trust me.'

'Luci?' Gabriel said.

She placed a hand on the archangel's chest. 'Nothing for you to worry about. It's all under control. All you need to think about is the fun we can have now this piece of shit is no longer watching over us.'

Gabriel looked down at the still figure of Mikhael curled up on the dark patch of grass, then pushed Luci's hand away.

'*What have you done?*' he said. 'I trusted you, Luci. You told me this would take away his power and free us all.'

'Yes,' she said quietly, looking out over the crowd of concerned faces. 'I *have* freed us all, but I've also got this now.' She held Mikhael's sword aloft.

'So *you're* in charge now?' Gabriel said, his eyes pleading with her to explain. 'And how does that make you any different to him?'

She ran her hand through her hair, her lips set in a straight line. 'It's *totally* different. Mikhael controlled us while hiding behind gods, religion, corrupt old white men in pinstripe suits. He never cared about humans, just power. He feared humans and angels uniting. He took away the rights of women and anyone who he couldn't benefit from. But I will change all of that. My blood, combined with that of Enzo's and Indie's, has bound us three eternally. It means *we* now decide what happens here on Earth as well as in our realm. We're now in charge of the whole wide world and we'll make it a better place.'

'That's ridiculous!' Ella said, running toward the crowd and standing beside Indie. Her daughter glared at her and moved away, but Ella wouldn't leave her side. 'My daughter is just a child, Luci. She's not a ruler of anything. You've dragged her into enough drama as it is.'

Luci rolled her eyes skyward. 'Ella, Ella, tiresome Ella. Your concerned mother bullshit doesn't wash with me.'

'Indie and Zac are the most important...'

'Really? Don't pretend you've spent the last twenty years pining for my son. You've had so many men in your life you didn't even know he was the father of your child. Gabriel told me everything...'

'Don't drag *me* into this,' the archangel mumbled, but Luci ignored him.

'He told me how you fucked your way around the south of Spain. How you got engaged to Josh within a week, then had sex with Zadkiel on the morning of your wedding day. You've always done exactly what you've wanted, even if those around you got hurt. Yet here you are, acting all high and mighty—a self-righteous *martyr*! I'm not saying I have many morals, but at least I don't *lie* to myself.'

'You're nothing but a jealous, possessive, vindictive…'

'*Quiet!* You're lucky I wiped away your memory and forced you back on your life path, because if I'd let you carry on with my boy, we'd all be dead by now and my granddaughter wouldn't even exist. Once again, I saved your life, Ella. So now it's *your* turn to do something for *me*. Don't get between me and my Nephilim, and keep the hell away from my family.'

'You're not my family!' Zac shouted, marching toward the three of them. 'Ella and Indie are my family. You're just a bitter old bitch who's been obsessed with revenge for so long you've forgotten what's important.'

Luci sighed. 'Son, if only you'd listened to me. It could have been us—you, me, and Indie taking over the world. A family dynasty. But sadly, you're too weak to stand up and be counted. Good job your daughter inherited some balls…and that I have another son.'

She placed a hand on Enzo's shoulder, who grew taller under her touch. But Zac didn't care about Enzo, he cared about his daughter, who was now glaring at Ella.

What was Indie thinking? What could she feel? Was she trying to match up all the vile things Luci had spewed with whatever emotions were emanating off her own mother? Ella was the only one everyone could feel—everyone but Zac and his mother. And he imagined Ella was feeling every possible emotion right now.

'What do you need from us, Luci?' Indie asked, although she looked directly at Ella as she said it. Goading her mother, trying to make a point.

Luci smiled at her granddaughter and stroked her cheek. It made Zac feel sick how much they looked alike.

'You're strong,' she said. 'And unlike your father, you understand that power comes from the collective. I have a treat for you, for all my Nephilim. You too, boys,' she added to both her sons. The glint in her eye made the hairs on Zac's arms stand on end. 'Let's see whether this sword lives up to its reputation.'

With an arc of her arm, Luci drove the weapon into the damp earth while muttering an incoherent incantation under her breath. Her hair flew out behind her like a black halo as she rolled her shoulders and laughed up at the clear bright sky. She looked every bit the madwoman the world had always feared she was.

As Zac watched on in horror, two dark shadows began to rise behind her back. At first, they curled like giant serpents, working their way over her shoulders, until slowly they began to unfurl like new leaves in the sunlight. Higher and higher they climbed, slick and glistening in the crisp winter light, until a pair of magnificent jet-black wings crested the fallen angel's back. Luci let go of the sword, which remained upright in the ground, and stretched out her arms.

'I've waited so long for this,' she shouted up to the heavens.

Something hard, cold, and heavy dropped into Zac's stomach. He should have known. Her outfit made perfect sense now. She'd been planning this from the very beginning.

Luci ran her fingertips along her new feathers, shuddering with delight. Then, arching her back, she raised the giant sword into the air and howled.

'Children of shadows,' she cried, plunging the sleek blade back into the earth. 'Join me!'

'No!' Zac shouted, but he was too late.

A searing pain shot up his spine, his legs buckling beneath him. The ground came up to meet him as he collapsed to his knees, clutching his stomach and curling up into a tight ball. A low moan escaped his pursed lips, his jaw throbbing as he clamped his teeth together in raw agony. Ella ran over to him and crouched by his juddering body. She was trying to talk to him, but he couldn't see or hear or focus on anything beyond the invisible talons clawing down his back. With one final cry his skin ripped in two, like tissue paper tearing down the centre, and giant sticky plumes erupted from between his shoulder blades.

Zac's wings had returned.

Just as before, they were a brilliant white, large and soft, and so much fuller than those his father used to own. Using Ella for support, he tried to stand and find his balance, regulating his breathing as the horrific scene surrounding him came back into focus. All the Nephilim, including Enzo, were crying out in pain, faces contorted in gargoyle-like agony. Gabriel and Rafael stood motionless, confused, worried. Ella was now running from one crouching figure to another, picking her way over mountains of feathers as she tried to find Indie. Her eyes were wide with terror as they met Zac's, a silent plea for help—but he couldn't move. What on earth could he possibly do to help? The immensity of what his mother had done was paralysing.

But Luci was smiling. The joy on her face was a cruel and sharp contrast to the twisted bodies surrounding her as they writhed in agony. His mother, the most evil of bitches, finally had what she'd always wanted—an army of winged warriors prepared to fight for her.

'Mum?' Indie stammered, stumbling as she attempted to walk. Ella gathered her into her arms, whispering calming words into her sweat-matted hair. 'It hurts, Mum. What's happening?'

The cries of his daughter startled Zac out of his shock, and he ran over, pulling Indie's coat off and loosening the scarf around her neck. He could see the sharp feathers already burrowing their way out of her bloody jumper. With gritted teeth, she blinked back tears of pain.

'Indie!' Blu shouted, crawling over to her. He grabbed her hand, fingers clasped between hers, squeezing them as huge wings suddenly erupted out of their backs simultaneously.

Hers were a mix of black-and-white feathers interspersed with a shimmering indigo blue—giant magpie-like plumes. They were soft and fluffy at the bottom, tapering off into long, elegant points with tips of vibrant sapphire.

'Oh my god!' Blu said, pointing at them. 'You're an... You have...'

'So do you,' she said, laughing.

'We're angels. *Fucking hell, Indie!* Luci has turned us into immortal angels.'

Still crouching on the muddy ground, their shock and relief turned to hysterical laughter while Zac and Ella looked on, hand in hand and mouths gaping in horror.

Indie's head swivelled from one side of the field to the other, taking in the multitude of vibrant feathers that had suddenly appeared like exotic blooms covering the ancient tourist attraction. Jade's wings were a light green with tips of gold like her father's, whereas Blu's were the reverse—gold, with a jade fringe. Indie reached out and stroked the edge of one of his feathers and Blu grinned.

'Well, that feels kinda different.'

Zac cleared his throat and they both stopped, eyes fixed to the ground.

'Are they OK? Kids, are you OK?' Gabriel shouted, running to his children and collapsing on the ground beside them. This time they didn't hesitate, letting him envelope them in an embrace, the three of them becoming a jumble of jewellike feathers glowing in the early morning sun.

Zac held on to Ella's hand so tightly he feared he was going to crush her fingers, but it was all he could do. He couldn't move—he didn't know what to say. He could only look on at his mother's new world. At a world where humans would no longer be guided to a future they'd been so busy destroying.

'They aren't that heavy, actually,' Jade said, stepping away from Gabriel and rolling her shoulders. She stumbled past Zac and Ella, laughing as her wings brushed everyone she passed.

One by one the new angels got to their feet, wobbling like newborn calves as they became accustomed to the redistribution of weight. Amber had no problem getting used to hers and was already running toward Rafael, her own bronze and white wings fluttering like an ornate kite in the breeze.

'Daddy! Can we go home and show Mummy?' she squealed. 'Will you teach us how to fly?'

Her brother Sol looked happy too, having already mastered the flapping of his wings and grinning over at his father.

'I take it you like your gifts,' Luci said with a smile. She was rewarded with a deluge of excited chatter from the young Nephilim.

'Do these babies actually work?' Scar asked, moving his shoulders up and down, trying to make his sharp carmine wings move faster. 'Check these bad boys out. I'm going to get so much action.'

Violet sighed, but she was laughing at the same time, her own wings softer than her half brother's and the colour of tropical coral.

'They match your eyes,' Jade said to Violet, breaking away from her father's embrace.

'Do they clash with my hair, though?'

'Yeah, a bit, but you look totally fierce.'

'So you like my new look?'

Jade nodded and brushed her lips against Violet's. With their arms wrapped around one another, their wings merged into a riot of colour.

Luci was glowing with pride at what she'd created. Her feathered children. Except she already had two children of her own, and it was Enzo that Zac was now looking at. In the space of a couple of hours this stranger had gone from a man Zac didn't entirely trust to revealing himself as his new brother and their mother's saviour. Zac had been around long enough to know nothing was ever that easy, and that people who had been on Earth as long as Enzo tended to have an agenda. Immortal beings weren't the easiest to please.

Enzo stood silhouetted against the early morning light as if he'd always worn wings. They splayed out behind him, large and black like his mother's but with flecks of silver. His eyes shone black, impossible to read, glinting like the multitude of rings on his fingers as he smiled over at Zac.

'Chill. It's going to be OK, brother,' he said.

Zac didn't like being told to chill.

'You don't know our mother as well as I do,' Zac replied, the only one in the stone circle not smiling.

Enzo's own roguish smile was unsettling. 'Things are about to get interesting. You'll see.'

'That's what worries me. Even when things appear to be going well, she has a talent for making everything worse.'

Enzo's smile dropped and his face turned serious. 'She won't. We finally have the chance to make the world better, to get rid of power-hungry dictators.' He nodded at the still, crumpled figure of Mikhael on the ground. 'We can finally stop hiding and be ourselves. Aren't you looking forward to seeing angels and humans mixing again? Other couples like you and Ella getting a chance to be happy? Mikhael was a tyrant—my aunt told me how he hunted the Sentients, what you call Nephilim, like they were nothing but rabid dogs. He murdered babies and punished any angel that defied him. He attempted to kill our mother, kill you, *and* get rid of the woman you love. Today is an important day. You should be happy!'

Maybe Zac should be, but there was something in the way Enzo was taking everything in his stride that made him uncomfortable. Ella had told him Enzo was a war photographer, but he was more than that—he was a soldier, a fighter, and the son of a pirate. Men like him always had a plan. A plan that benefitted only them.

'Why didn't you tell me who you were when you drove us here?' Zac asked, his eyes narrowed and voice just above a whisper.

His brother raised his eyebrows in amusement but didn't have time to answer as a deafening roar erupted from the heavens. The sound of a thousand sails battling a storm. Wings. As one, the Nephilim turned their faces to the heavens and Amber let out a piercing scream at the sight of dozens of angels descending and landing on top of the giant stones.

Like a terrifying flock of giant tropical birds, the remaining archangels, along with what was once Zac's Choir, jostled for space on the rocks. They stared down in horror at the charred remains of their previous leader, Mikhael, their jewellike eyes wide with either fear or shock. Zac imagined it was probably both. Archangels Saraqael, Jophiel, Uriel, and Chamuel stood out in their glowing glory, their wings higher and wider than the others and a haze of golden light emanating from their crowns. The three dozen lesser angels surrounding them were by no means the entire realm, simply those prepared to fight for their fallen leader.

'I was expecting you,' Luci shouted over the sound of nearly one hundred wings rustling in the breeze.

'We felt his pain,' Saraqael answered. If she was surprised to see Luci and Zac alive and sporting wings, she didn't show it.

Saraqael's dark skin shone in the pale light of the morning. It felt like a lifetime ago that Zac had worked with her at Indigo, remembering how she'd helped Mikhael pass 'judgement' on him and Ella all those years ago on the rain-soaked Spanish mountain. The way Ella was sneering at her, it was clear she too remembered the archangel holding her back and taking away her voice.

'We've come for our master,' Saraqael said. 'He belongs with us.'

'I was on my way to pay you all a visit. You saved me the journey,' Luci said, stretching her arms in an elaborate yawn. 'Mikhael stays with us.'

Saraqael's mouth turned down at the sight of her leader, his wings reduced to two sharp, charred sticks. 'What have you done to him?'

'Don't worry, I didn't kill him. He's no longer an angel though, and he won't be free to be a man either. I'm going to keep him in this glorious and painful state of in-between. He'll beg me for the sweet relief of death every day of his existence, which is eternal, but I won't give it to him. That way he'll have a tiny taste of *my* life over the last two thousand years.'

'You're crazy,' Saraqael muttered. 'You always have been, Luci. Always needing to be the best, the strongest, the most admired. You've got your wish now, you win. Just hand him over and we'll go peacefully.'

'You've never done anything peacefully, Saraqael,' Luci said. 'I keep him, and you join my team. That's the only option.'

'And if we don't?'

Luci picked up the sword. 'I have this, and it can do so much more than it could before. Before, it could only eradicate lesser angels, and stop humans from returning in future lives, but this time I can kill archangels, like you...and I can *create* them too.' She signalled to Zac, Enzo, and the Nephilim standing defiantly, shoulders back and brand-new feathers shimmering in the breeze. 'I also have the ability to make my people live forever. Think about it, Saraqael. Do you *really* want to be my enemy? That's a very powerful army you'll be fighting.'

'I can deal with that,' said Chamuel, jumping down from the stones and landing soundlessly on the ground before her. From his armour to his long grey hair, the Viking warrior was a vision of silver—except for his eyes, which shone a bloody ruby-red. 'You've been gone two thousand years, Luci. You can't come back, kill our leader, and take over as if it's nothing.'

'Actually, I can—because I just did,' she replied. 'Put your macho pride away, Chamuel, and think of your children. They need you.'

The archangel recoiled at the mention of children. His head turned from side to side, his strong brow creasing as he noticed the winged teenagers for the first time. Zac was clearly not the only one who'd been unaware of his role all these years.

Unlike Zac, Gabriel, or Rafael, Chamuel had never defied Mikhael in the past. He'd never been interested in relationships on Earth and would never have risked fathering a child. Yet most of the angels' loyalty had been tested after they'd witnessed Zac die seventeen years ago at the hands of their master. Once they'd learned of Mikhael's lies, and that he'd murdered Luci thousands of years earlier, a huge number of angels had rebelled. Chamuel, quite clearly, had been among them.

Scar and Violet took a hesitant step forward and the warrior angel's face, normally so strong and defiant, immediately softened. Anger melted into bewilderment as his gaze fell on Scar's crimson feathers, a smaller and less sharp version of his own, along with his son's bright red eyes filled with nervous hope. The girl was different, not as ferocious, eyes and wings a paler shade of magenta. The way they were looking at him told him everything he needed to know. They were of him.

'I didn't… I don't understand,' he stuttered.

'You want power, Chamuel?' Luci said. 'Then be the father these two need you to be. Nothing is more important in this world than showing your children the right way to live. They are part of my army now and they are going to lead the new world—a world where people will know we exist and will respect us as the deities we once were. Our job is no longer to guide humans in their lives, but to live out our own.'

Scar held out a hand to the archangel. It trembled a little, but he kept it extended, his eyes never leaving those of his father.

'I had no idea,' Chamuel said.

Scar kept his hand proffered. 'I knew you'd have to be someone great.'

The angel shook his hand and Scar visibly relaxed. 'I'm Scar and this is Violet. I only met her yesterday. She's a bit quiet and her hair is weird, but she's all right when you get to know her.'

Violet smiled shyly and nodded. The angel nodded back.

'You still want to fight me?' Luci asked. 'Because we have a long road ahead of us, and I'd prefer you on my side.'

Chamuel bit the inside of his cheek and turned to the other archangels. Saraqael was cutting eyes at him, but his face broke into a smile at the sight of Rafael and Gabriel standing beside their own kin, and Zac with Indie.

He walked over to the three of them. 'Is this some kind of dad's army?' he asked with a grin.

Gabriel clapped him on the back. 'I wouldn't grumble, Chamuel. At least we missed the potty training stage.'

Luci turned to Saraqael. 'As I said, I'd prefer you all on my side. Jophiel? Uriel? Is there anything you want to add?'

Uriel had been sitting alone on the top of one of the rocks, watching the happenings below them without saying a word. They looked surprised to have been named. With androgynous features, short white hair matching their unnaturally white skin, and delicate eyes of the softest lilac, Uriel was unlike the other archangels. When asked how they wanted to appear, they had said they wanted to just be Uriel. Not male, not female, just them. Uriel wasn't concerned with matters of relationships, passion, nor power—they simply wanted peace, and right now it was clear that they didn't want to get involved.

'It's nice to see you again, Luci. Albeit under these very dramatic circumstances.'

Luci smiled kindly at them. 'Likewise, my old friend.'

'What do you want from us?' they said quietly.

Luci shrugged. 'Nothing. I'm setting you all free to live your own lives. I'm just asking for your support.'

Uriel nodded. 'As long as no one gets hurt, then that's fine by me.'

'I promise that anyone who stands by me will remain safe—but I can't promise that no one will get hurt.' Luci's grip on her sword tightened. 'In my time on this planet I have stood up to men and women viler than Mikhael, but they keep coming back. Nobody learns. They die, and they come back a generation later, their souls as soiled and damaged as before. We can stop that cycle now. We can change the world. All you angels have to do is work with me...or keep out of my way.'

'Bullshit!' Jophiel shouted.

Always the last one to talk, Jophiel preferred to stay silent and observe before any attack. She was known for her wisdom and judgement, although Zac was yet to see her demonstrate either very well. Her face was delicate and elfin, her hair a vibrant crimson, and she wore her eye makeup heavy around her yellow feline eyes. Her feathers were small, cream, and flecked with silver. Just like last time when they had come to collect Zac on the stormy Spanish mountain, Jophiel's nose and ears were full of piercings and she was wearing jeans and a tight band T-shirt like she was on her way to a gig. The archangel looked young and care-free, but her appearance was deceiving. Along with Saraqael, she'd followed Mikhael's orders to hold Ella down as he'd pointed his sword at the crown of her head, intent on ending her life and every life to come. With Jophiel it was much more about the judgement than wisdom.

Zac squeezed Ella's clammy hand as she kept her gaze trained on the two female angels, fear dancing in her eyes.

'They'll never hurt you again,' he whispered. 'One way or another, this ends soon.'

'You have a problem, Jophiel?' Luci asked.

'Yes, I do. You can't go around making Nephilim into angels to suit your egotistical whims. You may have won over Uriel, but they tend to side with the easiest option, and Chamuel…' She looked over at the Viking angel and sighed. 'Well, you've always had a way of making anything with a cock fall at your feet. But Saraqael and I know you, don't forget. We were your friends eons before you used Mikhael to climb the ladder of power. You've never been happy knowing you were second best to him—it's why you thought having his child would make you his equal, but it backfired. So now what? You kill him and become our queen overnight? I don't think so.'

'That's not what happened,' Luci said quietly. 'You've allowed him to rot your brain and turn everyone against me.'

'Don't play the victim, Luci. I'm simply protecting our realm from further tyranny.' Jophiel arched her dark brows, eyes glowing like midday suns. 'Our way has worked for millions of years. Our job is to govern the human world and steer it to good—silently and subtly. You can't swoop in like some superhero, murdering the baddies and making the people you like into winged gods. That's not how it works.'

'That's *exactly* how it works,' Luci spat. 'The world's a fucked-up mess, Jophiel. Whatever we've been doing hasn't worked. I know because I've been living amongst unhappy humans for two thousand years. I've been a woman who hasn't been allowed to speak. A woman whose body has been used as a plaything. A woman who lost her babies time and time again and was left to suffer her loss alone. If the only way I can change the world is by using the same hate that currently governs it, then so be it. You're either with me or against me. What's it going to be?'

40

JOPHIEL AND SARAQAEL flew down from the rock, followed by their celestial Choir, their flapping wings creating a gust of wind so strong the Nephilim staggered, still learning how to keep their balance. The winged tribe landed before Luci, the two female archangels at the front and the others flanking them on either side.

Ella studied the lesser angels. Some looked like children, others like wise old men. Some had been created at the very beginning, others transformed into angels after dying—Nephilim who had chosen not to return in the next life. Their skin, wings, and eyes were all different colours, no two feathery formation the same. She wondered how many of these celestial beings had walked beside her unknowingly over the years. Some of the faces looked familiar, but from what lifetime?

Then she saw her. Paloma—the Spanish assistant who had pushed her and Josh together. The one that had gone running to Mikhael once fate had won, forcing the realm to take notice of Ella and preventing her and Zac from being together. She caught her eye, but the angel didn't flinch. She was no longer that same pretty, young girl who'd been all too eager to help Ella run her hotel. She was an ancient being straddling two worlds, fate's very own assistant. No hint of apology or remorse registered in her beautiful face. Paloma had always worked for the realm, and it was clear she and the other angels would follow Saraqael and Jophiel to the ends of the world.

Ella hoped it didn't come to that. Although the way the three female archangels were glaring at each other, the end wasn't very far away.

'Stand down,' Luci commanded.

Enzo bristled beside her, his dark wings merging with his mother's, forming an impenetrable black wall behind them. Gabriel joined Luci on the other side, standing so close he had to fold his wings to make room. The tips of his fingers brushed against Luci's and she closed her eyes, her lips curving upwards as she took a deep breath. When she opened them again, they burned a ferocious green.

Rafael joined them, as did Chamuel, followed by all the Nephilim.

'Indie!' Ella called out. Her daughter ignored her. Ella looked up at Zac, but his eyes were locked on those of his mother, who was pleading with him to join her.

'Go with our daughter,' Ella whispered.

'I can't,' Zac replied. 'I won't bring further destruction to this world.'

'Our daughter *is* my world,' Ella said. She marched toward Indie and the other Nephilim. 'Don't look so shocked, Luci. The enemy of my enemy is my friend, right? Plus, my daughter seems to like you, and she's smarter than me.'

Zac ran up to Ella. 'What are you doing?' he hissed. 'You're the only one here who has no powers, the only one who can die. I can't lose you, Ella.'

She shrugged. 'So stand by me and fight for what you love.'

Luci and Gabriel tried to conceal their smiles as Zac begrudgingly joined them.

'As you can see, Jophiel, I'm not alone. You may outnumber us two to one, but this sword of mine is the only thing that can kill anyone in this field. So, I'll say it again—stand down or die.'

What happened next was a frenzied flash of blood and feathers. The lesser angels launched into the sky, then descended on the Nephilim, using their strength and force to throw the teenagers onto the ground. With the absence of weapons, the children fought with what they had. Teeth, nails, fists, and magic. Luci, Zac, Enzo, and the other archangels ran to defend them, with Jophiel and Saraqael doing everything they could to stop them.

Hair and feathers were ripped out from their roots, only to grow back again in an instant. Blood stained the angels' hands, and clothes were torn from their bodies, but no scars remained. Wounds healed seconds after they were created.

'This is ridiculous,' Zac cried out at Luci as he pulled a small angel off Scar's back. 'No one is going to win this fight!'

He'd positioned Ella between two rocks and was standing in front of her, protecting her from the onslaught. The Nephilim were fighting well, using the skills they'd learned the day before to shield themselves from the blows and to work together to increase their power. But this battle was never going to stop while everyone had endless energy and immortality.

Luci looked around her at the carnage, impossible to decipher who was who amongst the whirlwind of coloured feathers. The only person who wasn't fighting was Uriel, who remained on top of the largest rock, their head in their hands.

'Get into position,' Luci bellowed, causing the Nephilim to jump up immediately and run to their markers. Those who had mastered flight used their wings, although the fighting had tired them too much to gather any great speed.

Luci checked, and they were all there, all accounted for. Indie, Enzo, Gabriel, and Rafael stood two by two beside her, and Zac remained protecting Ella. Blu was the last one to reach his spot, his golden wings crooked and bald in places. As soon as his foot touched the stone, the ground shook and the symbols on the rocks glowed brightly.

'I told you to step down!' Luci shouted, addressing the dishevelled angels before her. Saraqael stood in a warrior pose, her arms held up and ready to fight. Jophiel's yellow eyes flashed as she landed beside her comrade.

'I warned you,' Luci continued. 'But you didn't listen. You've given me no choice.'

The ground continued to shake, making the lesser angels lose their footing and crouch lower to the ground for balance.

And that's when Luci struck.

Launching herself into the air with the power of her giant wings, she swooped down, sword in hand, and hacked off the wings of those below her. Now her Nephilim where in position it was clear to see who her enemies were. It made no difference to Luci if the angels displayed a facade of a small girl with pigtails or a kindly old lady with a weather-beaten face; the archangel who once built the world was not going to let anyone stand in the way of building a better one. The sword cut through the air with a hiss as she systematically sliced the angels' wings clean off, feathers and hair sticking to its bloody blade. Archangels and Nephilim stood by, frozen, as the air hummed with the screams of murdered angels. Lesser angels, not being as powerful as archangels, crumbled to ashes as soon as they lost their wings. There was no time for the Choir to fight, hide, or fly away. All they could do was throw their arms over their faces and hit the ground as the new leader of the Angelic Realm, and the deadliest weapon in history, turned every single one of them to dust. In less than a minute, where an army once stood, all that remained was piles of ash and bent feathers blowing in the breeze.

Luci had eradicated the only supporters of the ancient realm—a kingdom that had governed over the human world since the first two atoms collided. Lucifer, the archangel of light and life, had been there at the very beginning. She had seen humanity grow from nothing to the thriving cesspit of wonder and destruction that had been her home for two thousand years. Without angels, people would be left to their own devices. There would be no path to follow, no preordained lives. Chance, opportunity, chaos, and luck would reign, and Luci would be its master.

Sword held aloft, Luci landed on top of the tallest archway. Her black wings billowed in the wind as the pale sun glinted off the sword firmly clenched in her hand. The Nephilim stared up at her, dirty and frightened. All that was left among the dust and ruin was Saraqael and Jophiel, their faces tearstained and wings drooping. The last to witness their kingdom turn to ash.

'Tell the rest of the realm, the true angels who refused to fight me, that they are now free,' she cried out to the two remaining archangels.

Saraqael shook her head slowly but made no other sound.

'Did you really think you could ever be stronger than a woman who has lost all that I have?' Luci shouted down to her. 'Now you've seen what I can do, I'll give you more than Mikhael ever did—a choice. Either you leave and I never see you again, or you stay and I also turn you into a smouldering heap of charred rags and bone.' She nodded at Mikhael. 'He still lives, but I can assure you it will be a life worse than death. What will it be?'

The archangels looked at one another then threw out their hands, screaming with rage. Their faces twisted with horror, their mouths wide and teeth bared like deadly fangs. Their collective force sent an invisible wave careering toward the rock formation on which Luci was standing, causing it to shake. She flew into the air as the boulders swayed and rocked from side to side, then one by one fell like thunderous dominos, the circle of boulders collapsing in on itself. The Nephilim ran into the centre of the clearing as the giant stones crashed into one another, smashing and crumbling as if they were nothing more than building blocks for children.

Saraqael and Jophiel didn't stay to watch the destruction of England's most powerful energy centre. They vanished into a cloud of dark dust and debris, disappearing back to a kingdom which no longer wanted them.

Of the Nephilim and archangels remaining, those who could flew up to escape the toppling towers of stone or used their powers to create a force field to shield themselves from the rubble. Every one of them remained unscathed. All except one.

The last thing Ella saw before she was crushed by the ancient pillars of Stonehenge was a wave of grey descend upon her. She may have escaped death so far in this life, but it had finally caught up with her and it was too late to do anything about it. She tried to scream, she tried to put her hands out to protect herself, she tried to call out to Zac and Indie—but she failed. All that came for her was darkness.

41

IT TOOK A while for the dust to finally clear, and when it did the Nephilim and archangels descended from where they'd been perched on top of the fallen stones, swirls of mangled feathers and clumps of grass settling at their feet.

Blu rushed to Jade.

'You OK?' he panted. He was searching for something, head swivelling from side to side.

'Yeah,' his sister replied. Her wings were crooked, and her face smeared in blood and tears, but she was unharmed. 'She's over there. Don't panic.'

He grinned and hugged his sister quickly before running up to Indie.

'That was intense,' he said. 'Your grandmother is… I mean, she's…'

'She's Luci,' Zac said, placing a hand on both their shoulders. 'You kids all right? Not hurt?'

They nodded, although Indie struggled to meet Zac's eyes.

'Listen,' he said to her. 'Luci said some awful things about your mother, most of which was not true. We have a lot to talk about. The love Ella and I share, our eternal connection, goes back millennia. It's complicated, but I want to be part of your life, Indie. And please know that I'll never try and take your father's place. He was a good man.'

Indie looked down and nodded, biting the inside of her cheek, although it did nothing to stem the flow of tears leaving tracks on her dusty face.

'I know,' she said with a sniff. 'I felt it, that connection. My parents adored each other but... You were always there. Her constant.'

'I was?'

'Yeah, she was never free of you. I felt you inside her soul. A piece of you, I guess, embedded deep in her heart. Everything makes sense now.'

Zac patted her on the shoulder, hesitantly. He didn't know much about teenage girls, but he did know how it felt to discover your real father too late. 'I'm sorry.'

'Don't be. I never saw it as a bad thing, more like a comfort.'

Zac nodded slowly but his heart was soaring. His daughter, who looked so much like his own mother, had wings and powers and could feel Ella's emotions. She was brave too, and she'd got through all this madness without him. Well, that was going to change. He was going to make things better.

'Where is she?' he asked

'Who?'

'Your mother.'

'I thought she was with you!' Indie said, her voice rising with panic.

The air was still thick with dust, and it was hard to see whose shadows belonged to whom. The metallic tang of angel blood coated the lining of his nostrils, the air smelling of hot copper coins. It took him back to that day in Fiesole, the slaughtered goats and Arabella, the first time he'd been faced with the stench of death and a love so strong he'd never be able to fight it.

Where was she? Perhaps Gabriel had protected her. She'd been standing between them both when the rocks came down.

A scream pierced the air and Zac ran blindly toward the sound. It was Indie, and she was crouched on the ground beside a large rock— one of many that had snapped in half when Saraqael and Jophiel had toppled the sacred monument.

There, by Indie's knee, was Ella's bruised face. Her hair was matted, full of mud and leafy debris, her eyes were closed, and her body was somewhere beneath the rock. Crushed.

'No!' Zac roared.

He pushed at the boulder, quickly joined by Gabriel and Rafael who'd rushed over as soon as they'd seen Zac fall to the ground. Even with their combined strength the rock was difficult to budge, only moving a little with each push, inch by inch.

'Don't look!' Zac shouted at Indie. 'I won't let you see your mother...' His voice broke. He couldn't say it out loud. He couldn't allow himself to believe she was dead.

'Boys, boys. You're being very heroic, but she's fine.'

Luci was at the foot of the rock, a satisfied expression on her flawless face. Zac scowled up at his mother, dressed in her ridiculous leather catsuit and giant jet-black wings. She'd just massacred half the realm, yet there she was grinning in her inappropriate outfit as if she were at a party waiting for someone to pass her a glass of champagne.

'What the hell are you talking about?' Zac cried. 'How can you smile when your granddaughter has just lost her mother?'

Luci sighed and with one swift twist of her wrist pushed the rock off Ella. Indie turned her head away, Blu and her friends quickly gathering around to comfort her, but Zac needed to see this. He had to witness Ella's lifeless body to believe this was finally the end she should have had six years ago. Had she been injured he could have healed her, but no one could survive a boulder of that size landing on them. This wasn't the first time Zac had lost Ella, but it *would* be the last.

Except her body was not crushed.

The scratches and bruises to Ella's face and hands began to disappear before them, dark blue patches fading and deep cuts stitching themselves back together, just like Zac's and Indie's had during the battle. Slowly the colour returned to Ella's cheeks and her eyes fluttered open.

'What am I doing on the floor?' she croaked.

As soon as she heard her mother's voice Indie threw herself on top of her, sobbing into her neck. Ella threaded her arms around her daughter's neck and pulled her closer.

'One of the stones fell on you, Mum. How are you alive?' Indie hiccupped.

'Oh, baby. I'm fine, honestly, I'm fine. Help me up.'

Zac took her hand and pulled her to her feet. Her back cracked as she straightened herself.

'Are you not in pain?' he asked, cupping her face in his hands. He let go and she leaned against him. It took all his willpower not to scoop her up in his arms and fly away from this dammed field. All he wanted was to be with Ella and Indie, somewhere far away where his mother's destruction couldn't touch them anymore.

'I'm a bit shaky,' she said slowly. 'My back's sore, but I'm fine.'

'Of course she's fine,' Luci said in clipped tones, giving Ella a quick smile and brushing clumps of mud off her coat. 'I have no idea how my own son can be so dense. Have you not worked it out yet, Zadkiel?'

He shook his head. Everyone had fallen silent, waiting for an explanation. Especially Ella.

'Your beloved was meant to die six years ago. Right, my son?'

He nodded. 'She was meant to die with Josh during the yacht accident, but she didn't.'

Indie's breath hitched, her face crumpling as she stared at her mother. Ella nodded and gave her a look that said she'd just found out herself.

'Gabriel, Rafael, how many people do you know who have avoided their death date?' Luci asked.

'None,' they replied in unison. 'Death always catches up with them,' Gabriel added.

'Exactly. When Zadkiel and I lost our wings, we changed. We came back with abilities we didn't have before. We can now control the minds of humans and we can also make them immortal.'

'How?' Zac cried.

'With our blood.'

He rubbed his face and let out a long breath.

'Blood?' he echoed. 'That's what you gave my daughter?'

'Yes. Although I have a feeling Indie may have been born immortal, because your lover here was already infallible before you got her pregnant.'

Zac put his arm around Ella, and she rested her head on his shoulder. His mother wasn't making any sense. Why hadn't she told him this sooner?

'I don't understand. How on earth did I make her immortal?' he said.

Luci rolled her eyes. 'Honestly, son, you really need me to spell it out? When I walked in on you both in the library, the day of her wedding after you'd...' Luci looked at Indie and stopped. 'Ella had blood around her mouth, and you had it on your face. She hit you, right?'

Zac nodded.

'Then she kissed you?'

Zac nodded again.

'I swallowed your blood,' Ella said slowly. 'I remember. Your eye was bleeding, and I kissed you and some went in my mouth.'

'Ew,' Indie cried.

Ella ignored her. 'Luci, are you saying I survived Indie's birth and the boat accident because Zac made me immortal?'

Luci sighed and waved her hands in the air. 'Bingo! You two are truly made for each other, both poodling along on the slow bus. Yes, my darling, you are immortal. You, Zadkiel, and Indie will never die. A family forever—just like Zadkiel, Enzo, and I. Can't get rid of each other, even if we wanted to. Isn't that right, son?'

Zac didn't answer his mother, kissing Ella's forehead instead and ignoring the look Indie was giving him. If he had to get used to having a winged daughter with superpowers, she'd have to get used to seeing him with her mother. Because he wasn't going anywhere.

As for Luci, Zac couldn't even look at her right now. The thought of all the secrets she'd kept from him was making him nauseous. How much easier would the last seventeen years have been had Luci told him he and Ella could have lived forever, together?

Except... He closed his eyes as the realisation dawned on him. Everything made sense now.

'Is that why you wouldn't let me say goodbye to Ella the day before she was due to die?' he shouted at Luci. 'Why you locked me up in that warehouse? So that I'd think she was dead and not leave your side? So I'd carry on helping you with your Nephilim quest? Honestly, Luci, you are one selfish bitch!'

'It was for your own good. I needed you.'

'I only helped you so we could do this stupid spell sooner and save Ella. She's the only reason I would have put myself through all this. I should have known you would find a way anyway. Happy now? Got everything you want?'

Luci shrugged with one shoulder. 'Kind of. I would have preferred not killing all those angels—they would have come in handy—but I can make new ones. Saraqael and Jophiel would have been good to have on my side too, but I don't think they'll try and fight me again. Uriel, are you OK, my darling?'

As soon as Luci had launched herself to the skies before the massacre, the angel had flown to the side of the field and watched on in sadness. They were now sitting far away from everyone else, playing with a blade of grass, their lilac eyes having lost some of their sparkle.

'I never wanted to be dragged into any of Mikhael's stupid games anyway,' they mumbled, getting up and heading toward the others. They settled on a rock on the periphery of the crumbled circle and scratched at the surface with their nail. 'I just want an easy life, Lucifer.'

'You'll have one now,' she replied, something resembling discomfort flashing over her still features. She looked behind her. 'Boys?'

Enzo, Gabriel, and Rafael looked exhausted. Their wings were pulled back and folded, their faces dark with shadows, but they were smiling.

'I'm happy to stick around a bit longer,' Enzo said.

'As long as you protect my babies, I'm in,' Rafael added.

Gabriel gave her a lopsided smile and raised one eyebrow. 'Do you even have to ask?'

She turned to her son. 'Zadkiel?'

'My heart is with my family.'

Luci smiled. 'Perfect, in that case we…'

'I didn't mean you.' He put his arm around Ella and lay his other hand on his daughter's shoulder. 'I meant my two girls. *They're* my family now. You've just proven to us what you really care about, Luci. Winning.'

The slight tremble of her chin was the only sign he'd rattled her. Gabriel reached out to lay a hand on Zac's shoulder, but he pushed him off.

'Are we free to go now?' Zac asked. 'I presume I have to ask your permission seeing as you're our grand master now.'

He knew goading her was never a good idea, but Luci didn't understand subtlety. She hadn't listened when he'd pleaded, she hadn't respected his space when he'd asked to be left alone, and now here she was pushing, *commanding*, that he join forces with her when all she'd ever done over the years was lie to him. She'd known Ella couldn't die, but instead of telling her own son the truth she'd kept him from his one true love and let him suffer. That wasn't love, that was possession.

'Don't go, son. You're one of us,' Luci said quietly.

'I'm nothing like you.'

'You are, Zadkiel. You want to be human, but you're not. Your daughter isn't. None of us know what it's like to be normal in this world. That's why we need to work together, as a team, to decide what the new world will look like.'

'You have Enzo now,' Zac said with a shrug, shooting his brother a look. 'And Gabriel will do whatever you ask him to. He's always been your lapdog.'

'Hey!' the archangel shouted. 'Not cool, bro.'

Zac's shoulders slumped forward. He was tired. Tired of the drama, tired of his mother, and tired of fighting for an easy life. He looked over at Ella and Indie, huddled together, and a lump formed in his throat. His immortal family. Not normal, but as close to normal as he could ask for right now.

'Bye, Luci,' he said, placing his hand on the small of Ella's back and guiding his new family around one of the fallen stones. 'I'm done with this shit.'

He expected Indie or Ella to say something, but they looked as exhausted as he was, happy to go home. To talk. To figure out what the hell tomorrow was going to look like.

'No.'

One word. His mother's favourite.

Zac turned around.

'What did you say?'

'No, I won't let you go.'

'You don't get a say in anything I do anymore.'

'That's where you're wrong,' Luci replied. Her teeth were clenched and nostrils flared. 'I get a say in *everything*. You and your daughter are one of us, whether you like it or not, and if Ella is the only thing getting in the way of you joining us then I *will* do something about it.'

Gabriel made a lunge for her arm, Blu shouted for her to stop, and Zac ran forward, but they were all too late. Sword in hand, Luci struck the long silver blade into the churned soil while muttering under her breath. The giant boulders, now lying cracked and broken around them, began to glow. Sparks erupted from the tip of her sword, sending a crackle of forked lightning shooting across the earth toward Ella.

There was a collective gasp from the Nephilim as they sheltered their eyes from the bright white light surrounding their friend's mother. A piercing scream carried on the winter wind, Ella's or Indie's or a mix of both, and Ella dropped to her knees.

'Stop!' cried Zac, grappling to pull the sword from his mother. 'What are you doing to her?'

His mother's sword, the same one Mikhael had nearly killed Ella with, had the power to end all human lives forever. Not just in this lifetime, but every single one to come. Even immortals could be finished with the power of that mighty blade. Nobody was safe from Luci's wonts.

Ella fell forward onto the grass, now a soft downy blanket of colourful feathers once belonging to dead angels. Curled up in a ball she held her stomach, her face creased with agony. Hands smeared in mud and jeans soaked to the knee, she managed to stagger onto all fours, her back arching like an angry cat. No words formed on her trembling lips, just howls and screams of pain. What was Luci doing to her? Zac lunged at the sword but was thrown back by an invisible force. Ella was now struggling to remove her winter coat, her back bubbling and rippling as if a beast was attempting to burrow out of her skin. Then slowly, like the tips of snowdrops pushing their way out of the spring soil, two sharp white buds began to grow through her jumper.

'No, no, no, no,' Zac muttered, looking up at his mother imploringly. 'Not her. She didn't ask for this. Make it stop, Luci. She's in *pain*.'

'Everything hurts the first time, my son.' A faint ghost of a smile hovered on Luci's lips. 'But she'll get used to it. One can get used to anything if they stick around long enough.'

42

ELLA'S WINGS GREW until they covered her shoulder blades, then her back, and eventually obscured her from view. Crouching on the ground, she looked like a giant downy snowball, shaking, fingers grasping at the churned soil. She stumbled to her feet and swayed with the new weight behind her, but Zac caught her. He held her upright, pushing her sweat-drenched hair from her face, and glared at his mother.

'You've done some things in your time, but this…'

Luci shrugged. 'I did her a favour, my darling boy. Now *none* of you are human. She's the same as you and Indie, the same as all of us. You can thank me later.'

She put her arm around her granddaughter's shoulders, but Indie pushed her off just as Zac ran at his mother. Snarling, fist raised, he launched himself, but Gabriel held him back.

'What you gonna do?' he shouted at his friend. 'Hit your mother? Really?'

'Look what she did, Gabe!' Zac screamed, spit foaming at the edges of his mouth. 'She can't just leave people alone, can she! Ella never asked for wings. None of us did. I came back from my own death, looking to lead a normal life with the woman I love and *now* look.'

He threw his arms around, signalling at the ground filled with broken rocks and bloodied feathers. The muddy earth had been churned into mounds and pits, puddles of Nephilim blood forming shallow icy puddles. The field, a sacred and revered site, was now full of exhausted winged children and the barely alive charred skeleton of an archangel who had once ruled two worlds.

'You can't force people to love you, Luci,' Zac cried. 'Love, respect, and trust are *earned*. Nothing about you is worth loving. *Nothing.*'

Zac's words cut through the thick silence hanging over the ruins of the sacred circle. In the distance tourists continued to take photos, cars drove past, and birds flew overhead, but behind their magical veil the angels were still. The only sound was the light rustle of wind blowing through their wings. Zac expected his mother to shout at him, throw him through the air, or reply with something equally vicious, but she didn't.

Luci was crying.

Large, round tears fell down the fallen angel's cheeks and onto her silent lips. She didn't speak nor wipe them away as she walked over to where the *Book of Light* still lay open on the stone altar. Zac flinched as she passed him, but the fight had left her. Turning the thin, yellow pages, she stopped when she reached the back of the book where three portraits had been sketched of her, now faint and blurred with age.

'I *was* loved once,' she whispered, running her finger over the faded pictures. 'Lorenzo loved me. Purely. Completely. He really did.'

'And then you murdered him,' a gravelly voice added.

Enzo had silently watched the exchange between his mother and brother, until now.

The younger Nephilim had backed away when Zac had turned on Luci, and were now hidden behind Gabriel, Chamuel, and Rafael. And Ella, with her new wings, had pulled her daughter tightly to her with no intention of letting go. But not Enzo. He hadn't moved from his place beside the sword, the sword he now held in his hands.

'Zac's right,' he said, taking a step toward Luci, the blade flashing its own bright smile. 'Our mother is selfish, power-hungry, and doesn't give a damn about anyone but herself, Luci. The demon that only knows how to destroy.'

Luci's chin trembled but she didn't look up.

'My father *did* love you,' Enzo continued. 'But he died so disappointed in you. Did you know that?'

Luci's eyes, which that morning had shone with determination, were now two dark smudges against a face pale as death. Enzo glared at his mother, years of hurt rising to the surface. He'd hidden it well, he'd played his part, but now the past had finally caught up with her. The woman tattooed on his arm. His biggest regret.

'What? Did you think I'd spent all these years searching for you to *thank* you?' he snarled. 'My father told me everything. He didn't die right away, you know. Oh no, it took him *years* to die, a slow and painful death. But you wouldn't know that because you never came back for us. You didn't keep your promise because he didn't matter to you anymore, none of us did. He'd failed to give you a living child, or so you thought, so you broke him in half and sent him away. Forgot about him. Probably moved on to another poor fool.'

Luci stretched out a shaky hand. 'Son, please, you don't understand…'

'You broke his back, the day I was born. For seven years he was only able to utter a few words a day, but he couldn't move. His sister fed him, cared for him, and raised me. Every day he asked me to look out of the window, to check the horizon for new boats. Told me my mother was ferocious, brave, and passionate. That she was indestructible and would never break her promise. Every day he told me my mother was coming back for her family.'

A loud sob escaped Luci's lips, but Enzo continued.

'Years passed where I was brought up on stories about the great Lucifer, the witch that couldn't be burned. My aunt taught me to read angelic font using your book of spells, and I learned every page word for word. When my eyes turned to this deep black, my aunt was there. Not you, her. My father passed away slowly, his days spent in agony and eternal hope. The day he died he turned to me and said, "Son, unlike me, you're going to live forever. Find Mikhael and kill him. And when you find your mother…"'

Luci rubbed at her blackened eyes with the back of her hand. 'What? What did he say?' she croaked.

'You don't deserve to know.'

Lifting the sword above his head with both hands, he swung around and swiped at the charred remains of Archangel Mikhael. With a thud, something black slowly rolled toward him, scattering dark flakes in its wake. He stopped it with the tip of his brown leather boot.

Mikhael's head. Luci cried out but Enzo ignored her.

'I know that book of spells better than you do, *Mother*,' he said. 'I've been planning this day for centuries. I added my blood to yours, which makes me one of the leaders of the new realm. And you, drunk on power and always so thirsty for admiration, were stupid enough to give me that gift. Well, you don't know the book as well as I do, because you were wrong. See? Mikhael *can* be killed—and so can you.'

43

WHAT HAPPENED NEXT passed in a blur. For years to come few would recount the same story. Who moved first, who said what. A myth, a legend, that would go down in celestial history.

Enzo, his handsome face now contorted into a hate-filled mask of rage and regret, raised the mighty sword to the heavens while Luci stood before him like a lamb to the slaughter. She didn't move. She didn't even try to defend herself. Something in the way she stood, shoulders hunched, head bowed, said 'you are right. I deserve this.'

Luci had survived two thousand years spurred on by only two things: the thought of exacting her revenge on Mikhael and keeping him in a constant state of pain and finding her son Zadkiel. But all of that was over. Mikhael had ceased to be, and neither of her sons loved her. The world didn't need her anymore, none of them did. Her firstborn had been right—she was unlovable…and she'd brought this upon herself.

Luci may have freed the realm, but she would never be truly free because the only person she wished to escape from was herself. Her anger. Her past. Her pain. But wherever Luci went, Lucifer followed.

As the ancient sword arched through the sky, its blade on course to finish her just as she had felled her own enemies, two things happened.

The Nephilim, the two archangels, and Ella ran to Luci. Creating a winged wall and shielding their leader, they raised their arms skyward, forming a force field, an invisible glass dome. The sword crashed down upon them and bounced off again. Ten winged beings strained against the force of the deadly weapon, pushing back, legs buckling under its power as Enzo tried to break through.

Then nothing.

Enzo was on the ground, blood oozing from his mouth and Zac looming over him. Zac didn't make mistakes. He should have listened to his instincts as soon as he first set eyes on this man. The fallen angel threw himself at his brother, sitting astride him, knees pinning down Enzo's jet-black wings. He punched him again, this time driving his fist into the man's onyx eyes.

Zac knew the damage wasn't going to last, that Enzo was healing as quickly as he was being hit, but it felt good. In fact, it felt glorious. The pain that shot through his fists and up his arms didn't hurt, not really, it simply reminded him of why he'd longed to live. The blood on his knuckles proof that there was something worth fighting for. Just one thing. A life worth living. With each punch he thought about the people gathered behind him, his friends, his family, his tribe—all brought together by one person.

At first, Enzo was too stunned to fight back. But by the third strike he raised his fist, the sword still firmly clutched within, and cried out as he lunged at Zac. The blade made contact with his brother's back—but he was too slow.

Twisting at the waist, Zac grabbed the edge of the mighty sword with both hands.

Blood seeped into Enzo's wide eyes, turning them into two burning rubies.

'You can't survive this sword!' Enzo roared. 'No one is strong enough to fight it.'

'That's where you're wrong.' Zac pulled at the blade with his bare hands as he got to his feet, forcing Enzo to stagger forward. 'I am the son of the great Lucifer and the almighty Archangel Mikhael. My strength is greater than yours, greater than anyone's. It was *my* feather our mother used in her spell, and when you killed my father, the last of his powers went to me. So now…' Blood ran in rivulets down his wrist as the blade cut into his hand. 'Now it's time to show you what a true ruler looks like.'

With one final punch, he drove his fist into Enzo's jaw with a deafening crunch. Dazed and stumbling, the Nephilim loosened his grip on the sword just as Zac pulled on the blade and sent it flying through the air. He caught it by the hilt with his right hand and pointed the tip of the blade at Enzo's throat before the pirate's son had a chance to wipe the blood out of his eyes.

'Brother,' Enzo whispered.

'I don't have a brother.'

'Why are you doing this? You hate our mother too.'

'You're right.'

'So let me finish her.'

'No. Hate is simple, but love isn't. Love is complicated and it lasts forever.'

'But she abandoned us.'

Zac took a deep breath, the sword shaking at Enzo's throat. He couldn't see his mother's face from where he was standing, but he could imagine it—because he'd been picturing her face since the day he'd lost her two thousand years ago.

'My mother never left me. The only thing she ever did wrong was not knowing when to let go.'

Zac's arm shook at the weight of the sword. He had a choice now, and whatever he chose to do would change everything. He could be a murderer, or he could walk away. He could save his mother, or he could save the world. It wasn't a difficult decision to make.

'Angels and humans have made life so complicated for themselves,' Zac continued. 'They created religion, rules of the realm, and human law. But when you think about it, there's only one commandment we ever needed to follow.'

Enzo stared at him blankly, and Zac smiled.

'You don't fuck with family.'

Keeping the tip of the blade pointed at Enzo's neck, Zac turned and gave his mother a questioning look. Her blank stare was void of any emotion.

'Go ahead,' Luci said with a shrug before turning her back on her boys. 'He's been dead to me for hundreds of years. I've already said my goodbyes.'

She walked away slowly, only flinching slightly at the gurgled sound of her youngest son meeting his death. She didn't see Zac drive the sword through Enzo's throat, or the way the blade slid through his neck with ease. She didn't watch as Enzo fell to the ground face-first, his wings creating a sparkling black canopy over his fallen body. And she didn't witness Zac, her blue-eyed boy with the softest of hearts, grasp a fistful of plumes and slice the wings from his brother's back, making Enzo's lifeless body explode into dust.

But she heard it all, including the final roar as Zac lifted his brother's wings above his head and threw them across the field.

'This is where it ends!' he shouted out to the retreating back of his mother, his friends, his family. 'No more death. No more destruction. The new world starts today. This is what you wanted, wasn't it, Luci?'

His mother stopped, but she didn't turn around.

'You wanted our world to merge with theirs,' Zac continued. 'And that's what's going to happen. No more realm, no more Mikhael, no one left to stop you. Just us. *We* are the future, Luci. All of us, together. And if I'm going to be a part of it then it's going to be done properly.'

44

LIFE'S WHEEL OF destiny had slowed down and ground to a halt. Ella was never going to die again and return as someone new. Indie was never going to get any older. Zac was no longer tasked with accompanying people on their life paths, ensuring that fate and destiny guided humanity to every end. Thanks to Luci, free will reigned and chaos ruled. Whether they liked it or not, that was the future now.

No evidence remained of the day the Angelic Realm was overthrown. Together, the remaining angels—old, new, and ancient—replaced the rocks and fused them together by magic. Luci formed a crater in the earth, filled it with the spilled blood and feathers of the fallen, and sealed it shut again. They left Stonehenge exactly as it had looked for thousands of years, all while tourists continued taking photos on the other side of the magical veil, unaware they'd just witnessed the end of the world.

Everyone was back at the house now and all was silent, each person quietly processing the horrors they'd witnessed, the myriad ways their lives had changed. Rafael had been the first to leave with his children, and Chamuel was still upstairs talking to Scar and Violet. Zac knew he too had a long conversation awaiting him with Indie, but they had time. Lots of time.

Ella stroked Zac's cheek and planted a kiss where her fingers had been.

'I'm an angel,' she said.

It wasn't right, none of this was right. 'I'm sorry she turned you into a monster like me.'

With a breathy laugh Ella ran her finger along the edge of his wing. A delicious ripple fluttered down his back and through every inch of his body.

'You're no monster, Zac. You're a miracle.'

He thought back to the first time they'd met, when she'd called him a god. He could tell by the way she was looking at him that she was recalling that moment in the river too.

'I've never touched anyone else's feathers before,' he said, stroking her back and enjoying the way her eyes closed in pleasure. 'Your wings are identical to mine.'

'Gabriel told me he'd never seen two identical sets of wings before. It's rare, apparently.'

'It is. According to legend, only soul mates get matching wings.'

'Well, fancy that.' Ella leaned into him so their feathers rubbed together—a new, heavenly sensation. It was strange for Zac to experience something new after having lived so long. But that was the wonderful thing about being alive—this crazy world just kept on giving. A shiver ran up his spine at the realisation that there was still so much left for him and Ella to share and explore in their new forms.

'So you're happy with your wings?' he asked her.

'Yes.'

'Really?'

She nodded 'We're finally the same, Zac. You, me, and our little girl.'

At the mention of their daughter his stomach twisted into a tight knot. Indie.

The girl's laughter rang out from the other side of the room. Indie had got changed and was lying between Blu's legs on the sofa. Zac homed in on them, surprised he was able to hear them from the other side of the room. It appeared that, thanks to Luci, all his angel powers had returned. Blu had his arms around Indie's waist and his head on her shoulder as they looked at something on her phone. They'd worked out how to fold their wings back inside their bodies, and now looked no different to any other teenagers giggling on the sofa together.

'So Jesse's OK?' Blu asked Indie, the boy's lips inches from her ear. She squirmed and smiled.

'Yeah. I've had four missed calls and about ten thousand messages from him. He's been asking why we didn't make the trip, and he's all excited because he got to share a room with Xavier last night.'

'Yeah? And?'

Indie rolled her eyes. 'Believe me, you don't want the details.'

'Luci properly brainwashed them after we left, eh? Glad our mates are OK though. What you typing back?' He buried his head deeper into Indie's neck, making her laugh.

'I'm saying we skipped the trip because you and I might have a thing for each other.'

Blu laughed and wrapped his arms tighter around her.

'Might?'

She stretched her arm back, pulling his face down to meet hers and kissing him.

'I'm loving our *thing*,' he murmured.

'Well, I could hardly tell him the truth,' she said.

'What? That we were kidnapped by your devil grandmother so we could overthrow the Angelic Realm, and now we're immortal winged beings who just watched a bunch of angels get murdered?'

Indie shuddered and he hugged her tighter.

'You OK?' he said.

She nodded. 'You?'

'Yeah.'

Zac tore his gaze away from the couple and was met with Ella's earnest face staring up at him.

'*Will* they be all right?' she asked. 'They're only children.'

He pulled her closer until she was resting her head against his chest.

'I don't think any of us will be all right for a while,' he replied. 'But we'll get there. We have time.'

There it was again, that word. *Time.* He was struggling to come to terms with their new reality—the fact that there was no longer a finite amount of years he could spend with Ella. A future where he no longer had to calculate how long they had left, or what he could or couldn't say. No more waiting, so much waiting, for her to return.

He had his mother to thank for that, in theory, but he wasn't in a very grateful mood.

Luci was sitting on the kitchen counter, a mug of coffee cradled in her hands. Head bowed, she was listening to something Gabriel was saying to her. The archangel hadn't left her side since Zac had driven his sword through Enzo's throat.

His mother had tried to fly away soon after, but Gabriel hadn't let her, dragging her down from the sky himself. She'd screamed at the archangel on that bloodied field, awful words filled with fear and spite and regret. She'd banged her fists against Gabriel's chest, telling him to let her go, that she wasn't worth saving, but he didn't. If Luci had never learned how to truly love, then Gabriel had never learned how to stop. With a ragged gasp, Luci had finally released a howl that had her falling into the archangel's embrace. His strong arms encircled her, and he'd held her close, rocking her gently from side to side and whispering into her ear until she'd finally subsided and allowed him to take her back to the house.

Luci hadn't said a word since. Not to Gabriel, nor to anyone else.

'Our daughter and Gabriel's son appear to be close,' Ella said, nudging Zac with her shoulder and nodding at Blu.

Zac made a grunting noise and she laughed.

'And the great archangel hasn't left your mother's side all day,' she added. 'I think he has feelings for her.'

'Gabe has loved my mother even longer than I've loved you,' he muttered.

'You don't look happy about it.'

Zac let out a long sigh. 'Because he only loves her for who she *wants* to be. He refuses to see her flaws.'

Ella stroked his cheek. 'That's no bad thing.' She glanced over at Blu and Gabriel again, the boy a carbon copy of his father, and shook her head with a laugh. 'This celestial world of yours is very messy, you know.'

Ella was laughing but it wasn't funny. None of it was funny.

'Hey, look at me.' Ella tipped Zac's chin up so they were eye-to-eye. 'You did the right thing back there.'

He rested his head against her chest. 'Killing someone is never the right thing, Ella.'

She stroked his hair, reminding him of when he was a boy and Luci would stay up all night stroking his head so he would sleep.

'Enzo was going to murder your mother,' Ella said quietly. 'Who would have been next? Indie? Me? You? He couldn't be trusted.'

'I don't like who I became out there.'

'A hero?'

'No. It's not that simple.' He looked over at his mother and Gabriel on the kitchen counter. She was talking now but he could only hear a faint murmur. Luci's eyes were fixed on her dangling feet while the archangel rubbed her arm. Zac hadn't found the courage to speak to her yet. Everything was still too sore, too fresh in his mind. There were too many wounds that needed to heal first. But he would, one day.

'What's the difference between a hero and a villain?' Zac asked Ella. 'A saint and a monster? An angel and the Devil? What are any of us? If I've learned anything in this world it's that there's no difference between the names that define us—it simply depends on who's telling the story.'

Tucking a strand of hair behind Ella's ear, Zac kissed her lips gently. Such a simple gesture, yet one he'd only been able to dream of for so long. Zac finally had everything he'd ever wanted, yet he was now more terrified than ever. Is that what happiness felt like? Never wanting to relax? Living in constant fear that a life filled with so much love, calm, and contentment could never last?

He kissed her again. 'How did I get so lucky,' he murmured into her mouth, 'to fall in love two thousand years ago with a woman like you?'

She closed her eyes, running her fingers through the hair at the nape of his neck. 'I can't get my head around the fact we're all going to live forever. Every single person in this house, stuck with each other for eternity. We're going to have to learn how to get along better with one another. You sure you're not going to get bored of me?'

He smiled down at her. His beautiful Arabella.

'Never.'

Yet what kind of future was left for them? The world was about to change in a big way—Luci had made sure of that. As usual his mother had focused on the things she had the power to do, never stopping to think whether she *should* do them. There were still hundreds of other angels who needed to be informed—Rafael said he would return to the realm later that day to impart the news. Jophiel and Saraqael were still out there too, and who knew what they would do next? And the Nephilim, how long until they decided their powers made them better than others? Stronger, more important, someone worth following? It was too much power for them. They were still children.

Could the human world and theirs really be successfully and peacefully combined? If they could, there was still a long way to go.

'Hey,' Ella said, smiling up at him. 'Why so serious?'

'Just thinking,' he whispered, looking over at his daughter, his mother, Gabriel, and his friend's children. Perhaps the big picture didn't matter right now. Perhaps the only world Zac should be worrying about was the one right there in the same room as him. His family.

'Perhaps it's time to move on. Forgive. The past is behind us for a reason. It's all about the future now.'

Ella cupped his face in her hands, their lips almost touching. 'And what *does* our future look like?'

'Well, thanks to my mother, fate and destiny no longer control us. So what happens next is completely up to us.'

Ella's lips brushed his and he pulled her to him, all of her, her mouth and her body pressed against his. And when he kissed her, he was kissing all the women she'd ever been and ever would be, and he knew she was kissing the only man she had wanted in every one of her lifetimes. The one she'd ached for. The only soul who could make her complete. Zac combed his fingers through her hair as their kiss deepened, hair that still smelled of the jasmine from his childhood, and her mouth as sweet as the figs they had shared the day he'd first fallen in love. And Ella remembered. She remembered every moment they'd shared. He was no longer alone in his love for her.

As their bodies merged into one, the tips of their wings touched on either side of them, creating a soft canopy of white. Her feathers stroked his, and they both shuddered in one another's arms at the new sensation. Beneath the shadow of their plumage, it was just them, Ella and Zac, as if nothing else existed. It never had.

They broke away, but his arms remained draped around her shoulders, his face still cupped in her soft hands. He was never going to let her go again. He didn't have to anymore.

'This is it, Zac,' Ella said, giving him the same smile that hadn't changed in two thousand years. 'This is our beginning.'

THE END

ACKNOWLEDGMENTS

In 2012 I had a dream about a girl lying in bed, waiting for a guy to sneak into her room. She was filled with anticipation and excitement, and a tiny bit of fear. It haunted me. I couldn't shake off that dream. I remember saying to a friend 'I'm going to write this story. I have no choice. These characters won't leave me alone, and I'll go mad if I don't at least have a go.'

After three long years my first ever book was finished. That girl was Ella, that boy was Zac, and the book was *The Path Keeper*. As I sit here writing the acknowledgments to the third and final book in the trilogy, I'm wondering where the last nine years have gone. Since that dream a lot has happened. I've moved countries, I'm writing my tenth novel, and the babies who I fed at all hours of the night while creating a world full of angels and witches in my head now help write my books.

But two things haven't changed—the love I will always have for this series, and the love I have for the people who have supported my writing.

You may have noticed *Children of Shadows* is a big book. To be honest, when my final edits came in even I had forgotten just how big this book is! But I had a two-thousand year love story to wrap up in a way so none of you would hate me—and that is not an easy thing to do.

So my first thanks goes to you, my readers, for sticking by me, Zac and Ella, and reading on until the bitter end.

Also a huge thanks to the BHC Press team. To Joni and Vern, and to my editor Jamie Rich for all their hard work and belief in this story. And to Cristina Galimberti, my foreign rights agent, working so hard to get these books out into the world!

None of this would have been possible without the support of all my family and friends. A special mention to my amazing writer buddies—Jacqueline Silvester, Anna Day, Isabella May, Emma Wilson, Emma Cooper, Alexandra Christo, Teuta Metra, Holly Seddon, Olga

Mecking, Kristin Anderson and Sarah Norris. Thanks for keeping me sane, girls (especially in 2020 when all we had was the internet and endless days of dread)! And huge gratitude to Jennifer Griffiths at Collab Writers and Elliot Grove at Raindance for all your support.

A big shout out to my online community, especially the support of everyone at The Fiction Café, The Savvy Writers Snug and MWHITL. In fact, my Loomies have been there from the start, and I know will be waiting at the finish line.

Huge thanks to all the bloggers and reviewers who have said such kind words about *The Path Keeper* and *Son of Secrets* over the years. I really hope you enjoyed meeting Indie, Blu and Enzo in this book. And as always, a massive squidgy hug to my ultimate gang of cheerleaders Claire Knight, Ellie Stone, Kristen Pullin, Liss Wheeler, Melanie Keeler, Phoenix Tier and Simone Birkholt.

To all my friends in the UK, Spain and the Netherlands who have no idea why I keep writing when all I do is moan about it—thanks for putting up with me.

And my family, well, you have always been by my side since the very beginning. You've read the books when they were half-finished, you've bought all your friends copies and you reply on every post on social media (you can stop now, Mum). Thank you, thank you, thank you! To my mum, dad, sister, Jemma, and stepdad, Bob—all of whom this book is dedicated to—I love you. And Angela, Wendy, Emily, Ana, Thomas and Chris and all the married-ins, plus Linda Drake and her enthusiastic sisters. You rock. So lucky to have you all supporting my writing adventure.

And now, the final words I will ever write of this trilogy (I'm not crying, *you're* crying), thank you to Pete for giving me the opportunity and encouragement I needed to follow my dreams. And Isabelle and Olivia for always being by my side. I've never known two people who have loved my books so much without being allowed to read them yet! I promise you will be able to one day.

Thank you, girls, you are my world. *In aeternum te amabo.*

Photo credit: Jeremy Standley

ABOUT THE AUTHOR

N J Simmonds writes fantasy and speculative fiction and is the author of The Indigo Chronicles series. Her stories are magical, historical and full of complex women, page-turning twists and plenty of romance. When Natali's not writing, she lectures on storytelling in business. Originally from London, she now lives with her family in the Netherlands and Spain.

Follow her writing adventures on:
njsimmonds.com
and at bhcpress.com

Lightning Source UK Ltd.
Milton Keynes UK
UKHW010734020222
398089UK00001B/196